the BASTARD IS DEAD

D'ARCY KAVANAGH

the BASTARD IS DEAD

A Paul Burke Mystery

Livonia, Michigan

Edited by Chelsea Cambeis
Proofread by Lana King

THE BASTARD IS DEAD

Copyright © 2020 D'Arcy Kavanagh

All rights reserved. No part of this publication may be reproduced, distributed, or transmitted in any form or by any means, including photocopying, recording, or other electronic or mechanical methods, without the prior written permission of the publisher, except in the case of brief quotations embodied in critical reviews and certain other noncommercial uses permitted by copyright law. For permission requests, please write to the publisher.

This book is a work of fiction. The characters, incidents, and dialogue are drawn from the author's imagination and are not to be construed as real. Any resemblance to actual events or persons, living or dead, is entirely coincidental.

Published by BHC Press

Library of Congress Control Number: 2019938909

ISBN: 978-1-64397-029-5 (Hardcover)
ISBN: 978-1-64397-030-1 (Softcover)
ISBN: 978-1-64397-031-8 (Ebook)

For information, write:
BHC Press
885 Penniman #5505
Plymouth, MI 48170

Visit the publisher:
www.bhcpress.com

For Lynda
...who helped me plot murder
while we cycled across Europe

PREFACE

THE FRENCH RIVIERA, KNOWN in French as the Côte d'Azur, extends along the Mediterranean coastline in the southeast corner of the country. It does not have an official border but is generally considered to extend in the east from the Italian border, through Monaco, on to Nice and as far west as Toulon, although some folks point to Marseille as the end. Along the route are internationally famous communities such as Cannes, home to arguably the most celebrated film festival in the world, and Saint-Tropez, made famous by legendary film star Brigitte Bardot.

The area has been inhabited since prehistoric times; primitive tools have been discovered in the area that date back one million years. As for its political history, the coastline has been ruled by Romans, Visigoths, Normans, the kingdom of Provence, the House of Grimaldi, the House of Savoy and, today, the French.

Thanks to its mild climate and beautiful seascape and landscape, the Riviera has been popular with artists for centuries, as well as tourists from around the world, who come to be mesmerized by the area.

The story that follows, however, isn't so much about beautiful scenery as it is about death—and other matters.

the BASTARD IS DEAD

CHAPTER 1

THE PELOTON OF 180 riders took a sharp right turn at fifty-five kilometers per hour and then lined up for the final push to the finish line by the Promenade des Anglais in Nice. Thirty thousand people lining the barricades of the 500-meter-long straightaway saw only a blur of color as the cyclists bumped and elbowed for space. The danger was palpable to the onlookers, most of them shrieking encouragement.

Behind the riders came a cavalcade of team cars. In the second vehicle—an apple-red Volkswagen Jetta used by the Global Projects team and piled high with six bikes—Directeur Sportif Pierre McManus yelled *"Allez, allez, allez!* Go, go, go!" into his radio speaker, although he knew his lead riders were too focused to pay much attention. But he was on an adrenaline rush, and so he yelled louder and louder.

As soon as the riders zipped by the turnoff for the team cars, two yellow-clad Tour de France officials hopped into the road and madly waved the vehicles off to the right and into the parking lot set aside for them.

"Allez, allez, Raoul!" McManus screamed at his top sprinter as he turned right, coming within ten meters of one wide-eyed official.

That's when his heart stopped.

CHAPTER 2

A DOZEN KILOMETERS AWAY, in the old part of Villeneuve-Loubet, Paul Burke poured a little water into his pastis while keeping an eye on the small, ancient television that Claude Brière had hooked up for the customers at his Café de Neptune. Burke sipped the licorice drink to ensure he had the right blend of water and alcohol, but quickly forgot about it as the cyclists, many of them standing on their pedals and feverishly maneuvering their bikes, sprinted the last two hundred meters to the finish line. He felt someone standing beside him but didn't take his eyes off the screen until the British favorite cleared the line first, a wheel ahead of the runner-up from Germany.

"I'm surprised you aren't there at the finish," came Claude's husky voice.

Burke looked up at the owner—a beefy man in his fifties who had grown up in this village and, as far as Burke knew, had always worked at the café, which had once been owned by his uncle.

Burke brushed the comment aside with a classic Gallic wave. "Not worth my time," he said in his fluent, Québec-accented French. He shrugged. "I have better things to do."

Claude, who was always cheerful, grinned. "Yes, I can see your Sunday is bursting with activity."

Despite himself, Burke laughed. He liked Claude. In fact, he liked almost everyone in the hillside community for their good spirits and jovial pessimism, which had taken a few months to get used to. These people were to be respected and appreciated. He felt differently about the residents of the neighboring developments. They were a well-heeled, self-absorbed bunch who cared little for the social niceties of a small community.

As for the tourists who were coming in droves to the expansive resorts being developed at an extraordinary pace, Burke did his best to avoid them. Too demanding, too elitist and too loud. The area was changing.

"Just killing time," Burke said.

"But surely you must feel some association or kinship with those cyclists," Claude persisted.

Burke and Madame Marois—the quiet, eightyish, pinch-faced woman from just around the corner—were the only customers. Burke had learned it was at such times that conversation was appropriate. It was even expected.

"My career is long over," Burke said, his mind suddenly filled with memories from a score of races, most of them not involving the Tour de France.

"Just, what, three years?" Claude asked. "That's not so long ago. Then you did television commentary, too. And you were good. You know strategy as well as anyone."

Burke smiled as they went through a conversation they'd revisited a dozen times since he had moved to the village. "I was crap, and everyone knows it. That's why I got fired so quickly."

"A bad decision by the television people," Claude said with a sympathetic smile.

"Ah, you're just being kind again, Claude. You know I was terrible. Everyone knows it. And it didn't help when I reported that last race pissed. Not a good decision by me."

During Burke's final telecast, he blurted out a string of curses on the air just as the riders had finished the race. Not only had Burke been fired immediately after, but his outburst had become a YouTube sensation and had led to a legislated change so there would be a minor delay in French coverage of sporting events to ensure no commentator ever unleashed profanities on the air with such enthusiasm again.

"Well, as you Americans say, shit happens," Claude said.

Burke smiled at their inside joke. Claude was fully aware that Burke was a Canadian expat who had grown up in Montréal, but he liked to tease Burke on occasion by lumping him in with American tourists.

"That's exactly what we Canadians say," Burke said. "Since you've got so much advice and so few customers, why don't you sit down and join me?

Madame Marois over there doesn't look like she'll need your services for some time."

Claude glanced at the old woman, who was swathed in a black shawl despite it being thirty-five degrees Celsius—a temperature that sucked the energy out of most people. As usual, the woman was statue-like, her eyes boring holes into the wall of an old stone house on the other side of the tiny courtyard. Beside her stretched her curly-haired Jack Russell, Plato, a ball of white fluff with caramel-colored ears and one sandy spot on his back. The dog moved as much as his mistress. Claude shook his head, then looked back at Burke.

"You're only in your late 30s, Paul, and you look fit, so maybe you could return to racing," he said.

Claude graciously ignored that Burke was starting to show a little more stomach and maybe drank a few too many pastises than average.

Burke sighed. "Get a pastis, Claude, and I'll tell you once again why I don't race anymore."

He watched the café owner go, catching the crooked finger Madame Marois extended to him, which meant she wanted another glass of rosé.

Burke thought about the rest of his day. Maybe he'd stay and have a salade Niçoise, which he had always craved during his decade of pro racing but had avoided due to the salty anchovies. And a bottle of a Bordeaux red would work. Pastis afterward, too. The French might frown on such a sequence of beverages, but screw them. They were a little too rigid about food and drink for his liking.

He turned his attention back to the television, where the stage winner was holding up the day's trophy—a piece of abstract sculpture that resembled a dog humping a leg. The crowd was cheering wildly.

He wished he'd experienced such a moment just once. His only win had been in an unnoticed, three-day event, when he had taken the last day's stage after all the favorites in front of him had crashed. The stage trophy had been a small teddy bear that looked like it had already been used.

Claude returned, nodding at the stage winner on TV as he sat down with his own pastis and another for Burke. "He's a prick, I think," Claude said. "I think all sprinters are like strikers in football, totally caught up in their own deeds without a care about others. They pretend they're good teammates, but they're just shits. I would very much enjoy telling them the facts of life, but no one takes me up on my offer."

Burke smiled. Yes, the salade Niçoise would work if it came with more of Claude's good company. *Life wasn't always so depressing*, he thought. Then after his meal, when he'd likely be feeling a little drunk, he'd go to the highest part of the village, near the old castle, and see how much of the Mediterranean he could see. It would be quiet up there, except for the diminished roar of distant vehicles on the highway, and the air would be perfumed.

And maybe he'd sleep well. He was tired of nightmares. Too many goddamn nightmares.

CHAPTER 3

THE NIGHTMARE WOKE HIM just after 5 a.m.

He had dreamt he needed to catch an airplane but had been inexplicably held up at customs by some jerk of an official, and, when finally cleared, he had seen the plane beginning to taxi. Bursting through the airport doors, he'd sprinted as hard as possible toward the departing plane, and just when it seemed he would reach out and climb aboard, it pulled away, leaving him to a terrible, unknown fate.

Then he woke up, not to the songbirds outside his second-story apartment bedroom, but to anxiety.

Again.

Sitting up in his bed with the sheet wet from sweat, Burke wondered if someone could please tell him what the hell was wrong. He had experienced such dreams for the last two or three years and hadn't a clue what was causing them. He just knew that sleep rarely brought pleasure or relief.

He also realized he had a thumping headache and a queasy stomach. He'd felt fine or close to it after the bottle of Bordeaux. Maybe it had been the four pastises afterward. Even Claude had suggested that maybe he was going a little too deep into the booze, but he had blown off the friendly suggestions to stop. He grimaced. Taking advice wasn't one of his strong points.

He stood and looked out the open window to see the start of a sunrise against a cloudless sky. It would be another beautiful, hot July day.

Burke had little to do.

His next blog for three Côte d'Azur newspapers and their websites wasn't due for another three days. He also had a column for the same publications but had another week to finish it. Maybe he'd base the blog on what Claude had discussed—the self-absorbed sprinters and strikers in sport who thought they were God's gift. Or maybe he'd do a piece about racing in abnormally hot weather. Or he could write about how crappy it felt to wake up with a hangover after you thought you'd solved the problems of the world the night before.

He stuck his head through the open window and let the slight breeze caress him. He loved early mornings in this part of France; they were so sunny and languid, and the birds were always chattering away at sunrise. He loved the smells and sounds of the world awakening. He closed his eyes, which seemed to accentuate his hangover, and took a couple of deep breaths. His problem, he knew, was that he had too many late nights.

He stepped back, a little wobbly, went to the bathroom and washed his face with cold water. That helped.

Burke then went into his tiny kitchen and started up the coffee. During his racing days, he had been a three-coffees-a-day man for the caffeine boost. Now he was putting down five cups of espresso a day because he found himself bored too often and without a lot to do. When in doubt, drink an espresso. Then later, drink pastis.

He promised himself that within six months, he'd have everything straightened out. Maybe he'd go back to Montréal for a visit, although there really wasn't anyone left he wanted to spend much time with. He chuckled at the thought of a few days with his older brother and his brother's family. If he showed up, they'd start finding excuses to disappear. Too much brotherly competition—and borderline hatred—over the years. To make matters worse, his brother's kids, both boys, were shitheads, and they weren't even teenagers yet. As for his sister-in-law, she was a chronic complainer. The family dog, Alvin, was the only one he liked.

He could go to Vancouver to see that young woman he'd hooked up with the previous autumn in Antibes. She was a doctoral student doing research on something involving plankton, and they had bumped into each other at the Picasso museum with her coming out and him just hanging around outside slurping down a gelato. She'd thought he was an art fan, and he'd gone along with it because she had great legs and enormous blue eyes that sucked him in. After a few days of mindless passion, she'd discovered he knew as much about art as he did about nuclear physics, and so she harrumphed and blew him off as some "stupid cyclist who doesn't understand the real world." He smiled. Picasso and plankton were the real world? Still, she'd been a lot of fun once they managed to get to a bed. Maybe he could make her forget his intellectual weaknesses and rekindle her passion.

Once the coffee was ready, Burke turned on the kitchen TV—it helped to cook if there was something to watch—and switched the channel to the news. He really wasn't any kind of journalist and was only doing Tour de France blogs and columns as a way to help pay the bills, but he did like to know what was going on in the world.

Of course, the lead item was the TDF, and the screen showed the wild finish of the previous day's race. The announcer discussed how the stage had played out and then, finishing the story, added a bit about the tragedy of longtime directeur sportif, Pierre McManus, dying just as the race was ending.

"Jesus Christ!" Burke said.

Officials had reported a heart attack was the cause of McManus's death.

"Damn!" Burke said.

McManus was dead? How does a nasty bastard who's got the constitution of a bear just pop off? Burke wondered. A heart attack? It didn't seem possible. McManus didn't have a heart. Burke had always figured his former directeur sportif would be right there at the end of the world with the cockroaches and crows.

"Shit," Burke said with less passion.

He surprised himself by feeling a little sad. He had only worked for McManus for two years, which was about two years too many thanks to McManus's driving ambition, psychological gamesmanship and endless criticism. But somehow, he had developed a minor appreciation for McManus's sense of cycling strategy. The bugger had produced some great champions over the years, and even Burke had to admit he'd learned a few tricks that had served him well. Of course, he could never forget the time he'd overheard McManus telling a team masseur to spend as little time on him as possible because "Burke can barely make the pedals go round. He's a useless turd who doesn't even deserve to be stepped on."

As soon as his contract, which had been signed under another boss, had ended, Burke found himself unemployed. The turd had been canned.

Burke watched the entire news hour and then took his third cup of espresso into the tiny spare bedroom that served as his office and a parking place for his Cannondale racing bike, which was starting to gather dust. There, he turned on his computer and started reading everything he could about McManus. Most of the stories were about McManus's talents and predated yesterday's events, but a couple mentioned how he had died at the wheel of a team car, which had stopped only when it crashed into another team's bus. It almost seemed a comical ending.

Burke shook his head. Yes, McManus had been highly strung, a total alpha dog who was always snapping at riders, team staff, the media and even sponsors. But he was a beast of a man who had somehow found time to exercise each day and whose eating habits were scrupulously proper, yet he'd been only forty-nine at the time of his death.

McManus dead? It barely seemed possible.

Just before eight, Burke went to the local newsagent's and picked up a stack of newspapers from the affable owner, Jean. He grabbed another coffee with water and sat at one of the two tables outside the newsagent's place. Then he started searching for anything about McManus.

There wasn't much new—just the same info about the heart attack and the team's statement that said riders and other staff were shocked by his demise and distraught over his death, but would continue in his name so as to bring him glory. Burke smiled at that. Unless McManus had changed beyond belief, he'd bet most of the riders and others on the team were probably shaking hands and toasting the unexpected passing of their directeur sportif.

There was also a short bio of McManus relating how he'd grown up in the Flanders area of Belgium, then became a pro racer with limited results but showed brilliance in developing race strategies. He'd gone from team to team, rising in the ranks, and built a reputation among the media as a savvy if ruthless leader. His teams had won a lot of races.

There was also a brief mention of McManus's tryst with a Hollywood actress, whom he'd met on the set of a cycling-related movie in Saint-Tropez. The actress had called him her "Belgian treat," which had stuck and led to plenty of behind-the-back snickering at McManus's expense. Burke had been sure that when she dumped McManus after three months for a rodeo cowboy whose first name was Buck, McManus would be surlier than ever, but that wasn't the case. In fact, after his bout with Hollywood fame, McManus had been abnormally pleasant, with hardly any barking or growling or biting. Then another racing season got underway, and McManus had gone back to type. *So much for the influence of a slightly good woman*, Burke thought.

Burke made up his mind. He'd write about McManus this week, exploring a little more than what the initial reports had included. He'd provide some color, a few anecdotes and maybe even hint at how miserable McManus could be in pursuit of victory. The price of glory and all that blather.

He figured he'd start by whistling down to Nice, where the teams would still be because the day's afternoon stage was starting at Cagnes-sur-Mer. And why not go by bike? He could definitely use the exercise—he'd seen Claude noticing his expanding tummy—and it might also be easier than driving, since the area would be jammed with cycling fans.

Back in his small apartment, he pumped up the tires on his red-and-white Cannondale carbon fiber bike, added a few drops of oil to the chain, put on cycling shorts and a cycling jersey and then jammed a tape recorder and notebook into one of the jersey's three back pockets with his wallet in another. He took a look at the helmet by the bike. *Screw it*, he thought. It would squeeze his head, which already throbbed thanks to his hangover. He left it there.

Outside, he waved at a couple of the local shop owners strolling to their businesses. They always seemed to be in a decent mood. He hoped that one day their bonhomie would rub off on him.

Then he was riding, and instantly, he felt at home, his long, lean legs punching the pedals with little effort, to his surprise. Of course, the first stretch was marginally downhill, but he felt strong. He was a believer that if you've done a lot of physical exercise, you keep a base of muscle and lung power that can be easily reasserted with a little work.

He passed a couple of middle-aged touring cyclists and then snuck past some crawling cars. He cruised through the first roundabout at forty-five kilometers per hour, and on the following straightaway, he cranked it up to fifty—but not for long. After about thirty seconds, he was wheezing and slowed to the low thirties. A good start to a new program, he figured.

He made it to the road by Nice Côte d'Azur Airport in under ten minutes, and then he punched the pedals hard again, moving smoothly with the traffic toward the main part of the city. He figured a couple of the teams would be staying at hotels just off the main area, so those would be his first stops.

Just as Burke was slowed, ready to take his first hotel turnoff, a man on a one-speed rental bike came off the promenade and collided with him. Burke, a veteran of a hundred crashes in his career, made himself go limp as he twisted and then landed against the side of a parked Citroën. Instantly, the traffic all around stopped.

Stunned but sensing no major injury except an expansion of his headache, Burke got to his feet. He did a brief body check. Nothing was broken. He looked at his bike and saw the front wheel was caved in with spokes sticking out in wrong ways. He looked at the other cyclist, who seemed fine and was standing by his bike, which looked undamaged.

"What the fuck are you doing?" Burke said in French.

The man, who looked to be in his mid-forties, stumbled over what Burke had said. Behind him was a pretty woman and a boy of about twelve years old, both on similar bikes. They were watching the exchange, looking a little worried.

Burke tried again, this time in English. "What the hell were you thinking?"

The man shrugged and offered a sheepish grin. "I thought there was a turn here, and I'm just real sorry," he said in some kind of Midwest American accent. "Are you OK? I'll pay for any damages."

Burke looked down at himself. He had a few rapidly developing bruises on his left arm and leg, but that was it.

"Let's move over here," Burke said, hauling his bike with him and letting the motorists get on with their travels. On the promenade and away from the bike path, he shook his head and said, "I'm fine, but I'll need a new wheel."

"Really? Are you sure?" asked the tourist, studying the wheel.

Burke wanted to lay into the stranger but remembered the bonhomie he wished to achieve. "I'm sure. I'm a pro cyclist, and I understand these kinds of things," he said, figuring no one but a cycling geek would recognize that he was a retired pro. "There's a decent shop about four blocks from here."

"Uh, how much are we talking about?" the man asked.

"I can't say for sure. Probably six or seven hundred euros," Burke said.

The woman behind the man gasped. The man himself looked like he had been slapped. The youngster suddenly seemed more interested and bent over to inspect the wheel.

"It's a pro machine," Burke added, hoping the exchange wasn't going to turn into a complete ordeal, though he expected it would.

"That's a lot of money," said the man.

"I can call the police," Burke said, spotting a cop about a half block away. He had no interest in involving the local constabulary because, in his experience, French police were often as challenging to victims as they were to the perpetrators, but he wasn't going to share that viewpoint with this tourist.

"No, no," the man said, relenting.

They agreed to walk to the bike shop and figure out what needed to be done.

Burke would have preferred to walk in silence so he could concentrate on reducing the thump in his head, but the tourist seemed to feel an obligation to fill the time with observations about Nice and France, anything. Burke wondered if the man was trying to be cordial to get the price of the repairs dropped. *Not a chance*, Burke thought.

Eventually, Burke felt compelled to ask a question. "What do you do back home?"

The man, who had introduced himself as Ron Henderson, puffed up. "I'm a pharmacist. I run my own pharmacy in Missoula, Montana. Been doing it for fifteen years," he said.

Henderson's wife was paying no attention whatsoever. The boy didn't seem to be enjoying the trip, although his head swiveled whenever a pretty girl—and Nice had lots of them—strolled by.

The pharmacist launched into a monologue about the different meals they had enjoyed since landing. Burke worked hard at tuning him out but perked up when he heard the American had developed a liking for steak tartare and pastis.

Finally, they were at the bike shop, a small but tidy operation run by André Rousseau, a longtime mechanic for a decent French pro team. Rousseau had finally given up the pro circuit at his wife's wishes and, with the backing of some pro racers, had opened his shop, which catered to many top-caliber racers in the region. Burke respected Rousseau's mechanical expertise and liked him for his dry wit. He figured Rousseau would support him in this dispute.

The mechanic took one look at the crumpled front wheel and told the pharmacist in flawless English that it was a write-off and would cost about seven hundred euros to replace. Henderson winced. His wife shook her head, looking a bit worried. The son stared out the window.

Rousseau removed the broken wheel and leaned it against the counter, then looked at Burke. "Mavic, same model?" he asked. "Or an upgrade?"

Burke would have liked an upgrade but said he'd manage with a same model as a replacement. Rousseau nodded and went into the back of the shop.

"An expensive day," the pharmacist said, managing a smile.

Rousseau was back in two minutes with a new wheel and tire, which he quickly put on. He slipped the wheel back onto the bike and then filled the tire with a pressurized pump.

"You're back in business," he told Burke.

After Henderson had settled with a credit card, they went outside.

"Sorry about your bad luck," Burke said, starting to climb aboard.

"Yeah, well, stuff happens, hey?"

Burke felt a strange obligation to extend the conversation a few more seconds. "Staying in Nice?" he asked.

"Three nights at the Hotel de l'Empereur," Henderson said.

"Good hotel," Burke said. "Have a good time and watch out for cyclists."

Burke started off, catching a *"Bonne journée"* from Henderson.

A few minutes later, Burke stood at the entrance of the hotel housing the Global Projects team, his bike safely attached to a nearby post by a thin cable lock. He flashed his media pass at the two security guards at the hotel entrance. They seemed unimpressed, which didn't entirely surprise Burke, given he was wearing spandex cycling bib shorts and an old KAS shirt with his notepad and recorder tucked in his back jersey pockets.

"I'm a journalist, but I rode here from my apartment," he explained. "I'm a former pro."

The security pair continued to look unimpressed. In fact, they seemed to be studying everyone else but Burke.

He spotted the hawk-like features of Mark Den Weent, a former teammate and one of the coaching staff. Den Weent was just strolling down the hallway and turned when he heard Burke call his name.

Den Weent came over and told the security duo that Burke could come in. Wordlessly, the pair stepped back, letting Burke walk into the large, brassy entrance of the glamorous hotel.

Burke looked at Den Weent. "Tough day?" he offered.

"Oh, you mean McManus," Den Weent said. Then he shrugged. "Well, it's difficult and definitely a surprise, but what can you do? We must go on."

Burke thought Den Weent, who looked a lot more ready to smile than cry, was managing just fine.

"You haven't been doing your miles on the road," Den Weent said with a grin, nodding at Burke's waist.

"Yes, well, it's the life of the journalist," Burke replied. "Not good for exercising."

Den Weent, still smiling, shook his head.

"How's the team doing?" Burke asked, leading Den Weent to a couple of vacant black leather chairs in the foyer.

"Are you asking as a journalist or my old teammate Paul Burke?" Den Weent asked, dropping into one chair.

"Both, I guess. I'm doing a piece on McManus, but I'm also curious how everyone's managing without the old—"

"—bastard!" Den Weent said, jumping in. "Officially, as we said at the news conference last night, we are devastated by the tragic loss of such a giant of the sport and such a key component of this team's success."

"You've been working on your PR skills, I see," Burke said, letting the leather chair swallow him.

"I've had plenty of instruction in the art of PR," Den Weent confirmed.

"And the non-PR take?"

"Everyone is breathing again," Den Weent said. "This last year, he was worse than ever, and I didn't think that was possible. We've got riders who've been close to breaking for months. They came here for more money and discovered very quickly that a better contract isn't worth shit when you've got a boss who believes he owns your life."

"And you? Did you get fooled by McManus?"

Den Weent smiled. "Same story. He had me by the balls."

"But not now."

"Now my balls don't hurt," Den Weent said. "After the press conference last night, the other two trainers on the team and I got pissed at the bar right over there. Everyone not on the team probably thought we were overcome by sadness and drowning our sorrows. Fuck that! We were celebrating."

They chatted for a few more minutes, and then Den Weent excused himself, citing a need to concoct the team's plans for the next stage. Burke was ready to head back outside when he spotted Eric Tilson, one of the most familiar faces in pro cycling and a consummate domestique with endless stamina, boundless understanding of race tactics and the gift of gab in five languages, which made him a media darling and a strong candidate for a TV commentator's job once he hung up his cleats.

"Big loss, eh?" Burke held out his tiny recorder, hoping it still had enough juice to work.

"Irreplaceable," Tilson said in his Aussie drawl, his dark eyebrows knitting into one solid line as he frowned. "We're all devastated."

"Tough to ride today?" Burke asked, sensing that Tilson would stick to the company line.

"Yeah, I'm heartbroken. I'll be thinking of Mac every kilometer," Tilson said, a slight twinkle showing in his gaze.

"Surprised by the heart attack?"

Tilson paused. "Yeah, I am. He was made of iron and could still ride like hell. He ate well and stayed away from booze. He looked like he was ready to live to be bloody one hundred."

Burke asked who was controlling the team now.

"Den Weent will still work the car. Shit, he's one of the best at dealing with stage tactics on the fly. But I don't know about who'll really pull the strings. No one does. And with looking for a new sponsor, we're all wondering what's next."

"You want to stay around, Eric?" Burke asked.

Tilson, who was thirty-five but looked almost fifty due to years of racing in all kinds of weather, shrugged. "I'd like to. Lots of talent here. With the right cosponsor, we could do very well for the next couple of years."

"Would you want to stay around if McManus was still around?" asked Burke.

Tilson laughed. "I learned a great deal under his guidance. It's a real loss, a real tragedy."

Burke put away the recorder. He wasn't going to get much else, but he didn't really mind since he had always enjoyed Tilson's company.

"Thanks, Eric," he said, shaking hands.

He had gone a few steps when he heard Tilson's voice behind him. "Be careful what you write, Burkie. People are a little sensitive these days."

Then he was gone, leaving Burke wondering what was behind the warning.

CHAPTER 4

THE DAY'S STAGE WASN'T scheduled to start for another two hours, and Burke didn't feel like heading home to wait. He figured he'd hang around, maybe chat with some of the ex-pros who often showed up for race starts and see if he could learn anything new. He doubted he would, but it was a beautiful day, and he always enjoyed the energy of a community hosting a Tour de France *étape*.

He climbed aboard his bike and wound his way through the stream of pedestrians, who all seemed headed in the same direction—the beach front.

When he got to the start of the day's TDF stage—with its banners and other decorations, it was easy to spot—he took to walking. Already, there were a few thousand people milling about, setting up chairs, watching race personnel put up barriers, hoping to get a photo of a cyclist or, even better, a chance to land an autograph.

Burke didn't look out of place in his cycling attire; there were several hundred other riders sporting similar clothing. It was a celebration of cycling in general, along with the Tour de France.

A bit hungry and starting to feel his headache weaken, Burke went to a small kiosk and ordered a *gaufre*, or waffle, with walnuts. He would start his diet the next day.

As he worked his way through the whipped cream and into the waffle, he found his mind wandering. Just a day ago, he'd been watching TV and another stage of the Tour, and now he was poking about trying to gauge the impact of McManus's sudden death. He laughed to himself; he was doing a journalist's job.

He found a spot away from the throng but with a decent view. He watched the riders sign in and then assemble for the start of the stage. No one was moving quickly. It was all about conserving energy.

It was almost race time.

First-time fans were probably expecting a wild and crazy start, but Burke knew a stage usually began like a procession, with most, if not all, of the cyclists riding casually and chatting among themselves. The first attempt at a breakaway might come in the initial kilometer, but Burke doubted it because the heat was already stifling, and the stage had some testing hills ahead. He figured some riders would wait until they were approaching Antibes before trying to distance themselves from the peloton.

When the starter fired the gun to signal the beginning of the race, that was exactly the approach the peloton took as the riders slowly disappeared toward Villeneuve-Loubet and on to Antibes.

Burke looked about. Many in the crowd didn't seem to care that the race was underway; they were laughing and telling stories. Some spectators, though, were clearly puzzled at the weak start after such a buildup.

He walked a bit with his bike until he was clear of most of the throng, and then he mounted. He figured he'd ride back home and write a quick blog about the day's start and some of the comments he'd gotten from Den Weent and Tilson.

"Hey, hey," someone yelled at him.

Burke looked around. The voice belonged to the Montana pharmacist who'd slammed into him on his bike. He tried to recall the guy's name. Then it came back—Ron Henderson.

Henderson was walking toward him, his wife and son in tow.

"That was pretty exciting," Henderson said when he got within range.

Burke shrugged. "Glad you liked it."

"I got some good photos," Henderson said, sounding like he wanted to replay the entire start. "I'm hoping we can catch up with the race another day. That would be outstanding!"

"It can be fun," Burke admitted, although he knew "fun" wasn't a word the riders would apply to any of the stages. "Brutal" and "exhausting" would be better descriptions.

Henderson adopted a sorrowful expression. "Again, I'm sorry about what happened before, to you and your bike," he said. "I was just plain stupid to do what I did. I hope you're OK and your bike is working again."

"I am, and it is," Burke said, smiling slightly.

He was going to pedal off when a thought came to him.

"I know anyone can have a heart attack, but doctors are getting better at diagnosing heart issues, right?" he asked.

Henderson looked surprised at the turn in conversation, but his grin returned. "I think it's safe to say the medical profession has made leaps and bounds in heart issue detection," he said.

"So it's a little unusual for a healthy, active man who sees a doctor regularly to have a heart attack while doing something he does every day, right?" asked Burke, figuring McManus would never have been far from a doctor, considering his job.

"I'm not so sure about that, although I can't speak with any authority since I'm not a doctor, just a pharmacist," Henderson said.

"As a pharmacist, you probably deal with a lot of people with heart issues, I expect," Burke suggested.

"Yeah, lots. They use all kinds of meds. ACE inhibitors, antiplatelet drugs, beta-blockers, inotropic drugs, vasodilators and all kinds of other drugs," he said. "Heart medications are becoming more sophisticated by the day. I have to work hard to keep up with the developments. Why? Do you have heart issues?"

"No, no." Burke shrugged. "Just wondering. Someone I knew died yesterday, supposedly of a heart attack. It was a total surprise to everyone. He was a beast of a man, and no one probably figured he'd go from a heart attack."

"Lots of people have undetected heart issues," Henderson said. "Some pro football players have died on the field or just after a game from heart failure."

Burke nodded and thanked Henderson for the info. Then, with a slight wave, he started pedaling away, a little surprised by his own curiosity and still somewhat puzzled by how McManus just popped off without any warning.

Back in old Villeneuve, Burke put aside his bike, showered, grabbed a chilled Kronenbourg 1664 and sat at his computer. He figured three or four hundred words on the race, plus McManus would keep his French blog editor, François Lemaire, in a happy mood.

To his surprise, Burke found himself finished within a half hour. Usually a painfully slow writer in both French and English, the words flowed out of him as he passed on observations about the race and reported mostly about McManus.

Now if he could only spell in either language.

His screen had plenty of underlined words indicating misspellings. The autocorrect had helped somewhat, but his misspelling of other words had been so bad that autocorrect hadn't known what to do.

After cleaning up his copy, Burke emailed Lemaire, adding the blog as an attachment. He wished he had a photo of the race or of McManus, but he could usually rely on Lemaire to find some kind of art to add to the blog.

He was sipping his second 1664 when he noticed a new email. It was from Lemaire, who had written:

"Good work, PB. Timely. Excellent quotes about McManus. Took out part about doctors failing to diagnose a heart problem. Too much speculation. Or did you talk to his doctor?"

Burke nodded to himself. He was prone to speculating too much, and he was glad Lemaire was a real journalist who caught such flaws in his copy.

He emailed Lemaire back, saying he hadn't talked to McManus's doctor.

Lemaire replied instantly, saying, *"There's a news conference tomorrow afternoon that will deal with the results of McManus's autopsy and so forth. You should go. Info below."*

The news conference was scheduled for 2 p.m. at the Nice City Hall.

Burke told Lemaire he'd go.

"Good," Lemaire countered. *"I'm assigning a reporter for the print news side. I want you to blog about the heart issue from a pro cyclist's point of view. Had McManus damaged his heart from too much riding as a pro? Had he used drugs when he competed, and did that contribute to his death?"*

Burke nodded at the last sentence. There it was—drugs and cyclists. The longtime story that had plagued the sport for years. The pro cycling world had improved dramatically the last couple of years in reducing drug use, but the previous decades had been devastating. It hadn't helped the sport's image when some TDF winners had their titles stripped for drug use.

Then Burke got a little ticked. McManus hadn't been a rider when he died; he'd been a middle-aged man in a car. He'd ask Lemaire's questions at the news conference, but he'd ask about other issues, too.

Feeling he'd actually accomplished something, Burke left his apartment for Claude's café.

When he got down to Claude's outdoor terrace, the TV was on and the TDF riders were in the last few kilometers. Burke was surprised that the terrace was two-thirds full; it usually had only a couple of customers at this time of day. There was a table with six tourists—their accents hinted they were from the southern United States—but they were ignoring the race, chattering away about the best way to get to nearby Grasse, the French capital for perfumes, from the new condo development a kilometer away. At another table, two local government officials who Burke had met a couple of times were sipping glasses of red wine as they studied the race, which looked destined to end in another sprint. At a table nearby sat a young couple from the village. They were locked on each other's eyes, and Burke figured they'd soon be leaving for their bed. Then there was Madame Marois, who, as usual, was staring at her wall, a rosé within reach, Plato stretched out by her feet.

Burke took a seat at a table for two beside Madame Marois.

"Bonjour, Madame," he said with a slight bow.

The old woman glanced at him and tilted her head ever so slightly in acknowledgment. Then she returned to staring holes into the wall across the courtyard.

Burke sat, knowing it would be impolite to ask Madame Marois how her day was. She was old-school French, uninterested in discussing her day or anything else with tourists or acquaintances. Burke sensed she'd be happy to keep her entire day's conversation to just ordering a rosé. And then he recalled that she'd even mastered that without a sound, getting a glass from Claude with only the crook of a finger. She had trained him well. She'd probably trained others that way, too.

Claude appeared at his table, his face flushed from having to bustle about with so many customers.

"Pastis?" he asked.

Burke was about to say yes but then changed his mind, ordering a Pelforth Brune, a malty, brown ale brewed in Marseille.

"Ah, a surprise," Claude said, grinning. "You are not always predictable, my friend."

"I try, Claude, I try," Burke said, wondering how predictable he had become over the last few years.

Claude then moved off, serving a variety of beers and wines to the American table before dispensing a bill to the amorous young couple.

A few minutes later, Claude's assistant, Hélène Rappaneau, who was twenty-two and also his niece, appeared with Burke's beer, which looked delicious in a goblet-type glass.

"Busier than normal, I see," he said, stating the obvious but happy to do so because Hélène was a bubbly young woman and, with large almond-shaped eyes, rich auburn hair and an athletic figure, an absolute stunner.

"That's why my uncle called me in," she said, studying the growing crowd as two well-dressed couples in their fifties came in together. "More and more people from the new condos."

"Then business is going to be good," Burke suggested.

Hélène laughed at that. "But Uncle Claude likes it quiet, I think. That way, he can spend more time talking to his few customers—as you know, Paul," she said.

"True, true," Burke replied.

Then she was gone.

Sipping his beer, Burke pondered the next day's news conference. He had only attended news conferences as the teammate of the subject, never as a journalist. He figured he'd better prepare a few questions beforehand. He wasn't the quickest person on his feet, and he didn't want to look the fool.

"Stupid people there," came a weedy voice beside him. "They know nothing. Nothing."

To his surprise, it was Madame Marois talking. The strange part was she was not addressing anyone. She was just staring ahead and muttering away.

She stretched out a thin arm and waved something invisible away.

"So stupid," she said and then was silent.

Burke was concerned. He had known her—*seen* her would be a more accurate description, he thought—for more than two years and had never seen her talk in such a way.

"Madame Marois, are you all right?" he ventured.

It was like she hadn't heard him. He repeated his question.

Slowly, she turned her head to stare at him, her eyes hard and her lips squeezed together.

"Your accent is not very pleasant," she said.

"My accent?" said Burke, surprised.

"Yes, you speak like you have no education. Maybe you are a foreigner," she said, nodding to herself.

"I live here, but I am from Québec—in Canada," he said.

"Stupid!" she said in a snarl. "I know where Québec is."

By this time, Claude had come over, having spotted the awkward exchange. He caught Burke's attention. Burke shrugged.

"Are you feeling well, Madame?" Burke asked.

"I'm fine if you'd leave me alone," she said, her head swiveling back to her usual view of the stone wall.

Burke gave up. "I'm sorry if I have bothered you. I just wanted to make sure you are feeling well."

The old woman shook her head, brought up her rosé and took a sip. She was obviously done with Burke. He glanced up at Claude with a look that silently asked if he had encountered Madame Marois in this state before.

"Life is a puzzle, my friend," Claude said to Burke, who nodded. The café owner then moved to visit with the newcomers.

The two government workers caught everyone's attention when they yelled *"Merde!"* in unison as the English sprinter beat a Frenchman to victory in the day's TDF race.

Burke didn't care about the stage winner.

He finished his beer, glanced at Madame Marois, who was once again a still-life figure, and then went inside to pay his bill.

"You're leaving so soon?" asked Hélène.

"Too busy for me," Burke said with a smile.

The truth was that Madame Marois's small outburst had bothered him. She'd sounded angry—not at him, but at something.

He didn't want any of her grief or pain to rub off on him.

CHAPTER 5

BURKE PUT ASIDE HIS bike and drove his old Citroën to the news conference the next day. He'd dressed up somewhat, wearing pleated black slacks and a gray sports jacket. With newly shined black shoes and a white, collarless linen shirt, he thought he looked relatively professional.

The news conference was in a large meeting room, and when he arrived, there were already twenty members of the media in the room. Half sat in chairs; the others stood behind TV cameras.

Burke looked around for the print reporter Lemaire had sent. He spotted him in an aisle seat and went over, sitting beside him.

Marc Boutillier acknowledged Burke with a smile. He was an affable young man, maybe twenty-five, not long out of university, a studious sort who wrote well and, by Lemaire's estimation, would be moving on to bigger and better things in no time.

They chatted for a few minutes. Neither had heard anything more about the cause of McManus's death.

Soon, a parade of a half dozen individuals entered the room, in which the media had doubled. A short, stocky man and a tall, willowy woman wore white lab coats. The other four—all men—sported dark suits. Everyone looked glum.

The first speaker turned out to be a representative of the World Professional Cycling Federation, which ran the world's major pro cycling races. He explained that the two doctors present would make brief comments. But first, he introduced the vice president of the WPCF.

His name was Jean-Guy Brandenheim, and with that mix of French and German names, Burke figured he came from the Alsace section of

France where there was often a blending of names thanks to control of the region switching between France and Germany over the centuries.

The VP's comments, however, were hardly bizarre. He expressed his and his organization's sorrow for the loss of the legendary McManus. A stage later in this year's TDF would be dedicated to the great man.

VP Brandenheim turned it back to the host, who ushered the short doctor to the lectern. According to him, the cause of death could now be officially declared as sudden cardiac arrest, which, he explained, was different from a myocardial infarction—a heart attack, in layman's terms. The latter is caused by the blocking of blood, and therefore oxygen, to the heart. Apparently, the heart can keep beating, and often, a victim survives the attack. However, during sudden cardiac arrest the heart stops beating altogether, which in turn stops blood flowing to the brain and other vital organs. The doctor said the result is usually fatal. He added that sudden cardiac arrest can happen in people who seem healthy and do not have any known heart disease issues.

"His heart simply could not keep up with the workload he placed on it," he explained.

The doctor then launched into detailed medical descriptions that hurt Burke's head. When Burke looked around, he saw that most of the journalists seemed equally lost. They wanted simpler language.

Someone asked if McManus's job might have played a part in the fatal attack. The doctor shrugged and said that stressful occupations can be hard on a person's physical and emotional well-being. Burke rolled his eyes at that one. Stress was bad for you? Hardly news.

Another journalist asked if McManus's condition had been known. The host jumped in and said, "No," then glanced at the two physicians, who both shook their heads, confirming this answer.

A reporter a few rows up wondered aloud if McManus's team had conducted proper physical examinations of its managerial staff.

In response, a small man approached the podium and introduced himself as Wayne Lavalley, director of sponsorship marketing for McManus's team.

"Every member of our cycling team staff receives a medical exam," he said in a high-pitched voice. "Mr. McManus showed absolutely no signs of having any health issues on any front."

The questions continued to focus on how McManus could have held such a job with a ticking time bomb in his chest. The cycling federation rep, the marketing director and the doctors took turns batting back answers that seemed reasonable to Burke, but didn't seem to satisfy most of the media there.

Burke remembered Lemaire's suggested line of questioning and stuck up his hand like a kid in school. The tall doctor pointed at him, prompting him to ask his question.

Burke stood and looked about. The volume in the room dropped somewhat as he spoke. "Is there any indication that Monsieur McManus doped when he was a rider, and if so, did that have anything to do with his heart attack?" he asked, hearing his own voice quiver with nerves.

The doctor smiled at him the way a teacher does at a small child who's conquered a task. "No, no physical evidence," she said. "And to be accurate, it was sudden cardiac arrest, not a myocardial infarction."

Burke mumbled, "Sorry," in response to the doctor's correction.

Beside him, Marc Boutillier followed up with a related question: "Is there any record anywhere—maybe within the cycling organization—that suggests or points to McManus having used illegal substances?"

The two doctors both turned to VP Brandenheim, who, for the first time, looked fully engaged in the Q and A.

"I cannot say we have such information indicating that," said Brandenheim, frowning. "The passing of Pierre McManus isn't a doping story. It's a tragic story about a man who contributed enormously to our sport. Don't make the story something it isn't."

Burke grimaced and looked at Boutillier, who looked newly energized.

The follow-up questions zeroed in on Brandenheim's response, and soon, the reporters were implying that maybe the WPCF had drug test records that related to the McManus case but weren't being released.

As the session got more confrontational, Burke found himself losing interest. The journalists wanted the truth, but they seemed to want a truth that would sell.

The news conference began to wind down. Some TV crews were packing and leaving. A couple of the suits that were at the podium had somehow disappeared.

Burke stuck up his hand for a second question. The host pointed to him.

"Do the police have anything to say about McManus's death?" he asked.

The host shook his head in disgust. Brandenheim jumped in. "It was a heart attack, nothing more," he said. Then he glanced at the two doctors. "Sorry, sudden cardiac arrest. Now, leave the man's legacy in peace."

And with that, the news conference ended.

Boutillier looked at Burke. "Interesting question," he said. "What made you think about that?"

"I figured I should ask at least one more question. Besides, a bunch of the questions mentioned drug use. That's illegal. That means the police might have been involved."

Boutillier nodded. "Yet no one was here from the police, or at least not that I noticed," he said. "Maybe we should give them a quick call. Better yet, let's go over and talk to them. I've got the time."

"Me too."

Ten minutes later, they were explaining to a desk cop that they wanted to talk to someone in authority about the recent death of Pierre McManus. Boutillier waved a press card to show he was legit. Burke fumbled around to show he had one somewhere. Before he ran out of places to search, the cop got on the phone.

"Wait there," he said after hanging up, pointing toward a bench behind them.

A couple of minutes later, the door to the restricted area opened, and a smartly dressed young woman of thirty-five marched out. She had a computer tablet with her.

She introduced herself as Annette Remus and said she handled media inquiries.

Remus led them to a side area away from the flow of people coming into the station. Burke figured she wasn't going to say much, since she hadn't brought them back beyond the restricted doors.

Boutillier asked if the police were in any way investigating McManus's death.

Remus looked at her tablet. Burke tried to peek over her shoulder, but she was as tall as he was, and he couldn't see anything without being too obvious. Remus screwed up her eyes as she studied the tablet.

"We just have a record of the vehicle he was driving striking another vehicle at the end of the race," she said. "We have the damages. No one has been charged—obviously. Just a sad occurrence."

"Did the police talk to the medical staff about McManus's heart condition or look into the autopsy findings?" Burke asked, surprising himself again at his newfound willingness to ask questions.

"We followed the usual procedures to ensure nothing unusual was involved—and it wasn't," Remus said. "End of story as far as we are concerned."

"No more investigation then?" Burke persisted.

"We have acted according to the evidence," Remus said. "Thanks for coming."

She spun and marched off.

Boutillier nudged Burke in the side. "Do you think something illegal happened to McManus?"

Burke pondered that for a moment. Then he shook his head. "No, not really. I just don't get how that bastard could pop off driving a car," he said.

"Like someone earlier said, it happens—a lot."

"I guess."

"Well, I've got a story to write and probably a follow-up after that to start working on," Boutillier said as they started toward the exit.

"What angle will you take?"

"How the team will replace him for the long term," Boutillier told him. "Maybe a sidebar on how teams examine the physical well-being of their training staff."

Burke wondered what he'd write about in the next day or two.

"Do a piece on the organizers' sensitivity to doping questions," said Boutillier, who had obviously picked up on Burke struggling to plot his next piece.

"That might work," Burke said with a nod.

It was time for lunch.

A seaside meal seemed like a delightful idea, so he drove just outside the new area of Villeneuve-Loubet to Roxie's, a restaurant by the boardwalk that overlooked both the beach and the entire bay, which stretched out to encompass Nice. It was one of his favorite restaurants on the Med.

He turned off the main street onto the side track where Roxie's was. Usually, parking was a problem, but he spotted an open space and pulled into it, considering himself lucky.

Burke thought about what he'd have for lunch. Maybe one of Roxie's fantastic seafood dishes or their specialty—tagliatelle with a black clam sauce. Then, from his right, came the sickening crunch of metal on metal as an old blue sedan drove into an idling van that was parked facing outward.

He stopped to watch. The driver's side door of the blue sedan opened, and an elderly woman eased herself out, one hand over her mouth, her face frozen in shock. Meanwhile, the van's engine was cut and the driver—a swarthy, balding man in his mid-forties—was quickly outside to inspect the damage. He then approached the woman.

Burke walked toward the fender bender, anticipating a problem. Then the man spoke to the old woman in a comforting tone, easing Burke's fear of a confrontation. "It's all right. Just a minor accident," he reassured her.

She responded by bursting into tears and collapsing against the side of her car.

The van driver opened the back door of her car and eased her down.

"Can I help?" offered Burke as he stood behind the man.

"She's very shaken," the driver said. "I told her it's nothing, but she's not listening."

The old woman looked up at Burke. Her eyes darted about, seemingly unable to focus on one subject.

"Who are you?" she asked. "Are you the police? Are you going to take away my license?"

Burke and the van driver exchanged worried glances.

"I'm just a bystander, madame," Burke replied, bending down onto his haunches and patting her hand. "I just want to make sure you're OK."

The van driver leaned down and smiled. "There's no real damage to your car and just a small dent in my old van, madame," he said. "It happens. Please do not worry yourself."

The old woman nodded to herself, but her eyes continued to flutter about.

"Where am I?" she asked, not looking at either of them.

"Just near the Hippodrome and by the beach," the van driver said. "Where were you going?"

She frowned. "I can't remember. I'm sorry, but I just can't remember where I was going."

"Do you have family nearby?" asked Burke.

"I have a daughter, Thérèse, who lives near the beach," she mumbled.

"Mama!" came an approaching voice.

Burke turned. A woman of about fifty came rushing toward them, her long, curly red hair trailing behind as she jogged.

"She's my mother," the woman said when she reached them.

The van driver explained what had happened. The daughter nodded and, seeming to note his gentleness toward her mother, thanked him for his efforts.

"I've been telling her it's a bad idea to drive, but she doesn't listen," she said, rubbing her mother's arm and then patting her hand. "She is forgetting things, and her sense of balance is not so good anymore. Maybe she'll understand this is the last time she should drive."

She checked out the damage and apologized. The van driver shrugged off the small nick by the front right light and said dents were part of his job as a delivery man. They agreed it wasn't worthwhile to involve the insurance companies, and so they shook hands, and the driver left.

"You saw it?" the daughter asked Burke.

"I saw the result," Burke said.

She shook her head. "I'm afraid her mind is getting cloudier. She has good days, but she has bad ones. This is a bad one. Old age isn't kind, I think."

Burke agreed, wished her well and then left for Roxie's.

Glancing back, Burke watched the woman help her mother stand. Then she embraced her.

Yesterday, it had been Madame Marois. Today, it was this old woman. Life could come to collect its tax at any time, and Burke told himself he had to enjoy it while he could. So, as he turned onto Roxie's outdoor terrace, he decided he would enjoy the moment and order the best seafood meal on the menu and wash it down with a good bottle of rosé.

He exchanged greetings with the owner and a couple of servers who recognized him, then took a small table under the shade of a palm tree. The view of the bay, with the Maritime Alps behind, was majestic and as beautiful as it got in Burke's estimation.

Burke started with his usual pastis and then moved on to a glass of excellent rosé with an opener of crab-stuffed tomatoes that were remarkably succulent. As he waited for the entrée of Greek shrimp saganaki, his phone rang.

It was Lemaire.

"Marc told me about the news conference," he began. "I think you should get me that blog by noon tomorrow, and it would be a good idea to do a race update after catching the stage to Mont Ventoux in a couple of days. Drop by here for your press pass."

"The Ventoux?" Burke said, echoing the name of the famous—and dreaded—climb in Provence.

"See how the teams are coping after McManus's loss," Lemaire instructed. "Or see if they even care. The setting couldn't be better. The Ventoux will be epic."

Burke had to ask. "Expenses covered?"

Lemaire sighed. "Yes, but within reason. One night's accommodation, mileage, a meal or two. No pastis, though. And, Paul, we'll probably get you to do a print piece as well as a blog, so take some photos, OK?"

The shrimp dish showed up just as Burke was trying to recall where the charger for his camera was back at his apartment.

"I'll get that blog to you today, François, and I'll leave tomorrow for the Ventoux," Burke said. "The crowds will already be lining up. I'll have to hurry."

Lemaire agreed, and they ended the call.

Burke sat back, sipped his rosé and, in his mind, saw the lunar landscape of the top half of the Ventoux. He had ridden the mountain twice as a pro, and both occasions had been miserable, pulverizing climbs made worse by brutal crosswinds that had almost blown away some fans on the roadside.

He smiled to himself.

He wouldn't be riding the Ventoux this time, *and* he'd be on an expense account.

CHAPTER 6

THE NEXT DAY, AFTER a couple of extra strength coffees and reading the *Nice-Matin* newspaper, Burke packed a small overnight bag and left his apartment.

His car was parked in the public lot a couple of hundred meters away. As he approached his Citroën, he saw Madame Marois sitting on a bench that overlooked the stream that ran by the old village. He was surprised. He had never seen her before noon, and here it was, not even nine in the morning.

Burke approached the old woman, who was staring at the slow-moving stream. A few meters away, Plato was sniffing the grass, stretching his leash to the maximum.

He figured he'd try the casual approach. "Bonjour, Madame."

No reaction.

"Are you all right?" he asked, bending toward her.

She didn't twitch.

"Madame Marois, are you all right?"

Asking this of her was becoming a habit.

This time, she jerked as if she'd been awoken. Without blinking, she turned toward Burke.

"Yes?" she asked.

"Bonjour," Burke said again, noticing that Plato had given up on the grass and come over for a visit.

"Bonjour," she said and then turned back to staring blankly at the stream.

"Are you feeling well today?" Burke asked.

Her body snapped once more, and then she turned sharply toward him. "Young man, I'm old, which means I'm never feeling very well, but I am otherwise fine. Why are you bothering me with such trivialities?"

It was like a light had turned on inside her.

"I just saw you sitting alone out here, and I wanted to make sure you were OK," Burke said.

"I am fine," Madame Marois said as she leaned down and scratched Plato's ears. "I will be better when I'm left to my own thoughts without being bothered."

Burke apologized, wished her *Bonne journée* and then left.

Old age is a bugger, he thought as he walked to his car.

Although his Citroën was more than ten years old, it still had guts, and Burke enjoyed driving it. With the latest CD from Bruce Springsteen keeping him company, he passed by Antibes and then Cannes, groaning at the idea of spending any time in that overexposed movie town. Soon, he was on the national highway, charging along at 120 kilometers per hour. Burke thought it a little odd that the older he got, the more he enjoyed driving.

Burke figured he'd end up finding accommodation a long way from Ventoux, given that as many as a half million people would be visiting the mountain for the stage race. His preference was to stay in the small town of Bédoin, which served as the unofficial start to the southern climb of Ventoux, but that would be impossible. All of the rooms in the community had likely been booked within a day of the Tour's route being announced the previous year.

After three hours of hard driving, Burke spotted the turnoff for the small city of Carpentras and, in a snap decision, took it. He'd try the first hotel or bed-and-breakfast he found. As he approached the outskirts of the city, he saw a *"Chambre D'Hote"* sign and turned off. His luck was good. The owner—a plump woman in her early sixties—had one available room in her B and B. He took it.

After dropping his stuff in the small bedroom, Burke figured he'd drive the forty kilometers to Ventoux and see what was happening.

He stopped in his tracks as a radio blared. There had been another unexpected death associated with the Tour de France.

"*...The Global Projects team trainer was found dead this morning near the team hotel just outside Avignon. Police have not released details but say the circumstances surrounding the death of Mark Den Weent are being investigated. Neither the team nor race organizers have commented.*"

Burke was stunned—Den Weent was dead? What the hell was happening?

The announcer continued: "*The death follows on the heels of the sudden passing of the team's directeur sportif, Pierre McManus. It is unclear if the team will continue in the race. The sixth stage starts this afternoon at 1:30.*"

"Monsieur?" came a voice close to Burke.

He turned. The landlady was watching him, puzzled at his mid-stride stance.

He explained he had just been listening to the radio report.

"Terrible, terrible," she said. "I heard it last hour. Two men dead in such a short period. Very sad."

Burke, feeling shocked, agreed. His cell phone rang. He excused himself and took the call. It was Lemaire, who asked if Burke had heard the news.

"I don't know what the hell is going on, but you're close to Avignon, so we can have a local voice if you hurry over," Lemaire said.

After Lemaire fired off instructions, Burke dashed for the car and was soon belting along a secondary highway to Avignon, which was just over twenty kilometers away. He didn't know exactly where the police station was, but he had a good idea. He also thought he knew where the Global Projects team hotel was.

As he flew along well above the speed limit, Burke tried to process what was happening. A few days ago, he had been sitting at home, not doing much except relaxing and pondering a topic for his next blog. Everything had been moving at a relaxed pace. Now, he was chasing the Tour de France and trying to find out why two men—men he knew personally—were dead.

CHAPTER 7

BURKE MADE IT TO the police station in thirty minutes, but parking was a problem. The streets leading to the station were completely congested. There were several TV trucks parked and scores of media people milling about with cameras, microphones and notebooks. It was bedlam.

He found a parking spot three blocks away and ran to the station while trying to sort out what he needed to learn. Lemaire had told him that the news services would provide the basics of the story. Burke's job was to get a different angle for a blog and a couple of quotes from someone the news agency people wouldn't think to approach. *What the hell did that mean?* Burke wondered. He was no journalist.

But Den Weent was dead, and he wanted to know what happened.

He elbowed his way through the media and into the station entrance, which was small and packed with more reporters and camera people. Four burly cops were ensuring that no media personnel got into areas where they didn't belong.

"Anything new?" Burke asked a pleasant-looking blonde.

She threw him a scowl in return. "What do you think?" she snapped.

He tried a fifty-something man who was scribbling on a notepad despite being bumped every second or two.

"Nothing yet," the reporter said. "The cops aren't saying much."

The reporter studied Burke for a moment. "Who are you with?"

Burke needed a second. "I, uh, do blogs," he finally said.

The man snorted and shook his head in disgust. "Are you fucking for real?"

"It's a living," Burke said, feeling a little prickly at the man's sudden hostility.

"You look slightly familiar," the reporter said.

"Ex-pro racer," Burke replied.

"You're Burke, Paul Burke. Right?"

"Yes."

"I remember your bit on TV. Fucking unreal!" the reporter said, chuckling. "Now you're a blogger?"

"Yeah," Burke said.

"Well, hang around for a few minutes, Burke, because I have an idea the cops will give us something a little fresher."

The veteran journalist was right. Five minutes later, two men in suits came out from the restricted area, introduced themselves to the horde—Burke didn't get their names, which he figured wasn't good—and then began a short briefing.

To his disgust, Burke discovered he'd forgotten his recorder in his car. He pulled out his small notepad and tried to scribble down some main points, but he knew that was a lost cause since he was painfully slow at note-taking. He hoped his memory was working.

The two men in suits were detectives. The police were investigating the death as a homicide. Burke heard reporters near him mutter that it was time for some real information.

Then someone in the scrum asked how Den Weent had been killed.

The older detective said a knife had been used. He wouldn't expand.

"When was Den Weent's body found?" shouted another voice.

"Between midnight and 6 a.m.," replied the other suit.

The grumpy journo next to him muttered, "That's fucking helpful."

The Q and A went on for another five minutes, but the police were making it clear they weren't going to give any in-depth info. The reporters were clearly frustrated, and when the detectives left, most could be heard complaining or cursing.

Burke figured the TDF might have some official comment but then reminded himself that he wasn't a reporter, just a blogger getting paid a few euros for offering some snappy opinions about bicycling.

So, he phoned Lemaire and told him about the police station news conference.

"Yeah, no surprise they didn't want to give out anything good," Lemaire said.

Burke told him he was considering contacting the TDF for a quote.

"We already have something from them," Lemaire said.

"So, what should I do?" Burke asked, feeling a little stupid.

Lemaire paused. "Do the team hotel thing again," he suggested. "Then file something, no more than three hundred words. After that, check with me. We'll go from there."

Burke hadn't signed up to chat about the recently deceased, but he didn't want to anger Lemaire, so he agreed to follow the plan. After he ended the call, Burke wondered if there was another way to make some money without having to rush about talking to police and team officials about dead guys. He promised himself he'd do a little research when he got home and away from this TDF chaos.

Burke had a few ideas where Global might be staying. He suspected that if he phoned, he wouldn't get anything from a receptionist, so he got in his car and started driving. He went to his first two choices, and from outside, it was clear no bike team was staying there. Outside the Hotel du Ciel was a Global Projects car, three police cars and several TV crews and other media people crowding the entrance.

He parked a block away and hurried back to the hotel. When he got there, he noticed a couple of familiar faces among the press pack, but he decided to keep to himself.

And saying nothing seemed to be the theme of the moment, because a team rep who Burke didn't recognize was telling the scrum of journalists that the team was saddened by the death but would say nothing more.

That, of course, didn't stop the reporters from asking all kinds of questions, but the team rep remained in control, repeating his message and then excusing himself.

Burke shook his head. It had been a waste of time coming here.

"Hey, you're Paul Burke, aren't you?"

The voice belonged to a thin, lanky, curly-haired fellow in his mid-twenties. He was unfamiliar to Burke.

The young man stuck out a hand. "I'm Matthieu Martin," he said. "I'm a reporter with *Le Journal* in Montréal. We did a piece a few years ago on your retirement. 'Local Cyclist Calls It a Career' or something like that."

Burke shook hands. "I remember talking to someone from your paper," he said. It was one of the last interviews he ever did.

"I'm here to cover some of the Tour," Martin explained. "Since there are a couple of big pro cycling races in the fall in Québec, my editors sent me here to do some color. The races are very popular, so they figured it's smart to get some extra buzz going."

"Makes sense," Burke said.

"But they didn't figure on all this shit happening," Martin added. "I mean, a top directeur sportif pops off driving the team car one day, and then another trainer dies, this time stabbed to death? Shit!"

"Know anything about what happened to Den Weent?"

"Nothing more than what the cops are saying, which is virtually nothing," Martin said. "The team reps aren't talking either." He paused. "Why are you here, Paul?"

Burke gave a short spiel about his blog and helping his editor out with some work for the print paper.

"So, you're a reporter now." Martin grinned.

Burke laughed at that one. "Not a chance. I'm just floating around, trying to get something that'll keep my editor happy enough that I can keep doing a blog," he said. "It's about paying the bills."

Martin smiled and then flicked back a couple of pages in his notepad. "Well, maybe I can toss something your way that might help you with your blog," he said.

When he saw Burke's surprised expression, Martin grinned and said, "I'm a good guy, and you helped our paper a few years ago."

"Thanks," Burke said, pleased about the younger man's generosity but doubtful he would get much that he could use.

"The only interesting aspect—besides the fact that Den Weent got himself killed—is that he was in his room one minute, and apparently the next time anyone saw him, he was dead in an alley not far from the hotel," Martin said, jabbing a finger at something he had scribbled.

"How'd you learn that?"

"I overheard a couple of cops back at the station. It's not much, but it's something," Martin said. He shook his head. "I've written seven pieces since I got here—four about the actual race and three about McManus's death. I didn't figure I'd be mixing it up like that."

"Three stories about McManus?"

"He was in Québec the last two years for our races, so he's fairly well known within the cycling community of the province. I interviewed him a couple of times. When he wasn't chasing women, he was working the media, although he seemed a bit of a jerk."

Burke considered McManus again. The trainer had been something of a womanizer. He remembered a handful of times when McManus had literally abandoned a conversation to chase down some attractive female who had strolled by—and how a couple of those women had responded not with a scream for the police, but with an unexpected coquettishness.

"He was a jerk for sure, but I forgot about him and women," Burke said.

"I don't think he was ever married," Martin said. "A wife would probably have gotten in the way."

Burke nodded.

"Well, I have to file soon, so I better get writing," Martin said, reaching to shake hands.

Burke took Martin's hand, thanked the reporter and wished him well.

"Thanks," Martin replied. "I'm here until the end of the race, so maybe I'll bump into you again. Where are you off to next?"

"I'm hanging around here for another day. Going to the Ventoux, then home," Burke said.

"I'm at the Ventoux tomorrow. It'll be a helluva stage. Maybe I'll see you there."

Burke nodded. He figured the chances of seeing Martin on the Ventoux would be next to zero, given there would be hundreds of thousands of people lining the route.

Back in his car, Burke called Lemaire, who grumbled about the lack of new findings but took Burke's info so he could write something up. Then he told Burke to do something with the nutty fans already lining the Ventoux route the next day.

"But come back tomorrow," Lemaire said. "We're not paying for another night in a hotel."

Burke ended the call and, relieved he didn't have to write a newspaper story about Den Weent's sudden death, drove back to his Carpentras bed-and-breakfast. The closer he got to his digs, the more tired he became. His mind was active though, floating from images of McManus chasing a woman to the last time he had seen Den Weent.

CHAPTER 8

AFTER AN EARLY BREAKFAST, Burke jumped into his car and drove hard toward Mont Ventoux. His chances of getting anywhere near the mountain would be nil because there would probably be at least a quarter million people lining the route on the flat parts of the stage with at least the same number perched by the roadside of the famous climb. He'd do what he could and then leave.

Still, he knew a Tour de France stage featuring the Ventoux would be special, and he felt himself getting excited to see some of the stage. It wasn't the highest mountain in France by any stretch, but, for Burke's money, it represented the toughest climb at twenty-two kilometers, with a 7.1 percent average gradient and winds that usually blew with ferocity. By the time the riders made it to the top, they'd be physically and mentally exhausted. Burke certainly had been when he'd done the Ventoux.

After two hours of speeding and then having to slow down to a pedestrian pace as traffic increased, Burke approached the small town of Bédoin, where the race to the Ventoux would really launch. He decided to try a country road north of the town. It would probably be jammed by fans by this time, but it was worth a try.

The road wasn't as busy as he expected, and he managed to get a few kilometers closer to the actual base of the mountain. He parked by the side of the road and near a farm that looked like it needed some attention. He had a kilometer to walk to get to the road where the cyclists would go by.

Walking along a potholed dirt path, Burke was still five hundred meters from the main road when all kinds of parked vehicles and then the outlines of thousands of people came into view. He cursed at having to do all this for a silly-assed blog or maybe a few words in someone else's newspaper article.

When he got within one hundred meters, sounds of merriment reached his ears. There had obviously been some serious partying going on.

He approached a group of eight middle-aged fans, who were each decked out in a red-and-white, polka dot replica cycling jersey that honored the leading rider in the mountains. They seemed sober, and that probably put them in the minority.

He introduced himself as a blogger for a newspaper. No one seemed impressed by that. He asked where they were from.

"Holland," said a bespectacled man.

Burke wondered why they weren't wearing jerseys featuring the Dutch national color of orange, but didn't ask. The quicker he got his information, the quicker he could leave.

A short, plump man in the group pointed a finger at Burke. The man's face was scrunched up in concentration. Then he broke into a grin, and Burke knew what was coming next.

"You're the Paul Burke who used to be a rider and who was on TV, yes?" the man said in English.

Burke nodded.

The others broke into smiles. They may not have recognized his face, but they knew something about the name. Burke silently cursed YouTube.

He went through a short list of questions he'd prepped.

How long they had been there? Two nights. *Had they come for the entire Tour de France?* Just for the Ventoux. *Was it their first time watching the TDF live?* No, they'd seen stages when the race had gone outside French borders into the Low Countries of the Netherlands and Belgium. *Did they have a camper?* Yes, two. *How did they pass the time while waiting for the race to show up?* They played cards. *Why did they drive so far for one day's stage?* Because the legendary "Giant of Provence" is not on the TDF course except every few years. *Were they having a good time?* Absolutely. *What would they do after the Ventoux stage?* Drive home, maybe stop outside Paris for a night.

He got their names, thanked them and then moved on to three young, happy-looking men draped in American flags. He went through the same routine. The answers weren't as thoughtful as the responses from the Dutch, but that was likely due to the beer the men had obviously been drinking.

Just as he thanked them for their comments, one of them piped out in a Texan accent: "What's the deal with these cycling coaches suddenly dying?"

"You mean Den Weent and McManus?" Burke asked.

"Yeah, those guys," he said. "I mean, that's pretty fucking strange, don't you think?"

Burke agreed.

"Gotta wonder if they're connected," the Texan suggested.

One of his friends scoffed at that idea. "One died of a heart attack, and the other guy, Den Weent, croaked from being knifed," he said. "You can't orchestrate a heart attack, dummy."

"Maybe not," he replied.

Burke nodded. The deaths had to be coincidence, but it was strange nevertheless.

He thanked them and was set to move on when the Texan blurted out, "Aren't you going to ask us who's going to win today?"

Burke had been surprised that the three were familiar with the deaths of the two men and that one of them at least knew Den Weent's name. Now they were willing to provide the names of the Ventoux winner?

"OK, tell me," Burke said, figuring these three might end up being the focus of his blog. They might be a little drunk and somewhat rowdy, but maybe they knew their stuff, cycling-wise.

The Texan went first. "Pieterangelo is my guy," he said, naming a tiny Italian climber who was useless on the flats and in time trials but went up the side of a mountain at an astonishing speed.

"He'll be close, but Alvarez will win," said another.

"Which Alvarez?" the Texan asked, impressing Burke even more with his knowledge. There were at least two riders named Alvarez in the race.

"The Colombian. The leaders will let him go because he's no threat to the overall title."

The third man offered his perspective. "Good picks, but the winner will be—drum roll, please—Pavel Kladinsky. He'll do it on a small breakaway."

Burke thanked them once again.

"Hey, dude, I bet you'll find a link between McManus and Den Weent if you try hard enough," the Texan said. "It would make a great fucking blog if you could get it."

Burke smiled at that as he left. The three had been impressive with their selections for the stage winner. As for finding a link between the deaths of the two trainers, Burke knew it was absurd to think the police hadn't double-checked that possibility, however improbable it seemed.

But he still had a niggling feeling that somehow, he might know something about McManus and Den Weent that could be valuable.

CHAPTER 9

BURKE MADE IT BACK home by 10 p.m. that night. It had been an exhausting day, and having to drive hours in sweltering weather without air conditioning did not help. He dropped his bag onto the couch and then washed up. He thought about going to bed, but his mind was still busy. If he tried to go to sleep now, his brain wouldn't permit it, and he'd be up most of the night.

As for his blog about the Ventoux, he had to have it done by ten the next morning. He told himself he'd do it after breakfast.

He went to Claude's café for a soothing nightcap.

"You look tired, my friend," Claude said when he spotted Burke sitting in his usual spot on the terrace.

"Exhausted, Claude," Burke replied.

"I'll come back, and you'll tell me why you're so tired," said the café owner.

Claude dropped off two glasses of red wine for a couple in their sixties dressed in white linen. Burke wondered if they were from one of the new developments. It didn't matter. They seemed quiet and polite, smiling at Claude when he made a small joke about the heat serving as an excellent weight-loss program.

Back at Burke's table with a pastis, Claude collapsed into the opposite chair like a sack of potatoes. He was probably more tired than Burke.

In a few sentences, Burke explained where he had been.

"Yes, I heard all about the murder," Claude said. "This has been a very strange Tour."

"Today, a person I interviewed suggested there could be a connection between Den Weent's murder and McManus's death. Stupid, really, but who knows what's going on? If I worked for Global Projects, I'd be writing out my will."

Claude chuckled at the dark joke. "I expect you have not heard about our little activity here," he said.

"What happened?"

"Our poor Madame Marois went for lunch alone—although Plato was with her as usual—at one of those upscale cafés by the marina. She parked her car and then ate. When she returned to her car, she couldn't find her car keys. She had her house keys in her purse, but not the ones for her car. They weren't in her purse. They weren't in the ignition or on the floor or on the driver's seat. She apparently became very upset. Some strangers tried to help her find her keys. They retraced her steps back to the restaurant. No luck. Madame Marois was in tears."

Burke was surprised to hear the old woman had reacted so emotionally. He would have wagered she had no tear ducts.

"Madame Marois wanted her daughter to come and help, but she couldn't remember the daughter's cell phone number," Claude continued.

"That's not good," Burke said.

"What is worse is that her daughter lives in Canada," Claude said with a shrug.

"Canada?"

"Yes. Vancouver, apparently. Do you know it?" Claude asked.

"It's almost four thousand kilometers from Montréal to Vancouver," Burke said, "but I know it. Very beautiful. By the way, how do you know all this?"

"Patience, my friend," Claude admonished, glancing around to ensure no one needed his attention. "The people helping Madame figured out that her daughter lives abroad. When they heard she also has a son, they asked where he lives. Well, he lives in Vienna, but she told them that even if he could be reached, he wouldn't help."

"This is getting sad, Claude," Burke said.

"Madame then said she knew where her car keys were."

"Where?"

"In her shoe," Claude said, arching his eyebrows.

"Were they?"

Claude nodded. "She had tucked the car keys into the side of her shoe. Madame explained she used to hide keys in her shoe when she was young. She didn't know why she had put them there this time."

"Bizarre."

"She then calmed down and seemed back to her normal self, but she did ask these strangers if they would follow her home in their vehicle because she was still a little upset."

"Did they?"

"They did," Claude said. "They were very good people. Not many like that these days. They watched her park and then go to her apartment. Since they were here, they decided to have an aperitif and a little something to eat, and so they came to my café. We chatted a little, and they told me about Madame Marois. They were very concerned for her welfare, although she was apparently fine when she got back up to the village."

"It's lucky they were around to help," said Burke as he finished his pastis. "I just hope what happened isn't the start of a trend for Madame Marois. Anyway, I'm tired, Claude, and need to get some sleep. So, good night, my friend."

When he was stretched out in bed in his apartment, Burke thought about Madame Marois. She wasn't a friend, just a familiar face, but he felt sorry for her. It was tough getting old. He told himself to use his time better, before the decay set in.

CHAPTER 10

BURKE WAS STILL TIRED when he awoke the next day. He told himself he had to get in shape. If he was in better condition, he'd have more endurance, and his mind would work better.

Of course, less pastis would help, too.

After his newspapers and breakfast, Burke sat down at his computer and wrote his blog about the Ventoux stage, which the Colombian Alvarez had won by the length of a wheel. When he was done, he reread it. He smiled to himself. It wasn't bad at all. He'd been lucky to meet some colorful people lining the side of the road, but he still felt pleased with himself. He hoped Lemaire would like it.

He thought back to the three Americans who had tossed out the idea about the link between the deaths of McManus and Den Weent. It was silly, of course, but he wondered if it was possible that something could have caused McManus's heart to stop without being noticed.

Burke went to his computer and typed *"drugs causing a heart attack"* into Google, even though the doctors at the news conference had said McManus's death was due to sudden cardiac arrest. He figured "heart attack" was close enough. A half second later, he had more than twenty-three million results. He groaned.

A shortcut occurred to him, and he punched in *"Hotel l'Empereur."* He got the number and called the reception desk, asking for Ron Henderson, the wayward pharmacist from Montana who had collided with him on the Promenade des Anglais in Nice. If Burke remembered correctly, Henderson was still around for another day or two. If he wasn't, nothing lost.

To his surprise, the receptionist put him through. And to his greater surprise, Henderson answered the phone on the second ring.

Burke introduced himself again and instantly detected reluctance from Henderson.

"I'm not calling about the bike," Burke assured him. "I have a question totally unrelated to what happened, and I'm hoping you can help me."

A small sigh of relief sounded on the other end.

"OK, that's good," Henderson said, his voice more lively. "How can I help you?"

Burke explained why he had called.

"Well, that's not an easy question to answer," Henderson said, sounding like a college professor at the head of a lecture. "For example, antibiotics such as erythromycin and clarithromycin can really increase the chance of a heart attack for someone who has a heart issue."

Henderson cleared his throat. He was just getting started, or so it seemed to Burke. He went on about antifungal drugs and antidiabetic drugs and appetite suppressants. He mentioned anthracyclines and talked about cardiotoxicity.

Burke's head was spinning.

"Did your person have cancer?" Henderson asked. "There can be a connection between some anticancer drugs and a heart attack."

"I don't think so," Burke replied.

"Well, I'm not a doctor, but an autopsy should indicate if the subject had drugs in his system at the time of death. Of course, some drugs can disappear in the system quickly and might not be noticed at all if the pathologist isn't looking for them and doesn't conduct the right tests."

Burke was done. He couldn't handle any more information. Moreover, he didn't know what to do with anything Henderson had provided.

"Thanks for your help," Burke finally said.

"The bill's in the mail."

Burke paused.

"Just a joke," Henderson added.

Burke thanked him again and rang off.

He wondered if the autopsy done on McManus had been basic or more extensive with specialized testing. And if drugs were in McManus's system, what kind of drugs? Recreational ones? Something for a medical condition?

Burke's cell rang. It was Lemaire.

"Good job, your best blog yet," he told Burke. "Take a breather. Float me some ideas in the next day or so for your next blog."

End of conversation.

Burke figured he'd take a break and go for a ride. It would clear his head and certainly help his fitness. He changed quickly into his cycling clothes, grabbed his bike and left. Outside, he wondered about a route. Nothing too substantial, but still testing enough.

He had it—he'd take the back route to Grasse, a nice twenty-kilometer-long climb that ended just above the old town. The ascent would be easy by pro standards, but he wasn't a pro anymore so it would get his legs and lungs going. He might try pushing the pace a bit.

With a small change purse holding his ID and fifty euros in a back pocket of his cycling jersey, Burke jumped on his bike, pedaled quickly to the main road and turned right. The incline was gentle, and his legs worked the pedals with ease. The more you rode, the easier it got—or so he still believed.

The bike was beautifully engineered and took the corners smoothly. When he put some muscle into his riding, the machine snapped forward. He told himself he'd treat it to a cleanup when he got home. If this was how it responded when it had been neglected for a while, it would be spectacular when completely cleaned and tuned.

As he rode, his mind once more drifted back to the events of the last few days: McManus, Den Weent, the old woman outside Roxie's, blogs, Lemaire, news conferences. He hadn't been this busy in at least three years.

He was halfway up the climb when he decided to clear everything from his mind by pushing as hard as he could. He stood on the pedals and increased his cadence until he was hitting thirty kilometers per hour. He couldn't hold it for long, but it felt good. After a kilometer, he slowed to give his heart a break.

When he glided into the top of Grasse, he checked his watch. He'd made the trip in forty minutes—hardly good for a pro racer, but not bad for an ex-pro trying to get into shape.

Riding past the bus depot, a couple of cafés and a few shops, Burke smiled. He loved Grasse for the way it stretched from down in a valley to way up on a hillside, where he was now. And his affection for the city's Old

Town, with its ancient, twisting lanes, continued to increase with every visit. As for the cafés, they were magnificent and could satisfy anyone's tastes or wallet. He also didn't mind the hordes of tourists who often descended on the city because Grasse was the world's capital of perfume. His final reason for loving this special place involved the annual Fête du Jasmin in early August. He especially enjoyed the parade, during which young women on floats tossed flowers into the crowd. Everyone went home smelling of perfume. Burke had attended the last two festivals and could see no reason for missing the next one in a few weeks.

Dismounting his bike by the gardens that overlooked most of the city and, in the distance, Cannes, Burke walked down the main lane. There were a few tourists around, but most pedestrians looked like locals.

Burke spotted one of his favorite cafés. It was in a pastel-yellow building that had probably been there for three hundred years, and its terrace was one of the largest in the Old Town. He enjoyed stopping there for seafood pastas, which were the best he'd ever eaten, and for the owner's two daughters—each in their thirties, tall, sassy and absolutely gorgeous.

He placed his bike against a giant flowerpot and then grabbed a small table. He had barely sat down when one of the daughters, Amélie, strolled over, offering him a dazzling smile.

"Ah, Paul, it is good to see you," she said. "It has been a while."

"Too long," Paul said.

They chatted for a couple of minutes, and Paul enjoyed the conversation, although he knew Amélie was engaged and, despite some flirting, would never do anything more than talk to him.

He ended up ordering what she recommended—mussels with angel hair pasta, covered in a delicate tomato sauce. Since he had worked hard to get to Grasse, he added a glass of midrange cabernet sauvignon.

The wine came, and it was brilliant—smooth and round with just a hint of spice. Burke let his first sip curl around his tongue before it slipped down his throat. He shook his head. Since he had moved to Europe to pursue a cycling career, he had become something of a wine snob. If his childhood chums could see him now, they'd be shocked.

He watched the action along the lane.

Most of the people strolling by were local mothers with kids in tow. Some popped into a chocolate store directly opposite the café. They also visited a nearby shop that offered handcrafted glass jewelry.

Then he saw Madame Marois. Right on her heel was the loyal Plato, his little legs moving like pistons.

She was coming up the lane, holding something in her hand. As usual, she wore black, although she wasn't as heavily dressed as usual. She glanced around, and her eyes fell on him. She stopped, a perplexed look on her face. Surprised by the sudden stop, Plato bumped into her legs. Burke smiled and waved.

To Burke's surprise, she smiled back and came over. As smiles went, it wasn't much—just a twist of the ends of her lips—but it was better than anything Burke had seen from her in two years.

"Good day, monsieur," she said in her brittle voice.

She reached out and showed him what she was holding. It was a cameo pendant on a gold chain.

"It's lovely, isn't it?" she said. "I just purchased it down the way there. It reminds me of one I had as a young girl."

Burke told her it was beautiful—and it was. He didn't know how much it had cost, but he would have wagered well over three hundred euros.

Madame Marois pulled back the pendant and carefully put it in her small purse. Then she looked at Burke through her dark brown eyes.

"I believe I might have been rude to you recently, when I had some difficulties," she said.

"I didn't notice," Burke lied.

"If I was, I must apologize. It is a matter of age. I regret if I said anything that might have offended you."

"You have nothing to apologize for, Madame," Burke said.

He thought about inviting her to share his table, but she checked her watch and tilted her head as if trying to remember something.

"I believe I have to be somewhere," she said, more to herself. "I'm just not sure where. Oh, well, maybe it will come to me."

And without another word, Madame Marois and Plato turned and started up the lane toward the gardens. She was now glancing around in a jittery fashion. He hoped she'd make it back home—or wherever she was supposed to be—without incident.

Burke's lunch soon came, and it was as good as Amélie had promised. They chatted a little more, and then a crowd of tourists arrived, taking over several tables. The noise level increased. Burke decided to skip dessert.

He took his bike back up to the gardens and climbed aboard. He had made a decision. He'd ride back home—it was almost all downhill—and then he'd drive to the police station in Nice and ask someone about McManus's autopsy.

CHAPTER 11

THREE HOURS LATER, BURKE made his request to a police officer at the front desk. She frowned and asked that he provide identification. He pulled out his beaten-up press pass from Lemaire. The police officer studied it. Then, without a word, she turned and disappeared behind a door. The power of the press.

As he waited, Burke wondered if he wasn't being profoundly stupid.

A minute later, the desk cop was back, accompanied by a fifty-something man wearing a gray suit that was more than slightly wrinkled. The desk cop introduced the man as Inspector Jean-Pierre Fortin.

Burke went through his routine again for the new man.

"We had a news conference just the other day," Fortin said. "Weren't you there?"

Burke nodded sheepishly. "I was there, but I've been wondering ever since if there have been more findings about the autopsy."

"There aren't," the cop said.

Burke didn't know what to say. Neither officer volunteered anything. The three of them just stood there, not moving, not saying anything.

"Can you tell me if the doctor who did the autopsy tested for any specific medications that might have contributed to McManus's death?" Burke said.

He figured he'd try to make an impression, so he tossed out some of Henderson's drug terms—erythromycin and clarithromycin—that he had practiced on the way over. To his surprise, Fortin told Burke to follow him and then led him through the heavy door into a restricted area.

Burke followed Fortin down a windowless, institutional hallway to an office at the end. The office was airless and hot. There was nothing in the room that suggested a personal touch. Fortin sat behind a desk and motioned for Burke to take the metal chair facing him.

"I've been looking into the McManus matter," Fortin said.

Burke nodded. He didn't know what to say next, so he said nothing.

"Why are you wondering about specialized medications like erythromycin and clarithromycin?" Fortin asked, his hands clasped across his stomach.

Fortin seemed familiar with the medical terms. Burke explained he was struggling to accept that McManus had suddenly died and added that he understood there were a variety of drugs that could be legally ingested but lethal.

Fortin stared at Burke. "You heard what we told you press people at the news conference?" he finally said.

"Yes."

"And you somehow suspect something else?"

"I'm not sure what I suspect," Burke said.

"Are you suggesting the autopsy was flawed?" Fortin asked, sounding slightly belligerent to Burke.

"No. I'm just wondering how detailed the autopsy was," Burke replied.

"You're a former pro cyclist, aren't you? And aren't you the guy who fucked up on TV, too?"

There it was again, his television screwup. It was like everyone wanted to remind him of it. As if he could ever forget it.

"That's me," he said.

"And now you're some kind of journalist or blogger or something, and you think we're doing something wrong in how we're handling the McManus death," Fortin said.

Fortin was making a statement, not asking a question. Burke was ready to leave.

"No, I'm just a blogger for a website, and I'm only doing some follow-up," he said, starting to stand. He'd had enough. "No insult intended."

"Your accent is Québec, right?" Fortin asked.

That stopped Burke mid-movement. "Yes. I'm from Montréal."

"I know it," Fortin said. "I've been there twice on holidays."

Burke sat back down. He didn't have a clue what to do next.

"Anyway, I can only tell you we're still examining McManus's death," Fortin said.

Fortin had just given him a hint that something was amiss with McManus's death. *What were the police checking up on?* Burke wondered.

"For what?"

Fortin sighed. "It's just standard practice," he added.

But Burke sensed it wasn't "standard practice" in this case.

He tried to go a step further. "Do you suspect someone was involved in McManus's death?" he asked.

Fortin shook his head. "As I said, it's a procedural matter. We want to ensure we have examined everything we need to," he said.

Somehow, Burke didn't think this was the way an interview was usually conducted. He sensed that Fortin was leading him somewhere.

"Have you found any links between McManus's death and the murder of Den Weent in Avignon?" Burke asked.

Fortin stared at Burke, as if evaluating him somehow. "We're working with investigators there. I believe the media have been told we have nothing definite yet."

"But you suspect something, don't you?" Burke said, figuring he had nothing to lose by getting a little more aggressive.

"As I said, we're examining the evidence," Fortin said. "Right now, we have a man who died when his heart suddenly stopped and another who was killed by an unknown assailant. Did you know either man personally?"

Burke nodded. "I knew McManus a little and Den Weent better. I hope you catch his killer. He was a good man."

"Tell me about him," Fortin said.

It was more a demand than a request. Burke figured a journalist wouldn't comply, but he wasn't a journalist, so he related how Den Weent had been a smart, strong rider who understood cycling tactics and, as a result, had become a good strategist in races. Burke paused. It felt odd to talk about Den Weent in the past tense.

"He wasn't married," Fortin said.

Once again, it wasn't a question, just a statement to probe for a response. Fortin's interviewing strategy made Burke feel uncomfortable, but maybe that was his intent.

"He was married several years ago, but he got divorced," Burke said after a short pause.

"Was he one for the ladies?"

"I don't know," Burke said. "Why are you asking me about his love life?"

"Just curious," Fortin said. He pointed at Burke. "There's a lot of doping in the sport, isn't there?"

Burke bristled. "It's gotten a lot better with the biological passport," he said. "It's a lot cleaner. Other sports should pay attention to what's happening in cycling."

"But it's a fair bet that some staff on pro cycling teams would know their way around a needle," Fortin said.

"Most of those individuals have been weeded out these last few years," Burke told him.

"Did you dope?"

"Why do you care?" Burke was getting annoyed.

"I take that as a yes."

Burke had doped for a small part of a single season and hated how he felt emotionally, so he stopped. Instead, he became fanatical about diet, although he certainly didn't practice good eating habits anymore.

"You take it whatever way you want," Burke said. "I think I'm done here."

He stood, and Fortin did, too.

As Burke was about to step into the hallway, Fortin added, "If you think of any connection between McManus and Den Weent beyond the obvious ones, let me know."

He handed Burke his card.

Burke walked down the hallway with Fortin trailing behind him. He had the feeling the police in Nice and Avignon suspected the deaths of McManus and Den Weent were both murders—and were connected.

Burke tried to decide if there was a blog there. *Screw it*, he told himself. His brain was on overload. He'd decide later if he would blog about McManus and Den Weent.

It was time for Claude's café.

CHAPTER 12

AFTER CHANGING INTO BEIGE linens, Burke strolled down to Claude's café. He didn't want to think about Fortin, McManus or Den Weent, so he focused on the beautiful flower pots positioned by the stairs as he went down toward the café.

It wasn't working. His mind was still spinning with Fortin's comments. This was getting a bit silly. He wasn't a journalist, nor was he a private investigator, yet he was now consumed by two deaths associated with the Tour de France and chasing a link between the two.

Since it was late afternoon, the terrace of the café was occupied by just a handful of people—none of whom Burke recognized—sitting and nursing glasses of wine.

Burke wasn't in his chair for more than a few seconds when Hélène showed up with a pastis and a wide smile.

"Where's your uncle?" Burke asked, although he was quite happy to have Hélène around.

"He's off to some meeting about a new development on the other side of Villeneuve," she said.

"I didn't know there was a meeting," Burke said. He wouldn't have gone even if he had known.

"Uncle Claude wants to tell everyone that enough is enough," she said with a shrug. "He keeps telling me the town is big enough."

"I agree with him," Burke said.

"Well, this new development is going to be really big, and the locals will probably have to pay more taxes for all kinds of services that will be needed as a result," Hélène said. "At least that's what Uncle says."

"Do you think the area needs another resort or big condo development?" Burke asked.

Hélène shrugged once more. "I don't know. I live in Nice, so it doesn't affect me. But maybe Uncle is right."

Then she was off. Burke finished his pastis and then returned to his apartment, which was being baked by the late afternoon sun. He thought about cooking something but felt lazy, and so he pulled out some cheese and sausage from his small fridge, poured a glass of rosé, grabbed a chair and posted himself right by the dining room window. He was soon sweating from the sun, but he didn't care. He took in the view over the tops of his neighbors' houses—new Villeneuve-Loubet with the turquoise Mediterranean beyond. It would only get better when the sun starting drifting down.

For the first time all day, he wasn't thinking about anything.

CHAPTER 13

THE NEXT MORNING, BURKE decided to change his routine. After a quick coffee and a croissant, he went for a ride, opting for the sea route from Villeneuve-Loubet to Antibes and then around the Cap d'Antibes, a scenic stretch with a kilometer-long hill he could test his legs on.

He felt strong as he pedaled along the coastal bike path beside cars, trucks and scooters, which he hated because of their mosquito-like noise. He charged through the Old Town of Antibes, rode by the Picasso museum, which he promised himself he would one day visit for real, dashed down from the Bastion and then rode by the beaches. From there, it was a sharp turn to the left and onto the scenic route around the Cap d'Antibes—home to the super rich and the merely wealthy.

He loved this area for its panoramic views of the Côte d'Azur. It was a quiet route that went by some mansions and a couple of hotels whose clientele sometimes comprised some of Hollywood's biggest names. Burke was on the hill, and he hammered the pedals. By the time he reached the top, he was breathing heavily, but he was pleased at his performance; it was the strongest he had been on the bike in a couple of years.

He flew down the other side of the hill and into Juan-les-Pins, a bustling resort community with gorgeous sandy beaches that were far superior to those in Nice. He didn't quite know where Antibes ended and Juan-les-Pins began, but it didn't matter. They were both beautiful.

As he rode, he wondered how much development could occur in this region. It had to be one of the most densely populated regions in the country.

After he got to the far end of the beaches in Juan-les-Pins, he stopped and took in the view. Cannes was to the west. To the east was the Cap. Behind were the hills that fed into the Maritime Alps. There was an abundance of scenery. It was no wonder this part of the world attracted so many visitors. Even though it was only 9:30, the beaches were starting to fill. By noon, even though it was a weekday, they'd be jammed.

Burke wondered if the day was coming when he wouldn't be able to afford to live where he was. He wished it wouldn't be for many years—if ever—but he suspected that day might be just two or three years away, and when it came, he'd have to look elsewhere, unless he could increase his income. His savings were getting a little thin, and his blog efforts weren't going to make him rich.

He turned his bike around and took the same route back. Still feeling strong, he shot up the hill even faster.

In Antibes, he went to the Old Town, grabbed a couple of newspapers and then went to the daily market, where there was a tiny café that was always busy, and for a good reason. Its food, although simple, was wonderful.

With his bike leaning against the café window, Burke sat and ordered an omelet and a coffee. He studied the vendors and shoppers in the market. Watching the French discuss food at a good market—and Antibes's was a terrific one—was one of his favorite pastimes. He loved eavesdropping on the conversations, so full of passion and knowledge. There was always an argument going on someplace, but usually, the disputes ended politely with good wishes from both parties.

The aromas trapped under the market's sprawling awning were enticing: fish and fruit and spices, plus soaps and perfumes. And flowers.

He opened his *Nice-Matin*.

And saw Claude's face.

In a large photo at the bottom of page three, his friend was gesticulating angrily at someone. Behind him, several other people were equally animated.

Burke read the accompanying story. It related how the committee responsible for land use in the Villeneuve region had given initial approval for a development permit for the construction of a condo complex. The proposal involved three large, connected buildings, each having one hundred units. If further permissions were given—and there seemed to be a couple more steps to be taken, in the usual French bureaucratic fashion— construction could begin in six months and be completed in eighteen.

The value of the project was estimated at 280 million euros.

The approval was given at a public meeting, and several people had spoken against the development. Claude was quoted as saying, *"We are losing our community to industrialized tourism."* Burke frowned at that. He'd have to ask what "industrialized tourism" meant. But, then again, maybe he wouldn't.

The developer was FP Developments, a big company out of Paris with interests in Germany, Austria, Switzerland and Italy. It had French resorts in Biarritz on the Bay of Biscay, and in Menton and Saint-Raphaël on the Riviera.

He read another quote from Claude, who was concerned about *"the value of land becoming so expensive that French locals will have to move."*

Again, Burke wondered if he'd be gone in the next two or three years. Shit!

His cheese omelet came. He took a bite. If it was any lighter, it would have floated off the plate. The cheese was delicate yet sharp, and the eggs had been done to perfection. If he had to move, he'd miss such meals.

He sipped his coffee.

"Hello, Paul."

Burke looked up. It was François Lemaire, his boss, standing over him with his crooked smile in place and clutching a bag weighed down with all kinds of vegetables from the market.

Burke stood up, and they shook hands.

"Please, join me," Burke said.

He liked Lemaire, who was a few years younger but came across older, thanks to a world-weary style that he probably got from the movies—maybe from Humphrey Bogart in *Casablanca* or Jean-Paul Belmondo in a score of films. Lemaire was smart, funny and, as far as Burke could see, unusually patient, which was probably a little weird for a newsman.

"Thank you, Paul," he said, pulling out a chair and squeezing in. It was now official—there wasn't a vacant chair in the café.

Lemaire ordered only coffee, explaining he had to be in the office within the hour.

They exchanged niceties about the market. If they'd been in Canada, they would have started by discussing the weather, but in summer, the weather on the Riviera was totally consistent—hot and hot—which didn't provide enough variety for discussion. That left the market and food. The French were always ready to discuss food. That stereotype was totally accurate.

Soon, they got to some business. Burke mentioned he'd have a blog prepared that afternoon. Lemaire nodded and smiled as if he didn't care if he got the blog or not. As Burke knew, Lemaire's focus was split between news stories for both the print and internet version of the paper.

"This is good timing. I was going to call you this afternoon," Lemaire said. "How are you with video?"

"As in, do I like to watch videos?" Burke asked.

Lemaire laughed and shook his head. "You're such a Luddite, Paul," he said. "No, I mean shooting video with a camera or smartphone and posting it to a website or YouTube."

"Me?"

"We need more video online, and one way to achieve that is to have the bloggers do a video blog as well as a written one."

Burke instantly started to weigh the grief of learning how to do a video blog against maybe getting a bigger check.

"I can see you're considering how much extra you might make," Lemaire said, his smile still in place. "I can also see the idea scares you."

Burke shrugged and took a bite of his omelet. When he began handling his own contracts years earlier, he'd learned that the first person to talk in contract negotiations ends up being the loser.

Lemaire said he'd have the paper's tech expert show him how to use a video camera and offered to add some pointers of his own if needed.

Burke kept quiet. He took another bite.

"Ah, I see you are in negotiating mode," Lemaire said.

Burke relented, and soon they were discussing payment. In the end, they agreed that Burke would get the same price for doing a video version of his blog. Burke wasn't sure if that was a good deal, but he wasn't going to turn down the money.

"You see, we're entering a relationship with a communications company," Lemaire explained. "This company works with TV and the internet. Lots of different delivery mechanisms. And the people who are in charge want changes very quickly."

"So, is this good for you?" Burke asked.

"It's good for everyone, Paul, and you can't say that too often these days," Lemaire replied. "It's all about going bigger. Bigger audiences, bigger partnerships, bigger everything. I mean, look at our little slice of France—we're growing and growing, even though it doesn't seem possible."

"What do you mean, it doesn't seem possible?"

Lemaire pointed to the lead story Burke had just read.

"Look at the size of that proposed development," he said. "Hundreds of millions of euros. They say 280 million, but that's in today's euros. The cost will be much bigger when they get down to building it."

"I suppose so," Burke said.

"I'm hoping we can get an interview with the chairman of FP Developments while he's here," Lemaire continued. "That would be a coup. I don't think it'll happen because we're small, but if you don't ask, you don't get."

Burke glanced down at the paper. He couldn't remember the chairman's name. Yves Something. It didn't matter. He wasn't involved. And he didn't really care.

They worked out a basic schedule for Burke to learn how to video blog. Then Lemaire stood, saying he had to get his veggies home before he went to the office.

"I forgot, did you hear the latest about Den Weent and McManus?" Lemaire asked.

"No," Burke said, alert.

"I was talking to one of my reporters—the police are now saying McManus's death wasn't accidental. And they're not ruling out a connection between his death and Den Weent's."

"What? Are you sure? The flics are saying he was killed?"

"Yes, and they said they have 'someone of interest' in the case," Lemaire said. "But don't worry, you're not doing anything on this. Not a blogger's territory."

Burke's mind was popping with questions, but he couldn't ask more because Lemaire was gone, swallowed by the crush of shoppers.

CHAPTER 14

AFTER A QUICK RIDE back home, Burke checked his computer for news reports involving McManus and Den Weent. The information wasn't much fresher than what Lemaire had told him, but a new development caught his attention. Apparently, Global Projects had withdrawn from the TDF. The police in Avignon, supported by the Nice constabulary and other French law officials, had determined team members would be involved in a series of follow-up interviews. Under those circumstances, Global couldn't compete.

This was turning out to be the strangest Tour de France he had ever heard about—and there had been some wild ones.

He flicked on the TV. Maybe there would be something on the news.

The lead item on the newscast wasn't about the TDF, but about the development permit hearing the day before. The story included an interview with FP Developments chairman, Yves Vachon, who seemed comfortable in a media scrum, answering questions with the aplomb of someone who had done it a hundred times before.

"We recognize people's concerns," said Vachon, who looked like a film star with graying hair, an aquiline nose and strong jaw. "I can guarantee we are being vigilant about following not just the legal procedures and requirements facing the project, but in ensuring we do the right thing in terms of incorporating the development into this lovely area."

A lot of words just to say FP Developments was trying to avoid trouble.

"We believe this part of the Riviera is indeed special, and we want to ensure it retains those unique qualities," Vachon continued.

Burke admitted Vachon was smooth and eloquent. The TV cameras certainly loved him. When someone in the scrum asked if FP Developments was going to use local contractors if it got final approval for the complex, Vachon's face lit up.

"FP Developments has always believed in local investment in its projects, so I can guarantee we will be contracting local companies to help us with this development," Vachon said.

The story went to a clip of some protestors outside, and then, to Burke's surprise, there was Claude's face on the TV screen.

"Our elected officials must take a stand. Enough is enough," said Claude, his face red with anger. "If this development goes ahead, we will lose even more of what makes this region special. The Riviera has changed too much and not for the better. The little person can hardly find a way to stay here. It's terrible!"

Burke had never seen Claude so angry. The man on the news was a volcano, not the jovial, peaceful owner of a village café.

The story concluded by mentioning the general timeline for future approvals facing FP Developments. It seemed the company could get through all the steps within another six weeks. Burke sensed from the TV report, and from what he had read earlier, that FP Developments was going to get all its approvals without too many obstacles, Claude and a few protestors included.

Intrigued by the newscast, Burke decided to stroll down to the café and see if Claude was there. If he was, Burke hoped they could manage a few minutes to chat.

He was about to turn the last corner to Claude's terrace when he saw Madame Marois coming down a set of stairs nearby. She was moving slowly and maintained her balance by trailing a hand against a stone wall. Beside her was Plato, who was watching his mistress, clearly puzzled about which direction to go.

Burke waved and said, "Hello," but Madame just looked through him, as if he wasn't there. It was sad. She was nearing a time when she wouldn't be able to navigate the stone stairs of the village, which would mean she'd have to move, and that would be tough. He had the feeling she loved old Villeneuve-Loubet.

Burke went on. Claude was watering one of the flower boxes at the side of his terrace. He touched the petals of a couple of roses, and then, not knowing Burke was watching him, he bent and smelled the flowers. He stood, his eyes closed, as if trying to memorize the gentle aroma of the roses.

No one else was on the terrace. Too early.

"You look very relaxed, my friend," Burke said.

Claude's head snapped around. When he saw Burke, he smiled and waved him toward his usual table.

"Will you allow me to join you?" Claude asked, brushing his hands down his white apron.

"I was hoping you would," Burke said.

Claude turned toward the indoor part of the café, but Burke called out, "Claude, no pastis for me. A Perrier with ice, if you would, please."

Claude stopped. "No pastis? Are you not feeling well?"

"I'm on a fitness program, and I'm reducing my intake of pastis."

Claude nodded and went inside. He came back with two glasses, a Perrier and a bottle of pastis. He put them down and then joined Burke at the table.

Hélène came out from inside, saw Burke and winked. Then she checked that each table had everything laid out just right.

Burke told Claude about the newscast. The café owner chuckled.

"I was in form," he said. "But I said what I wanted to say, and that was good."

"I didn't know you're an activist," Burke said, sipping his Perrier and wishing it was a pastis.

"Normally, I am someone who stays on the sidelines," Claude replied, then sipped his own pastis. "It's too difficult to run a café and be out protesting. But this development is bad for this region."

Burke just nodded.

"And you know that bastard Vachon? He's got some chateau in the hills just beyond Nice," Claude said with a resigned shake of the head. "He should know better."

"He lives here?" Burke said.

"No, he just comes down for a few days' holiday now and then," Claude said. "He normally lives in Paris. Bastard!"

Claude looked away. Burke followed his gaze. It was Madame Marois. She was standing at the edge of the stairs that lead into the tiny square and

Claude's terrace. She looked at her wristwatch, back to the square and then once more at the watch.

"That's odd," Burke said.

"I think our Madame Marois is starting to feel her age, if you know what I mean," Claude said.

The old woman lifted her purse arm and jabbed the index finger upward, as if she had just remembered something. And with that, she turned from the square and continued down the stairs and out of sight.

"I think Madame might need some watching over," Claude said. "Too bad her children live so far away, although I'm not sure it would matter."

"What do you mean?" Burke asked.

Claude scanned the area. No one was coming. He had time.

"Many years ago, after she first moved here, Madame told me about her two children," Claude said. He folded his hands on his ample stomach. Burke knew the pose—it was storytelling time.

"She does not advertise she has children, although she did mention it to those Good Samaritans the other day when they helped her find her car keys at the café," Claude continued. "I believe it's because they're estranged from her. The daughter, as I told you before, lives in Vancouver. As for the son, he got into trouble in the 1968 Paris riots, and when everything died down, he left the country and apparently lives in Vienna. At least that's what Madame told me."

Burke did some calculations. That would put the son in his late fifties at the youngest. More likely, he'd be in his sixties.

Claude scratched his chin.

"I think the son actually spent time in prison because of something that happened during the riots," he said. "Attacking a flic maybe. Madame wasn't specific, just hinted he had confronted the police and wound up in jail. She was also annoyed with him for having drugs another time."

"And the daughter?" Burke said.

Claude shook his head. "No idea, except that Madame mentioned she was an idealist. She seemed disgusted, as if that was a terrible thing."

Burke was surprised how interested he was in Madame's story. Maybe it was because of seeing her in Grasse or having just witnessed the old woman's fragility a few minutes before.

Burke asked about Madame's husband.

"She told me he died years ago before she came here," Claude said. "He was some kind of businessman in Paris. He must have done well, because I've never noticed Madame lacking the better things in life. For example, when she comes here, she always orders the best wine. And her shoes, according to my ex-wife, are usually Christian Louboutin or something like that. Very fancy, very expensive. And you'll see her wearing Hermès accessories and some Versace clothes."

"How do you know about fashion?" Burke asked, surprised by the café owner's unknown interest.

Claude laughed. "Through my ex-wife Jeanne," he said. "She liked to imagine a life in which she could afford high fashion, and so she was always studying what Madame Marois was wearing. To me, it's always been the same—black, black and more black—but Jeanne knew what was what. I think Hélène does, too. She likes to serve Madame just so she can look at what clothes and accessories she's wearing."

"So she just spends her days getting through her days," Burke suggested.

"I like that way of describing it," Claude said. "You are a writer in training. I also believe you're correct about Madame Marois. I think she'll soon be a different person—and not a better one—and that will be sad. There's no joy in getting old, but it's a fact of life that it awaits us all. Most of us, anyway."

"You're still young at heart, Claude," Burke said with a grin.

Claude nodded and slapped his chest. "I am. Yes, I am."

Two well-dressed couples in their thirties came around the corner and over to Claude's terrace. The man in front pointed from Claude to a distant table. Claude nodded, then stood.

As the foursome walked to the table, Claude bent down to Burke.

"I would wager they are from one of our new condo resorts," Claude said. "If they spend some money on good wine and a fine meal, then I will admit there are some advantages to these resorts coming in. Money over idealism, you see?"

Claude laughed and took a couple of steps toward his new guests. He turned back to Burke and pointed at the Perrier on the table.

"And that is just not right, my friend. It will kill you."

CHAPTER 15

BURKE AWOKE AT JUST after 6 a.m. the next day with more energy than he'd had in months, maybe even years. He wasn't sure why, but he took advantage of it by going out for a snappy one-hour ride around the Cap d'Antibes.

Back home, he polished off a new blog, focusing on how the world was looking differently at the TDF thanks to the deaths of McManus and Den Weent. He had to admit that he'd hardly covered new territory with the blog, but he felt that his phrasing—and passion—had never been better.

Then, still enjoying his spurt of creativity, he wrote his column, in which he expressed hope that the world would be able to look beyond the deaths and still see the TDF as the magnificent sporting event it was. He smiled, leaving out some of the event's dubious past, such as champions being stripped of their titles because of drug usage. Blemishes on the TDF's record aside, he truly thought it was a great race and hoped it would regain its old luster.

Finally, he treated himself to breakfast. It was just a coffee and two croissants, but he enjoyed it enormously. The day was feeling good.

His cell phone rang.

It was Lemaire.

His editor was his usual laconic self and mentioned how he liked both Burke's blog and his column.

"There's nothing new in what you said, but the way you said it shows me you're developing some real writing skills and you're bringing a little more depth to your observations," Lemaire said.

"I must be getting smarter," Burke replied. "That's good. I was worried I might still be dumb."

Lemaire laughed and reminded Burke about his first lesson in doing a video blog.

"And I think it's appropriate if you learn by actually doing a real one," the editor added.

Lemaire said they should meet in an hour at the eastern entrance to the Old Town in Antibes.

"Bring a copy of your blog with you, Paul," Lemaire added. "That's what you'll work off. If you can memorize it from now till then, even better."

"What should I wear?" Burke asked, feeling a little embarrassed.

Lemaire paused and then said, "Ride down on your bike and wear some cycling clothes, although nothing too promotional."

Burke agreed.

He showed up a few minutes before the designated time. He put his bike against a palm tree and studied the view—a busy marina, a stone parapet jutting into the sea, the turquoise of the Mediterranean and the dark blue of the Maritime Alps in the distance. He had been in this spot dozens of times, and he was always impressed.

Lemaire showed up soon after. He got out of his car, along with a huge, bearded man in his mid-thirties who had to weigh 150 kilograms, not comprised of muscle. The massive man had a camera bag with him.

"This is Antoine Pastore," Lemaire said, introducing the man beside him.

"Hello," Antoine said in a soft voice.

Burke's hand disappeared in Antoine's when they shook. Fortunately, the huge man had a mild handshake.

They sat on a nearby bench, and Antoine took over, showing Burke two cameras—one a digital SLR with plenty of video capacity. The other was an amazingly light video unit that, as a sideline, could shoot stills. Antoine showed the basics of both and then showed how to set up both on a tripod.

Then Antoine, who was clearly enthusiastic about the topic, got into tougher terrain, explaining how to use the settings for maximum effect. He talked about automatic versus manual, ISO, white balance, JPEGs and other aspects that made Burke's head swim.

"OK, I can see I am beginning to hurt you, Paul," Antoine said with a smile.

He then suggested Paul speak on his topic for about thirty seconds. Antoine would film it, and then they'd check it out.

"You should be OK at this, I think," he said.

"Really? What makes you say that?" Burke asked.

"You've been on TV before, as I recall," Antoine said, his smile turning into a playful grin.

Burke shrugged. "Ah, yes, my reputation."

Except for bumbling two words, Burke managed a usable first take. On the second, he was flawless, if a little stiff. On the third, he added a little more passion. Lemaire and Antoine loved it.

They spent another half hour working on improving the lighting and sound. Then they talked about how Burke would deliver the video. To his surprise, Burke found himself enjoying the process.

"Antoine, film that boat coming in," Lemaire suddenly said, pointing to an enormous yacht sliding into the marina.

Antoine did as ordered, using the small video unit.

"Why do you want me to shoot it?"

"I think that boat belongs to Yves Vachon," Lemaire replied. "I've seen it before. He's a big one for sailing about the Med. It wouldn't hurt to get a little video and a few still shots. Vachon is stirring up a lot of shit these days."

Lemaire took the digital SLR and jogged across to the marina. Antoine followed. Burke figured he might as well join them, so he grabbed his bike and brought up the rear.

The sleek yacht was about twice the size of most of the other boats. It was gleaming white except for blue and red striping on the hull. Its name was *La Gloire*, or *The Glory* in English. It seemed an odd name to Burke.

On board, three men dressed in light blue T-shirts and khaki trousers directed the yacht to its mooring.

"I wonder if Vachon is on board," Lemaire said.

"He's not," Burke said, pointing to two men leaning against a parked black Mercedes sedan. "He's there."

Lemaire grabbed his notebook and jogged over toward the car. Vachon, who was wearing gray espadrilles, gray slacks and a short-sleeved white shirt, spotted the oncoming Lemaire and stood straight. The other man stepped in front of Vachon. He was tall, broad-shouldered and very capable looking despite wearing a businesslike black suit with a white shirt and blue tie.

Lemaire dropped to a fast walk. He cracked a smile, and Burke could hear him begin to introduce himself as he got closer to Vachon.

The other man took three steps toward Lemaire and held out a warning hand.

"Monsieur Vachon is busy and does not wish to talk to anyone," the man said in an even voice.

Lemaire slowed his approach but still continued forward. "Is that right, Monsieur Vachon?" he asked. "I just want to ask a couple of questions."

Vachon smiled his Hollywood smile and pointed to the oncoming yacht and shrugged. "We're busy," he said.

Lemaire took another step and made to go around the other man, who reacted by extending an arm against Lemaire's chest.

"Hey, screw off!" Lemaire said.

When he tried to go around again, the man in the suit barely moved his arm, but it resulted in Lemaire grabbing his stomach and falling to his knees, gasping for air. The man had punched him in the solar plexus.

"I told you," he said, standing over Lemaire.

Then he backed up.

Antoine rushed toward the man in the suit. A moment later, he, too, was rolling on the ground, only he'd been kicked in the kneecap. While Lemaire was gasping, Antoine was groaning in pain.

The man in the suit looked at Burke, who'd made up his mind to stay a good distance away.

Vachon shook his head in disgust at the two men on the ground.

"It would be wise to leave," he said. "We do not wish to have you prosecuted for assault, whoever you are."

Burke figured that last bit was to avoid possible trouble down the line. Vachon was suggesting his bodyguard had attacked some strange man who had run at them. Lemaire hadn't identified himself as a member of the press, although the minder didn't give him much of a chance to do so.

Vachon didn't wait for a response from either Lemaire or Antoine. Instead, he turned and walked toward his yacht, which was being tied up to the dock by his staff. His expressionless minder took up a position behind him, but kept an eye on Burke and the two men on the ground.

Antoine was now sitting upright and rubbing his left knee where he'd been kicked. Burke went to Lemaire and instructed him to stretch out. Then he folded Lemaire's legs and drove them back and forth a couple of times into Lemaire's chest. That got the editor's lungs working together. After a couple of hesitant breaths, Lemaire seemed recovered.

Burke turned back to Antoine. "How's the knee?" As a former pro cyclist, Burke had seen a lot of leg injuries.

"I don't think anything's really damaged, but it sure hurt when he kicked me," Antoine said. "It happened so fast. I wasn't going to hit him. I was just going to tell him to back off."

Burke had a feeling that Antoine couldn't have hit the minder even if he'd wanted to. Vachon's man was obviously a professional bodyguard, maybe ex-military.

"That tells us something about Monsieur Vachon," Lemaire said, slowly getting to his knees. He was grimacing and holding his stomach. He didn't look well, but Burke expected he'd recover soon enough.

"Asshole!" Lemaire grunted, straightening up.

"Bastard!" added Antoine.

The three of them watched as Vachon and his man walked onto the gangway and then onto his yacht. There was some shaking of hands. Vachon turned and pointed at Lemaire, Antoine and Burke, shaking his head and looking disgusted. The head of FP Developments was a showman. It was all about appearances.

Burke suggested they retire to a café to recover. He said a glass of wine or a good beer would help.

Lemaire wasn't interested.

"I'm going back to the office, and I will talk to the police," he said. "If nothing else, I want it on the record what he did."

"Are you sure that's a good idea?" Burke asked.

After all, as far as Burke could see, there had been no other witnesses. If there had been, they had disappeared. So, it was Lemaire's word—plus

Burke's and Antoine's—against Vachon and his man. He doubted Lemaire would get much understanding from the police.

"He can't simply have his man beat someone up whenever he wishes," Lemaire said.

The color was returning to Lemaire's face, and he was obviously feeling a good dose of righteous indignation.

"You didn't really identify yourself, and that might be an issue," Burke said.

Lemaire nodded. "That's true, I didn't, but his dog didn't give me a chance." He paused, and Burke could see him weighing the situation. "Maybe there's not much hope for me to get some revenge, but there is the paper."

Burke said nothing. Lemaire's face pinched in concentration.

"I know, I know, I'll have to be careful," he told Burke. "Vachon is a bully—a well-dressed one, but a bully nevertheless. We French are a revolutionary people, and we don't take such an attitude very well."

His speech over, Lemaire motioned toward Antoine, and they left.

Burke grabbed his bike as Lemaire and Antoine disappeared into the heavy traffic heading toward the Old Town. He turned to see what Vachon was up to. The head of FP Developments was no longer visible, and the boat was well away from the dock and starting to pick up speed.

It was only just approaching lunchtime, and it had already been a busy day.

He wondered what the afternoon might bring.

CHAPTER 16

AFTER THE SCUFFLE INVOLVING Lemaire, Antoine and Vachon's man, Burke needed to blow off some energy. So, he decided to ride to the Old Town in Nice as hard as he could go and then reward himself with lunch afterward.

The distance was not quite twenty kilometers, and despite some heavy traffic, Burke covered it in just over a half hour. It helped that the wind had been behind him, but Burke sensed he was getting fitter by the day.

By the time he got off the bike and was ready to walk through the archway into the Old Town, he was feeling more relaxed. The biggest surprise to Burke, though, was how much more sharply his brain seemed to be working these days. Maybe it was the exercise and a slightly better diet. Or maybe it was all the excitement around McManus and Den Weent. It could also have been because Lemaire was challenging him to do more and to do better. Regardless, Burke felt a little more attuned to events around him.

It hit him that he was starting to grow up. After retiring, he hadn't done much, acting more like a twenty-year-old without any interests beyond catching some sun, drinking some pastis, watching TV and chasing women.

What a waste those years had been. For the most part anyway.

Besides re-examining what had happened in the last week, Burke decided he needed to put together some kind of plan for how he was going to start living from now on. He needed a steadier income if he wanted to stay in the region. He needed to drink less and exercise more. And if he met someone nice, he needed to be more mature.

Burke stopped at a small café along a winding lane in the Old Town. It was one of his favorite spots, and he ordered a full plate of grilled anchovies, plus a bottle of water. The grilled anchovies weren't the wisest meal for someone trying to improve his diet, but they were so damned tasty that Burke figured he could give himself a break now and then.

He grabbed a spot at one of the tiny tables by the takeout window and settled in to watch the action; since it was a market day and just past noon, there was plenty to see. Still, Burke found his mind drifting back to the marina in Antibes. He had never been involved in anything like that before, and it had shaken him.

Burke looked down and discovered his anchovies had disappeared. He had eaten them all without noticing. His water was almost totally gone, too.

He took it as a signal to do something else. He got up, grabbed his bike and rode over to André Rousseau's bike shop to see if his friend had any new gear. If nothing else, Burke figured he'd get a couple of water bottles since his old ones hadn't been washed out and were likely inhabited by all manner of bacteria.

It took just ten minutes to get to Rousseau's shop. Although he was French in virtually every way, Rousseau didn't shut his store for lunch, so Burke walked right in, wheeling his bike beside him.

Rousseau was sitting beside the counter, talking to a stocky, balding man of about thirty. He smiled when he saw Burke.

"No more broken wheels for me to replace?" he said.

Burke smiled back. "No broken wheels. I'm avoiding tourists on bikes these days."

The other man looked familiar, but Burke couldn't place him.

"This is Léon Petit," Rousseau said, introducing the man beside him. "He's a mechanic with Global Projects."

Petit offered a gap-toothed smile that suggested he wasn't particularly happy.

They shook hands.

Burke excused himself and took a stroll around the shop. Behind him, the two men talked about Petit working at the shop, at least temporarily. Rousseau seemed open to the idea. That wasn't a surprise to Burke, since Rousseau often seemed on the lookout for staff.

Rousseau and Petit agreed to talk the next day and then shook hands.

On his way out, Petit looked at Burke. "I remember you," he said. "You were a good rider."

Burke thanked him and watched the man leave. He turned back to Rousseau and asked his friend about his seemingly growing staff.

"It's all the fallout from what's been happening with Global Projects," Rousseau said. "The team is stopping operations, and the support personnel are looking for work, at least until matters get sorted out."

"Did you work with Petit in the past?" Burke asked.

"Just for one season, when I was with RMS," Rousseau replied. "He's talented. Good, fast worker. Picks up new things very quickly. Not much for talk, but that's OK. He can work in the back shop while I charm the customers. I could use some help for the next few weeks, so I think I'll take him on. He's a local boy, so that helps, too."

Burke nodded. "Well, his team's in a mess," he said.

"As if cycling doesn't have enough issues, we get this Den Weent murder," Rousseau said. "And there seems something's wrong in McManus's death, too."

As he listened, Burke picked up a fancy heart monitor. The price tag was two hundred euros, but he wondered if it might be a good purchase. If he was serious about getting in shape, it would be wise to pay attention to how his heart handled the new fitness regime.

"Did Petit just walk in?" Burke asked, sticking to the topic at hand while looking at the options on the monitor.

"He called me a couple of days ago, said the team was in trouble and that he was looking for a way to pay the bills, although he lives with his mother when he's not on the road," Rousseau said.

"I guess it's too late to hook up with another pro team," Burke said.

"Yeah, all the other teams have the staff they need for this season."

Burke asked if other staffers on Global had contacted Rousseau.

"Just Petit, but then the only ones I'd be interested in would be mechanics," Rousseau said.

Burke agreed that made sense. He wondered what the other support staff might do. They'd definitely need to find a way to make some money, unless the team intended to pay everyone a full wage until everything was sorted.

Burke told him he needed to think about the heart monitor. That seemed fine for Rousseau.

The bell on the door rang, and a young couple came in. Burke said goodbye to his old teammate and left, noticing that the young man who just entered studied his bike with some envy. Clearly, that cleaning job had been a good idea.

Burke headed home. On the way, he spotted Madame Marois driving along a side street. She didn't see him. Beside her, propping himself on the dashboard to get a good view, was Plato. Madame Marois had one hand on the wheel, and the other was scratching her dog's ears. She was grinning—something Burke had never seen her do before. Burke didn't know Plato's age but hoped he had many years ahead, because he seemed to be the only real companion the old woman had.

Burke wondered if he should get a dog. He had no other obligations, and his landlord didn't care if he had one. Burke liked dogs, too. He could handle a small one like Plato. He'd think on it. A dog might be a good change and a nice taste of responsibility.

Back home, Burke showered and then phoned Lemaire to see how he was doing.

"I'm fine now," Lemaire said, "but that jerk Vachon won't be. I might only be an editor in some small newspaper chain, but I'm going to make sure he goes under the public microscope. If he's dirty or if he misses a step, I'm going to let the world know. And I think he's dirty."

Lemaire hadn't voiced that take before today, and Burke sensed the editor was still steaming about what had happened at the marina. But given the fierce tone of Lemaire's voice, he said nothing.

Lemaire shifted topics and told Burke he had an idea for his next video blog.

"I think you should do something about how major condo and resort developments will make it far less safe for those who indulge in the number one sport in this area—cycling," Lemaire said.

Burke kept quiet. Lemaire still had Vachon on the brain.

"Nothing to say?" said Lemaire. "Well, I think it would be a good blog. It's timely, and it affects a lot of people. So, I'm telling you to make it your video blog. For your regular blog and column, just rework the theme."

"OK," agreed Burke. Lemaire was still livid, but Burke had to admit the suggested topic did have some value.

Burke ended the call, almost sorry he had phoned Lemaire.

He sat in the sunlight in his small living room for several minutes. He tried to think about nothing, but had only limited success. His mind was too busy with recent events, and so he gave up trying to relax, opting to make an egg white omelet with mushrooms and peppers instead.

After the meal, he headed to Claude's for a nightcap, or maybe just a coffee. Usually happy to be alone, Burke felt a strange need to be around others. He had no clue why.

The terrace at Claude's was nearly full, with just a single vacant table tucked in a corner. The inside of the café was bustling, too. It was a busy night.

Burke took the vacant table for two. He felt he shouldn't take a table just for a coffee and decided he'd add a crème brûlée to his order. Claude or his main chef usually did a great job on the dessert, and he could afford it after the day's events.

Like any good café owner or server, Claude always noticed who was arriving or leaving, and he nodded at Burke as he carried some plates to a table of four. He wasn't the only one serving. Hélène was working quickly, and Claude's occasional third server, Eric, was also going at full speed.

Hélène came over, smiled and took his order.

"A little busier than normal, it seems," Burke said, gesturing to the crowded terrace. He recognized some faces, but most were unfamiliar.

"We had several reservations from people in the resorts," Hélène told him. "It's been like this since seven."

Then she went off. Burke watched her move. She was indeed pretty.

He sat back, feeling better. The noise of various conversations was strangely soothing.

He tuned into the discussion of the middle-aged foursome at the nearest table. They were English and were going over some travel plans for the next day that involved a trip to Ventimiglia for the market. They weren't sure if they should drive or try another method of transport.

One of the two men caught Burke half listening. "Hello," he said. "Would you know anything about Ventimiglia?"

Burke usually found English tourists to be either a little arrogant or simply loud.

"I do," Burke replied. And, having ridden all around the coastal resort, he knew the region and the town fairly well. It was a lovely place, more a working-class stop than a destination for the rich and famous.

The Englishman asked for advice on getting to the Italian resort. Burke told him that the train would work best, if they didn't mind walking once they arrived. The route by car to Ventimiglia could be busy and sometimes unnerving.

The man's wife asked about the market, and Burke told her it was large and excellent.

"You don't sound like a local, although I expect there are plenty of people who reside here who are not from this region, or even France, for that matter," she said.

"I live just up that path there, so I am a local," he said.

"But you're American," she said.

"Canadian, I venture," her husband suggested.

Burke nodded at him. "You've got it right, but I've been living in France for several years," he said.

They chatted back and forth, and, to his surprise, Burke found himself enjoying the conversation. He normally wished only to talk with people he knew.

The group wondered what had brought him to Villeneuve-Loubet, and Burke explained how he had been a professional cyclist and had fallen in love with the village, thanks to its pace, climate and proximity to great training rides.

"We saw the stage that English fellow, Hudson, won," said the man who had started the conversation.

"It was a good win," Burke said.

"Pity about everything going on with the race, though," the Englishman continued. "And a murder as well. Not good at all."

Burke asked where they had come from.

"By the way, I'm Simon," said the Englishman, reaching out to shake hands. He introduced his wife and the other couple. "We're from London, but we have condominium units near here. We arrived ten days ago and go back in three days."

"Do you come here every year?" Burke asked.

"We bought in the spring, so this is our first time as owners," Simon said. "We've all been on the Riviera several times before and liked it enough, so when the price was right, we took the opportunity to purchase."

That caught Burke's attention. "Lots of discussion about new developments in this area. Do you know Yves Vachon?"

"Well, he's the head of FP Developments which is responsible for our project," Simon said. "I met him once on business matters, but that's all."

Burke asked if the resort was meeting their expectations.

They all nodded and praised FP Developments for constructing a good property with lots of special touches.

Slowly, the conversation drifted away until the two English couples were back talking among themselves, leaving Burke alone with his own company.

"May I sit for a moment?"

It was Hélène, who was motioning to the chair opposite Burke.

"Absolutely," he said.

She sat and gave him a gentle smile. It was her eyes that were so captivating. The rest of her features were nice too—strong cheekbones, wide mouth, golden Mediterranean skin. She was dressed casually this evening in a beige peasant blouse and sky-blue cotton trousers. It was a simple outfit, but Burke thought she looked better than good.

"My feet are a little tired," Hélène said, waving a sandal-clad foot at him. "I was hoping to quit a little early tonight, but Uncle Claude says he'll need me till eleven. Eric can help after that with cleanup."

Burke looked around. There were now a couple of vacant tables. Otherwise, every table was occupied with diners working on a meal.

"One of these days, maybe you and I can go for a drink," Hélène said.

Burke was surprised. "You and me?" he said. "For a drink? Is there something you need to talk about?"

Hélène smiled. "Not at all," she said. "I'm a perfectly happy woman. I thought it would be nice if we both escaped together for a drink."

His mouth was wide open. He closed it and tried to remember how long it had been since he'd gone out with someone, but it had been so long he couldn't be precise. It might have been a year. Maybe longer.

He studied Hélène. He had never thought about her in any romantic fashion, but she was undeniably attractive and, he realized, becoming more attractive by the minute.

"But your uncle—"

Hélène interrupted. "Don't worry. He's not my father, and he knows that. Besides, he likes you."

Burke digested that and then nodded. "OK, let's do it. When?"

Hélène started to stand. "You're making me do all the work, Paul. I have tomorrow off, so how about then?"

He said he'd pick her up at 7 p.m. and they'd figure out where to go then. She gave him her address.

"You should find it easily," Hélène said. "You know, Paul, you are fortunate you're not a detective—you miss too many clues."

And then she went back to work.

Burke caught Claude looking at him and smiling. The café owner seemed to know what had transpired between Burke and Hélène.

It had been another unusual day.

CHAPTER 17

BURKE AWOKE AT MIDNIGHT to someone yelling and a dog barking. He leaned out his bedroom window. The noise was coming from an apartment fifty meters away.

The voice sounded like an old person's.

He spotted a couple of men who lived nearby running to the building. A woman followed them.

Another yell. More barking.

Burke thought he knew the voice—it belonged to Madame Marois. It dawned on him that she was yelling "Fire!" Plato was providing the barking.

He quickly dressed, grabbed his keys and ran out to see if he could help. If there was a fire, people better be notified. While the buildings were made of stone, he expected a lot of the homes were cluttered with furniture and would be primed for going up in flames. He doubted many neighbors would have fire extinguishers.

It was indeed Madame's place, and as he approached, he saw smoke. Not much, only a few clouds floating out an open window. He dashed up the stairs to her front door, where he almost bumped into Jean, his neighbor who owned the newsagent's shop.

"It's all right," Jean told him. "No flames, just smoke. Madame Marois forgot to turn off an element on her new stove. The pot got too hot and started to smoke. I turned it off. The pot's useless now, but no other damage. Now I have to try to get back to sleep so I can wake up at four."

"How is she?" Burke inquired.

Jean motioned for him to go in. Bianca, Jean's wife, was inside, sitting beside Madame Marois, patting her hand and gently telling the old woman that everything was fine. Another neighbor, Pierre, was wafting smoke out of the kitchen and out of the apartment.

Madame Marois looked shaken. She wasn't saying much, just nodding at Bianca's sympathetic comments. She interjected once to tell Bianca she had been reading when she smelled something from the kitchen and then she had forgotten about it for some reason or other.

"When I did smell the smoke, I was very afraid," Madame Marois added.

She sniffed at the memory and pulled the black shawl she was wearing tighter around her shoulders. Plato, who was curled up by her feet, looked up at his mistress.

Burke checked with Pierre to see if he could help. Pierre shrugged and told him the only damage was to the pot. Together, they used towels and flagged away the rest of the smoke. As they worked, Burke noticed with envy that the kitchen was triple the size of his and had old-style brass pots and pans neatly aligned in various corners.

When they were done, Burke and Pierre went into the living room. Madame Marois seemed to be recovering from the shock. Lucky she had been awake, even though it had taken her a while to react. It could have been far worse—not just for her, but for her neighbors.

He glanced about the living room, which was much larger than he had thought it might be from the outside. Although the building had to be a century old at least, the room had a severe, modern feel about it, with a medium-sized LCD TV hanging on the wall, a black leather couch and chairs, and brass lamps and tables. The only older touch came from two Impressionist-looking paintings hanging on a wall.

The dining area shared an open space with the living room. Again, the design was modern, with a black metallic table set for six. A side table made of the same black metal held up three bloodred ceramic pots.

As he suspected, Madame Marois seemed no stranger to money. But her style, for what it was worth, surprised him. Given her affection for the pendant she'd bought in Grasse, Burke would have guessed she'd go for oak or mahogany furniture with lots of old-time knickknacks around, instead of the modern, severe approach she'd taken.

Burke got the overriding sense that this was a woman who wasn't strongly connected to her apartment. It was an austere setup with no photos of family or anything sentimental. It was also an apartment for someone who liked space. There was lots of room to wander about. He wondered if Madame Marois had employed an architect to redesign the layout of the apartment, or maybe she had bought two apartments and had them merged into one.

Burke thought of something and returned to the kitchen. There was no smoke detector. So much for taking precautions. Of course, he didn't have one either.

Back in the living room, he watched as Madame Marois got to her feet and thanked them for their help.

"It's time for you to return to your beds," she said with a feeble smile. "I am grateful. I'm becoming a forgetful old woman."

On the way out of the building, Jean suggested there were dark days ahead for Madame. His wife nodded and added it was a pity the old woman was alone.

Back in his apartment, Burke undressed and returned to bed. He couldn't sleep, at least not at the outset. He kept thinking about Madame Marois and the "fire." Once more, he told himself not to take life for granted and to start doing a better job of living it.

When he awoke after only four hours of sleep, Burke was surprised to find he wasn't exhausted. Yesterday had been a full day and had finished with sadness, yet here he was on a new morning feeling a decent burst of energy.

He had a couple of coffees and was about to get his newspapers when his phone rang.

"I just read that Pierre McManus's funeral is today, over in Saint-Raphaël," said André Rousseau. "I'm going. Want to join me?"

Burke had forgotten about a funeral for McManus. The police had spent so long examining his death that the funeral had been postponed.

Although he hadn't really known McManus, and what he had known about him was hardly positive, Burke decided he'd go, if for no other reason than curiosity. Besides, he didn't have anything else planned until his date with Hélène. Rousseau said he'd pick him up in a half hour since the funeral was at eleven.

Rousseau, good to his word, was there in precisely thirty minutes, and they set off in his Toyota Corolla for the working-class resort of Saint-Raphaël. If the traffic wasn't too bad, they'd make it within an hour.

Burke wondered who was looking after the shop while Rousseau was gone.

"Well, Petit was going to start work today, but he's going to the funeral as well, so I have a part-time person doing it," Rousseau said. "So, no problems. I definitely couldn't ask Petit to skip the funeral to look after business, and I definitely didn't want to miss it either."

"Why are you so eager to go?" Burke asked.

Rousseau laughed at that. "Curiosity, nothing else. I want to see who's there to say goodbye to the bastard," he said.

Burke wasn't impressed by that, but then realized he essentially felt the same. He was curious, too. Would there be ten people or one hundred? If he was a bookmaker, he'd have put up odds on a small turnout.

Rousseau, who drove like he wanted to race Grand Prix, knew the fastest route. He got them there in forty-five minutes. The funeral wasn't for another half hour, and yet the parking lot outside the church was full and cars were lined up for blocks.

This was going to be quite a show.

They got out, and Burke scanned the crowd for familiar faces. He saw several—all from the pro cycling world. A couple recognized him and nodded. He waved back. He noticed that none of the cycling people were lost in sadness; a handful almost looked like they were sharing a joke.

The church inside was nearing capacity. Rousseau and Burke got a couple of seats in a side pew near the rear. A few minutes later, people were being forced to stand. An overflow crowd. Who'd have guessed?

Burke spotted some Global cyclists near the front. They were reasonably easy to spot; they were wearing the team's blue-yellow-and-white cycling jerseys—a statement of support. Then he caught a quick glimpse of Petit, who was with the team and sporting a jersey as well.

As the crowd waited for the mass to begin, Burke looked about. He saw some executives with the International Union of Professional Cyclists. They all seemed appropriately sad, although he expected their glumness was all an act. Then he saw another familiar face—Jean-Pierre Fortin, the detective from Nice. Fortin was whispering into a woman's ear, and Burke guessed she was a cop, too. They were probably on the job, although Burke couldn't figure out for what purpose.

Finally, the priest and altar boys came out, and the mass began. Burke wasn't a practicing Catholic anymore but found himself following along with the proceedings.

When it came time for the priest to do his readings and address the audience, Burke wondered what he would say. McManus might have had good qualities, but if he had, they'd certainly been under wraps and hadn't included anything to do with being friendly or kind or generous or helpful.

It soon became evident that the priest had not known McManus, because he made sweeping comments about McManus's devotion to his sport, to his teammates and to family and friends. He said McManus had demonstrated that a "life lived seriously and well is a gift itself."

When the priest said that, Rousseau snorted and said, "What a pile of shit."

Burke checked to see if anyone had heard, but it seemed no one had. In fact, most of the faces around were showing little expression at all. They were just watching. A couple of times, he spotted people pointing at something or someone as if sharing an observation or secret.

Many people in the audience probably didn't even know McManus. They were there because his name had been all over the news. He was a celebrity, and for some people, that made his funeral a special event to attend. It was the same the world over—the media covers a person's death, and people want to be at the funeral to share some of the limelight and get some fodder for future stories they'd tell friends and family.

Two others spoke about McManus. One was a team rep, and one was a first cousin. Both had obviously known him and recounted a couple of whimsical anecdotes that made Burke frown in disbelief. McManus was the last person on the planet to be whimsical, but the two had a job to do and showed off the trainer in a good light.

And then it was back to the mass, which thankfully ended in another twenty minutes. After, McManus's casket was carried out by pallbearers— half wearing Global team jerseys—followed by the congregation, which trooped out appropriately solemn.

Burke and Rousseau finally made it outside, joining the others as the casket was loaded into a white limousine. The vehicle wasn't moving yet, though. More visiting had to occur.

Burke and Rousseau moved toward a group of ex-pros they knew. They all shook hands and made serious noises, but it took just a couple of minutes before the wisecracks started. They had all known McManus, and not one was a fan.

As they swapped progressively nastier anecdotes about McManus, careful to ensure no one overheard, Burke noticed the deceased's family had congregated near the limo. They definitely looked upset.

He tore his eyes away and glanced around. It was like a Who's Who of the professional cycling world. Lots of team managers and plenty of great ex-riders had shown up to bask in the limelight.

"A big show, eh?" Rousseau said, nudging him in the side.

"It just needs the red carpet," Burke said, noticing TV cameras taking video from the roadside.

He caught Petit looking at them and waved. The mechanic raised a hand in return. He had an arm draped around a frowning middle-aged woman. Petit whispered something in the woman's ear, and she nodded.

"That woman with Petit seems a little upset," Burke said to Rousseau.

"Maybe she's an old flame," Rousseau said. "McManus had a way with the ladies, although that always seemed unbelievable to me."

"McManus with women, now that's a scary thought," Burke said. "I bet it's Petit's mother. There's definitely a resemblance."

Rousseau looked carefully at Petit and the woman. "You're right; they do look alike," he said. "He's mentioned his mother, but I've never met her."

"Well, everyone has a mother," Burke said.

"Even McManus had one, although it's hard to believe," Rousseau replied.

Burke spotted Fortin and excused himself. He approached the Nice detective who crooked an eyebrow when Burke got near.

"Are you here on business?" Burke asked.

Fortin shrugged. "A good day for a funeral," he said.

Burke looked at the woman beside Fortin, who introduced her. The woman was his sergeant, Sylvie Côté. She nodded at him. She was short but sturdy, and Burke figured she was mostly muscle. She had penetrating brown eyes that made him slightly uncomfortable.

"Anything happening with the McManus case?" Burke inquired.

Fortin smiled and shook his head. "No change, Monsieur Burke," he said with the exaggerated patience of an adult addressing a young child. "And that's all I'm going to say."

Burke smiled back and excused himself, returning to Rousseau and the others.

They agreed with the other ex-riders that a drink at a seaside café would be a good way to end matters.

Ten minutes later, there were a dozen of them seated around two conjoined tables. They'd just come from a funeral, but it definitely didn't seem like it. They were laughing and swapping yarns. A few times someone commented on a pretty passerby.

Burke spotted Petit on the boardwalk with the woman, her arm linked inside his. She wasn't frowning anymore. They looked like they were out for a casual stroll. Everyone had recovered, it seemed.

Burke didn't join in the ribald conversation at his table. Instead, his mind drifted to a blog about the funeral and the strangers in attendance. After he finished his pastis, he pushed Rousseau to leave.

They were approaching Rousseau's vehicle when they encountered Petit and the woman.

Petit seemed uncomfortable, but still managed to introduce everyone. The woman was indeed his mother, Karin Petit, who nodded shyly at Burke and Rousseau.

"Did you know Pierre McManus, madame?" Burke asked. He was growing uncharacteristically nosy these last few days.

"I knew him a little," she replied. "Léon worked for him."

"McManus was an interesting man," Rousseau said.

"He was unusual," Madame Petit said.

Burke nodded. "It's hard to believe he's gone," he said. And that was true.

"His time came," Léon Petit said. "Ours will, too."

And with that, he directed his mother down the sidewalk.

"Like I told you, our Léon isn't much for conversation," Rousseau said.

The drive back went quickly and quietly. Rousseau stopped in the Villeneuve-Loubet village parking lot to let Burke off.

"Well, that was not the most exciting funeral I've attended," Rousseau said, "but it was still interesting. I'm glad I didn't bet on how many would attend."

"Me, too."

"I still can't believe Pierre McManus died of a heart attack or whatever the heart issue was," Rousseau added, shaking his head.

And neither could Burke.

Back in his apartment, Burke was surprised at how easily the words fell out of him and onto the computer screen. When he reread his work, he thought he might be getting the hang of this writing business, although he wasn't ready to write a novel.

He fired it off to Lemaire.

Next up—a date with Hélène.

CHAPTER 18

AFTER A SUPERB BOTTLE of wine and some hors d'oeuvres at Roxie's, followed by a stroll along the promenade, Hélène suggested they have a nightcap at Burke's place. A little surprised, he happily agreed.

Hélène walked into his apartment, looked around and then turned to Burke. She stood for a moment with a coy look in her eye, and then she reached out and pulled him to her. She kissed him—not gently, but with an eagerness that surprised him. She tasted mildly of garlic and wine.

She pushed him back. "You're not going to say 'no' tonight," she said. Then she kissed him again.

He didn't need any encouragement, and soon, they were tearing each other's clothes off, stumbling from the wall to the couch, where she directed him into her. When they were done, they were both covered in sweat. Burke looked at Hélène. Her eyes were closed, and she had a slight smile on her lips. She was lovely and undeniably sexy.

"I've wanted to do that for the longest time," she said, as if she had just read his mind.

"I never knew," Burke said.

"I gave you plenty of hints," she said, looking at him.

"I'm just a pretty young thing who isn't very observant," he joked, and she laughed.

"When we were at Roxie's, I couldn't wait to get through those drinks and the escargot," Hélène said. "And then we went for that long walk on the beach, and the entire time, my mind was stuck on what would happen next. All that time, I just wanted to get you up here."

"And if I had said no?" Burke wondered aloud.

She laughed. "I knew you wouldn't."

She reached over and grabbed her purse, pulling out a cigarette. "You mind?" she asked.

"Not at all," he said, and with his foot, he pushed over a small plate for the ashes.

She lit up, took a long pull and then let the smoke drift from her nostrils. Burke had never been a fan of smoking, but he admired the languid way she puffed on the cigarette. It was almost sexual.

"When I'm done with this, I hope you will be ready," she said.

Her intent was plain.

And he was ready. He carried her into his bedroom, and there they made love, almost falling off the bed in their enthusiasm. When they had sex a third time, it was the same—passionate and uninhibited.

Hélène, finally satisfied, said she was hungry, and they went into the kitchen, where they made shrimp crepes and opened a bottle of red wine.

After they ate, they went to his bedroom. Hélène soon fell asleep with her head on Burke's chest. She actually snored, but not loudly.

Burke was exhausted and felt like all the bones had been removed from his body. If he was any more relaxed, he'd be a puddle. He smiled at that. He was starting to think descriptively.

His last thought involved Hélène wearing her peasant blouse but nothing else, and then he fell asleep.

A few hours later, Burke awoke to Hélène's hand exploring his chest, then his stomach and then his groin. He looked at her. She was staring back like a cat eyeing a mouse. When her hand grabbed his rapidly hardening penis, he gasped.

He wondered what Uncle Claude would think if he knew what was happening.

And then Hélène made Burke completely forget Claude.

They had breakfast looking out the window at the perfect morning before them. Burke had on his shorts, while Héléne was wearing his shirt, mostly unbuttoned. Every few seconds, he snuck a glance at her. She was even sexier in this quiet moment. How could he have missed all her signals before?

"I'm wondering about your uncle," Burke finally said.

Hélène laughed. Burke liked her laugh. It was full and passionate, and she didn't care if it was too loud.

"My uncle is a smart man," she said, patting Burke's hand. "He knows this is part of life, and besides, I think he approves of you, even if you spend a lot of time not doing much."

"I keep busy," Burke said defensively.

"Yes, of course you do," she said, clearly not meaning the words.

Burke knew she was right, although these last few days had been a different matter. If anything, he had been overly busy trying to sort out new experiences.

"Can I see you tonight?" Burke asked, knowing he was coming across like an anxious puppy.

Hélène laughed again and shook her head. "Ah, you have a little taste and you want more," she said. "That makes me happy. I can't do tonight, but I am sure we will have other times, *chéri*."

Burke smiled back at her. "That would be good," he said.

"You Canadians, you are so polite," Hélène teased. "You don't get an answer you want, but you accept it and say thank you."

"I didn't say thank you."

"Well, you should have," Hélène said, and she stood. "It's time for me to get home."

She showered quickly, dressed and then left, but not before kissing him tenderly at the door and saying, "Soon, *chéri*."

He hoped so.

After he cleaned up, Burke went to the newsagent's for his papers. As he stepped inside, Jean motioned for him to come over.

"That was bad at Madame Marois's home," Jean said, looking serious.

"She was fortunate it wasn't worse," Burke said.

"Bianca thinks we should meet with her this evening and talk about her safety," Jean continued. "Too often my wife likes to get involved with other people's business, but I think she's right in this case."

"Who's 'we'?" Burke asked.

"Those who were at her place for the fire and a couple of other neighbors," Jean said. "I think Claude would like to be there, too."

Burke didn't have anything planned, so he agreed.

"Does Madame know about this?" he asked.

"Not yet," Jean said. "We wanted to make sure we had some people who could come."

"What if she says no?"

Jean shrugged. "That's possible. Madame can be a little difficult. But we need to try. It's a shame her children live so far away."

They agreed to contact each other later in the afternoon to discuss details.

"Bianca is thinking nine tonight, after dinner, but we will see," Jean added.

Back home, Burke read his papers, but didn't get much from them. He struggled to concentrate, thanks in part to the proposed meeting with Madame Marois, but mostly because images of Hélène kept showing up in his mind.

His thoughts were interrupted by the phone.

"Good blog," were Lemaire's first words. "Your comments about McManus's funeral are thought-provoking, but don't let it go to your head."

Burke wondered what the editor was alluding to, and then he recalled how he had written about strangers showing up and mixing with people from the pro cycling world in a kind of odd ritual that wasn't about McManus as much as about being seen. *"Sometimes,"* he had written, *"the dead are ignored at their own funerals."*

"As a result," continued Lemaire, "I've put your name forward to represent us in a panel discussion about professional cycling."

"What're you talking about?"

"Partly as a result of McManus and Den Weent, the University of Nice Sophia Antipolis is planning a special forum on the subject called Secrets of the Pro Cycling World," Lemaire said. "They're having it in three days. They asked me to be involved because we've run a lot of stories, blogs and video on it, but I'm no good before a crowd. Besides, you're closer to the information, so I suggested you instead, and the organizers were very happy."

"Me?"

"You should be getting a phone call or email today," Lemaire said. "You'll be great."

"Who else will be on the panel?" Burke asked.

"Some professor of law at the university, that TV sports person in Nice—uh, Gerard Something or other—a rep from the professional cyclists' union and a couple of others—plus you."

Burke had serious doubts, but Lemaire, seeming to sense them, kept working on him till Burke finally relented.

No sooner had he hung up that the phone rang again. It was an organizer for the Secrets of the Pro Cycling World forum. He was persuasive and flattered Burke by saying Burke was "not just a well-read commentator, but an ex-pro racer who understood the sport inside and outside." The organizer also said there would be plenty of media coverage.

After the organizer's pitch, Burke agreed. He got some instructions, and the call ended.

Another new experience on deck, although Burke guessed he'd likely be overwhelmed by the event and wouldn't contribute much.

Burke wanted to give his brain a rest, and the best way to do that was to go for a bike ride. He changed, grabbed his Cannondale and headed out, opting to climb over to nearby Vence. It wouldn't be far, but it would be strenuous. When he reached the old village that seemed to be stuck in medieval times, he thought he might grab a coffee, and then maybe he'd pop inside the old chapel, where there were stained glass pieces done by Henri Matisse. He didn't know much about art, but he'd always liked anything by Matisse, even his cut-and-paste paper creations.

As Burke was leaving old Villeneuve-Loubet, he spotted Madame Marois walking Plato by the small green strip near the stream. The old woman was watching her dog root around in the bushes, and then she suddenly darted forward, kicking something away from Plato. She pulled him back, scolded him and then pushed the dog in another direction.

Burke thought about approaching her to see how she was managing, but dismissed that idea. Someone else was going to talk to the old woman about having a meeting, and he didn't want to upset any planning.

If there ended up being a meeting, Burke expected it wouldn't be pleasant.

CHAPTER 19

WHEN HE WALKED INTO Madame Marois's living room that evening, he saw Jean and Bianca, Pierre and four others whose faces he recognized but names he didn't know. He also saw Claude wedged into a small chair in the corner. His friend nodded at him and then tossed in a sly smile.

Madame Marois was tucked into the side of her couch, looking like she wanted no part of this meeting. Plato was in her lap.

"That is everyone," Jean said, taking control.

Introductions were made. Madame Marois barely looked at the others in the room. She had a small glass, filled with what looked like cognac, and sipped it occasionally. She sat rigid, stroking Plato's head. The small dog had its eyes half closed, enjoying the attention of his mistress and ignoring the strangers in the room.

Jean, who sat beside his wife on the couch, started by explaining that the people assembled were there because they wanted to make sure Madame was healthy and safe.

"You're sure it's not because you are afraid for yourselves?" Madame said.

Jean batted that one away. "Not at all," he said, adding a warm smile. "We are here because we've noticed you have had a few—what is a good way to put it?—problems recently."

"I have not," Madame snapped.

Jean ticked off the kitchen fire, the occasions when Madame Marois had forgotten a task, and the lunch when she lost her keys.

"All things that could happen to anyone," she said. "Life is complicated, and it is natural to have moments of forgetfulness."

Jean was persistent and discussed other occasions, and he did so in a quiet, unassuming voice. He might have been a newsagent, but he sounded like a social worker.

He continued, "Now, if your children were—"

"No!" said Madame Marois. Her eyes flashed at Jean and then scanned the room. Her sudden energy was palpable. "I will not discuss my children, and I will not permit you to either."

"But, Madame, it is important to make sure you—"

The old woman pointed a thin finger at the newsagent. "I said no."

Jean stopped. No one said a word.

"How can we help you?" asked Bianca in a soft voice. "You need to be safe."

Madame Marois's eyes no longer blazed. She tilted her head and looked at Bianca.

"I will have someone come in and help me with meals," she said. "I have a maid for the apartment. I will ask her. I believe she can cook."

She stood, forcing Plato to jump to the floor.

"Thank you for your kindness," she said. "But now I must take Plato for his evening walk."

And with that, the meeting was over. It had lasted three minutes at most.

Burke hadn't said a word, and he doubted his presence had added anything. As he walked out of the apartment with the others, he imagined everyone felt it had been a total failure. Still, he believed doing something was better than doing nothing, and Madame Marois certainly needed to know she was not alone.

He just hoped there wouldn't be any more fires.

Someone grabbed his elbow. Claude leaned toward him.

"Maybe you have time for a little drink?" he asked Burke.

"Sure," Burke said. "Your place or maybe mine?"

"Yours will make for a nice change," Claude said.

Burke led him to his apartment, where he poured them both a cassis, adding some water to thin the rich liqueur. They sat in the living room, which was still warm despite the hour.

Burke figured Claude wanted to discuss Hélène, and he didn't have to wait long to find out he was right.

"I think you like my niece," Claude said. "Am I right?"

Burke wondered how carefully he should select his words. He decided to be candid.

"I do, Claude. She's a very nice girl."

Claude laughed and waved a hand at Burke in mock exasperation. "A 'very nice girl'? That's it? You can do better than that."

"All right, Claude, she's terrific. Attractive and smart," Burke said.

"That's more like it," Claude said. "Now, before you think I'm here to ask what your intentions are, I just want to say that Hélène knows her own mind and makes her own decisions. So don't be nervous around me. Watch out for my niece. She's a woman who means to get the most out of life."

Burke nodded. Claude's words had a sense of truth about them. Hélène had initially struck him as a young woman who was serious and had set goals in life. He now knew she was also passionate.

"Now, let's discuss Madame Marois," Claude said, surprising Burke by the change in topic. "As we all know, she is not as sharp as she once was."

Burke said nothing. Claude's point was indisputable.

"I think it might be worthwhile to ensure Madame does indeed get more help at home," Claude said. "She can certainly afford it."

Burke had no doubt about the last point either.

"But why didn't you talk about this when we were at her place?" Burke said. "We were all there."

"Because I knew it would do no good," Claude said. "I have known Madame for many years, and I understand how she reacts. She is a very solitary person. She likes what she likes and is not open to other things. I told that to Jean when he was trying to organize the meeting, but he didn't really hear me. I went along with the meeting, knowing nothing would happen. I believed the others needed to see that for themselves."

"Now I understand. You wanted us to see what Madame Marois is really like."

"That's right and now you know," Claude said. "For some strange reason, I rather like Madame and want to help her. She can be miserable and demanding, but I think underneath those characteristics, she's a good woman. So, if someone else has a good idea that might help her, I would like to hear it."

Burke shrugged. "OK."

"We were talking about Madame getting more care. In fact, I have done some homework and learned that Madame can afford at least a little help," Claude said. "Her husband made one fortune in Paris and then added a second one from other investments. He then got into real estate in the south and made even more money."

"Who are you, Sherlock Holmes or Inspector Maigret?" Burke said.

"It's amazing what you can find with Google," Claude said. "Here, pour me another cassis and I'll give you more information about Madame."

Burke tipped more of the sweet, dark liqueur into Claude's glass, then sat back and waited.

"Madame and her husband became quite the socialites in Paris. They also gave away a fair amount of money, which made them even more popular. Then came the riots of '68."

Burke couldn't recall much about those riots. They happened before he was born, and Burke had never been one to read history books.

"I was just a young boy when they happened," said Claude, seeing Burke was struggling to recall the riots, "but I remember watching television with my parents and seeing all the violence. It started with university students going on strike against the discrimination among the different classes, and it went from there. Tear gas, rock throwing, beatings, arrests. Students and professors and workers. Very, very ugly. De Gaulle made a mess out of it. It was probably the end of him politically."

"So what did the riots have to do with Madame Marois and her husband?" Burke asked. "And what does all that have to do with Madame needing help today?"

"Patience, my friend," Claude said.

Burke nodded. "Sorry, I'll listen."

"Well, their son was arrested and convicted of all kinds of things," Claude continued.

"What did he do?"

"It sounds like he might have been one of the ringleaders. Anyway, his real troubles began when he preached for a communist overthrow of the government and suggested violence would work," Claude said. "He made it worse when he attacked a policeman during a riot and beat him into a comma."

"Damn!"

"He was arrested and sentenced to four years in prison," Claude said. "Apparently, when he was in the dock being sentenced, he screamed all kinds of foul things at everyone and included his parents in his rant, calling them the 'new aristocrats' and saying they profited from the misery of others."

Burke thought of Madame Marois back in her apartment and how she had reacted when Jean had suggested bringing her children into the picture.

"A number of years passed, and then Madame's husband lost a large portion of the family's fortune with some bad investments," Claude said. "Not long after that happened, he died from a heart attack. He was much older than Madame. It made the news, since he had been such a prominent businessman for a long time."

"What about the daughter? Did you find anything out about her?"

"Ah, the girl, yes, I did," Claude said. "She was arrested during the riots as well, but she was released without any criminal record. Apparently, she wasn't quite the same believer her brother was. She moved away a few months later."

"Any idea if Madame stayed in contact with them?" Burke asked.

"I don't know, but I do know that shortly after her husband died, Madame became involved in business," Claude said. "It turns out she had a very good mind for it, too. She was involved in a number of big projects and made back some of the money her husband had lost. In fact, as I've just learned, she was also involved in the early years of FP Developments."

"In what way?"

"She sat on the board for a number of years in the 1980s," Claude replied. "She actually got involved with FP Developments not long after the company hired Vachon, although he wasn't the big shot he is now. Back then, he was just another vice president."

"I wonder if she knows he's around here these days," Burke said.

"I don't know."

"What happened to Madame after the 1980s? Any ideas?"

"Google isn't as helpful for that period, except for a suggestion that Madame gave away more money and then moved from Paris," Claude said.

"To here?"

Claude shrugged. "She's been here for years and years, but I would wager she lived elsewhere after Paris."

"Who did Madame Marois give her money to?"

"Some went to various arts projects, but most went to a private clinic dealing with mental illness," Claude answered.

"Interesting woman," Burke said. "Do you know anything more about her kids beyond where they live today?"

"On Google, the daughter, Sophie, is mentioned a couple of times for being a volunteer with some parents' organization. There was a photo of her on one website. Very handsome woman. A younger version of her mother."

"And the son?"

"His name is Gabriel. He was involved in some anti-development protests in the early 1990s in the Alsace region, but that seemed to be the end of his protesting days. After that, it seems he settled down, even got involved with a few small businesses. These days, he runs an antiques store in Vienna. Maybe he's waiting for her to die so he might collect an inheritance, although with what Madame said about him, he might not be in the will."

"There is definitely some animosity, at least on her part," Burke said.

"The question remains—how can we help her?" Claude said.

"I think we can only monitor her from a distance," Burke said. "Maybe we can talk to the helpers she hires. I guess we could also talk to someone in social services to see if they can help. Beyond that, I doubt we can do much more."

"Those were my thoughts as well, Paul," Claude said. "I think I'll chat with her helpers in the next few days. And I'll phone social services and tell them there are people in the village willing to help. But mostly, like you, I will watch out for her and hope for the best."

Claude lifted his glass. "To our Madame Marois. Let us hope she lives well in her last years."

"Absolutely," Burke said, clinking glasses with his friend. Looking after neighbors was something he had never done before, and he was surprised by the odd sense of loyalty he felt.

CHAPTER 20

THE NEXT MORNING, BURKE read that Mark Den Weent's body had been released. A funeral would be held in three days back in his hometown of Apeldoorn in the Netherlands. If it was closer, Burke would go, but Apeldoorn was just too far away.

After a quick breakfast, Burke decided to go for a ride and end at Rousseau's shop, where he'd buy the heart monitor he'd been looking at the other day. If he was going to be serious about getting fit, it would be wise to log his efforts, and a heart monitor would help.

A typical July day, it was already hot and sunny by 9 a.m. Some people complained about the heat and humidity in summer, but not Burke. He didn't have air conditioning, and there were times when he baked in his small apartment, but he loved the summer weather because it rarely demanded a jacket. As for winter on the Riviera, it sometimes got wet and chilly, but it could never compare with the often brutal winter conditions in his hometown of Montréal.

He wheeled his bike down the stone alley and by the small park that bordered the stream. The birds were singing up a storm in the bushes and trees.

Madame Marois was there, sitting on the same bench he'd seen her on the other day. She was watching Plato sniff the grass with an intensity that suggested he was on the trail of something special.

Burke was about to get on his bike and ride away, but decided he should say something to the old woman.

"Bonjour, Madame," he said.

Plato stopped his survey of scents and studied Burke closely. The little creature then looked at his mistress, who waved him away. He seemed content to go back to cataloguing odors.

"Bonjour," Madame replied.

"Beautiful day," Burke said.

Madame Marois said nothing. She was back to watching her dog.

"I hope you understand that last night we were only trying to be helpful," Burke said. "We don't want to see anything bad happen to you."

Madame shook her head. "It's my business," she finally replied. "I am fine. I know there have been some occasions where it has been awkward, but I am managing."

Burke didn't know what to say to that. He didn't want to push his concern.

He looked down. Plato was sniffing by his feet.

"He's a good dog," Burke said.

Madame turned and looked at him. "He's an excellent dog," she said. "He's well behaved and very intelligent."

Plato went to his mistress and sat contentedly against her left ankle.

"He's certainly loyal," Burke added.

"He's more than that," Madame said. "He's highly sensitive."

Burke hadn't heard a dog described as sensitive before. "What do you mean?" he asked.

"He understands my moods," she said, "and he reacts accordingly."

Burke studied the small dog. At that moment, Plato was the essence of relaxed, having given up exploring the different odors of the outdoors. His head was half dropping, and his eyes were almost closed as he curled around his mistress's feet. It was nap time.

"If I ever get a dog, I'd like one like Plato here," Burke said.

Madame did something that surprised Burke—she smiled at him.

"You would be fortunate," she said. "Are you fond of dogs?"

"I had dogs when I was young," Burke said, recalling a couple of lovable terriers his family had owned. "But I haven't had one in years because I did so much traveling."

"Do you travel much now?" she asked.

Burke realized the old woman knew little or even nothing about him. That wasn't a surprise, though. Why should she know anything? They had rarely exchanged more than a few words at any one time.

"Not much," he said. "I was a pro cyclist. Now I'm retired."

"You're still very young, probably not even forty," she said. She looked at Plato and smiled. "You should get a dog. They are always loyal, always faithful and always protective. You can rely on them."

Madame Marois turned her gaze to the flowers beside her.

The conversation was over. Burke wished her a good day and then walked away, getting on his bike in the adjacent parking lot.

He rode to Nice, zipping along by the Promenade des Anglais. He pedaled around the Old Harbor, which, as usual, was busy with boaters and tourists. Then it was up the hill to Villefranche-sur-Mer. The hill wasn't much, but Burke liked how it twisted and bent, forcing him to lean into the curves at the top and on the slight decline into Villefranche.

Burke loved Villefranche almost as much as he loved his home village. A town of 6,500, Villefranche was embedded into a steep hill that rose from a beautiful bay to the Moyenne Corniche, a road that climbed east to Èze and then Monaco.

As he rode through the new part of Villefranche, Burke looked down at the bay, which was dotted with sailboats and, at that moment, being visited by a massive cruise ship. He remembered the first time he'd seen this picturesque community. It was on TV; he and his parents had been watching the movie *Dirty Rotten Scoundrels* with Steve Martin and Michael Caine. He'd thought the region was so beautiful that he'd like to visit it one day. His dream had come true.

Burke turned off the main road and went up a steep switchback through a residential section. It was tough cycling, but Burke was loving it. He was slowly getting back into form, and he liked how his body was beginning to feel.

Soon, he was on the Moyenne Corniche and flying toward Èze, a small village that offered one of the best views of the entire Mediterranean coast of France. Once there, he stopped to watch a couple of busloads of tourists enter the Fragonard *parfumerie*, which attracted visitors from around the world. Then he turned and headed back the way he had come.

He covered the return trip to Nice in a third of the time, plunging down the descent at speeds up to eighty kilometers per hour. Back in Nice, sweating heavily but feeling better than he'd felt in months, Burke cycled to Rousseau's shop.

"Are you coming to buy something today, Paul?" Rousseau said when Burke walked into the shop, which was busy with customers.

Burke laughed. "I am, André. The heart monitor I was looking at the other day. That one there," he said, pointing at the item in a display box on the counter.

"Good selection," Rousseau replied.

Burke told his friend to attend to the other customers while he looked around.

"All right, but please don't stink up my shop too much," Rousseau said. "You've been riding hard, it seems."

Rousseau moved to a couple checking out some carbon-frame racing bikes, the cheapest of which probably cost two thousand euros.

Burke put his bike against a wall and poked around. Rousseau carried quality stuff for the pro rider and good gear for the amateur. Burke checked out the latest edition of an electronic shifting system he had heard about. It looked heavy, but then he picked up the main component and was surprised how light it was. The price tag was high enough that he put it back.

"It's a good piece of equipment," came a voice beside him.

It was Petit, who was rubbing some cleaner cream on his hands. Petit nodded at the system. "Soon, everyone will be using this," he said.

"Well, I think I'll keep what I've got on my bike for a while yet," Burke said.

"Sounds like the thinking of some pro teams I know," Petit said. "They're afraid of change and refuse to use the latest technology or new training methods, or even new ways of massage."

"It sounds like you keep up with changes," Burke said, surprised at how chatty the mechanic was today.

"I work hard to be current with equipment, nutrition, massage and homeopathic remedies. I could work as a *soigneur* if I wanted."

Burke couldn't tell if Petit was boasting, because the man didn't show much expression. If what Petit was saying was true, he had some strong skills. Burke couldn't recall hearing of anyone who had the knowledge to be both a mechanic and a *soigneur*—someone who works with riders on their physical well-being during competition.

"You could do a few jobs on a team," Burke suggested.

"And I have. I've done massage at times, when my mechanical duties were complete or when a *soigneur* was ill. I've also worked with the team chef on introducing high quality nutritional aides."

"You're a busy man," Burke said, starting to feel that Petit could be a little overbearing once he started talking. On top of that, the man seemed to be devoid of a sense of humor.

"I like to stay busy, and that's why I'm here. I could wait till the Global situation has been sorted and not work until it is, but that's not my way."

"No family to keep you busy?"

"No, just my mother, and she keeps herself busy with her work," he replied.

"Yes, I met her at McManus's funeral," Burke said. "By the way, she seemed to know McManus."

"She only knew him a little. She was there to show support for me. I better get back to work, or Rousseau will get angry."

Burke shrugged and watched Petit return to the back shop where repairs were done. Then he went to the counter and paid Rousseau for the heart monitor.

He rode easily out of Nice and toward Villeneuve-Loubet. He wondered if he was losing any weight with his new program. Probably too early for decent results.

A kilometer from home, he saw three police cars and a police van speed by. They seemed to be heading into the area with all the new condo developments and resorts.

"It's getting to be a noisy neighborhood," he told himself as he took the turn to his village.

CHAPTER 21

BURKE WATCHED THE EVENING news and learned the reason for the speeding police vehicles he had seen—there had been a protest at the new FP Developments work site, and it had gotten violent. The report said several protesters were arrested after scuffling with security personnel for the company and then with the police. No one was injured, but the reporter quoted the police saying there had been "the potential for real violence."

As for FP Developments, a spokesperson for the company said in one video clip: *"There were members of the protest group who wanted nothing more than to cause trouble. We haven't even started real work on the site because we are awaiting final approval on some permits, and yet these people were there to create chaos. There is a system involved here, and we are playing by the rules. Those protestors don't care about such matters."*

Burke noticed in the clip that among the journalists surrounding the spokesperson was François Lemaire, his editor.

Another clip included brief comments from a couple of protesters, who complained that security staff had originated the problem by demanding the protesters leave even though they were not on FP Developments property.

Burke wondered if Claude had been involved. He expected he had been. He called Lemaire at work to get details.

"I'm busy, Paul, so I can't give you much time," Lemaire said.

"Who started it?" Burke asked.

"I was there right from the start, and the FP Developments' thugs got a little heavy with some of the protesters, probably under Vachon's orders."

"How did you know when it was going to start?" Burke asked.

"Protesters rarely conduct a protest without alerting the media. If there's no coverage, what's the point?" replied Lemaire. "Once the media showed up, the protestors got busy, even though the only work being done on the site these days is leveling the ground, since final construction permits haven't been approved. I expect their efforts will be on the evening news tonight. If that's the case, they got what they wanted—exposure. We're definitely running a story, too."

"Do you know a café owner from here, a middle-aged guy named Claude Brière? His place is the Café de Neptune?"

"I know him. I've had some excellent meals and wines at his place, and I've interviewed him as part of the fight against FP Developments' new project," Lemaire said.

"Was he there today?"

"At the protest? Oh, yes. Claude was a ringleader and right in the middle of all the pushing and shoving," Lemaire said. "In fact, I think he might have punched one of the FP Developments workers."

Claude would have been a load to move, even if his weight was not all muscle. He figured Claude, with his beefy arms and huge hands, could do some damage with a punch.

"And he's one of the protesters who got arrested," Lemaire added.

Burke shook his head and asked how long Claude might spend in jail.

"It depends on what he's been charged with," Lemaire told him. "He could be out now, or he might be in overnight—or longer. It depends."

"One last question?"

"OK, but make it a short one."

"Was Vachon there?"

"Not that I could see," Lemaire told him. "I would've been surprised if he had been there. He does his work in boardrooms. Now I've got to go. By the way, you need to get me a couple of blogs soon, right? And start preparing for that forum you're doing in a couple of days."

"I will."

Burke went to the Café de Neptune to see if Claude was there.

He wasn't.

But Hélène was and gave Burke an enormous smile when she spotted him. She couldn't stop though, because the terrace was busy once again with nonlocals, and she and an unfamiliar young woman were the only servers. Burke decided he'd grab a quick pastis and hope for a lull in the action.

The other woman who was serving came over to Burke and asked what he'd like. About the same age as Hélène, she seemed like someone who had done this kind of work before.

Burke peered around the woman's shoulder to see if he should wait for Hélène.

"Ah, you must be Paul," the woman said with a finger pointed at him and a sly smile.

"I am," he said. "How do you know me?"

The woman, who was petite with a thin, pretty face and short black hair, nodded toward Hélène. "Someone told me what you look like," she said. "I'm Marie, Hélène's friend. Hélène asked me to help because her uncle is in jail and the other server is ill. I've done lots of this work before, and so I said yes."

"I heard Claude had been arrested. Is he still in jail?"

"He's still there, or he was when we last heard," Marie said.

Hélène appeared with a pastis and nudged her friend with her elbow.

"I see you've met," she said, placing the pastis before Burke. "Paul, I'm sorry, but tonight is crazy, thanks to my uncle getting himself locked up."

"I understand," Burke said. He felt like a schoolboy with a terrible crush on the girl next door, but he didn't care; she was special. "I just came down to check on your uncle—and to see if you were around."

"Maybe we can meet tomorrow," Hélène said. "By then, I hope Uncle Claude will be out of jail."

The two women went back to work. Burke took his time with the pastis, partly so he could watch Hélène and partly to think about Claude. After almost an hour, he paid and left, getting a quick wave from both Hélène and Marie as he turned to go home.

Back in his apartment, Burke checked Twitter and then some news sites to see if there was any update on the protest. There wasn't.

He turned on the TV and watched a movie—*The Horseman on the Roof*—but he had trouble focusing, even though it featured one of his favorite actresses, Juliette Binoche, who looked like a slightly older version of Hélène. When it ended, he could only recall that a lot of people had died from cholera and there had been a great deal of horseback riding.

It was likely a good movie and worth viewing another time when his mind wasn't drifting.

After the credits rolled, he went to bed, but he couldn't sleep. Too many thoughts and too many images. He lay sweating on his sheets and wondered what was happening to Claude and what might happen with Hélène. At about three in the morning, he drifted off.

CHAPTER 22

THE NEXT DAY, BURKE checked the papers and internet for any mention of Claude, but he found nothing. He called Hélène, waking her, but she hadn't heard that her uncle would be released. She said she was going to the police station to check on him and asked if Burke wanted to come along.

"Absolutely," Burke said. He was as interested in being with Hélène as he was in seeing how Claude was managing.

Shortly after they hung up, Burke got a call from the organizer of the forum coming up the following day. The organizer provided details about when Burke should show up for the sound check and how he should dress—a sports jacket, a tie only if he wanted and absolutely no stripes. Then the organizer gave the format—three hours with six panelists—and told Burke what he'd be expected to contribute.

"It should be very easy for you," he told Burke. "There will be discussion of the changes in the sport, from the technology to the biological passport."

"I'm just a little worried that it could become a complete attack on cycling," Burke said.

"Well, there have been some rough times these last few years, but I expect you and the other panelists will be able to discuss how the sport is lifting itself out of that difficult period."

Burke wasn't so sure, but he had committed to participating, and so he went along, ending the call soon after.

An hour later, he buzzed Hélène in her apartment, and she came out, her hair wet from the shower. She wasn't wearing makeup, but then, she didn't need any. In her usual loose cotton blouse and linen skirt, she was striking.

She greeted him with a gentle kiss on the lips that made Burke tingle.

The main police station was busy. For several years, Burke had lived in the area but hadn't a clue where the station was. Now he was becoming a regular visitor.

Burke wondered if Claude's case was more for the Gendarmerie Nationale, since the protest had occurred not in Nice, but in a smaller area. He couldn't recall what the news reports had said, but figured he'd find out soon.

"You again," came a voice that was becoming familiar.

Burke turned and looked at Jean-Pierre Fortin. Not surprisingly, his sergeant, Sylvie Côté, was beside him.

"This is becoming part of my routine," Burke said, adding a smile that was not returned.

"And why are you here today? Still interested in the McManus death?" Fortin asked.

"Not this time," Burke replied.

"Good. Nothing new in his case anyway," Fortin said.

"I'm here to ask about Claude Brière, who was arrested at that riot yesterday at the FP Developments work site in Villeneuve-Loubet," Burke said. "Was he brought here? Or is he elsewhere?"

"I'm not entirely involved in the case, but he's here because the matter involves more than the jurisdiction of the Gendarmerie."

Burke, who wasn't entirely clear on the various jurisdictions within the French police system, sensed Fortin had wanted to say something negative about the Gendarmerie but had thought better of being critical.

Burke looked at Hélène. He'd been doing the talking, but Claude was her uncle, her family, and maybe she should take control. However, she looked at him and seemed fine to leave the questioning to Burke.

"Just check at the counter there," Fortin said. And with that, he and Côté walked out of the building.

Burke went to a counter manned by a burly cop in his forties. Burke asked for Claude and mentioned his friend had been arrested in the protest yesterday.

"Are you family?" the cop asked.

Burke nodded at Hélène. "She is. She's his niece. Is Claude going to be released soon?" Burke asked.

The cop looked at a computer screen, punched in something and then turned to Hélène.

"As it turns out, he will be released in fifteen minutes," he said. "You can wait over there."

He pointed to a couple of benches. Half the seats were taken.

Burke and Hélène sat down, but they didn't talk. He could sense her discomfort. In fact, she looked frightened. Burke attempted a distraction; he told her about the last time he was here—when he had come asking for the latest on the death of Pierre McManus.

"How did he die?" she asked.

"His heart suddenly stopped, but I get the sense from our friend Fortin that there might have been more to his death than that," Burke explained.

"Like what?"

"I really don't know, but maybe someone initiated what happened to him."

"I don't understand," Hélène said.

"Maybe someone gave him a drug that caused it, but I'm just guessing here."

"Was he the type of man someone would want to see dead?" Helene asked, starting to take more interest.

"He was hardly a monster, but he was difficult and could be mean—even cruel," Burke said. "He had a reputation as a good tactician in races and a miserable bastard otherwise."

A familiar laugh sounded. "So what kind of trouble are you both in now?" asked Claude with a grin.

Hélène jumped up and hugged her uncle. When she was finished, she wagged a finger in front of him.

"You cannot do this to me again," she scolded. Then she softened. "It hurts my heart too much to see you in trouble."

She hugged him again, and Burke spotted tears in Claude's eyes. When she pulled back, Burke hugged Claude too.

Claude pointed to the front door. "Let's go," he said, leading the way. "I don't want to spend any more time here."

Burke nudged him and asked what charges he was facing. Claude shrugged and said he was being released without charges.

"The police do not really have time to spend on small-time villains such as myself," he said. "Just one protester has been charged, and that's because he punched a flic in the nose."

"But didn't you punch someone?"

"I might have, but no one wants to make a big deal out of it," Claude said. "They're charging the other guy because he's been in trouble before."

"So why did they keep you in jail overnight?" Hélène asked as they walked outside into the brilliant sunshine.

"They were afraid we would cause more trouble," he said. "I think they also wanted to frighten us."

"Did it work?" Burke asked.

Claude nodded. "Oh, yes. Jail is not a good place for a man like me. As you know, I am cultured and sensitive."

Claude laughed. Burke and Hélène exchanged a glance.

"But, seriously, it is not a place I would like to return to," Claude added.

"I think maybe we need to take you to lunch," Hélène said.

Claude seemed to like that idea. "But I'll need to change," he added. "I'm a little sour to the nose."

"You are," Hélène said. "And by the way, you are buying lunch because of all the worry you caused me."

"I will buy," Claude said with a resigned shrug. He turned to Burke. "Did you see the TV coverage of the protest? We did what we wanted to do."

"You mean you wanted to get arrested?" Burke asked.

"Not really. We wanted to get the media to notice. We wanted people to learn that the protests against FP Developments haven't ended. And we wanted the politicians to see that it might be unwise to let the development go ahead."

"Well, if you go to any more riots, Uncle, do not finish up in jail," Hélène said.

It took about an hour to go to Claude's place—he lived a half kilometer from Burke—and for him to shower and change clothes. Then they opted for Roxie's.

They drove there in Burke's car. They took a table at the far end of the terrace under the protection of a palm tree.

On Claude's recommendation, they ordered some tapenade and sautéed prawns to start with and a bottle of chardonnay to accompany the hors d'oeuvres. It seemed an odd mix to Burke, but Claude swore the taste of the wine worked well with the tapenade and prawns.

Burke took a prawn, chomped it down and then sipped his wine. It was a perfect blend of tastes. He tried some tapenade and then took another sip. Same result. It was fantastic and more proof that the French, especially a café owner, knew how to eat well.

"I do not believe it," Claude said, looking past Burke and Hélène, who were sitting opposite him.

They turned. Yves Vachon, his minder and two other men, all dressed in dark suits but no ties, sat at a table under the shade of another tree.

"He's here to ruin my lunch," Claude growled.

"Who are you talking about?" Hélène asked.

"The bastard with the silver hair," Claude said. "That's Vachon, the chief of FP Developments and a man who cares only about his wallet."

Claude was almost vibrating with repressed anger.

"Drink your wine, Claude, and enjoy your freedom," Burke said, touching Claude's wine glass with his own.

Claude glared at Burke for a couple of seconds and then visibly relaxed, breaking into a smile.

"You're right, Paul," he said. He took his glass and held it high. "To freedom and sunshine and a wonderful niece—and a good customer and friend."

They toasted together, and Burke hoped the worst was over, but he could sense Claude's attention wavering from them to Vachon.

After their hors d'oeuvres and seafood pasta, they ordered a cheese plate to be followed by coffee.

Before the server walked away, Claude pointed to Vachon's table.

"The man with the silver hair over there who looks like a Hollywood movie star," Claude said. "Is he an actor?"

Burke wondered what Claude was up to. Claude knew Vachon. Why was he quizzing the server?

The server shook his head. "No, he's a businessman. Monsieur Vachon. A regular visitor here when he's in town. He often has both lunch and dinner here. He likes our food, but I think he likes the view better."

The server nodded at three comely young women strolling along the boardwalk. They were wearing skimpy sundresses. Burke glanced at Vachon and saw he was noticing the women going by as well.

The server went away, and Burke saw Claude nodding to himself.

"Why did you ask if he's a movie star when you know who he is?" Hélène asked.

"The servers seem to be giving him special treatment, and I was curious to know if he comes here often," Claude said. "I figured the Hollywood approach would end up getting me an answer."

"What does it matter if he's a regular, Claude?" Burke asked.

Claude shrugged. "I wanted to know if he parachutes into our area to check out his latest big deal or if he's a regular visitor, that's all," he said.

"You're making too big a deal about him and this place and everything," Hélène said.

"He's a pig as well as a bastard," Claude said, staring at his niece. "I love this restaurant, but I'm afraid it's time to boycott it after today."

"Don't be silly, Uncle," Hélène said.

"I'm not being silly, *chérie*," Claude said. "That man and others like him will change this area beyond recognition. We will not be able to afford to live here. It will be nothing but tourists and the rich. So, no, I am not being silly. I am fighting for my community and for my people."

The cheese plate came, and they ate its delights without conversation. When the coffee came, the only talk was of Burke's participation in the upcoming forum on cycling. Neither Claude nor Hélène seemed interested. The meal ended in sourness.

Burke dropped Claude off at his place, and then he asked if Hélène had plans for the rest of the day.

"I do, Paul," she said. "I have to work later at Uncle's. It will be a long night, I think."

Burke was disappointed, and it must have shown, because Hélène reached across and brushed his cheek with her fingertips.

"But I am available tomorrow—if you're interested," she said.

"I am, but I have that forum in the afternoon," Burke said.

Hélène smiled coyly. "I was thinking more about something we could do in the evening and later."

Burke knew he was probably doing his boyish grin again, but he didn't care. An evening and more with Hélène would be perfect.

They agreed to get together after the forum, and then Burke dropped Hélène back at her place.

He drove leisurely back home, thinking tomorrow promised to be an active—and terrific—day.

CHAPTER 23

BURKE AWOKE EARLY, BUT skipped a bike ride to prepare for the forum instead. He might know his sport, but he sensed some tough questions on deck, and he wanted to be prepared. Before he started his homework, he strolled down to the village newsagent's.

Jean had his head buried in the Nice newspaper.

"Anything big happen?" Burke asked.

Jean's head snapped up.

"Ah, Paul, yes, something big happened last night," he said, nodding toward the rack behind Burke.

Burke looked over his shoulder at the newspaper and read a headline that caught his breath:

"FP DEVELOPMENTS EXECUTIVE KILLED IN HIT-AND-RUN"

There was a photo of a covered body and an inset shot of Yves Vachon. Burke wondered about Vachon's minder. After all, it seemed the businessman never strayed far from his protection.

"What happened?" Burke said.

"He was coming out of one of his favorite restaurants when he was hit by a vehicle," Jean told him. "It sounds like this FP Developments guy was killed instantly."

Burke shook his head.

"The story says the police haven't made an arrest yet, but are investigating," Jean said. He looked up at Burke. "That's about it."

Burke picked up a copy of the Nice paper, along with a national newspaper with a similar headline about Vachon's sudden death. He paid for both and told Jean he had an appointment, then jogged back to his apartment.

He went online and saw plenty of stories about Vachon. He checked Twitter and discovered Vachon's death was starting to produce a fair number of tweets, some of which suggested it wasn't a bad thing that the FP Developments boss was gone. He wondered if the police checked Twitter.

His cell phone sounded.

It was Hélène, and she seemed upset.

"It's Uncle Claude," she said. "The police picked him up again."

"For what? Another protest?" Burke hadn't heard anything about another altercation.

"No, he's being questioned about that FP Developments executive and his bodyguard who were killed in a hit-and-run," she said.

"Yves Vachon?"

"Yes, that's his name. Anyway, the police just came over to Uncle's place and arrested him. He managed to contact me."

"What did he say?"

"Not much. He asked me to get him a good lawyer who is not too expensive," she said.

"No such thing," Burke interjected.

Hélène ignored his comment. "We have to do something," she said, her voice firm.

Burke agreed, but he didn't have a suggestion. He tried to sound calm, but he was far from that. He couldn't believe that the day after Claude promised them he would avoid trouble, he was being linked to Vachon's death.

Had Claude actually done it? Burke didn't think it was possible. Claude didn't mind creating some trouble, but killing someone was outside his character.

"Let's go to the station," Burke suggested.

"Where we were yesterday?" Hélène asked.

"It's a good place to start."

Less than a half hour later, they were back in the foyer at the police station. It was noisier this time, with reporters and TV crews looking for information about Vachon. After all, it wasn't every day that an international business star was the victim of a hit-and-run.

Jean-Pierre Fortin came out of a side door and stopped to check out the action. Burke grabbed Hélène's hand and pulled her along toward the detective, who was soon joined by his shadow, Sylvie Côté.

"Ah, you again," Fortin said when Burke stepped in front of him. "And what is it this time?"

"The hit-and-run deaths of Yves Vachon and his minder," Burke replied.

"Well, I'm not the investigating officer," Fortin said. "You'll have to ask someone else."

"But can you tell us if any charges have been laid?" Burke said.

"As I said—"

"My uncle, Claude Brière, has been arrested," Hélène said. "Can't you tell us anything? Please."

Fortin looked at her but said nothing.

"They arrested him, but he didn't do anything," she continued.

Fortin remained silent but glanced at his partner, who shrugged.

"Uncle did not like Vachon, but he would not hurt a fly," Hélène added.

Burke tried to warn her off from making more comments, but she was locked onto Fortin.

Fortin began, "You'll have to wait for—"

"Can I talk to him?" Hélène asked, panic sounding in her voice.

Fortin pointed to the front desk. A crush of journalists hurled questions at a pair of desk officers, who were abstaining from providing any answers. Burke figured a spokesperson would soon show up to handle the reporters.

"Please help us," asked Hélène with tears in her eyes.

Côté took the initiative and turned to leave. Fortin began to follow, and then he turned to Hélène and said, "Ask for Inspector Jardine."

Then he left.

Burke was surprised that Fortin had provided any help. He hadn't given them much, but it was something, and Hélène seemed slightly calmer.

"Let's wait a minute and then ask for this Inspector Jardine," Burke said.

"We'll ask now," she said.

Instead of joining the crush of media at the front counter, Hélène pulled out her phone, did some scrolling and then punched in a number.

"I would like to speak to Inspector Jardine," she said with authority.

A few minutes ago, Hélène seemed like she was about to fall to pieces. Now, she looked fierce and determined.

"Inspector Jardine, my name is Hélène Rappaneau, and my uncle is Claude Brière," she said into her phone. "He is being held in connection with the hit-and-run death of Yves Vachon and his bodyguard."

To Burke, Hélène sounded like a lawyer speaking to a witness at a trial—all facts and very businesslike.

Jardine must have said something, but Burke couldn't hear.

"Has he been officially charged with a crime?" Hélène asked. Then she added, "I should let you know that I am a freelance journalist as well."

Burke wasn't sure if Hélène's strategy was a good one. He doubted you could intimidate a flic by saying you were a journalist. And if the police checked and discovered she wasn't, she might find herself scrambling to provide some answers.

"If he has not been charged, when will he be released?" she asked.

Clearly, it was not the answer she'd been hoping for, because she frowned and then snapped, "That is unacceptable. I can assure you we will be acting on this."

She listened for a few seconds, then the call obviously ended.

"It sounds serious, but it doesn't seem like he's a main suspect," she said. "In any case, Uncle Claude might be released today, although this Jardine said they can hold him longer."

Burke wondered what she intended to do next.

"He might need a lawyer," Hélène said. "I have a friend whose father is a lawyer here in Nice. Maybe he can help."

Hélène had taken control and had a plan of sorts. He couldn't offer anything else but support.

"Thank you for helping me with this," she said to Burke. She touched his cheek with her fingertips. "It's nice to have a good friend."

Burke didn't know how to reply, so he just nodded.

"I think you need to start getting ready for your public forum," she added, tapping her watch.

Burke had forgotten about the forum, which would start in three hours. He'd been worried earlier about not being properly prepared, but all that seemed inconsequential now with Vachon's death and Claude's arrest.

"Forget the forum," he said. "I want to help you."

Hélène smiled. "No, you must go," she said. "I'll handle this. After your forum, call me. Maybe Claude will be out. If he is, I will lock him in his room and not let him out for a month. Sometimes, he can be such a child."

Burke was surprised at how her spirits had changed in the last few minutes.

He dropped her off at her apartment with a quick peck on the cheek, and then he drove home. He parked his car and was heading to his place when he saw Madame Marois walking Plato, the two of them moving along briskly, both noses up in the air. The leash was always loose, as if the dog anticipated his mistress's every move.

When Burke caught her eye, he waved. She stopped and waved back. Then, for a split second, she looked a little lost, but then resumed her stroll. Burke moved on as well, pulling up short when he heard her reedy voice calling out to him. Madame was motioning him to come to her.

"Yes, Madame?"

"Have you seen my keys?" she asked, looking perplexed.

"Your keys? To what?"

"To my house," she snapped.

Burke looked down at Plato, who seemed to be perfectly content to be sniffing the air.

"No, Madame, I haven't seen them," he said. "When did you lose them?"

"That's a silly question," she said. "If I knew when I lost them, I would know where they are. This has not been a good day. I've lost my keys, and this morning, I couldn't balance my bank book."

Burke asked what route she had taken so he could retrace her steps and maybe find her keys.

The question was simple, but it left Madame speechless and obviously puzzled.

"I can't remember exactly where I've been on my walk with Plato," she said.

"By the small park? The stream? The garden?" Burke offered.

"Yes, yes, that way," she said.

"Wait here, and I'll go back that way and see if I can spot them," Burke suggested.

He jogged off, did a loop of the area but found nothing. When he turned to go back to Madame, she was gone.

He jogged toward her apartment building and spotted her unlocking the main door.

"You found your keys," he said.

Madame Marois looked at her hand. "Oh, yes, I did," she said. "They were in my purse, at the bottom."

"I'm glad you found them," Burke said.

"How did you know I had lost them?" she asked. There was a short pause. "Oh, yes, I told you, and you went to search for them. Thank you for looking for them."

And then she disappeared inside.

Yes, Burke thought, *she was losing it*.

Back at his apartment, Burke started prepping for the forum but struggled to concentrate. Claude's situation took some of his attention. Hélène's varied reactions stuck in his brain, too. Then there were Madame Marois's signs of dementia or some similar ailment.

He was halfway through his preparations when François Lemaire called.

"Paul, I want to warn you that some police may be coming to see you," Lemaire said.

"What are you talking about?"

"Yves Vachon is dead," Lemaire began.

"Yes, I know."

"Well, it has come to the attention of the police that I recently had a physical altercation with his minder and that I have been overheard saying Vachon is—was—a pig," Lemaire said. "Then there were my editorials against Vachon and FP's Developments' latest project."

"Why do they want to talk to me?" Burke asked.

"Because you were there when we were attacked by Vachon's thug," Lemaire said.

"Have the police talked to you?" Burke asked.

"They just left," Lemaire said. "They seemed to hear what I told them, but you never know."

"Who talked to you?"

"Some cop named Fortin," Lemaire said. "He had a female sergeant with him. Côté, or something like that. Very tough looking."

"What did you tell them?" Burke asked, surprised to hear Fortin and Côté were on the case. So much for Fortin telling the truth about who was handling the investigation of Vachon's death.

"I told them I'd only been doing my job as a journalist," Lemaire said, sounding more anxious than authoritative.

"Well, there isn't much I can tell them."

"I understand, but I wanted you to know in advance," Lemaire said.

Burke's doorbell sounded.

"I think that might be your police," Burke told Lemaire.

They rang off, and Burke opened the door.

Fortin and Côté entered. Fortin smiled slyly, while Côté's face showed little expression.

"We need to ask you some questions about an incident at the Antibes marina five days ago," he said.

"What incident?" Burke asked, deciding to play as if he didn't know.

"May we sit?" Fortin asked.

Burke shrugged and waved them to the couch. He took a chair opposite.

"It seems you may know why we're here," Fortin said.

Burke was surprised by the statement. But then, cops are trained to know when a person is lying or disguising the truth.

"I might," Burke admitted. "I expect you mean the incident when Yves Vachon's minder attacked two members of the Antibes press."

"Let us make that determination," Fortin said. "For the moment, we just want facts from you, Monsieur Burke."

Fortin launched into a series of questions about the incident. He wanted both an overview and details. Côté asked a couple of follow-up questions and took notes. She also stared with an intensity that made Burke feel like he was prey.

The questions weren't difficult, and Burke answered only what they asked. He had a sense that Côté, on occasion, was annoyed with his answers, but Fortin remained placid throughout the half-hour interview.

When it seemed the interview was over, Burke asked his own question.

"Why did you lie to me back at the Nice station when I asked if you could provide some information about Vachon's death?"

Fortin offered his sly smile once more. "I did not lie," he said. "I told you I wasn't the investigating officer, and that's true. I am not in charge."

"So you're here to ask questions for someone else," Burke suggested.

"That would be correct," Fortin said.

It seemed to Burke that Fortin was splitting hairs.

The two officers stood.

"If we have more questions, we'll contact you," Fortin added, nodding at Côté.

"What about Claude Brière? Is he going to be released? You may not be the investigating officer, but you probably know," said Burke, standing and following the two to the front door.

"Once again, I'm not in charge," Fortin said. He paused. "If you know of anything that might help us with this hit-and-run, please contact us."

He gave Burke his card.

After they were gone, Burke made himself a coffee and sat down. Fortin seemed to suggest he was just a flic following orders, but Burke had a strong sense the detective missed nothing and had a ruthless streak to him.

And if he was right about Fortin, he hoped he, nor anyone he cared about, ever ended up on his bad side.

CHAPTER 24

BURKE WAS A FEW minutes late for sound check. He told the organizers he had been helping a friend and couldn't leave her in a difficult situation. They didn't seem amused, but he didn't care.

After the sound check, Burke sat offstage with the other participants and listened to the forum moderator, who was host of a Nice TV talk show, explain how it was going to play out. The event would start with introductions, and then the moderator would make some opening remarks. After that, the moderator would initiate discussion by introducing a series of subjects. After an hour' the forum would open up to questions from the audience. If there were enough questions, the forum would extend to three hours.

The other panelists seemed familiar with the plan, nodding confidently as they received their directions and making small remarks that suggested they knew exactly what to do or, as one panelist joked, how to perform. As he'd been told on the phone a few days earlier, the panelists were a mixed bag: a sociology professor, an old-time sportswriter, a sports physician, an Olympic official dealing with drug use, a former cabinet minister who once ruled over French sports, and Burke.

Then it was showtime.

While waiting to be introduced, Burke peeked at the audience through the curtain. He had expected a few dozen. Instead, he saw a crowd of at least five hundred. He also spotted several TV cameras. He groaned.

"Our next panelist is a former professional racer, a former TV commentator and a current blogger about the sport with a wide following—Paul Burke," intoned the moderator.

Burke smiled at the remark about "a wide following" and walked onto the stage to polite applause. He took his spot beside the sportswriter.

After the introductions, the moderator embarked on a lengthy preamble. It seemed the TV host would have liked nothing better than to be the only speaker; he was clearly in love with the sound of his own voice and his own importance. But eventually, he had to share the spotlight.

As he had for most of the day, Burke struggled to concentrate. His mind wandered when he wasn't speaking, and twice, he got caught not listening and was forced to ask for the question to be repeated. He joked once that he was struggling with his hearing, which drew a few chuckles from the audience.

The professor didn't contribute much except long-winded, lecture-like statements about the changing culture of cycling and sports in general. The Olympic official wasn't much better, providing all kinds of dry info about testing methods. The ex-politician spent most of his time promising the audience that the current government was ensuring due diligence was being taken by all sports bodies when dealing with amateur sports.

The veteran sportswriter was another matter, making wisecracks and offering remarks as if he was writing snappy headlines. When he suggested the moderator was interrupting the panelists too much, Burke almost burst into laughter. The other panelist—the sports physician—was the best and had all kinds of stats, which she delivered with conviction. She was particularly effective when describing how the pressure from the media, sponsors and fans was creating an "atmosphere of great risk for great financial rewards—but only for a few."

As for his own initial efforts, Burke gave himself a C minus. He should have done more homework before attending the forum. His answers lacked depth. But he did get a couple of good laughs from the crowd when he shared some of his stories.

The session opened to the audience. Within seconds, a dozen people were lined up at the various microphones set up in the theater.

The people asking the questions were looking for blood.

The first questioner, who identified himself as a university student, went after the Olympics official, asking why the Games organizers seemed to struggle with consistency when "everyone knows the Chinese and Americans dope the most." The Olympics official denied that those two nations were worse than others and said the Games' drug scientists and technicians were the world's best. That prompted the student to reply in a sarcastic voice, "That's reassuring." The crowd applauded.

The next person said the government's sports budget included hundreds of thousands of euros for politicians and bureaucrats to travel around the world to attend various sporting functions. He then related how some youth groups had had their budgets slashed so significantly that the groups ended up shutting down operations. He asked the politician to respond. When the politician said the numbers were misleading and added that the government was being vigilant by sending representatives to various events, the crowd booed.

Burke was surprised by the crowd's increasing hostility. The opening hour had been placid, even boring. The audience had sat back and listened. Now, they were angry and edgy, almost like they'd been given a collective shot of adrenaline.

Someone questioned why the sports doctor couldn't speak in everyday language and explain why cheats seemed to be winning the drug battle. Another blasted the sportswriter for both the media's lack of attention to drug use and its sensationalism in a few cases.

Burke thanked his stars he hadn't been asked anything.

Until the next person stepped up to the mic. Burke looked at her. She was middle-aged—and familiar, but he couldn't place her.

"I want to ask Monsieur Burke a question," she said. She seemed nervous, grasping the standing mic in a death grip with oversized hands.

Burke leaned forward toward the mic before him on the table.

"Why does pro cycling not tell the world about the terrible people within its ranks?" she asked.

Burke didn't have a clue what she was talking about and asked if she could be more specific.

"Everyone is saying Pierre McManus was a successful sportsman who died tragically of a heart attack," she said.

And then Burke recognized her. She was the woman who'd been with Léon Petit at McManus's funeral in Saint-Raphäel. His mother.

"But he was not a good man," she said. "He was mean and cruel and a liar."

The moderator tried to interrupt her, but she wasn't having any of that.

"...and everyone like you who knew him, knew him for what he was. He helped no one but himself. If I'm wrong, you tell me now."

Burke felt his face flush. He had never expected such an outburst.

"Pierre McManus could be a difficult man," he began.

"He was a bastard," she said. "And all of you allowed him to do what he wanted."

"I was just a rider, madame," Burke offered feebly. "Every sport—every business, every government department—probably has people who can be difficult, who anger others. It's part of a working life."

"A working life?" the woman said, her voice still high. "Do not patronize me. All of you—you riders and management and you in the media—do little to protect the victims of such people."

Burke said nothing. He was still perplexed by her explosion.

"Do you have a legitimate question, madame?" the moderator asked, his voice booming in the suddenly silent theater.

The woman glared at him and then shifted her attention back to Burke. She spoke deliberately.

"Do you believe Pierre McManus should have been a role model for anyone?"

Burke took a moment. The crowd was leaning forward in anticipation. It was like they were watching a chess match.

"I don't believe sports figures—or actors or other performers—should be role models just because of what they do for a living," he said, his brain racing to find the right words. "I believe role models should be a parent or a friend or someone who has sacrificed to help others. A sportsman is just someone who plays a game or does some kind of race."

Burke thought he sounded pious and pompous, and was probably echoing what others had said in the past, but he also believed what he was saying.

"We're here today because of the pressures that the media and the public put on athletes," he continued. "We're discussing how sports has been corrupted, but why do sports get corrupted? Because we put too great a value on what happens in sports, on who wins and who loses. I've made a living from professional sports for many years, but I have often wondered if that's because I haven't grown up."

He was starting to sound like the professor on the panel, but the urge to continue was overwhelming—and surprising. He felt like some alien had taken over his brain.

"Paying athletes millions is ridiculous; although in my sport, most riders get little money or just enough to pay the bills. We also need to stop hero-worshipping riders and footballers and golfers. Pro athletes are just people, which means they're flawed. We have to expect them to mess up. But it's the media—and it's the fans—who want to make them so godlike. That makes those athletes willing to do anything to succeed, to live up to the public's expectations. There's so much at stake. It's insane. We need to find some balance."

He figured he'd get off his soapbox at that moment. Besides, he wasn't saying anything that was new.

"And what about Pierre McManus?" the woman persisted.

Burke figured what the hell and said, "You're right, he was a bastard—but he didn't become a bastard on his own. He got lots of help from lots of people."

"That's what I wanted to hear—finally," said the woman, looking satisfied. "It's about time someone in the media told the truth about some of the terrible people in sports."

She left the mic and walked right out of the theater. Many in the audience turned to watch her departure.

"Is the Tour de France doomed?" asked the next speaker. "There have been so many scandals, and now there's even been a murder."

"Who do you want to answer this question?" asked the moderator.

"Monsieur Burke," said the young man. "He's the only one who has said anything that's real."

There was a small round of applause.

Burke cursed under his breath and leaned back toward the mic.

"No, it's not," he said. "The Tour remains a wonderful event despite its troubles. It's a race for the people. Everyone can attend. You don't need money or influence to see it. You just go and watch.

"But it's more than that. Most people have ridden a bicycle, so they know what's involved. I believe they also understand how difficult it is to ride such distances at such speeds, possibly over such tremendous mountains. We riders talk about 'suffering,' and that's the essence of the Tour. We suffer on roads in the world's most beautiful country because we love the challenge, and we embrace the obstacles. And we love that people come out in the millions and applaud our efforts. It's almost as if we're all working together to get to the end. That's why we can still forgive the people who cheat and drug."

Burke figured he was now sounding like a philosopher, so he shrugged and stopped talking.

To his surprise, there was more applause. The French usually embraced cynicism and not idealism. Of course, the nation had exploded in revolutions due to idealism. Maybe one day, he'd give that observation some in-depth thought.

For the next hour, the bulk of the questions focused on the Tour, its intricacies and its history. There were also requests for predictions on who would win. Virtually every one of the queries was directed at Burke.

When the forum ended, Burke felt exhilarated and yet exhausted. He had talked more that afternoon than he had in a very long time.

"Lucky for the forum, you were there," the old sportswriter said to Burke as they strolled off the stage together. "The rest of us weren't doing shit. We were just filling the room with words. You provided a small dose of passion."

Burke thanked him.

"I didn't know ex-riders could be so profound," the sportswriter said, grinning. "You're a veritable Descartes or Sartre."

Burke didn't know the names, but assumed they had to be famous French thinkers.

He was about to leave the theater when a TV reporter approached him and asked for a short interview.

"Why me?" Burke asked.

The reporter—a young blonde with fashionable clothes—smiled at him.

"You were the one who said the most," she said.

So he did the interview, repeating a little of what he'd said before about athletes being unwisely venerated and about the values of the Tour de France.

"That was excellent," she said, thanking him. "It will probably be on the news tonight and maybe again tomorrow."

Outside, Burke noticed people looking at him. He nodded a couple of times and received smiles and waves in return. It was strange.

Léon Petit's mother, Karin, whose question about McManus had prompted the fireworks, was sitting on a bench nearby. She stared at him. Burke wasn't entirely sure, but it looked like she had been crying.

Beside her was Léon Petit, holding her hand.

Burke thought about going over, then opted to stay away. Petit seemed to be comforting her and oblivious to Burke.

He turned and walked toward his car. This was one of the strangest days he'd had in a long time.

CHAPTER 25

RELAXING ON HIS COUCH and feeling more than a little tired, Burke phoned Hélène.

"How is Claude?" he began.

"They've released him again," Hélène said, relief evident in her voice. "The police cautioned him against getting involved in any more trouble."

"So they obviously think he had nothing to do with Vachon's death," Burke said.

"How could they?" Hélène said. "He can be loud and a pain, but he wouldn't hurt anyone."

Burke remembered the photos of Claude he'd seen in the news. He wasn't so sure Claude was opposed to some degree of violence if he thought the matter warranted it.

"He told me he thought the police were full of shit, but I believe he was truly frightened this time," Hélène continued. "I don't think he'll get into any more trouble."

"Did you get him a lawyer?"

"I did. He helped Uncle get out. I think they're meeting right now."

Burke asked if anyone had been charged with the hit-and-run deaths.

"Uncle said he hadn't heard anything," Hélène answered. "He said the police mostly talked to him about his car and searched it."

"Probably for damage from the accident, but since he didn't do it, they wouldn't find anything," Burke said.

"Yes, exactly."

"What is Claude doing after he meets with his lawyer?" Burke asked.

"He wanted to work at the café tonight, but I persuaded him not to. Bad timing. The staff and I will make sure the café is fine."

Burke told her he might come down to the café later.

"But, Paul, I won't be able to be with you," Hélène said. "I'll have to close up, and then I want to see how Uncle is doing, even if it's late."

"I understand."

They talked a little more and then rang off.

Paul remembered the news on TV and turned on his set. He watched a short item on a mysterious cougar once again being spotted in the hills above Vence, and then came the story about the forum he'd participated in.

It wasn't a long spot, maybe forty-five seconds or a minute, but Burke was surprised at how much he was featured in the piece. There was a clip of him discussing the value of the Tour de France, and then, at the end, there was part of the exchange between him and Petit's mother.

To his surprise, Burke thought he looked reasonable, and when he agreed on how McManus had been falsely depicted, he looked positively judicial, even though his words were harsh.

"A new career," Burke said to himself with a laugh.

A few minutes later, François Lemaire called.

"I just saw the news. You were very eloquent, Paul," the editor said. "I thought you'd be acceptable, but that forum showed a different side of you. And your defense of the Tour was especially strong. I'm glad I recommended you."

"Thanks."

"And as for your comments about the real character of Pierre McManus, they were very powerful. It will be interesting to see people's reactions."

"I wonder about that, too," Burke said. It was time to change the subject. "So, have you had any more visits from the police?"

"They did come back and checked my car, but didn't find anything of interest," Lemaire said. "I think they've taken me off their list of suspects."

"Did they say that?"

"They didn't say much," Lemaire said. "That Fortin just asks his questions. I had to be very careful with him."

"But you didn't do anything wrong," Burke said.

"I'm not so sure that matters much to Fortin," Lemaire said. "He just wants a result. I expect he's being pushed hard by the examining judge. There are a lot of people watching this Vachon case. He was a big deal."

Lemaire then switched topics and reminded Burke that he needed to do a written blog and a video blog within the next two days.

"Yes, I remember," Burke said, though actually he had forgotten. "I'll spend all day tomorrow on them."

"Then get a good night's sleep so you can produce good work," Lemaire said.

"You know, François, you sound a much happier man than when we last talked," Burke observed.

Lemaire chuckled lightly. "Being taken off a suspects list will do that."

They hung up.

Burke poured himself a small pastis—he *had* cut back, he told himself—and thought about how two people he knew had been implicated in the Vachon hit-and-run case and how both had just been exonerated—sort of.

Who could have killed Vachon? A man like Vachon had to have had enemies. Of course, maybe it was just bad timing and the driver hadn't even known the victim's identity before speeding off into the night. It happened.

Burke thought about it for an hour, getting nowhere, and then made himself a panini.

He would stay home and get a good night's sleep. Hélène wouldn't be coming over anyway.

CHAPTER 26

AFTER A SNAPPY NINETY-MINUTE ride into the nearby hills, Burke decided he would launch into the regular blog and then the video version without any distractions.

However, he immediately faced a problem: he didn't have a topic for either blog. For ten minutes, he went from subject to subject, dismissing each one. What was it Lemaire once told him?

"Write what you know and write it well" had been the advice.

Then it dawned on Burke that he could write about yesterday's forum for the written blog.

And that's what he did.

He didn't put the focus on himself. Instead, he examined the types of questions that were asked and how the audience members reacted to the given answers. It was all about people's *"diminishing hopes and expanding cynicism,"* he wrote.

He added that such negative emotions mirrored what was happening elsewhere in society. He paused. Was he going too far? *Screw it*, he thought. It was true. Besides, if Lemaire didn't like it, he could edit it out. That was his job.

He finished the piece inside an hour. When he reread it, he thought it was his best work yet. He wasn't much of a writer, but he was improving, especially in delivering his message.

He fired it off to Lemaire with a comment that he was going right into working on the video blog.

He thought about doing it on the forum, but that would be duplication. Again, he recalled Lemaire's advice: *"Say something new, say something people care about, say it once and then move on."*

It was Saturday, and if he went anywhere near the beaches, there would be noise from all the people seeking some sun. He wasn't sure how much background sound could be eliminated, and he didn't want to produce something and then be told it wouldn't work because of background noise that could have been avoided.

A minor brainwave struck him—he'd do his video blog in his village's little park. The noise from the nearby shops wouldn't be too bad. Besides, the flowers were in full bloom, and they would make for a colorful scene.

He planned to use the tranquil setting to talk about how people needed to appreciate the beauty in life and how the Tour, despite its flaws and two deaths in the last several days, remained a thing of beauty. Was it new information? Not really. Did people care? They were forgetting to care, and Burke believed that was his hook.

It was corny, but Burke thought it might work.

He began writing a short script. He gave his first effort a "crap" rating. His second was far less preachy and pompous. It might just do the trick. He read it through once more. Yup, he'd use it.

Burke grabbed his video camera, tripod and instructions from Lemaire and Antoine, and walked to the small park. The village was unusually busy with shoppers. The local bakery was especially active. So, too, was Jean's newsagent's shop. There were lots of tourists, or maybe they were new residents from the nearby developments.

There was noise, but in the park, it seemed distant. And the flowers were indeed beautiful. Lots of red ones and multicolored ones, too. Burke recognized roses, but beyond that, he didn't have a clue. One year, he'd have to attend Nice's Festival of Flowers in February and March for more than the partying. He would go for the endless displays of brilliant flowers that attracted people from around the world. It was a big deal. He recalled that Henri Matisse had supposedly painted a bunch of pictures of it.

"They are lovely, aren't they?" came a thin voice behind him.

It was Madame Marois. Beside her was Plato, staring intently at Burke with his tail wagging.

Burke was surprised the old woman had initiated the conversation.

"Yes, they are," he replied. "I just wish I knew more about them."

He meant it. He was about to do a video blog about recognizing beauty around oneself, and here he was, to his own surprise, discovering he truly wanted to expand his own experiences and knowledge.

Madame Marois pointed to the roses. "You know those, I expect?" she asked, arching an eyebrow.

"I do," Burke replied with a smile.

Madame then identified several other flowers, doing so with considerable speed and adding little bits of background.

"You must be a gardener," Burke said.

Madame Marois's face hinted at a smile. "No, but I have employed many gardeners over many years, and I discovered what I liked and didn't like at an early age," she said. "I have a few plants in my home—"

"I saw them," Burke interjected.

Madame Marois paused for a moment, almost like she wished to pretend Burke's visit to her home a few days earlier hadn't happened.

"As I was saying, I have some plants, but it's outdoors where the true beauty of flowers is found," she said.

As if to contradict his mistress, Plato moved to his left, lifted a leg and squirted on some flowers that Madame had identified as petunias.

"Oh, Plato, you little rogue," the old woman said to her dog, who, instead of feeling shame, seemed to take the comment as a compliment, perking his ears in response.

"His diet is exceptional, so he cannot hurt the flowers," she added, and her smile expanded slightly.

She then asked what Burke was doing. He told her.

"This is my normal time to be here, so do you mind if we sit and watch?" she asked. "Plato will be quiet—unless he sees a cat."

"That would be fine," Burke told her.

With that, Madame Marois sat at a nearby bench and watched Burke, who felt like he was under some kind of microscope.

He worked on getting the camera set into the tripod and then putting the tripod into a good spot. He fumbled the job slightly, but heard nothing from Madame Marois, who sat watching him, still as a statue. By her feet, Plato stretched out and studied Burke's progress.

"He's a handsome dog, Madame," Burke said, figuring it would be less awkward if he could eliminate some of the quiet as he set up.

"He is. He knows me well, and that's good," she said. "I think sometimes he knows me better than I know myself, especially these days."

"These days?" Burke asked as he lined up his camera angle. He tried to remember what Lemaire's techie had told him about white balance or shadows or something like that.

"I'm afraid my memory is not what it used to be," Madame Marois said. She lowered her head. "I believe you might have learned that recently."

Burke looked at her but said nothing.

Madame stared at Plato. "He understands all my moods. I can't fool him. I've occasionally tried to be happy when I've actually felt sad, but he knew the truth and comforted me. And sometimes, I've pretended to be angry, but he knew I wasn't being sincere and ignored my outburst. He's an exceptional little animal."

It wasn't the first time Burke had heard her praise Plato, but this time, she seemed more melancholic when she discussed him.

"He's such a devoted companion, very calm and quiet for his breed," Madame said in a soft voice. "I like to take him wherever I go although that's not always possible. I'm fortunate to have him."

Burke smiled and nodded. Then he got back to work. Finally, he had his camera properly set.

It was time to do the video blog.

He stood in front of the camera and clicked the remote button in his hand. That activated the camera.

He lasted about ten seconds into his take before he messed up. The second time, he went twenty seconds before he misspoke. The third time was the worst yet, with Burke having to stop filming after only five seconds.

"May I help you?" Madame Marois asked.

Burke couldn't believe what he'd just heard.

"Yes, thank you," he said.

He wasn't sure what to have her do. Run the camera? Provide some script hints?

He opted to have her start and end the segment by pushing the ON and OFF buttons. It would be one less thing for him to think about.

And it worked perfectly.

He did his video blog on the very next take.

"Thank you, Madame," he said. "You must have calmed me down."

Madame Marois accepted his thanks with a nod and then returned to her bench, where Plato had remained.

Burke checked the video. It was fine. Heck, it was better than he'd expected. And it was colorful.

Perfect.

He packed up his gear, then turned to Madame Marois, who was suddenly looking around.

"Madame, are you all right?" he asked.

"My pills, I have lost my pills," she said, her voice anxious.

At least it wasn't her keys again. He dropped to his knees and started scanning the grass.

"My pills, I need my pills," she said.

"Are you sure you dropped them?" Burke asked after coming up with nothing.

"Yes, young man, I am sure," she said. "I had them a moment ago, and now I do not."

Burke had another peek around and found himself almost nose to nose with Plato. Neither of them had any luck.

"What will I do?" Madame said, her hands on her face. "I need them, I need them."

Burke was flummoxed. He didn't have a clue what to do next. Finally, he asked if he could check her purse.

"You won't take my money, will you?" Madame asked, sounding frightened.

She was a totally different woman from the one helping him a few moments earlier.

Burke patted her hand. "No, Madame, I will just double-check to see if your pills are there. You can watch me," he said.

Madame Marois nodded.

Burke patted Plato, who was now stretched out and enjoying the sunlight. So much for the small dog being in tune with his mistress's moods, Burke thought as he pushed himself to his feet.

He went through Madame Marois's purse and, within seconds, found a small container. He opened it and found a cache of about twenty pills.

"You found them!" exclaimed the old woman. "Thank you, young man. Thank you. I don't know what I'd do without them."

He offered to walk her back to her apartment, and she accepted, standing and putting her arm over his elbow.

"You must think me a silly old woman, losing my pills in my own purse," Madame said as they approached her home.

"It's easy to forget things, Madame," Burke said.

"I wish that was the case, monsieur," she said, sounding back in control. "But I believe I'm having some issues with my memory."

It was becoming a familiar scene to Burke.

As they approached her place, Burke spotted Claude walking toward his café. His friend saw him, too, and waved. He stopped to watch Burke and Madame Marois negotiate the last few steps to her home.

"If you need help, Madame, I'll do what I can," Burke said, although he wasn't quite sure what kind of assistance he could provide her.

"Thank you," she said. "I'm not driving much because I have found myself lost once or twice in recent days. I might need someone to take me to a doctor's appointment or something like that."

Burke was surprised. Madame Marois's pride had always seemed endless, and he wouldn't have guessed she would ever consider seeking help. Besides, she had enough money to take taxis everywhere.

She went inside, a little shaky. Plato followed her, keeping to her pace perfectly.

"That looked odd," Claude said when Burke approached him.

Burke explained what had happened.

"Like I said the other day, the old woman is losing it," Claude said.

"Maybe, but Claude, are you losing it, too?" Burke suggested. "I mean, two trips to the local jail? Maybe next time you will find yourself in the Château d'If."

"But I am not the Count of Monte Cristo, and so the police won't send me to his old prison," Claude replied with a chuckle, his good spirits clearly restored. "I'll just spend my evenings at my café or at home."

"At least you can't get into trouble at either place," Burke said.

"Well, you never know," Claude said. "Come to my café with me, and I will tell you my adventures."

Burke promised he would within the hour. First, he had to file his video blog.

"You've become a fan of technology, Paul," said Claude, who made Burke look like a software engineer.

"An hour, Claude," Burke said.

"Good. I have much to tell you."

CHAPTER 27

THE LUNCH CROWD AT the café was larger than normal. Claude and Burke chatted for a couple of minutes about Claude's recent misadventures, and then the café owner had to excuse himself to help handle customers, leaving Burke to relax over a glass of rosé.

When Burke spotted Hélène walking toward the café, obviously to start a shift, his heart beat a little faster. He caught her eye, and she smiled and waved. As she approached, he grinned, excitement growing inside him.

She kissed him on both cheeks and then gently on the lips.

"I have to work, *chéri*," she said with a shrug. She nodded toward Claude. "And I have to make sure Uncle doesn't get into more trouble."

"I understand."

"Tomorrow, maybe? I don't have to work, and it is Sunday. We can spend the day together."

"That sounds perfect," Burke replied. And it did. "I'll call you in the morning."

"But not too early, *chéri*," Hélène said, waving a finger for emphasis. "I'll need my beauty sleep."

"I'll call you at eleven," Burke suggested.

"Perfect. Maybe a little lunch, a visit to the beach and then…" said Hélène, leaving the rest unspoken but understood.

She went off. Burke pondered having another drink and maybe something to eat, but in the end, he opted for neither, paying his bill and waving goodbye to Claude, who seemed surprised to see Burke leave so soon.

Back home, Burke stretched out on his couch. He suddenly felt drained. He put it down to the mental work he was doing, not the morning's bike ride, which hadn't been anything too strenuous. He laughed at the notion that he was overworking his brain.

He rested for a half hour and then decided to go for another ride. When he was tired, a ride would often snap him out of his lethargy.

Soon, he was pedaling toward Vence and feeling rejuvenated by the effort. He didn't stop at the historic village. Instead, he kept going east until he cycled down into Nice.

The city was bustling with its July tourist trade. There were thousands of people on their way to the beach or coming from the beach. Even the locals seemed to be out in record numbers. A couple of times, Burke had to dodge a vehicle going outside its lane to escape traffic congestion.

He turned toward the lovely Old Harbor, with its lively cafés and bustling marina, and then climbed out of town. He didn't stop until he reached the more peaceful atmosphere of neighboring Villefranche-sur-Mer. He stopped for a quick drink of water by the tourist information center, the gardens of which were more colorful than ever. Then he turned around and rode back, charging down the hill into Nice at seventy kilometers per hour—fast enough to earn a substantial speeding ticket if he got caught.

He headed to André Rousseau's bike shop once again. It wasn't so much that he wanted to talk to André. He was actually hoping to have a chat with Léon Petit if he was working today. Something was bugging Burke, and he wanted to explore it.

Léon was working, toiling away in the back shop truing a wheel. He didn't look up when Burke said hello, just acknowledged him with a quick nod.

"Léon often doesn't have the best people skills," whispered André, noticing the exchange.

Burke wasn't bothered. It seemed talking to people was a stretch for the mechanic, although Petit had been almost chatty the other day. He seemed much more comfortable alone, working on bikes. Or with his mother.

Burke talked a few minutes with André and then left him so he could attend to two young cyclists who had just walked in. Burke returned his attention to Léon, who was putting the wheel back onto the bike. In the background, a radio played some pop music.

"I saw you outside the forum yesterday with your mother," Burke said.

Léon shrugged.

"Were you in the crowd at the forum?" Burke said.

"I was."

"What did you think about it?"

"I didn't think much about it at all," Léon said, putting aside the restored bike and grabbing a top-end racing machine and hoisting it onto the bike stand.

"Boring?"

"A little."

That gave Burke his opening. "Your mother added some spice, though," he said.

Léon looked up at him. He didn't say anything.

"If she hadn't spoken, I don't think the forum would have been interesting at all," Burke said.

"She speaks her mind," Léon said as he applied a small screwdriver to the front derailleur, which played a major part in switching gears.

"So she knew McManus?" Burke asked.

"A little."

"Enough to think he was a bastard," Burke said. "When did she meet him?"

Léon stopped working on the racing bike and stared at Burke.

"Why are you interested?" he asked.

"Well, it was clear at the forum that she knew him and that she didn't like him," Burke said. "And I did agree with her about McManus. He was a bastard."

Léon shrugged again.

"She seemed very upset afterward," Burke said. "I saw you both sitting outside the theater."

"She has trouble speaking in front of people, and it took a lot out of her to go to the microphone."

"Why did she go up and speak if she gets so nervous?" Burke asked.

"You'd have to ask her."

"When did she first encounter McManus, Léon?" Burke asked, hoping he sounded friendly and not like a flic.

"I'm not sure. Years ago, I believe," Léon said. He paused. "I don't know. It isn't important."

"It was important enough that she told everyone what she thought of him."

Léon said nothing.

"Are you from around here, Léon?" Burke asked.

"Nice."

"So you grew up on the Côte d'Azur? Lucky guy," Burke said.

Léon ignored the comment and kept his attention on the front derailleur. Something was slightly off-kilter with the mechanism.

The time was now for him to pursue what had been truly bugging him.

"Is your father dead, Léon?" Burke ventured.

Léon turned and stared at Burke. "Yes," he finally said.

"My dad just died recently," Burke said. It was a lie, since both his parents had been killed in a car crash when he was a teenager, but Burke hoped it might free Petit to talk a little bit about his father, whoever he was. "Did yours pass away a long time ago?"

"Why do you care?"

"Just curious," Burke said. "I miss my father, so sometimes I search for ways to deal with that. Asking people how they've coped with losing their own father sometimes helps me."

"If you're so sad, maybe you should talk to a professional," Léon suggested.

Burke waited. Then he asked what Léon's dad's name was.

"My business," Léon said.

Another pause. He had to ask. "You know, it's strange, but you look a lot like Pierre McManus," he said.

And it was certainly true. In fact, the more Burke looked at Léon, the more he saw McManus's rough, squat features and the piercing brown eyes and arched eyebrows. They also had the same stocky, muscular build.

Léon was rigid. Not a muscle moved—not even his eyes, which were locked onto Burke's.

"I'm working, so maybe you can stop with the questions and just fuck off," he said in a low, threatening voice.

Burke nodded. "It's just that you could be his younger brother—or even his son. You have the same look."

Léon moved toward him, his hand now grasping a heavy wrench. His face was flushed, and his eyes blazed.

"I told you to fuck off," he said, stopping a foot away from Burke.

"What's going on here?" Rousseau stood just inside the shop.

"He's distracting me from my work," Léon replied, moving back to the bike stand.

Burke looked at André and shrugged. "I know when to leave," he said and walked through the door and into the main shop.

Rousseau followed, looking annoyed at having to stop a disagreement between his mechanic and his friend.

"What the hell was all that about?" Rousseau asked in a low voice, even though the back-shop radio probably drowned out what was being said.

"I was asking Léon about his mother," Burke said.

"Why do you care?"

Burke told him how she'd appeared at the forum in such an angry state and had asked questions that changed the entire tone of the gathering.

"I understand Léon is close to his mother, but there had to be more than that for Léon to get so pissed at you," Rousseau said, his voice still low. "He looked like he was going to clobber you with that wrench."

"I also told him he looked a lot like Pierre McManus. He didn't seem to like that."

Rousseau paused. He took a step back, glanced into the back shop and then returned his attention to Burke.

"Now that you say it, Léon does look like McManus a fair amount," he said. "Maybe the cat got into the milk a long time ago. McManus always was one for the ladies."

"My thoughts, too."

"Paul, you are becoming quite the troublemaker," Rousseau said.

"Have you ever heard Léon say anything about his father?"

"Never."

"Interesting," Burke said.

"OK, enough of the detective work. If you aren't going to buy anything, maybe you should go investigate elsewhere," Rousseau said with a smile, gently leading Burke and his bike to the front door.

Burke nodded at his friend and then stepped outside. Rousseau wasn't angry. On the contrary, he seemed almost equally curious about Petit, his mother and a possible connection to Pierre McManus.

Burke wondered if there was any way he could learn who was listed as "father" on Léon Petit's birth certificate.

CHAPTER 28

THERE WAS.

A quick Google search told Burke that the French had been registering births, deaths and marriages for more than two hundred years. Of course, some areas of the country were better than others at doing so, and there had been issues during various wartimes, but the French were a bureaucratic people and had done an exhaustive job with their record keeping.

He tried to find a website that would provide what he was searching for, but it soon became a struggle. One site turned him over to another. He began bumping into unfamiliar terms. Then there were sites that provided all kinds of methods for obtaining the desired results, but not the actual information he wanted. More than a few sites were subscription based.

After two hours, he decided he needed help.

François Lemaire's tech staffer, Antoine, came to mind. He called the Antibes office, hoping some staff would still be working Saturday afternoon, and luckily was put through to Antoine. Burke apologized for disturbing him and was happy to hear Antoine wasn't busy. Then Burke explained what he was trying to do.

"Do you have the person's full name, date of birth and place of birth?" Antoine asked.

Burke felt stupid. He didn't.

"You'll need it," Antoine said.

Burke rang off and then called André Rousseau. He told his friend he needed information about Léon Petit without Petit knowing it.

"What are you up to, Paul?" Rousseau asked. "Does this have something to do with your argument in the shop today?"

"It does, André," Burke admitted. "You know I've been involved with the coverage of Pierre McManus's death, and I have this funny feeling that your man Petit is somehow mixed up in what happened."

"And you want me to provide you some information?"

"Yes, without letting Petit know I want it."

Rousseau paused for a few moments. "All right, I'll do what I can, but you owe me," he said.

Burke told him he needed Petit's full name and date of birth. He hoped Petit had filled in the usual employment form.

"Give me five minutes, Paul," Rousseau said. "By the way, the reason I'm helping you is that I have some strange feelings about Petit, too."

Burke was surprised but chose not to explore Rousseau's comment. He wanted the information fast so he could get back to Antoine.

Rousseau was good to his word, providing the information Burke had requested within five minutes. Then Burke got back to Antoine, who suggested Burke pop down to the newspaper office.

"It relates to a video blog, right?" Antoine said, giving Burke a clue that their efforts had to be work related, if only for official purposes. "It isn't good to hack into computers for personal reasons."

Burke understood the nuance and agreed.

Fifteen minutes later, Burke was sitting in a small, cramped office with Antoine, whose bulk seemed even greater in the tiny room.

"Were the parents of this person—Petit—married?" Antoine asked. "I did a little legwork waiting for you and learned that for generations, if a woman had a child out of wedlock, it was common for the mother's parents to be listed instead of the father or father's parents."

"I don't know," Burke said. "If I was a betting man, I would say they were not."

"Well, let's see what we can do."

For a huge man, Antoine's oversized hands and thick fingers danced over the keyboard at an astonishing speed, so quickly that Burke could hardly keep up with what was happening on the screen.

Burke asked a couple of questions, but soon sensed his queries only served to distract the other man. He kept quiet and tried to follow along.

Once, Lemaire popped his head into the office and asked what was happening. Without turning, Antoine said he was helping Burke with his video blog. The suggestion was they should not be disturbed. Lemaire said, "OK" and left.

"François thinks he knows tech stuff, but he's essentially clueless," Antoine told Burke with a sly grin. "He doesn't appreciate what can really be done with all the new software, and he definitely doesn't find any joy in a good hack."

"And you do?"

"I don't hack for the pleasure of it or to create chaos, which is what too many self-important idiots do," Antoine said, his fingers still dancing on the keyboard. "If I do a hack, it's for a good cause."

"But you're good at it, right?" Burke said.

"Maybe," Antoine said.

After twenty minutes, Antoine exclaimed, "Success!" and jabbed a meaty finger at the screen.

"I found a way into the statistics site for Nice, where your man was born," he said. "Now, we will see."

Fifteen more minutes passed. Burke didn't know why, but he felt tense.

"Voilà! I have it," Antoine said.

Burke moved closer to the screen.

There was the information about Léon Petit's parentage that he had been seeking. Mother: *Karin Petit.* He looked for the identity of the father, expecting to see her parents' names, whatever they were. Instead, he saw: *Pierre McManus.*

Burke's wild guess was true. McManus was Léon Petit's father.

For whatever reason, Karin Petit had wanted McManus's name on the record as being the father of her child. Had they been living together? Had they been engaged? More questions.

Burke expected this connection between Petit and McManus would be a giant surprise to Rousseau and many others in the pro cycling world.

But what did it mean beyond that?

Burke didn't know, but he had to find out.

CHAPTER 29

BURKE THANKED ANTOINE FOR his efforts. He told him he wasn't sure what he was going to do with the information—which was true—but that he would do something, and when he did, he'd tell Antoine. The big man nodded and said he had enjoyed the challenge.

"A successful hack can be a good thing," Antoine said.

In his car, Burke called Rousseau as he had promised and related the information, asking him to keep quiet. He knew his friend would adhere to his request.

"This is getting a little strange," Rousseau said. "In fact, this is getting a lot strange."

"Can you talk?" Burke asked. "Is Petit still there?"

"I can," Rousseau said. "Petit just left for the day, and there's no one else in the shop."

"You know Petit better than I do, André," Burke said. "Has he ever talked about McManus?"

"No, not at all. The only conversation he's had about McManus that I know of was that argument you had with him."

"Did he seem sad after the funeral?"

"He acted just the way he usually does—quiet, focused on the job, hardworking," Rousseau said. "He mentioned his mother once or twice, but not in any depth. He comes in, does what he has to and goes home—I think."

"He's a good mechanic, right?" Burke asked.

"He's as good as I am, and I am very good," Rousseau replied with no false modesty. "He can diagnose a problem in seconds and make the appropriate repairs in hardly any time. He may not be sociable, but he's a smart man. Lots of skills."

Burke recalled that Petit was qualified as a masseur and knowledgeable about nutrition.

"About the only time he talks is when he critiques my lunches which happens every second day," Rousseau added. "But he's great in the back shop and that allows me to work with the customers in the front."

Burke paused. He wasn't sure what the information added up to, if anything.

"What are you doing with this information, Paul?" asked Rousseau, interrupting Burke's train of thought.

"I don't know, André," Burke said. "I'm just curious about some stuff. I'm not sure the police care much anymore about McManus—or about Den Weent's death either. I haven't read or seen anything recently in the media about them."

"I haven't either," Rousseau said. "Maybe everybody is concentrating on the death of that Vachon guy. You know, the FP Developments bigwig. I saw more stories in the national papers today about the company and the developments that FP was involved with down here."

Burke had missed those articles and asked for a condensed version.

"The papers just said FP Developments would continue to proceed with all projects as planned," Rousseau said. "Full speed ahead. As for replacing Vachon, I guess the company expects to have someone appointed within two weeks."

"That seems fast," Burke observed. "I really don't know anything about big business, but Vachon was the face of the company. He has to be hard to replace."

Burke thanked his friend and was about to hang up when he had another thought.

"Does Petit have any scratches or cuts on his knuckles or at the base of his fingers?" he asked.

"Why do you want to know?"

"Just being curious again," Burke said. "I didn't think to look before."

"You really are becoming Chief Inspector Maigret, Paul," Rousseau said with a chuckle. "Anyway, I did notice he has a couple of scrapes, but maybe he got careless on a job."

Burke knew that top-notch bike mechanics on the pro tour worked so efficiently that they rarely ended up with dirt on their hands, let alone any cuts. They were that good.

And Petit, according to Rousseau, was as good a mechanic as he was. That meant he was among the best.

Burke chose not to tell Rousseau that his question about Petit's hands was prompted by an old TV crime show in which the lead investigator had commented how knife-wielding attackers often ended up with a cut finger or knuckle after stabbing someone. The power of TV.

He thanked his friend once more and hung up, but not before promising to keep him abreast of any developments.

Burke didn't have a plan for the rest of the day, and so he decided to drive home by way of the new FP Developments project that had been the scene of the protest.

He was at the work site within ten minutes. Sure enough, the site was busy with at least two dozen workers doing a variety of tasks, even though the company was still awaiting final permits to be approved and it was a weekend. Burke's sense of French construction staff was they did good work but at a leisurely pace. These people were almost jogging to get stuff done.

And then to his shock, he saw Claude at the corner, waving a placard. He was in a group of about a dozen protesters.

He cursed his friend.

Burke parked his car and marched to where Claude and the others were yelling, "FP—out!" to the construction crew.

"Claude, what are you doing?" he said when he was within earshot. "You said you were going to stay out of trouble. Besides, I thought you were working today."

When he saw Burke, Claude's face turned red, like a kid who'd been caught stealing a treat.

"I heard there was going to be a small protest, and I had some time to join them in showing opposition to the decision by FP Developments to continue this project," Claude said.

"You promised you'd keep a low profile after your problem with the Nice police," Burke reminded his friend.

"Well, I changed my mind," Claude said. "This is a serious matter, and I still believe what I believe."

Several of the other protesters were now paying more attention to their exchange than to the construction work.

"And if the police come back?" Burke asked.

Claude checked out the audience around him. He went for bold and brave.

"I would tell them to fuck off!" he said, thumping his chest theatrically with a fist.

Burke wondered if Claude told Hélène where he was going when he skipped out from the café. He doubted it. Hélène would be livid if she knew her uncle was back protesting at the site.

"And what would you tell Hélène if she discovered you were doing this and could get into more trouble?"

"I'm not in trouble, and if I was, I would tell her that this protest is important to me, to her, to all of us," Claude said.

His little speech got some support from his fellow protesters, who were starting to look at Burke like he was the enemy.

"It's your life, Claude," Burke said, starting to move away.

"It is, and I will use it to fight the good fight."

It seemed Claude was now playing to the others around them. His comment worked though, because they gave him a small round of applause for his last statement.

Burke walked back to his car, wondering if Claude would really stand up to the police again if they showed up. With the other protesters watching him, Claude probably would, and that could lead to more trouble with Fortin.

He decided not to tell Hélène he had seen Claude. She didn't need more frustration.

And he wouldn't visit the café for an evening drink. He had had quite enough of his friend.

CHAPTER 30

BURKE SLEPT WELL, BUT when he got up just after seven, his mind immediately went to Claude, and his anger was renewed. It was one thing to protest, but another to potentially put oneself back into the spotlight in a murder investigation. The police were still trying to pin Vachon's death on someone, and Burke was not sure Claude was entirely free of suspicion.

He drank a coffee, but that only seemed to make his mood worse. Grabbing his bike and a banana for energy, he set out for a short ride to take off the edge. He didn't want to be in a bad mood when he got together with Hélène in a few hours.

Burke loved early Sunday mornings in summer on the Côte d'Azur. Since almost everyone got up late, there was little traffic and noise, making it a great time to go for a bike ride. A cyclist had fewer vehicles to worry about and more time to catch the splendid views of the fabled coastline and beautiful hillsides that cascaded to the sea.

Of course, that would change in late morning when the family-oriented French and hordes of tourists took to the beaches and parks for hours of play and relaxation.

Burke charged down to the sea and then turned toward Antibes. The traffic, by Côte d'Azur standards, was almost nonexistent. Within fifteen minutes, he was in Antibes. He stayed on the main road and took his favorite route into the Old Town and up to the Bastion. From there, he kept close to the sea and powered his way onto the road that led around Cap d'Antibes.

Burke figured he had probably lost two kilos in the last several days, and he felt significantly faster than the last time he'd ridden the route. That was the day he'd seen Claude's photo in the paper after the protest that had turned violent.

He went up the kilometer-long spine of the Cap, reaching the top at almost thirty kilometers per hour. He was sweating heavily but enjoying it. He was becoming fitter, not professional cyclist fit, but much better than before.

When he hit Juan-les-Pins, he stopped and gobbled his banana.

Bunches of tourists crossed the street ahead to get to the beach. With the forecast predicting a temperature high of thirty-three degrees Celsius, the beaches along the coast would soon be packed.

He turned and headed for home.

As he got close, he detoured to the FP Developments site. It wasn't as busy as the day before, with only a half dozen construction personnel working, but it was a Sunday, and a handful of other workers were walking onto the site. Not for the first time, Burke wondered if FP Developments knew something others didn't about its chances of getting those final permits approved—and soon.

He saw no protestors or any damage. He wondered how long Claude had stayed.

Back home, he showered and shaved. The ride had worked, and his mood was brighter, although his mind was still partly occupied by Claude, Vachon, McManus and Léon Petit. He had somehow become a different man over these two weeks. Before, he would have been only thinking about when he'd have his first pastis of the evening, or if he should take a siesta after lunch.

He called Hélène at eleven. Her voice sounded thick from having just gotten up.

"Busy evening," she mumbled. "And Uncle disappeared for a couple of hours, which didn't help."

"Where did he go?" Burke asked, trying to sound only mildly curious.

"He said he had to run a couple of errands for the café. He was back by seven, so he was there for the main crowd, but it meant we had to delay some chores."

Hélène clearly didn't know about the protest. And evidently, Claude had not had any issue with the police. All was good.

They agreed Burke would collect her in forty-five minutes and they'd go for lunch someplace.

When he arrived to pick her up, Burke noticed once again how stunning Hélène was, this time dressed in a white linen, sleeveless blouse and an orange linen skirt that flowed just below her knees. How could a regular guy like him find himself with a woman as vibrant and beautiful as Hélène?

For lunch, they decided they'd try a small café in Èze Village. The café was a little expensive and usually busy, but it always provided wonderful food and spectacular views of the coastline far below. The drive took just minutes, even though traffic was starting to get heavy. From their lofty perch on the café terrace, they watched a giant cruise ship sail toward the bay by Villefranche-sur-Mer, where it would anchor and then shuttle passengers in on small launches. It was all very impressive—and a little scary. How much more could the Côte d'Azur handle? Burke figured the answer would be "lots" if there was enough money to be made.

When he moved into the region several years earlier, he'd needed a few months to adjust to the frenetic action along the coast. He had made the move because the area was popular with a number of pro cyclists, thanks to its climate and varied landscapes, and it was a strategy that definitely helped his career. By the time he retired, he couldn't think of anywhere else he'd rather be. Now, it was all about being able to afford to stay.

"You're thinking of something far away," Hélène said.

Burke had been caught drifting. "You're right," he said. "I was thinking how much I like living here."

"I'm glad you like it here," Hélène said, "because I love this area, too."

"The trouble is, it's becoming so expensive," Burke added. "I wonder if there will come a day when people like you and me can't afford to stay here."

"You sound a little like Uncle Claude, but I think you're right to worry," she said. "I'm afraid as well. What happens when my salary can't pay for food or the rent?"

Burke felt slightly depressed at that thought. He didn't want to have the lunch spoiled by such matters, even though he'd brought up the subject, and so he gave her his best smile and said they'd have lots of time before any serious changes occurred—if at all.

"Maybe," Hélène said.

"Time for dessert, I think," Burke said, deciding an entirely new topic was needed. "We're both so slender, we can afford something rich."

"You might be able to have such treats because you're a cyclist, but it's different for me," Hélène said, smiling.

"Well, we could both have dessert and wear it off later," he said slyly.

"Yes, there is that possibility," Hélène said. She paused thoughtfully, touching her chin with a finger. "In fact, I believe, *chéri*, it's more than a possibility. Let's order dessert."

And they did.

After spending an hour at the Villefranche beach, until it became overrun with tourists, they went to her place, where they wore off the rest of their dessert calories—and a lot more.

That night, with Hélène sleeping inside the crook of his arm, Burke found himself wondering about the changes facing his little world. The FP Developments project would drive up land prices and taxes. The next major development—and Burke knew there would be one sooner than later—would spike them even more. More ships, more hotels, more condos, more people.

More money.

And then what would happen?

Burke studied the woman sleeping beside him.

Some tough decisions lay ahead.

CHAPTER 31

BURKE GOT UP EARLY, made himself a coffee and then showered and dressed. By then, it was 8 a.m. He returned to the bedroom, kissed Hélène gently on the forehead and whispered, "*Bonne journée.*" She smiled in response before drifting back to sleep.

He drove back to his village, then went to Jean's to pick up a couple of newspapers, wondering if he'd find anything about Vachon and FP Developments.

He didn't have to wonder. The company had done the unusual and held a Sunday news conference, emphasizing how it intended to do business as usual, even without the charismatic Vachon at the helm. The FP Developments vice president, who served as spokesperson for the company, praised the police for their efforts and then managed to criticize them in the next breath for not having arrested anyone. Consequently, several papers, including most of the big nationals, featured major pieces about the news conference and about the progress—or lack of it—in finding Vachon's killer.

"The flics are in the fire with that Vachon death," said Jean, noticing Burke reading a story in *Le Monde*.

"Not really surprising," Burke said. "It's been several days and nothing."

"There's a comment somewhere from the justice minister that the investigation has to find who was responsible," Jean said. "If nothing happens in a couple of days, I expect the president will add his displeasure as well. I wouldn't want to be the police officer who's handling the Vachon investigation. It's going to get ugly."

"I might know the detective who's in charge," Burke told Jean. "He's tough. Smart, too. At least I think he's smart."

Jean's eyebrows lifted. "Did he arrest you, Paul, for one of your many crimes?" he asked.

Burke laughed. "I was lucky—he let me go. My good looks, I think."

"Ah, yes, those."

Burke liked how Jean usually made him smile and often made him laugh.

He wished the newsagent a good day and was about to head back home when he spotted Madame Marois walking Plato. They were moving quickly, in perfect harmony.

"She looks good now, with Plato, but I worry about Madame," Jean said to Burke.

"For good reason," Burke said.

"She's doing more walking," Jean added. "In fact, I see her almost every morning going for a walk. They go up to the end of the road and then come back. Then they spend a few minutes in the park just sitting. I'm not sure she drives much anymore. I think she might be afraid to go out in her car. Sometimes, we have a brief word, but she's usually distracted."

"Too bad," Burke said. "But it may be good she's not driving much these days."

Back home, Burke had just started reading the papers when his cell phone rang. It was Lemaire, and he got right to the point, saying the Vachon case was so big that the McManus-Den Weent story was getting lost.

"I want you to do a blog on how the police have nothing after two weeks and have probably given up to concentrate on the Vachon case," Lemaire said. "Put some anger into it. Piss someone off."

"What about the Vachon story and the FP Developments news conference?"

"I have someone doing a local angle about the news conference, so that part is covered. Just get yourself down to the Nice police and make them uncomfortable. They're dropping the ball on this, and as the new wise man of cycling after your forum performance, you're the one to tell the world about such incompetence."

"I'm no one's wise man," Burke said.

"Not true," Lemaire said. "There are a lot of people out there who think you have something important to say. I'm not sure I'm one of them, but let's capitalize on your new celebrity while we can."

"OK," said Burke, feeling more than a little uncomfortable with his new assignment.

"And I'd like your blog by the end of the day. It would be ideal, Paul, if you also did a video version. Same deadline."

"I understand," Burke said. "I better get busy then."

He rang off, not entirely sure about how to approach his blog. He scanned the papers to see if there was any mention of McManus or Den Weent. There wasn't. But Vachon got plenty of ink. And by connection, FP Developments did, too.

Burke figured his only option was to track down Fortin. He doubted the Nice detective would give him the time of day, but he had to start somewhere.

A half hour later, Burke walked into the Nice police headquarters. It was quiet except for a couple of officers talking to a man in plain clothes. Burke approached the front desk and asked for Fortin, adding he was there to get some information for his newspaper.

"You're a reporter?" asked the officer at the desk—a burly veteran who looked skeptically at Burke.

"I do a blog for them," Burke replied, pulling out the ID Lemaire had given him when he started the job.

"A blog? Well, that makes it special," said the flic with a significant dose of sarcasm.

Before Burke could reply, the officer went to another desk and used the phone. Burke couldn't hear what he said, but he expected he was calling Fortin. Or at least Burke hoped that was what he was doing.

"He'll be out in a minute," the desk cop said when he came back.

Sure enough, Fortin soon appeared, looking like he hadn't slept in days.

"What are you looking for?" Fortin said, getting right to the point.

"My editor thinks the Vachon case has taken over your department's priority and that the McManus and Den Weent deaths have been forgotten," Burke said.

Fortin grimaced and shook his head. If he was looking to portray disgust, Fortin deserved a ten out of ten.

"Come with me," Fortin said.

To Burke's surprise, Fortin led him through the security door, down the corridor and back to his small office. The main room in the station was at the end of the corridor; it was bustling with both uniformed and plain-clothes police officers.

Fortin motioned for Burke to sit in the beaten-up old chair facing his cluttered desk. Fortin took his seat behind the desk and leaned back, folding his hands over his stomach. Burke waited, thinking Fortin wanted to tell him something; otherwise, why would he have asked Burke back to his office?

"First, we have not forgotten Monsieur McManus or Monsieur Den Weent," Fortin said. "I've just been given full control of the case by the investigating judge and I'm telling you we're being active in pursuing leads."

"Why you?" Burke asked, noticing how Fortin had lumped McManus and Den Weent into a single case.

"Because the detective who was working the case has been assigned to other matters," Fortin said.

"Who's the investigating judge?" Burke asked.

Fortin shook his head. "That's not for public notice."

Burke thought this information was hardly a reason for Fortin to bring him back to his office; the detective could have told him that in the foyer by the front desk. Burke wondered if he was trying to diffuse a potentially awkward story, but he rejected that notion because, more and more, Fortin seemed clever and manipulative. Fortin probably didn't give a damn about some blog or news story—he had something else on his mind.

Figuring he had little to lose, since so far, he was getting nothing substantial, Burke asked if there were any new toxicology reports on McManus. He didn't expect any real answer.

Fortin nodded. "We're examining some new results," he said.

So they were looking for something different. They were no longer satisfied with the initial results.

"Can you say without any doubt if McManus's death was natural? Or was it a case of murder?" Burke asked, once again surprising himself by asking such direct questions.

"I can't tell you the results, but I will say we are reviewing them closely," Fortin said.

It seemed Fortin was leading him somewhere, but Burke didn't know where.

"Did someone check to see if masking agents were used?" he asked.

"The report takes into account several matters," Fortin said, and Burke thought that meant the answer to his question was "yes."

"Did the Nice police, and whoever is working on Den Weent's death, interview all members of the Global Projects cycling team?" Burke asked.

"That would have been routine, for both us and the Avignon police," Fortin said.

"So you did?" Burke persisted.

Fortin didn't say a word or even move.

"Do you know that Pierre McManus was the father of one of the team's mechanics?" Burke said, firing his biggest shot at Fortin.

Fortin showed no change of expression, but, to Burke, his gaze seemed to intensify.

"How do you know that?" Fortin asked.

"I just did a little research," Burke said. "Did you know about the connection?"

Fortin ignored the question. "What else do you know about Léon Petit?" he asked.

Burke wondered if this was the point where, if he were a regular journalist, he would reply that his job was to ask questions and not provide police with information.

He'd try answering by asking another question. If Fortin could do it, he could too.

"Did you also know Petit is a skilled masseur and a knowledgeable nutritionist?" Burke asked.

Fortin was leaning forward now, staring hard at Burke.

"We have information about his skills," Fortin replied. He paused, then pointed at Burke and said, "You seem to be implicating Léon Petit in the death of Pierre McManus, Monsieur Burke."

That was exactly what he was doing. He wasn't sure if Petit was truly involved, but there was something about the mechanic and his mother that made him uneasy. If Petit ever learned that Burke was implicating him to the police, Petit would be livid and maybe dangerous. Burke realized at that moment that he thought Petit was capable of violence—real, serious violence. He shuddered.

"I'm only asking questions for my blog," Burke said. "Are you considering Petit a suspect?"

"I can't tell you if we have any suspects," Fortin said.

"But you believe the deaths of McManus and Den Weent are connected," Burke said.

Fortin said nothing.

"Otherwise, you wouldn't have said you're investigating 'the case.'"

"I am not confirming anything about the death of Pierre McManus, or Mark Den Weent, for that matter."

Burke was out of questions and scrambled for something to say.

"When did you last talk to Mark Den Weent?" Fortin asked.

Burke told him. Fortin nodded.

"At that time, did Den Weent seem to think McManus had died of anything other than a heart attack?"

"No."

"Den Weent, it seems, had a reputation as someone who didn't miss much," Fortin said. "Is that how you would describe him?"

Burke agreed.

"You've had some conversations recently with Petit," Fortin said. It was a statement, not a question, and Burke wondered how the detective knew that.

Burke confirmed that he had talked with the bike mechanic recently.

Fortin asked what Burke had talked to Petit about. Burke gave him a condensed version, leaving out Petit's volatility when Burke had persisted about Petit's mother and McManus.

"Would you describe him as angry during those conversations?" Fortin said.

"At times, he was upset," Burke said.

"Is he an angry man normally?"

Burke said he didn't know Petit well enough to make that judgment.

"Why did you mention masking agents in connection with McManus's death?" Fortin asked.

"Given McManus's fitness level, it just seems improbable he would die from his heart suddenly stopping, despite what that doctor said back at the news conference," Burke said. "But then, I'm not a doctor, and I could have the whole thing totally wrong."

"I understand you and Petit's mother had an interesting discussion during a public forum on drugs in sport," Fortin said.

"We talked," Burke said.

"She was angry about McManus," Fortin said. "In fact, it seems she might have hated him."

Burke was hearing more statements from Fortin than questions.

He nodded at Fortin.

The door opened, and Fortin's shadow, Côté, walked in. Fortin gave the briefest of nods. Côté stood in a corner.

"When a mechanic is working on the Tour, does he get much free time?" Fortin asked, rapidly changing the subject, which he was making a habit of.

"Only to sleep a few hours," Burke said.

"Does a mechanic come and go on his own, or does someone need to know where he is at all times during a big race like the Tour?"

Burke didn't have a clue why Fortin was going in this direction.

"During the Tour, a mechanic is on call virtually all the time," Burke said. "He is at the beck and call of riders, the directeur sportif, other management, other mechanics."

"It sounds tiring," Fortin said.

"It's an exhausting, stressful job. I wouldn't want to do it."

"And the pay?" Fortin asked.

Burke figured Fortin knew the answer to that as well.

"Enough to pay the bills and probably not much more," he told the detective. "They do it for love of the work, for the most part."

"Indeed," Fortin said.

For a brief moment, Fortin appeared deep in thought.

"I have a couple of final questions for you, Monsieur Burke," Fortin said.

"About what?" Burke asked.

"You're an ex-pro cyclist, and you cover the sport to some degree these days. When a cycling team dopes, who dispenses the drugs? The team doctor? A trainer? Someone else?"

Burke said nothing. Fortin could find the answers elsewhere.

"I understand your reluctance to say anything, Monsieur Burke," Fortin said. "If you answer my question and save me some time, I might be able to help you with whatever story you're working on that involves Yves Vachon."

Fortin was using the Vachon matter—and Claude's possible involvement—as a hook. Burke was still reluctant to talk much about drugs, but he expected Fortin would keep prying.

Fortin leaned toward Burke.

"I will tell you right now," Fortin said, "that your friend, the café owner, is off the hook for the Vachon death, but there are people who are pushing for his rearrest and conviction for conspiracy in helping create a riot that led to the willful destruction of private property. They also want him to be charged with premeditated attacks against police officers. And they want him for tax fraud."

"Claude, a conspirator and a tax fraud?" Burke blurted out.

"A conviction on any of those charges could lead to some serious time in prison. A conviction on all three would lead to several years."

Burke didn't know what to say. Claude really was in a mess and didn't know it. Claude, and his lawyer, thought he was free.

"As I said, there are people pushing for action against him," continued Fortin. "But there's some counterevidence that suggests those charges could be a little weak."

Burke finally saw the game.

"A few minutes ago, you gave me some information about Léon Petit," Fortin said. "Now, I'm asking for information that's more general. I'm asking for you to help save my time, and these days, time is even more valuable, especially when your friends in the media are putting a spotlight on us."

It was a trade. If Burke was a journalist, he would probably protest—hard. But he wasn't. And Claude was his friend.

"When I was racing, I took drugs twice, and then I quit because I hated how they made me feel—not physically, but emotionally," Burke began. "When I refused to dope, I got into deep trouble with the team."

"And most teams doped back then, right?" Fortin said.

"Not now, but back then, it happened a fair amount," Burke admitted.

"So who would have known?" Côté interjected.

"Just about everybody," Burke said. "The doctor would likely have been the person who would supervise the doping. He would probably do most of the actual doping, too. But sometimes, he'd have someone else do it."

"Like a masseur or..." Fortin began.

"*Soigneur* is the actual title. It refers to someone who handles several tasks to help a rider recover and then prepare for the next day's race or training," Burke said.

"And a mechanic? Would a mechanic know?"

Burke saw Fortin was thinking Petit. *What the hell*, he thought. Tell Fortin the truth and let Petit fend for himself.

"Like I said, virtually everyone would know," Burke said. "I expect that a mechanic ran a doping errand here or there. But a mechanic who is also skilled in massage and nutrition might have a little extra understanding of how to help a rider cope."

"And it's possible no one would ever check a mechanic's private toolbox for any, say, drugs?" Fortin wondered aloud.

"Mechanics share some tools, but mostly, they use their own, and no one dares to borrow anything without permission," Burke told him.

Fortin nodded. He looked at Côté, who nodded back. Fortin stood.

"You gave us nothing that was earth-shattering, but it has been helpful, Monsieur Burke," Fortin said. "If you think of anything else, please tell us. It would help us—and maybe we could do even more for Monsieur Brière."

Burke sensed Claude had just about wriggled free but not quite.

"Here's a small observation, Inspector," Burke said. "A truly good bike mechanic on the pro circuit has to work quickly and efficiently. Speed is everything. So is quality of work."

Fortin looked a little puzzled but remained patient.

"He completes tasks he has done hundreds, maybe thousands of times before, but the mechanic is always focused. He has to be. One mistake could cost a racer a win, or result in some terrible injury. When the mechanic completes the work, his hands are usually clean—maybe cleaner than yours are now. He is so good that he doesn't get dirty. He's so good..." Burke paused for effect, "that he doesn't get cuts or nicks on his fingers or knuckles."

Fortin was seeing the light.

"Monsieur Petit's hands are a little chewed up," Burke said.

"And Petit is good?"

"A friend who knows about such matters tells me he's as good as it gets."

Fortin nodded. He looked at Côté, then back at Burke.

"Your friend, Monsieur Brière, could be all right after all, with the right influence," Fortin said. "Inspector Jardine is in charge of the Vachon matter, but I might be able to have a word with him."

Burke didn't know exactly what "have a word" meant, but he figured it couldn't hurt Claude's situation.

"Thank you," Burke said.

Fortin pointed a finger at Burke. "You're more than what I thought you were, Monsieur Burke."

Burke left the office under the guidance of a uniformed officer. He glanced back and saw Fortin talking animatedly with Sylvie Côté. He wondered what Fortin had learned from him—and what he had learned from Fortin.

Burke exited the building and went to the closest bench. He pulled out his notepad from his shoulder bag and jotted down some of what Fortin had said. Then he scribbled a couple of sentences for his blog. He reread them and saw they weren't anything special.

"Shit," he mumbled to himself.

He looked up.

Fortin and Côté were walking quickly down the street like they were late for an appointment. Burke could only speculate where they were heading in such a rush.

CHAPTER 32

AFTER BUMBLING HIS WAY through a video blog with the police station in the background, Burke drove home. He wasn't sure Lemaire would be impressed with the product, but he had other matters he needed to handle.

He had to talk to Claude, and he had to convince him to keep a low profile. No more protests, no more confrontations with police.

After parking his car, Burke jogged to the café, hoping Claude would be there.

And he was.

"We need to talk, and we need to talk now," Burke said.

Claude looked like he was going to make a joke, but Burke's face must have convinced him otherwise, because he said nothing instead. He got a server to handle his tables, and then he led Burke to his tiny, windowless office just off the kitchen.

"You look like something bad has happened, my friend," said Claude, dropping into an ancient swivel chair that squeaked under his bulk.

Burke sat opposite and related what Fortin had said about possible charges. Claude's face lost color at the mention of prison.

When he was finished, Burke waited for Claude to say something, but the older man didn't say a word. A minute passed. Burke still waited.

"We supposedly live in a free society, but this justice system of ours is corrupt," Claude said. "They want to put me in prison? I'm not the one ruining our little world here. I'm not the one who's trying to drive away the common people. I'm not the one—"

"Claude, this is goddamn serious!" Burke said, angry. "You need to understand that you could end up in prison for a long time if you get into any more trouble. Forget your right to protest. Look after yourself. You've said some stupid things, and people have noticed."

"Stupid things?" Claude exclaimed.

"You heard me, Claude," Burke said. "You're in trouble because you decided to provoke people. Now you could pay the price."

Claude opened his mouth to speak, but then pressed his lips back together. Burke watched as he calmed down. His friend sunk deeper into his chair and nodded. His energy was gone, and he looked exhausted.

"I know you're helping me, Paul, and I'm grateful," he said. "All of this makes me angry, but mostly, it makes me sad. I promise to stay out of trouble. I'll look after my little café here and keep my nose clean."

"You've promised that before," Burke said.

Claude nodded. "That's true, I have," he said. "But this time, I won't break my word."

Burke studied his friend and believed him. Claude looked beaten—and a little scared. Burke decided not to include how Fortin suggested Claude could be off the hook in return for Burke providing information.

"I should get back to my customers," Claude said, getting slowly to his feet. He offered his hand to Burke, who shook it. "You're a good friend, Paul. So much more than a regular customer. I won't forget."

Claude went back outside, Burke in his wake. They nodded to each other, and then Burke went home.

There, he packaged his video blog and sent it off to Lemaire. He figured the editor wouldn't be happy with the product, but at least it was something.

Sure enough, a few minutes later, Lemaire was on the phone telling Burke that the blog was rough, but would be usable with some extra editing.

"You can do better, and you need to do better, Paul," Lemaire said. "Were you rushing?"

"I was. Sorry. I figured I had to get it to you as fast as possible," said Burke. It wasn't exactly the truth, but it would work.

"Apology accepted," Lemaire said. "Now, I have the sense you believe the Nice police might actually produce a result involving McManus and maybe even Den Weent."

"I didn't want to mention in my blog anything that might not happen, but I think we're going to hear something soon from the police," Burke said.

"Are you holding back some information, Paul?"

"No, I'm just saying the police sound a little more optimistic about finding out who might have killed McManus and Den Weent. I think they now believe the two deaths are linked."

Burke considered giving Lemaire all the details of his conversation with Fortin about Petit but, in the end, opted not to. It was still too early.

"If you hear anything, you must alert me, Paul," Lemaire said. "Understand?"

"I understand," Burke replied. "Since we're talking about crime, is there anything new on the Vachon murder? I read the nationals this morning."

"My reporter didn't get much different, and he's good," Lemaire said. "But with all the pressure on the police, I think they'll produce some result very soon."

"It's all a little odd that the police have nothing," Burke commented. "I mean, isn't this the age of video surveillance and satellite imagery and all that stuff?"

"Yes, well, video surveillance is slowly getting bigger along the Riviera, especially in Nice, but there are some politicians down here who oppose its use," Lemaire said. "They don't want us to be like the Brits, who seem to have a camera or two on every street corner."

"Does your reporter know if there's any video of Vachon and his minder getting hit by the vehicle?" Burke asked.

"He said the police aren't making any comment whatsoever about what they have."

That wasn't a surprise. He asked if the reporter knew if there were any street cameras in the area where Vachon and his bodyguard were killed. If there weren't, then the matter of video would be irrelevant, unless some bystander happened to catch the accident with a smartphone.

"He said there are a couple of video cameras, but they're a fair distance away," Lemaire replied.

Burke wondered if the hit-and-run driver knew the position of video cameras before running over Vachon and his bodyguard.

They ended the call a few moments later, with Burke again promising to let Lemaire know if he learned anything new about the McManus and Den Weent deaths.

For the next hour, Burke relaxed on his couch. Once more, he was mentally exhausted, and yet he couldn't stop his mind from spinning from thought to thought.

The phone rang. It was the sports anchor at a Nice TV station.

"Next Sunday, we're doing a weekend show about the cycling season, especially the Tour de France, since it ends then. We would like you on the panel, if you're available," said the anchor.

"Me? Why me?" Burke asked.

"Your performance at that Secrets of the Pro Cycling World forum made the news, and lots of people liked what they heard. They want to hear more from you. We'll pay you to do the show."

Burke could hardly believe it, but he agreed, especially when he heard what he'd be paid. The anchor seemed pleased. They made the arrangements.

Ten minutes later, the phone rang again.

"It's Matthieu Martin."

Burke didn't recognize the name, but the accent was definitely from Québec.

"We met a few days ago in Avignon at the police station," said the voice. "I'm a reporter with a Montréal newspaper."

Now Burke remembered. "I'm surprised to hear from you," he said. "And I'm curious how you got my number."

"I'm a reporter. I can get someone's number without too much trouble," Martin said with a laugh. "Anyway, my editor wants me to do a profile of you—an updated version. Your comments at the recent forum made the wire service, and I pitched the idea you'd be worth a follow-up piece."

"Are you here in the Nice area?" Burke asked.

"No, I'm still following the Tour, but we can do it by Skype, if you're OK with that," Martin said.

"I don't have Skype," Burke said.

He'd heard about the software but had never had a need for it.

"It's easy enough to set up, especially if you have a laptop with a camera built in," Martin said.

Burke's computer was indeed a laptop, and it had a camera.

"So, Paul, do you want to do the interview?" Martin asked. "I have to file today's story soon. I could Skype you tonight, and we could do the interview then."

Since he seemed to be in the habit of agreeing to proposals that came his way, Burke said he would. Martin quickly took him through the Skype download, step by step. Then came the sending of emails to establish a connection between them on Skype. Finally, they set a time for the interview.

"This will be good exposure for you," Martin said and then rang off.

Burke felt energized, his lethargy shaken off by the two phone calls. He had to admit that it was somewhat exciting to have media people want his opinions after years of being mocked or ignored.

CHAPTER 33

BURKE AWOKE EARLY, RESTED and in a better mood than the day before. He made a coffee and, with all his windows wide open, listened to the early morning birdsong outside. He'd come to enjoy all the different sounds. One day, he planned to get a book to figure out which bird was producing which sound. He wondered if appreciating birdsong was a sign he was getting old.

Burke then recalled his interview the previous evening with Matthieu Martin who had said his editor was very interested in Burke serving as some kind of "special European cycling correspondent" starting in August.

"We have those big pro races in Québec in September, and he thinks a column every two weeks from you might help build excitement around the events beyond what I'm doing and what others are doing," Martin had told him. "Our paper has become a sponsor now, so my boss thinks it's a big deal."

Martin added that the editor would be contacting Burke in the next few days to see if Burke was interested and to talk payment.

Burke told Martin he'd be open to any offers.

And he would. Money was always good.

Burke finished his coffee and drifted down to Jean's newsagent shop, where he picked up his usual newspapers. As was their custom, the two men engaged in a conversation about overnight news events and what might happen today. Burke figured Jean knew more about world events, as well as French affairs, than anyone he had ever met, even journalists.

"Ah, look, Paul, Madame Marois is heading out in that old car of hers," Jean said, pointing and then waving at the old woman as she slowly eased her way down the lane near them, Plato perched against the dashboard.

Madame Marois gave a half-wave in return and slowly turned the corner. She was obviously aiming for the main road.

"That Plato is a lucky dog, although I don't think he knows it," Jean said. "He goes almost everywhere with Madame. Walks, restaurants, rides. I expect he has his own side of the bed, too. And his own plate at the dinner table."

Burke laughed and agreed. Madame Marois definitely loved her dog.

Back home, Burke's mind drifted to Karin Petit. He wasn't sure why, but these days, his mind seemed to be a lot more active and definitely more curious than ever before. Maybe it was like exercise in that the more you worked a muscle, the stronger it got. And with that thought, he realized he'd probably wasted the years after his pro cycling career by largely doing as little as possible. He promised himself he wouldn't go back to that state.

He called André Rousseau at his shop, hoping it wasn't too early, since the shop would not open for another hour.

But he was.

"Is Petit there yet?" Burke asked.

"We're back to Léon, are we?" Rousseau said. "Well, he isn't here yet. He won't be in until ten."

"OK, I have another request to make," Burke said.

"I'm not surprised," Rousseau said, adding a theatrical sigh for emphasis. "Go ahead."

"Do you know where Léon's mother works? Léon must have mentioned it at one time or another."

Rousseau took a moment and then said, "I do remember him saying she looks after plants for hotels and government offices."

"On a full-time basis?" Burke asked.

"I think so, because I remember Léon saying the work is hard and that she's usually very tired at the end of a day. In fact, I think he'd like it if she didn't have to work at all."

Burke asked if Karin Petit was self-employed or worked for someone else.

"She works for a small company," Rousseau said. "Léon says the company pushes her to work longer than she wants."

It took a few moments, but Rousseau recalled the name of the business.

"Thanks for the information, André," Burke said. "I owe you."

"The bill is getting long, Paul," Rousseau replied. "Before you go—you aren't going to do anything dumb, right? If she thinks you're harassing her, she could tell Léon, and I don't think you want him coming after you. He can be a little intense, as you know."

"I'm just going to accidently bump into her on her break and ask her a simple question or two."

"About what?"

"Why it meant so much for her to talk at that forum, for one."

"And that's important to you?" Rousseau said.

"Let's just say I'm curious," Burke told him.

"That seems to be your usual state of mind these days," Rousseau said.

"I have an evolving personality."

"OK, but you know our arrangement—you have to tell me what you learn, Paul," Rousseau said.

"Agreed," Burke said and then hung up.

Burke knew it was silly, maybe even stupid, for him to find Karin Petit and to try to talk with her. If he learned anything, what would he do with it? Still, he sensed there was something beyond the normal mother-son relationship between the Petits, and he truly wanted to know what that was. Of course, if Léon found out about his inquiries, it might be a different matter.

Burke punched in the number of the plant business, hoping Karin Petit would be there. If she was out on a job, he didn't think they'd tell him where. But it was worth a try.

When the receptionist answered, Burke said he'd received a recommendation from a friend for a certain gardener with the company—Karin Petit. Was she around?

"I'm afraid she's not here," said the receptionist. "But she's not far. She's across the street on a job, and I expect she should be back in about an hour."

Burke thanked her and rang off. He jumped into his car and drove to the plant business. He studied the buildings in the area. Most were single-story retail shops, but he did spot a two-story office building. He thought that would be his best chance to find her.

His plan was simple—if she came out, he'd get out of the car, casually bump into her on the street and strike up a conversation about the forum and how she'd made it so much more interesting. Burke recognized the whole plan might be in vain. She might be somewhere else in the area. And if he did spot her, she could easily ignore him when he tried to strike up a conversation. But he had time to waste, and so he waited.

Just past noon, Karin came out of the two-story building with two other women, both much younger. All three were in clean blue overalls, unique attire for the Riviera. The two younger women watched as Petit applied some kind of bandage to the palm of her right hand. One of the young women flinched as Petit attended to her injury, whatever it was. Otherwise, it looked like they might have just been having a nice chat.

The two younger women stopped a few steps later and lit cigarettes. They leaned against the wall of the building. Karin Petit gave them a small wave and started strolling down the street on the opposite side of where Burke was parked. She wasn't in any rush and was definitely not heading to the office. She looked like she wanted to stretch her legs for a while.

Burke hopped out, then scanned the sidewalk for a good spot to "accidently" bump into her.

Karin Petit was coming up to the corner. He could cross and catch her right there if he hustled.

"Madame Petit?" he said when he got close, adding a surprised look for effect.

She stopped and looked at him. Burke could see that his face registered in her memory.

"I'm Paul Burke," he replied, sticking out his hand to shake. She took it gingerly because of her injury. "I was at that forum the other day, the one where you got up and really got everything going."

"Yes, monsieur, I recognize you," she said.

"You made a strong impression," Burke said. "I think the organizers were pleased at what happened because of you."

Karin Petit didn't say anything, and Burke thought she was done with him. He decided against filling the pause, hoping silence would prompt her to talk. He didn't actually mind looking at her while he waited. She was likely in her early fifties, average height and maybe a few kilos too heavy, but on her tired face, there were indications she'd once been an attractive woman. She had large, beautiful green eyes—Léon's eyes were green too—strong cheekbones, smooth skin, a long nose and wide mouth. If she dropped five kilos, got some rest and added some makeup and a decent dress, she could still command attention.

"I had things I wanted to say," she finally remarked.

"Mostly about Pierre McManus," Burke said. "You called him a 'bastard.' I thought that was a good word."

Karin Petit nodded.

"How long ago did you know him?" Burke asked. "I got to know him when I was racing professionally."

He hoped sharing his opinion of McManus might prompt her to say more.

"I knew him when I was much younger," she replied. "I thought he was nice, but he wasn't. He was a—"

Burke filled in the word: "Bastard."

Karin Petit nodded, looking off into the distance, almost like she was seeing herself and McManus so many years before.

"Was he a boyfriend?" Burke asked, knowing this question might end the conversation.

Karin Petit looked at Burke and smirked. "Boyfriend? What a strange word that is," she said. "I don't think he was anything. Not in the end."

Burke softened his approach. "Did you occasionally bump into him over the years? I sometimes did and never liked it when it happened. He was the same bastard every time I had to deal with him."

Karin's gaze lingered on Burke's face, and he realized she was evaluating his sincerity.

"Not really," she finally said. "I didn't see him at all for a very long time."

"Did you see him recently?"

She shrugged. "It's not important. He's dead."

Her face had tightened with her last remark.

"Are you happy he's dead?" Burke asked, figuring this would definitely end the conversation.

Karin Petit glowered at Burke. Then, slowly, her face softened.

"No, I'm not," she said. "He was a very unpleasant man, but I don't wish anyone to die."

"You were very angry at that forum," Burke said.

"I should not have gone and said what I said," she replied. "It was very unwise. My comments ended up on television and in the newspapers. I didn't want that."

"What did you want, madame?" Burke asked.

"I'm sorry, monsieur, but I should get back," she said.

Burke expected she still had plenty of time on her break, but chose not to push her any further.

"Nice to meet you again, madame," he said, once more putting his hand out to shake. She took it again without saying a word and then turned back toward the building where she'd been working.

Burke dodged a couple of cars and got back into his vehicle. He wasn't sure what to make of Karin's comments, but he sensed there was something interesting just beneath the surface.

And he wondered how she'd hurt her hand.

CHAPTER 34

IT WAS MIDAFTERNOON, AND Burke forced himself to put aside all thoughts of Karin Petit and Léon Petit. He didn't know what to make of it all and figured if he was distracted by something else, his mind might work away on its own and produce some kind of epiphany. Or not.

Tucked up on his couch, he decided to watch the day's Tour de France stage. He hadn't been diligent in following the race the last few days, even though he was supposed to be providing some blogs about it from time to time. Today would give him a good sense of the overall winner. There was less than a week to go, and today's stage was going to be, in cycling terms, "epic."

That was because the stage was going to end on the legendary Alpe d'Huez—a 13.8-kilometer ascent around twenty-one hairpin bends that climb to a ski resort. It was the most famous climb in all of professional cycling. If it wasn't the toughest, it somehow always turned out to be the most dramatic.

The last time he raced it as a pro, he had somehow found himself with the lead group as it approached the mountain. Usually relegated to bringing up water bottles to more talented members on his team or shielding those same riders from the wind on flat stages, Burke was pacing his team leader to the base of the climb. He had "good legs" that day and had caught expressions of surprise from the contenders when they'd glanced across and seen him there. He had been an intruder among the elite, and it had been thrilling.

Until the Alpe's start—a leg-crushing first five hundred meters.

As soon as the road turned upward, almost everyone stood on their pedals. Then one of the main contenders put in an attack. The other team leaders followed. Burke's team captain yelled at him to go faster, and to his shock, he'd managed to comply.

The crowd that day was estimated at 750,000, but Burke believed it had to have been more than a million people. Whatever the true number, it had been bedlam with everyone screaming at the top of their lungs. The noise had been deafening.

And Burke had kept up with the leaders, riding with more strength than he had in his entire career. It had felt almost magical as he stomped out a fierce cadence.

Eventually, a lithe Spanish climber decided it was time to go for the win and quickly distanced himself from the other contenders, going faster and faster. Burke clearly remembered watching the Spanish rider begin to disappear and then hearing his team leader yelling, "Follow him, follow him!" in panic.

So Burke had. For about another 750 meters. Then his legs had called it a day.

Now, sitting on his couch years later and waiting for a new generation of riders to attack the mountain, Burke thought it must have looked funny on TV when his body had decided to surrender. He probably slowed from almost thirty kilometers an hour to ten within seconds, as if he'd tossed out an anchor. His team captain had been alert enough to avoid his rear wheel, and when he passed Burke, he'd yelled, "Shithead!" which was the least of Burke's problems at the time.

That's when l'Alpe d'Huez became the worst day of cycling Burke had known as a pro.

His legs barely functioned, and he just couldn't get enough air. All his energy had disappeared—a result of skipping food at the last feeding station so he could keep up with the leaders to the Alpe.

The leaders, of course, quickly vanished ahead of him. Burke focused only on turning the pedals, hoping he wouldn't slow so much that he'd fall off. He had twelve more kilometers to go, all of it ferociously uphill.

It had only gotten worse as the kilometers passed.

His legs cramped, and his lungs ached. Little black spots clouded his eyes, and his temples throbbed. At the infamous Dutch Corner, where long-partying Dutch fans had set up shop three days earlier, he'd taken a bad line and had to be pushed to avoid falling sideways. A few kilometers later, he threw up on himself, bile staining the front of his blue-and-white jersey.

When Burke crossed the finish line, he turned the pedals one final time and then lost control of his bike. Fortunately, a team mechanic had caught him. He hadn't cared that he finished forty minutes behind the Spaniard who won the stage and would go on to win the entire Tour de France. The next day, barely able to get out of bed, Burke had withdrawn from the race, much to the annoyance of his team's management.

Now the racers of a new era were flying toward l'Alpe d'Huez. Burke wished them well, or at least hoped they would avoid a total collapse like he had suffered.

His phone rang, disturbing his focus as the riders neared the start of the climb.

It was Jean-Pierre Fortin. Burke wondered how many other people had his number.

"Are you home?" the detective asked.

"Yes, I'm just watching today's stage of the Tour," Burke told him.

"Don't go anywhere," Fortin said. "We'll be there in fifteen minutes."

"Why?" asked Burke.

"We have to talk," Fortin said and then hung up.

Burke was puzzled and a little worried. He hadn't done anything wrong, but a visit from the police was rarely good.

Fifteen minutes later, Fortin—with the inevitable Côté by his side—was in Burke's living room.

"What can I do for you, Inspector?" Burke asked.

"Sit down," Fortin told him.

Burke didn't like being told what to do in his own home, but he did as ordered.

Fortin sat opposite him. Côté remained standing. Burke wondered if she ever relaxed.

"You had a conversation this morning with Karin Petit," Fortin stated.

"How do you know that?" Burke asked, surprised. "Are you following me? Or her?"

"That's not your business," Fortin said. "What is important is that you stop going around and asking questions of people linked to the McManus and Den Weent investigation."

Burke was angry. "It's a free country," he said, feeling instantly foolish for uttering such a cliché.

"Really?" Fortin said with a smirk. "Just listen. We don't want you talking to people linked to this case. If you do so again, we'll charge you with obstruction."

"For asking questions?" Burke said, still feeling ticked off. He needed to get control of his emotions.

"I'm telling you this in person because it's important you understand my warning," Fortin replied.

Burke glanced at Côté, who looked a little more intense than usual.

Fortin continued. "I will admit, you have helped us with our inquiries, but it's time for you to desist," he said. "We're working a case, and we can't have you contaminate it. Understand?"

Burke wondered how he could "contaminate" the investigation, but he didn't say that. A bit calmer now, Burke nodded.

"I hear you," he said.

"No more questions then?" Fortin said.

Burke nodded. It wasn't his business anyway. Besides, he had other matters to deal with. Behind Fortin, the cyclists were on the Alpe, coming up on the point where his race had exploded.

"Now, tell me, what did you talk to Karin Petit about?" Fortin said.

Burke sighed. Feeling he had little choice, he told Fortin what Karin Petit had told him. Côté jotted a couple of notes during his retelling of their meeting.

"Was she still angry in your estimation?" Fortin asked.

Burke thought about it. She had seemed angry at McManus at the start of their brief chat and clearly loathed the directeur sportif, but she had calmed down by the end of their conversation. Burke told that to Fortin.

"Does Léon Petit know you talked to his mother?" Fortin said.

"I don't know," Burke said.

"And what's your sense of their relationship beyond being mother and son?"

Burke didn't know exactly what Fortin was looking for, but he managed a response: "I'd say they're close and very protective of each other, maybe a little more than many mothers and sons. But as I said, I don't really know."

Fortin asked a couple more harmless questions, which Burke answered, and then he stood and nodded to Côté, who closed her notebook.

"Thank you for your time, monsieur, and don't forget my advice," Fortin said. "I don't want to visit you again on this same matter, because if I do, it won't be pleasant for you."

"I got it," Burke said, standing as well. He decided to be bold. "Now I have a request for you."

"I didn't make a request of you, monsieur, but go ahead and ask," Fortin said.

"If you find out what happened, will you let me know?"

Fortin shook his head. "That's what the media are for, monsieur."

And then they left.

Burke went to his window and watched the two officers walk toward their car. He sensed Fortin was getting close to some answers. Or maybe all of them.

CHAPTER 35

SEVERAL HEADLINES ON DISPLAY at Jean's newsagent's shop suggested eco-terrorists might have been responsible for the death of Yves Vachon.

"What do you think, Paul? Do you think eco-terrorists killed Vachon?" asked Jean.

"It seems a little odd," Burke said. He scanned the first paragraph of one story. "Two days after the national media criticize the police for lack of progress in the investigation of Vachon's death, we hear that eco-terrorists might be behind what happened to him. That hardly seems coincidental to me."

"That's what I thought, too," Jean agreed. "I read a couple of the stories, and the spokesperson for the police said they aren't ruling out eco-terrorists."

"Did they identify any particular group?" Burke asked.

"No," Jean told him. "The spokesperson said it could be a group that is known or some radical group that no one knows anything about. Or it could be neither."

"You know, Jean, I'm not even sure I know what an eco-terrorist is."

Jean laughed. "Me neither. It sounds like something you would hear about in a movie. But maybe I'm not keeping up with the latest news."

"I doubt that," Burke said. "You read more papers than anyone I've ever met."

"Anyway, besides selling more papers, I bet this eco-terrorist thing takes a little heat off the flics," Jean added.

The story worked well for both the police and the media—for the moment.

But was it possible that eco-terrorists—whatever that label meant—were really behind Vachon's death? Lemaire had said protest groups often alerted the media when they took action, and with that in mind, Burke thought it was unlikely that eco-terrorists were responsible for Vachon's death. There had been no public statement from any such group, and mention of them seemed too coincidental. It seemed clumsy to bring eco-terrorists into the discussion about Vachon's demise.

His head swam with various plots, but before he could get carried away, Burke decided to postpone further analysis—for a couple of hours, at least. He bought his usual three papers and added a couple of extras to read later when his mind had cleared. As he bid adieu to Jean, Madame Marois drove by, Plato propped against the dashboard for a good view, as usual. Burke waved, but she didn't seem to spot him.

"Two days in a row," Jean said. "The old lady must be feeling better. She isn't the most sociable person, but it's good to see her getting out more regularly."

Back home, Burke put aside his papers and turned on his computer. He couldn't take a break from whatever was happening; his mind wouldn't let him. He typed, *"eco-terrorism"* into Google. There were almost 675,000 results. He tried *"eco-terrorism and Yves Vachon,"* and links to recent news stories appeared.

He spent the next hour reading Vachon-related stories, but they didn't contain much new information, just speculation about some group potentially being responsible.

During his research, Burke noticed an Irishman had won l'Alpe d'Huez the previous day. He'd forgotten all about the finish in the wake of Fortin's visit.

It was time for a training ride. Maybe his mind would allow him to enjoy it.

He'd told himself he'd work on a blog later, and following that, he would do a little research for the upcoming panel scheduled right after the finish of the Tour de France.

Burke rode for almost three hours, covering just over one hundred kilometers along the coast and in the hills behind. He liked how he felt as he rode back into his village—a little tired but energized. He could have gone longer, but there were things to do.

He dismounted by the little park, figuring the short walk home would be good for his legs. He turned a corner and almost bumped into Claude, who was clutching a couple of newspapers, the headlines of which read, *"eco-terrorists."*

Claude looked startled. "Sorry, Paul," he said. "I was lost in reading this crap."

"Yes, I saw them earlier," Burke said. "A new development in the Vachon case, it seems."

"It's all shit!" Claude snarled. "This is all about the police and the politicos trying to make a statement."

"What's the statement?"

"That they're working hard and the only people who would kill a good man like Vachon are the terrible, murderous eco-terrorists," Claude said. "I can't believe the papers ran this garbage."

Burke shrugged. He didn't disagree.

"You know, it was probably some drunk teenager who hit him and his bodyguard, got scared and drove off, probably in Daddy's car," Claude said. "But the police can't find him, so they've come up with other ideas to take the heat, because, after all, Vachon was a big shot, and his death needs to be solved."

It seemed plausible. Burke had his own doubts about what the police were chasing.

"This whole eco-terrorist crap is going to get in the way of any protests against the FP Developments project, and that's the worst part," Claude said.

"Claude, are you getting involved in more protests?" Burke asked. "You know you have to stay away from that stuff. The police are watching you. I've told you that. And you promised to keep out of trouble."

Claude waved away Burke's concern.

"I'm not planning to get arrested again," he said. "I got your message before. But others will continue the fight, and it's a fight worth waging."

"Well, be careful, Claude," Burke said. "That's all I'm saying."

Claude broke into a smile. "Yes, Father, I'll obey," he said.

Claude exhausted him. "Forget the jokes," he said. "Just be smart."

"And treat my customers better, too, right?" Claude added, still smiling.

Burke relented. "Yes, and treat your customers better."

"Of course, if anyone gives me a difficult time about my soufflé or cassoulet, I can't be held responsible for my actions," Claude said.

"That's a different matter, Claude," Burke said. "When it comes to food in France, all crimes of passion are forgiven."

"As they should be."

They parted, Claude off to prepare for his lunch crowd and Burke to shower and start working on his next blog.

In his apartment, as he put away his bike and stripped off his sweat-stained cycling clothes, Burke questioned if Claude really would stay out of trouble.

He had doubts.

CHAPTER 36

FIVE HOURS LATER, BURKE knew the answer.

Claude had been arrested yet again and, according to a very upset Hélène, faced several charges, the most serious being conspiracy to commit murder.

"When did this happen?" Burke asked Hélène over the phone.

"Two hours ago," she said, her voice cracking. "Didn't you see the police cars? Two police detectives came right to the café terrace, along with another four officers who had their guns drawn. It was so frightening. They grabbed Uncle. The two detectives—"

"Were the two detectives the ones we met the other day at the station?"

"They were," she said. "I knew I recognized them. They were calm, but the police in uniform were very rough as they dragged Uncle away."

Fortin and Côté. And others.

Burke pictured Claude being dragged away, the customers scattering and Fortin looking more than a little smug as he watched the action. Côté might have appeared calm but probably wanted to either kick or punch his friend.

But why were Fortin and Côté working on the Vachon death? Had they been transferred from the McManus and Den Weent case? Burke shook his head. It didn't matter why Fortin and Côté were involved in the Vachon investigation, at least not at the moment. His friend was once again in police custody and in the most serious trouble yet, this time facing charges that could earn him a long prison term. As for Fortin's earlier comments about Claude being off the hook, they had been either lies or something had happened after the detective had made them.

"Where are you now?" Burke asked Hélène.

"The police station, but no one will talk to me," she said, starting to cry. "What do I do now? This is horrible! Uncle Claude promised he wouldn't get in any more trouble."

"I'll be there in twenty minutes," Burke said. "Call his lawyer in the meantime."

He thought about telling Hélène it would all work out, but he didn't really believe that, so he said nothing and hung up.

For the first time, Burke questioned Claude's innocence.

When he arrived outside the police station, he spotted Hélène talking animatedly with a short, slender, middle-aged man. Burke guessed he was Claude's lawyer.

He was. Olivier Richard.

"It's OK to talk to Paul," Hélène told the lawyer. "He's a friend of Uncle's, and he knows most of what has happened recently." She took Burke's hand. "He's also with me."

Richard nodded.

"I can provide only basic information," Richard explained. "It's a matter of confidentiality with a client."

"I understand," Burke said.

"The police apparently developed some suspicions about another man who had been involved in the same protests as Claude," Richard said. "So, they got legal permission to check this individual's emails and texts. Some of those emails recommended more dramatic action."

"Dramatic action?" Burke said.

"They advocated for violence beyond a confrontation with police," Richard said. "There was mention of personal intimidation against some of the executives of FP Developments. There was also mention of explosive devices."

"Bombs?" Burke said in a voice loud enough that a couple of passersby swiveled their heads to look at them.

Richard gestured for Burke to calm down.

"Sorry, sorry," Burke said. "Was Claude involved in any of those emails or texts?"

He feared the answer.

Richard nodded. "He wrote several to this person. In a couple," the lawyer said, "he critiqued the strategy being suggested."

"And what did Claude say in those emails?"

"That is where I must stop discussing the case," Richard said, but his face and his shrug told Burke that Claude had likely supported some violent action against the now-dead boss of FP Developments.

"What a mess," Burke said.

"It will not be an easy case," Richard said, looking at Hélène.

She nodded.

"I don't think he'll be released this time," the lawyer added. "I expect he'll be considered a flight risk, if not a threat to offend again."

Richard excused himself, saying he had to make some arrangements for Claude's initial court appearance. Looking glum, he marched off.

This was worse than Burke had thought. He glanced at Hélène. She was distraught, struggling to find any words.

"Let's go to your place, away from here," he said, draping an arm over her shoulders. "Monsieur Richard seems to be doing all he can. You need to trust him."

Burke kept his worries that Richard would be able to get Claude off the hook to himself. Emails and texts discussing violence against someone who then showed up dead? Not good.

Once in her place, Hélène seemed to unwind, dropping onto her ancient couch. She closed her eyes, as if trying to block out everything that had happened in the last few hours. It was apparent how much she loved her uncle.

Burke got two glasses of wine, but Hélène hardly touched hers. He tried to get her to talk about non-Claude-related events, but she barely answered. At supper time, he made a salade Niçoise. Hélène ate a few bites and discarded the remainder.

It seemed there was nothing he could do to lighten her mood.

He stayed the night, holding her in his arms while she slept, wondering how his world had been turned upside down.

CHAPTER 37

BURKE WOKE JUST AFTER six, having finally drifted off to sleep at 2 a.m. He was becoming an early bird, whether he liked it or not.

Hélène stayed in bed, snoring slightly as she slept. Burke hoped she'd keep sleeping for a few more hours. Her dream world had to be better than the reality that awaited her.

After gently shutting her bedroom door, Burke made himself some coffee and turned on the TV to catch the morning news.

That's when he learned Léon Petit was in custody and had been charged with the murders of both Pierre McManus and Mark Den Weent. A clip showed him being bundled into the police station by uniformed officers. Unlike so many others, Petit walked stiffly upright, his face open to the world without any coat draped over his head to hide his features. He looked both proud and defiant as he went up the station stairs.

For just a second, Fortin and Côté appeared in the background. They were watching Petit intently.

The reporter at the station stated that recent evidence had led to the arrest. Burke wondered if "recent evidence" meant some of the information he had provided Fortin and Côté.

The story then went to a clip of Fortin commenting that the complexity of the case had made it difficult to make the link between McManus's death and Den Weent's murder, but that recent information indicated Léon Petit had been involved in both cases.

When asked how McManus had died, Fortin turned to the camera and said, "The accused has skills few knew about."

Then he left, his statement leaving the reporter and viewers confused.

Burke shook his head. Fortin had used whatever—and whomever—he needed to get a result. Burke guessed the inspector hadn't gotten his rank by just luck or politics.

A while later, as he sipped his fourth cup of coffee, Burke's cell phone rang.

It was François Lemaire, breaking the news about Petit.

"I've heard," Burke told him.

"Well, you're plugged into the news," Lemaire said with some admiration in his voice. "And I expect you have also heard about Claude Brière, your friend?"

Burke said he had.

"Everything is before the French courts, and that's a system that doesn't move quickly," Lemaire said.

Burke remained silent.

"What are you doing Saturday and Sunday?" asked Lemaire.

"I don't know, François," Burke replied with some exasperation. "I'm sort of busy right now, especially with Claude."

"Like I said, nothing will happen quickly now," Lemaire said.

"I didn't know you were a lawyer," Burke snapped.

"Easy, Paul. I'm not, but I know the French judicial system. It only moves at one speed—glacial."

"So?"

"So I want you to go to Paris on Saturday and come back Sunday. I want you to blog about the final stage of the most controversial edition of the Tour de France in decades, maybe ever. I mean, besides the racing, we've had two murders and a team mechanic charged with those deaths—and you've somehow been in the middle of it. After Petit's arrest, I ran the idea by my boss this morning, and he totally supports you going. Expenses paid, of course."

Normally, Burke would have enjoyed a trip to Paris on someone else's coin, but not this time. He told Lemaire that. He added he wanted to help his friend and be there for Claude's niece who, he admitted officially for the first time, was his girlfriend.

"I know you're worried about your friend and your girlfriend," Lemaire said, dropping his voice to sound sympathetic. Burke wasn't buying it, though. "Take your girlfriend. It would probably do her a world of good to get away for a couple of days."

Burke figured there was no way Hélène would leave Nice when her beloved uncle was in jail and facing serious charges.

"Well, I really need you to go, Paul," Lemaire said. "You can fly up Saturday morning, come back after the race on Sunday afternoon. You need to do this for me—and for yourself. It will be great exposure."

Burke didn't care about more exposure. Then he recalled his involvement with the Nice TV show on Sunday after the final stage of the race.

"What time is the show in Nice?" Lemaire asked.

"9 p.m."

"You should have no trouble getting back in time," Lemaire persisted.

It was apparent that Lemaire had gone out on a limb with the Paris idea and couldn't go back to his boss now and say his blogger refused to go. After more discussion, Burke finally relented. They sorted out a few details and then ended the call.

A few minutes later, Hélène shuffled into the room. She had slept for ten hours, but still looked exhausted. Burke got her a coffee.

"That's better," Hélène said after a couple of sips.

Burke told her about Léon Petit, but Hélène didn't seem interested. He expected her mind remained occupied with her uncle's plight. Then he told her about his Paris assignment for Lemaire.

"You have to go?" she said.

"François made it difficult to say no," Burke told her. "You know, you could come with me. I'd pay. It might be good to get away, although it's just an overnight trip. I know you're thinking about Claude, but there's nothing that can be done for a while. His lawyer is the one who's in charge now."

She shook her head and looked at him. She seemed a little disappointed.

"I can't go, not just because Uncle is in jail, but because he'll need me to help out at the café," she said.

Burke had forgotten about the café. He nodded. She would be busy. Paris was unthinkable.

He made Hélène an omelet for breakfast, but she only toyed with the food. Then they showered separately and dressed in silence.

Hélène's phone rang. It was Olivier Richard, and he wanted to meet with Hélène within the hour if possible. She agreed, asking what he wanted to discuss. She listened for a few moments and then rang off.

"What's happening with Claude?" Burke asked.

"You're interested?" Hélène asked icily.

Burke bit back a sharp response and smiled. "Of course, I am," he said in a soft voice. "He's my friend."

Hélène smiled sadly back at him. "I'm sorry, *chéri*," she said. "You didn't deserve that. You've been good to Uncle and good to me. I know you care."

Burke just nodded.

"Monsieur Richard says he has some instructions after meeting with Uncle early this morning," Hélène said.

"Then let's get down there—if I'm invited?"

That sparked Hélène, and she grabbed her purse. "I would like you there," she said. "Four ears might be better than two."

They left the apartment and drove to within a block of the Old Harbor, fortunate to find a parking spot about fifty meters away from the building where Richard's office was located.

Richard worked in a small firm of five lawyers, but clearly, they did well, because the company's furnishings were elegant. Burke expected Richard charged a lot and wondered how Claude could afford the fees. Maybe his friend's café was doing much better than he thought.

The receptionist—a middle-aged, well-dressed woman who looked like she didn't miss a thing—took Hélène's name and then disappeared for a moment. When she returned, Olivier Richard was with her. He looked surprised to see Burke there, but shook his hand after kissing Hélène three times on the cheek.

"I'd like Paul here, Monsieur Richard," Hélène explained. "As I said before, he's a good friend of Claude's and of mine."

"As you wish, Mademoiselle," Richard said, bowing slightly and then leading them back along a hallway to his office, which had a spectacular view of the Old Harbor.

While the outer office was elegant, Richard's personal office was severe. The desk, which had a huge computer monitor sitting in the middle of it, along with two stacks of folders, was large and gunmetal gray. Behind Richard's black swivel chair were two gray filing cabinets. Richard's university diplomas hung between the filing cabinets. They were in his guests' line of sight but hardly given much prominence.

Burke's attention was drawn to one element in the room—well, two actually. The lawyer had two prints by Henri Matisse. One was identified as *Dishes and Fruit*. The other was titled *Open Window, Collioure*. Somehow, facing each other on opposite walls, the two prints gave the impression of color exploding in the room.

There was money here. Burke wondered if it came from defending café owners or from other sources.

"Your uncle will not be released anytime soon," the lawyer began. "In fact, he has limited privileges to contact the outside world other than through me. We're living in a time when authorities are extremely concerned about potential acts of terrorism, and they're taking a variety of stern measures. Your uncle is trapped by those concerns."

"They think Uncle Claude is a terrorist?" exclaimed Hélène.

"Unfortunately, the police have linked him to an activist group that takes environmental protests beyond the occasional demonstration," Richard said. "I believe his role in that group hasn't involved any criminal activities, but the police clearly believe otherwise."

Hélène was leaning forward, and her mouth was open.

"I will be working with your uncle to have the charges against him rejected by the court, but that isn't why I asked you to this meeting," the lawyer said. "Your uncle wants you to take over running his café."

"I was planning to help out as much as possible," Hélène said.

"I'm not talking about 'helping out.' I'm saying your uncle wants to transfer ownership of the café to you as soon as possible—this morning, if you accept. You might call it a precaution, although there are no guarantees about it."

"Me? Why? What's happening?" Hélène asked.

"For a variety of reasons, some legal and some not, it's possible the future of the café could be in jeopardy, and any potential future sale could be ruined by the current investigation. I know this sounds sudden, but you need to recognize how quickly matters can change, at least when it comes to dealing with business operations owned by people who find themselves involved in the criminal justice system."

"Why is it different if I take it over?" Hélène asked.

"You're family. You would 'inherit' the café from your uncle. It would be different than if he tried to sell out. French law can be complex on such matters, but there's no doubt a transfer of deed would provide some protection."

"But what happens if he's released?" Hélène said.

"You could deed it back to him after a certain time," Richard said.

"I don't know," Hélène said.

It was obvious she had never expected this twist. The café was her uncle's pride and joy. For him to give it to her came as a surprise even to Burke, and it seemed to suggest Claude didn't think he'd win his case.

"I don't have any money to pay taxes or anything like that," she said.

Richard waved aside her concerns, explaining Claude had financial resources elsewhere that would handle all related costs.

Burke wondered if those resources would also cover Richard's bill.

They discussed the transfer, and then Hélène agreed, signing a series of documents that had obviously been drafted that morning.

"Now, we need to discuss the charges against Claude, and I need to ask some questions of you both—but privately," Richard said. "It's possible you'll both have to testify in court."

Burke hadn't considered that, but it made sense.

Richard then asked Burke to leave the room so he could talk with Hélène alone. Fifteen minutes later, Hélène came out, and Richard ushered Burke back into his office.

The lawyer asked Burke whether he had heard Claude mention any specific group or individual connected to protests against FP Developments. Burke told him he had not. The lawyer probed to see if Burke had ever heard Claude discuss a "plot" to stop the company's new project. Burke said he hadn't. Then he asked Burke to describe Claude's mood over the last few weeks, and Burke did his best to recount a couple of situations. He hoped he got across that his friend had been angry about FP Developments but was hardly the type to do anything beyond complain.

"Good, very good," Richard finally said, standing and reaching out to shake Burke's hand. "Your responses have been both instructive and helpful. Thank you."

The lawyer led Burke back to the reception area and said that he would keep them up to date on Claude's situation.

"I anticipate I'll meet with him again this afternoon and definitely tomorrow," Richard said. "I'll let you know how we're proceeding. You must hope for the best, although it may seem difficult to do so at this moment."

Once outside, Burke and Hélène compared notes about their private sessions with Richard. They agreed they had said nothing to shake the lawyer.

"It doesn't sound good, Paul," Hélène said.

Burke took her hand. "We know your uncle, and we know he wouldn't do this," he said. "He has a good lawyer. Monsieur Richard seems very capable. We need to do what he said—hope for the best."

CHAPTER 38

OLIVIER RICHARD DID MEET with Claude that day and the following morning, but nothing had changed. He told Hélène that her uncle was holding up well in detention and had even joked to a couple of other inmates that they needed to try his latest specialty at his café when they were all released.

Still, Burke could see Hélène wasn't convinced her uncle was managing well at all. More than once, he spotted her brushing away tears.

Burke tried to contact Fortin but got nowhere. He left messages, but they weren't returned.

Meanwhile, the media seemed to have stopped howling, given that an arrest had been made in relation to the Vachon case. They were also busy examining the case against Léon Petit. Some facts were provided, but Burke felt most were missing in the reports. A spokesperson for the Nice police sounded positively puffed up on TV when she discussed how the two cases had been solved. Now it was all about what would happen in court.

On Saturday morning, Burke kissed a sleeping Hélène goodbye and drove to the Nice airport for his early flight to Paris.

Burke had been to Paris two dozen times before—maybe more—and he loved the city for its architecture, its museums and its cafés. He always spent hours walking around its various districts, up and down its narrow streets and along its magnificent boulevards. This time, without Hélène and with his thoughts clouded by Claude's predicament, he doubted Paris could work its magic on him.

He dropped his stuff off at his small hotel in the Marais district—it was too early to get into a room—and wandered about with his notepad and camera in his shoulder bag. Soon, he was caught in the horde of people marching toward the massive Les Halles shopping complex. They were like a mass of lemmings, and it took some effort for Burke to escape them. He was no fan of going underground to spend money in huge amounts.

He went into the condensed Jewish area, which was historical, funky and one of his favorite spots in the city, and decided to have lunch at a café he always checked out when he was in town. As usual, it was busy, and Burke found himself sitting an elbow's distance away from a middle-aged couple from Toronto who initiated a conversation by asking if he knew any English and, when he said he did, wondered if he could point them in the direction of the Luxembourg Gardens.

"We're tracking down some of the sites used in that Woody Allen movie, *Midnight in Paris*," the woman explained. "It was a wonderful show, and we decided we had to see those places personally."

Burke told them they were on the wrong side of the Seine River and then provided details on how to get there.

"You speak very good English," the woman observed.

Burke shrugged. "Thank you," he said. "I'm actually from Montréal."

"That would explain your French," she said.

"I live in France, although not here," Burke said, grateful for the distraction. "Down south, in a village just outside Nice."

"We're going to Nice next week," her husband said. "We hear it's a beautiful area."

"I like it," Burke said.

"Sorry to be so inquisitive, but what brought you over to France to live?" the woman asked.

Burke had time, so he told them how he'd been a pro cyclist, racing all over Europe and living in Spain and then the Netherlands before basing himself in Nice.

"Those deaths linked to the Tour de France are terrible," the woman said. "We've been reading all about them and seeing it on the news. Did you know anyone involved?"

"Not really," Burke lied. He had no interest in going further.

"Do they have the death penalty in France?" she asked after another pause.

"No," Burke said.

"Good," she replied.

After lunch, Burke decided it was time to do a little work, so he wished his new friends a good trip and walked to the rue de Rivoli. There, an army of workers was setting up barricades for the next day's final stage of the Tour de France, when close to a million spectators would watch the riders go round and round on the concluding circuit. It would be a magical moment for the riders after more than three weeks of punishing racing. Burke had finished only once, and he had been thrilled, if exhausted, when he crossed the finish line. Then he had gotten incredibly drunk.

Burke chatted with some of the workers and then got into a conversation in English with some Dutch fans who were staking out an area near the Place de la Concorde for the next day's final stage.

"It's been a very unusual Tour de France," said one of the Dutchmen—a towering man draped in an orange T-shirt, wearing an orange baseball cap. "I don't think the organizers planned on people getting murdered."

The other three Dutchmen in his group nodded.

"If you ask me, I think it's because there's too much pressure on the riders and their teams," the tall man continued. More nods from his friends. "When the pressure gets too great, people break. Of course, I think the media are happy about what happened. It makes for more interest."

Burke asked if he could film them for his video blog, and the Dutchmen readily agreed. The tall man did most of the talking, reiterating what he'd said before, while his friends added a few similar comments.

Burke thanked them and turned to leave.

"You're the Paul Burke who swore on television, yes?" called out the tall Dutchman, pointing a finger at Burke.

"Too much alcohol," Burke said with a shrug.

The four Dutchmen laughed.

"There's nothing wrong with having drinks," the Dutch leader said. "Tonight, we will have too much alcohol. We will hurt tomorrow for the final stage, but who cares? This is Paris, and this is the Tour de France. It's a time to party. We just won't get the chance to swear on TV."

Burke smiled politely and wondered if his lapse of judgment would end up on his tombstone: *Here lies Paul Burke. He swore on French TV. Now he's dead.*

Burke walked to the Champs-Elysées where several hundred more workers were busy preparing for the next day and where tens of thousands of people were strolling along, more than a few decked out in TDF clothing. He wondered how many people knew about the arrest of Léon Petit.

He thought about Claude. And Hélène.

He went to a nearby kiosk and got a panini and a can of Kronenbourg 1664. Then he found a bench, sat and texted Hélène, asking how she was doing and if she had talked to her uncle.

Ten minutes later, his smartphone alerted him to a text. It was from Hélène. She said she was doing OK and, according to Olivier Richard, so was Claude, although he remained in custody. Then she asked how Burke was doing in Paris.

He told her he was talking to lots of people and added that he missed her.

"I miss you too, chéri," she wrote back.

Burke sensed that Hélène was struggling, and he wished he was back there with her.

And that's when Burke realized he was probably in love with Hélène.

CHAPTER 39

THAT EVENING, BURKE SENT in a blog and posted his video version for Lemaire's perusal. He thought his efforts were reasonably good, thanks to the observations of the Dutch bunch and the excitement surrounding the next day's final stage of the race.

Fifteen minutes after sending in his stuff, Burke's phone rang.

"I received both your written and video blogs, Paul," said François Lemaire. "Some good work, although you still need to work on your spelling."

Burke, who was exhausted, thanked him.

"I have some good news for you," Lemaire said. "I had Antoine check up on followers for your blog."

"Oh, yes?" Burke replied, trying to sound interested.

"Your written blog has 21,575 followers and is growing by the day," Lemaire said.

"Is 21,575 good?"

"It's not bad at all. In fact, it's better than I had expected. The way it's going, you might get up to fifty thousand one day."

"That sounds good," Burke said.

"And that's just followers. A couple of your blogs had thirty-five thousand hits."

That seemed impressive to Burke, though he wasn't entirely sure he understood the difference between followers and hits. He was too tired to ask.

"And your video blog has gone from 250 followers to, the last time I looked, just over ten thousand," Lemaire continued.

"Good."

"Antoine dug into the analytics and discovered some other interesting facts," Lemaire said.

"Analytics? What are those?" Burke asked.

"It's a way to see who your readers or viewers are—or at least where they're from—and how much time they spend on a site or a page. Want to know where most of your followers come from?"

Burke didn't really care but told Lemaire he wanted to know.

"A third of your followers come from France. Another third come from elsewhere in Europe, especially Italy and Spain. About one-sixth come from the United States, and the rest come from around the world, including your homeland and a bunch in South America. A lot of people like what you're doing."

Burke was now interested. Besides the French, people in other European countries, the U.S. and even South America were interested in his viewpoints? He wondered who was reading him back home in Canada.

"And when they check out your blogs, both written and video, they're staying on several minutes, long enough to go through all of your material," Lemaire added.

"Good," Burke said, finally meaning it.

"But don't let it go to your head, and don't expect a raise," Lemaire added quickly.

Burke laughed. "OK, I won't. At least for the moment."

"Good. Talk to you when you're back here," Lemaire said and then hung up.

Burke ran the numbers through his head again. There were indeed a lot of people checking out his work. He'd have to polish his writing with that many following every word he wrote or said.

And down the line, he would talk to Lemaire about a raise. If taxes went up, as it looked like they would, he'd need extra money.

Burke went to bed, but it took a couple of hours before he slipped into sleep. Too many thoughts, starting with Lemaire's information and then going back to Claude and Hélène—and even Inspector Fortin.

On Sunday, Burke got up early, had a quick breakfast, checked out and then headed to the Champs-Elysées, his small overnight bag slung over his shoulder. He figured he'd mingle with people and then find a good spot close to the finish.

He eschewed the metro to walk there and was soon glad that he did. Even though the racers wouldn't be showing up for another four or five hours, the party atmosphere had already settled in as people of all ages and in all kinds of garb made their way toward the loop the riders would be doing. The good feelings were infectious, and Burke found himself putting aside thoughts of Nice, Claude and Hélène to eagerly chat with other spectators. It felt good to escape reality, if only for a while.

The day was perfect for racing. Warm, generally sunny and only a slight breeze. When he had ridden his final stage in the TDF, it had been unseasonably cool and wet.

He found a spot about two hundred meters from the finish line. He wouldn't be in the front row, or even the third or fourth, but he could still manage to see because he had a small mound to stand on.

When the riders finally flew onto the Champs, the spectators, who probably totaled more than a million, erupted into a deafening cheer that rumbled along the route. Burke wondered if it was like that every year. When he raced, he hadn't noticed much noise. He'd been focused on getting through the laps without crashing or getting left behind by the peloton.

Even though they were racing uphill and over cobblestones, the racers had to be pushing sixty kilometers per hour. Surely exhausted in every bone and muscle, they were feeling the adrenaline rush that came from riding in the finale of the biggest bike race in the world.

Burke found himself cheering and clapping along with everyone else as the peloton charged by.

Burke wished everything back home was different and that Hélène could be there with him, drinking in the energy of a million people and the pageantry of the final kilometers.

It was magnificent.

And then it was over, with a stocky Brit winning the stage and a whip-thin Spaniard winning the overall event.

Burke scribbled some notes and shot some video of the final ceremonies, and then it was time to leave. He had a plane leaving for Nice in two hours.

He considered himself fortunate to catch a cab two blocks away. If he'd had more time, he would have gone by the metro and then the RER to the airport, but he was in a rush, and besides, Lemaire would cover the expense.

When his plane landed, Burke sped to his car and drove quickly to the Nice TV station where he was going to be on the panel. He looked rumpled and tired, but he didn't care. Maybe the makeup people would freshen him up.

But they didn't. One woman crooked an eyebrow in disdain when he arrived, asking if this appearance was his usual state of affairs.

"I know," Burke said with a shrug. "I just got in from Paris and haven't had time to clean up."

That didn't seem to placate her.

The panel was made up of the TV sports anchor, the veteran sportswriter Burke had met at the forum, a long-retired former racer in his sixties and Burke.

They rehashed the day's final stage and then went through the surprises of the race. Burke contributed his share of comments but was a long way from being engaging. A couple of times, he found his thoughts drifting to what was happening with Claude.

"After all this discussion, though, the real reason that this race will linger in many people's memories long after today are the deaths of Pierre McManus and Mark Den Weent," the sports anchor said. "The Tour de France went from the sports pages to the front pages, from race results to murder."

Burke was back to paying attention.

"It was not the kind of publicity the Tour needed," the sports anchor added.

"It wasn't good for McManus or Den Weent either," interjected the sportswriter in a frosty tone.

Clearly not happy with the interruption, the anchor glared at the sportswriter, who glared right back. Burke remained silent as he waited to see what would happen next. The program was virtually live, with only a delay of a few seconds, partly due to his own shenanigans a few years back.

"Well, there has never been a doubt about that," the anchor replied. He turned to Burke. "Paul, my understanding is you've been close to the investigation of the two murders. In fact, a source told me you had some information that proved useful to the police."

Burke wondered how the anchor could have learned that.

"Not really, Pierre," he told the anchor. "I attended a news conference, talked to some police, but that was about it."

"You're being modest," the anchor continued, seemingly glad to have eliminated the sportswriter from the discussion. "I believe you uncovered some connections no one else knew about."

Who could have leaked the information? Fortin? Hardly. Côté? She seemed like she'd rather cut off her tongue than talk to the media. Someone else? Maybe another cop?

"I did learn a little bit about the case that didn't come out in the media," Burke admitted. "But it wasn't much, and the police didn't really seem to care much."

He wasn't sure if the last part was really true, but he had to distance himself from the investigation.

"I understand, but do you think the case against Léon Petit is strong, given your inside knowledge?" the anchor asked.

Everyone's eyes burned into him.

"Well, my 'inside knowledge' isn't much, and since I'm not a lawyer, I can't say if the case is strong or not," said Burke. "However, I don't think the police would have arrested him if they didn't believe they had a good case against him."

"Ah, Paul, now you sound like a politician," the anchor said with a smirk. "Come now, take on the detective's role as you apparently did over the last two weeks and give us something more."

"I'm not a detective, and I'm not a politician," Burke said, his anger threatening to ignite. "I'm just an ex-racer who didn't do well and now writes a blog. I only know what you know."

"Why do the police think Petit murdered Pierre McManus and Mark Den Weent?" the anchor continued.

"I don't know."

"Or won't say?"

"No, I don't know."

The anchor finally backed off, and the panel wrapped up with a few predictions for the following year's race.

When the show ended, the anchor and the director thanked Burke and the other participants.

The anchor then pulled Burke aside.

"You know why Petit murdered McManus, and I think you have some idea why he killed Den Weent as well," the anchor told Burke. "You could have shared that with the audience. It would have made for good TV."

"As I told you on air, I don't know. I might have some ideas, but I'm not sure about any of them," Burke said.

The anchor smiled. "No matter," he said, clapping Burke on the arm. "It was a good show. A lot more people know about you now. I expect you'll get noticed on the street from now on."

"I hope not."

"Really? Oh well, fame isn't for everyone," the anchor said. "Today's show is part of a new weekly segment I'm producing. It has a panel format and deals with the week's issues in sports. I'd like you to be on it."

"Every week?" Burke asked, stunned at the offer.

"Every week," the anchor said. "I've taken the liberty to talk to your editor, François Lemaire, and he has no issue with you appearing on the program in the future."

Burke wondered when Lemaire had known about the offer—and why he hadn't said anything to Burke.

"I'll think about it," Burke said.

The anchor smiled. "It would not be for free," he said. "You would be paid—and paid quite well."

A moment earlier, Burke had been ready to reject the offer. He wasn't interested in being on a regular panel; he didn't know a lot about other sports. Plus, he wasn't comfortable in front of a camera. He also wasn't sure about being tied down to a Sunday telecast every week. But the offer of being "paid quite well" changed his attitude; he could use the money.

"I'll think about it," Burke repeated, although he would probably accept. He just didn't want to seem too eager for the extra income.

The anchor could obviously see a change in Burke's thinking, because he smiled. "That's fine," he said. "I'll contact you tomorrow to talk about it. I think you'll find it's good for you, good for us and good for the viewers."

Burke wasn't entirely sure who would profit from his regular participation in the show, but he agreed to provide the anchor with an answer the next day. In return, the anchor told Burke what the pay would be. It was a nice amount—more than Burke expected.

And that's when he knew he'd definitely say yes.

On his way home, feeling tired and yet exhilarated from this latest development, Burke wondered what would happen next.

The old, slow days were long gone.

CHAPTER 40

IN THE MORNING, AFTER breakfast, Burke phoned Hélène, but she didn't answer. He had planned to call her the night before or to drop by the café, but once home, he'd collapsed on his bed and slept right through the night.

A few minutes later, Burke's phone rang.

It was Inspector Fortin.

"I want to talk with you this morning," the detective said. "Can you come to the station in the next hour or so?"

"Why?"

"I can't say on the phone, but I think you might find it very interesting," Fortin said.

With no other commitments, Burke agreed. He promised to be at Fortin's office in an hour. Then he took the initiative and called the anchor at the TV station. Burke said he would participate in the panel. He got some instructions for the following week's show and rang off.

After a quick shower and another coffee, Burke tried Hélène again. No luck. He texted her to let her know that he was back and trying to contact her, then left for Nice and Fortin.

A half hour later, he was sitting in Fortin's austere office. Côté, as usual, was nearby, this time sitting in a chair in the corner.

"If you were a regular member of the media, this would never happen," Fortin began. "But since you're not and since you provided us with some information that proved quite useful and since you will likely have to appear in court—"

"Court?" Burke interrupted. "What are you talking about?"

"Relax," Fortin said. "When I say, 'appear in court,' I mean to testify."

"Testify?" Burke said.

"The information you provided will need to be heard in court as part of a sentencing report," Fortin said.

"I don't understand," Burke said.

"Léon Petit has confessed to the McManus and Den Weent murders," Côté interjected.

"He has?" It was the last thing Burke had expected to hear.

"Monsieur Petit confessed last night," Fortin said. "He admitted to providing doctored nutritional pills that led to Pierre McManus's sudden cardiac arrest."

"Really? I wondered if he had," Burke said.

"I know you did. In fact, your questions prompted a re-examination of McManus's body by the pathologist. A new toxicology screen was done, and some new evidence was found. When we told Petit about that new finding and linked his background to the crimes—again thanks to some information from you—he gave himself up. Just told us the entire story."

"That surprises me," Burke said.

"Why?" Fortin asked.

"Because Léon Petit is a hard case and doesn't seem the type to confess," Burke said.

"Maybe, but he was definitely willing to talk and it's quite a story," Fortin said. "He told us that McManus planned to dump him from the organization and replace him with the son of a major supporter of the team. The son had some good skills, though not as good as his, and McManus figured getting him on board would ensure the dad was indebted to him. McManus told Léon it was the nature of the business to have a job one day and be gone the next, but Petit didn't agree, saying he'd been loyal and deserved to keep his job. McManus said he wasn't going to change his mind."

Fortin explained that when Karin Petit heard from her son what McManus was intending, she went out of her way to confront McManus for the first time in decades. She told him it was wrong to get rid of Léon, and besides, McManus would be firing his own son if he did so.

"Apparently, McManus didn't react well," Fortin said. "He told her he didn't have a clue what she was talking about and wouldn't accept the notion that Léon was his offspring. He said he didn't remember Karin, and then he called her some unpleasant names and threatened to sue her if she proceeded with any of her wild allegations."

Fortin said Léon hadn't known McManus was his father, but Karin finally relented and explained everything to him as a result of her meeting with McManus.

"Léon confronted McManus and argued with him again about his future with the team but got nowhere," Fortin said. "In fact, according to Léon, McManus promised to get him off the team even earlier if he could. And then McManus did something he shouldn't have—he called Karin Petit a whore and a blackmailer and a psycho.

"That's when Léon decided he would eliminate McManus by substituting drugs for nutritional pills."

"Did Léon tell his mother what he had done?" Burke asked.

Fortin shook his head. "He says he didn't, and everything suggests that's the truth. He's very close to her and very protective. Almost a clinical case, if you ask me."

Burke asked what had led to Den Weent's murder.

"Léon says Den Weent was a nosy guy. Soon after McManus's death, Den Weent asked Léon about all the pills he carried about, saying it was highly unusual for a mechanic to have such a haul of nutritional aides.

"And then over in Avignon, Léon found Den Weent poking through his stash. He told Den Weent to bugger off. That evening, when he saw Den Weent go out for a late-evening walk, he caught up to him and stabbed him with a knife he had. He said he had no other choice; Den Weent could've easily connected the dots. So, he killed Den Weent, although he says he didn't really want to. Then he took Den Weent's wallet and watch to make it look like a robbery."

"Den Weent was a good guy," Burke said.

"Léon told us he thought he'd be arrested the next morning, and when nothing happened, he started to believe he had gotten away with it."

"But why did Léon confess?" Burke asked. "It doesn't make a lot of sense."

Côté jumped in. "He didn't want his mother involved, and when we showed up to talk to her—thanks to you—he heard about it and got very nervous. And when she told him the types of questions we were asking, he was ready to tell the truth. This is one screwed-up guy who really only has feelings for one person in the world—his mother."

"Two people are dead because of his devotion," Burke said.

"That's about it," Fortin said. "This is a guy who's probably needed serious therapy since he was a kid. He just needed a trigger to set him off. McManus was it."

"What will happen to him?"

"He'll go to prison for a very long time," Fortin said. "As for his mother, she's devastated by all this and has been hospitalized since late last night. A total collapse."

"What a waste," Burke said, mostly to himself.

"We deal with that a lot," Côté said, surprising Burke with her gentle tone of voice.

Burke had a brainwave.

"So, since I'm here, what's happening with Claude Brière?" he asked. "He's a friend, and I know what you're going after him for."

Fortin looked down and shook his head.

"That's a different matter, and we are not at liberty to say much," he said. Then he paused. "But it might not end up as bad as you think. It won't be good, but it won't be the worst."

Burke asked what Fortin meant, but the detective wouldn't elaborate. He ended the conversation, saying it was time for Burke to leave.

Outside police headquarters, Burke phoned Hélène again. This time, she answered. She seemed relieved to hear his voice.

Then she told him why she had been difficult to contact.

She'd managed a visit with her uncle in the company of Olivier Richard and found him in decent spirits, if a little quieter than usual. She also learned that he'd be pleading guilty, but not to the worst charges. Instead, he was pleading guilty to conspiracy to commit willful damage. It seemed her uncle had been busy emailing a variety of options to other activists protesting the project by FP Developments, and some of those ideas involved destruction of company property. In fact, Claude's suggestions, if enacted, could have resulted in maybe millions of euros in damages.

"In the end, the police decided Uncle didn't kill this Vachon and his bodyguard," Hélène said. "They didn't say if they have someone else in mind, but they said Uncle is off the hook for the deaths. Thank goodness."

Burke felt some small relief.

"Monsieur Richard said Uncle will probably have to spend six months in jail," Hélène added, the words catching in her throat. "But they both said it could have been much worse. He could have received a much longer sentence, because the government wants to look strong when dealing with any acts that could be considered terrorism or industrial attacks. Besides, they will likely send Uncle to a place that won't be too rough or dangerous. It will probably be a new facility in the suburbs of Lyon. It hasn't been open too long. Thank God he won't be going to one of those nineteenth century dungeons."

That was good news. There had been recent stories in the media about the terrible quality of French prisons, with tales of rats, open wires, stifling air, backed-up toilets, horrible food and so on. If he was in a new facility, he might be OK.

"He has signed over the café to me, too," she said in a quiet voice. "He knows he can't take care of it, and he doesn't want it affected by the court action. So, I'm the new owner of his café."

Burke wasn't sure she wanted to take over the café for the long term since she was starting to develop career plans involving interior design, but he knew she wouldn't go against her uncle's wishes. Maybe in six months or a year, Claude would take it over again.

"And you agreed?" Burke asked to make sure.

"Of course," Hélène replied. "I'll have to postpone school for a year or more, but I'm young. Besides, I don't mind running the café. I might even change the menu a little."

Her voice was lightening up, and she managed a chuckle. "That would drive Uncle crazy, but it seems a new dish or two might be a good idea."

She said she would be spending her afternoon at the café trying to hire some additional staff to make up for Claude's absence.

"Maybe you can come over before dinner for a pastis," she suggested. "And for a hug. I need one. I want to feel your arms around me."

"I'll be there as requested, Hélène," Burke said. "And by the way, I need a hug from you, too. If I don't see you for a couple of days, I sort of miss you."

There it was—his statement of affection.

There was a pause at the other end of the line.

And then Hélène spoke. "And I feel the same, *chéri*."

They ended the conversation there. Hélène would be busy at the café, even before the dinner crowd showed, but even a few minutes with her would feel good.

Driving home, he turned his thoughts to that morning's activities. Léon Petit was going down for the murders of McManus and Den Weent—and Claude wasn't for the death of Yves Vachon.

And he had a new paying gig on TV.

Once again, he thought about how dramatically his life had changed in just three weeks and, given the morning's events, would be changing still in the next few days. Then he'd be back to a quieter life.

"Or maybe not," he told himself.

CHAPTER 41

CLAUDE'S CAFÉ — NOW Hélène's—was busy when Burke strolled down just after 7 p.m. Once again, he sensed most of the clientele came from nearby condo developments. They had discovered the quality of the café's food and atmosphere, and were starting to make it their own. That was fine by Burke.

He found a quiet table in a corner of the terrace. He caught Hélène's eye as she hustled by and got a wink in exchange. His server turned out to be a new addition to the staff—a tall, thin young man with a goatee.

"Hélène told me I had to look after you with special care," he announced stiffly before breaking into a broad smile. "I'm Henri, one of her old friends from school. I just started here."

Burke reached across and shook hands, then ordered a glass of rosé. Henri bowed slightly and hurried off.

He watched Hélène go from table to table, taking orders and working the clients with the same skill as her uncle. She might not want to do this type of work for long, but she was a natural.

Madame Marois was sitting a few tables away, as bolt upright as ever, with Plato dutifully stretched out by her feet. She was ordering something from Henri and waving a finger at him. He nodded a couple of times, did his bow again and beetled off. When he walked by Burke, he raised his eyebrows.

So Madame Marois was back to her old difficult self.

Burke sipped his wine and relaxed. He felt bad that Hélène was exceptionally busy while he clearly was the opposite, but she didn't seem to mind, stopping once to give him a quick peck on the lips and a couple of times to offer a little extra wiggle as she went by on her way to another table.

When he caught Madame Marois's eye, he nodded and smiled, lifting his glass in her direction. The old woman looked frostily back at him and tilted her head with the slightest of movements. Then she returned to gazing at her distant wall, lost in her thoughts and putting up her standard "don't bother me" barrier.

Burke finished his wine and decided he'd have dinner at home. He paid his bill, left Henri an oversized tip that left the young man pleasantly surprised, and waved at Hélène. Then, on the spur of the moment, he walked over to Madame Marois.

"How are you this evening, Madame?" he asked.

She stared at him for an extra couple of seconds. "I'm well, young man," she said with effort.

"The café is busy tonight," Burke said, waving at the occupied tables.

"Yes, it is—and unfortunately noisy, too," Madame replied. "Too many of these tourists don't understand the elegance of a quiet drink and meal."

"Yes, it seems a little noisier than usual," Burke admitted, not bothered by the extra energy. "But it's still a welcome escape. And Hélène will do a good job ensuring the café retains its quality."

Madame's eyebrows shot up. "What do you mean?" she asked.

"Hélène has taken over the café from her uncle," he said.

"Because he's in trouble for the Vachon affair?"

"In a way," Burke said. "But he's not guilty of the hit-and-run deaths, according to the police."

"He isn't?" Madame said. "The newspapers and TV certainly seemed to suggest he was the one who did it."

"You'll get the latest story tomorrow or maybe on the TV news late tonight, but he's off the hook," Burke informed her.

"Have they got someone else for the hit-and-run?" Madame asked.

"I don't know," Burke told her. "I don't think so, but they don't inform me."

Madame paused. "Well, that's good for Claude. But why is his niece taking over the café?"

Burke told her it was Claude's wish, then excused himself before he revealed any other news that wasn't his to tell. When he glanced over his shoulder on the way out, he noticed Plato was standing and Madame was patting his head and saying something to the dog.

Burke wasn't back in his apartment for more than a few minutes when he received a phone call from Olivier Richard asking if he could meet with Claude the following morning at the police jail cells. Since it was evening and he didn't think lawyers made late calls unless it was crucial, Burke wondered if there was an emergency, but the lawyer dispelled that notion, saying Claude just wanted to discuss a couple of personal matters in the morning with Burke and no one else—an obvious reference to Hélène. Burke agreed. Olivier added that he'd be there for some of the conversation, and then he rang off, leaving Burke to ponder what Claude wanted to talk about.

A little while later, Burke turned on the evening news.

Sure enough, the announcer told the audience that the charges of vehicular manslaughter and hit-and-run against Claude had been dropped, but that the café owner faced other charges involving conspiracy to damage private property.

The announcer added that two others were also charged in connection to plans made to stop the new FP Developments project in the area.

The investigation into Vachon's death was continuing, the announcer reported, and then there was a clip of—who else?—Jean-Pierre Fortin talking about how the Nice police and "other forces" remained optimistic about getting a result.

After the news, hoping that Hélène might drop over after closing the café, Burke found himself drifting off.

CHAPTER 42

THE NEXT DAY, BURKE met Olivier Richard at their designated time of 10 a.m. at the front of the Nice police station.

"What's this about, Monsieur Richard?" Burke asked.

"I believe he wants to get his affairs in order before he leaves us for a while," the lawyer replied diplomatically.

Burke followed the lawyer into the station and to a special side desk. There, Richard spoke quietly with a uniformed officer, who then led the two of them to a back room. There, under the watchful eyes of two guards, they sat and waited for Claude to show up.

When he entered the room fifteen minutes later, Burke was shocked at the change in his friend. He had lost at least ten pounds in just a few days and, for the first time since Burke had known him, looked somewhat trim.

He also looked exhausted as he dropped into the metal chair opposite them.

Claude must have noticed the look of surprise on Burke's face, because he said with an expansive smile, "What do you think of my new physique? Pretty soon, I'll be able to ride in the mountains with you—except for this minor inconvenience involving jail."

Then he leaned forward to Burke.

"The problem is the food here," Claude said in a theatrical whisper. "They have no sense of cuisine. I mean, the things they do to potatoes should be banned by law. As for the pieces of meat, I truly do not want to know their origins. Ghastly!"

Burke smiled back. Claude's eyes, though tired, still had their usual playful spark. He was in trouble, but he was keeping his spirits up. Or he was doing a good job pretending he was.

Burke glanced at Richard, but the lawyer's face showed no emotion.

"I'm hoping you can do me a favor, Paul," Claude said, growing serious.

"If I can, Claude," Burke replied.

"I know you're seeing my niece, and I know you have learned she's taking over my café while I'm away," Claude said.

Burke nodded.

"Hélène is a strong young woman, and I'm confident she will handle the responsibility of running the café—although I'm concerned she'll worry too much about making sure everything is operating just right. Mostly, though, I'm concerned she'll worry a great deal about her old Uncle Claude. We're close, much closer than a normal uncle and niece. More like a father and daughter."

Burke nodded. He had seen the strength of their relationship.

"I think it's possible she will try to do too much for me," Claude continued. "And I think she might crack under the pressure—if she doesn't get some support. That's where you come in, my friend. I can see you care for her in a way that's more than just a brief encounter, and so I want to ask you to support her as much as you can."

These were deep waters. But he couldn't disagree with what Claude was saying; he did care for Hélène.

"Will you be there for her—and for me? I know you and I have a history that isn't long, but we understand each other, I think, and that's why I'm asking you this favor."

"I'll do what I can," Burke said.

"But here's the tough part," Claude said. "I don't want her to visit me in prison. Not once. It would be very difficult on her, but it would be harder on me. I need to be strong, and if I see her, I'll weaken. So, please, do what you need to do to keep her away from Lyon."

Burke could see Hélène objecting to that idea. In fact, he assumed there was no way on earth she would be kept from visiting her uncle.

"Maybe you need to talk to her about that," Burke said.

"I will, but I know my niece," Claude said, nodding. "She'll argue with me at the start, and then she'll agree, but then, later, she'll change her mind. Please, Paul, do whatever you can to keep her from Lyon."

"I'll do whatever I can," Burke said. He paused. "What about other visitors? Like me?"

Claude shrugged. "That's different," he said, smiling. "It would be good to see a friendly face. I might even have some requests for you from time to time."

Burke didn't know what Claude meant by "requests," but he agreed.

"What about other friends? Do you want them to visit, too?" Burke asked.

"Ah, my other friends," Claude said. "I'll see some of them. They're good men. They'll know when to come and when to stay away."

"Maybe you'll have access to a computer," Burke suggested.

Olivier Richard jumped in, saying the conditions of Claude's soon-to-be sentence would preclude him from using a computer in the prison library.

"That's because of Claude's use of a computer in the commission of a crime," Richard explained.

They chatted for a few minutes, and then Claude ended the conversation.

"Make sure you don't get too thin, Claude," Burke said, standing. "Maybe the prison will let you work in the kitchen and make some decent food."

That made Claude smile and shrug. "Maybe," he said and then waved goodbye.

Outside on the street, Burke asked Richard when Claude would be appearing in court for his sentence.

"The end of this week," the lawyer said. "They want to get Claude's case out of the way as soon as possible. They know that the media will be back asking about Vachon's killer. There are a lot of politics involved in this case."

Burke nodded.

"In fact, I believe the police are now looking for a specific type of vehicle—a large, black automobile," Richard said.

"A lot of cars fall into that category," Burke said.

Richard nodded. "I think they have more information, but they aren't willing to give it to the lawyer of a man previously accused of Vachon's death. They just provided me with some basic information when they changed the charges against Claude."

"Was it Inspector Fortin?"

"It was," Richard replied. "He's in demand after solving the McManus-Den Weent case. He's been appointed to lead the Vachon investigation and put some movement into it. He's in total charge of the case for the investigating judge, and that's not likely a good thing for the true perpetrator. I know Fortin. He's not a likable man, but he's a very clever one. I've seen him in action a number of times, and he has the ability to make connections that lesser minds can't."

"But he seemed so anxious to lock Claude up," Burke said.

"His superiors needed some kind of result to silence the media's criticism and that of the government. The bosses ordered Claude to be served up, temporarily at least, as a solution. When it became clear to Fortin that Claude wasn't the one who killed Vachon, the charges were changed."

"So Fortin never really believed Claude did it?"

"I don't think so," Richard said. "I think he was just going along with his superiors. Along the way, he learned about Claude's emails and texts."

Burke nodded.

"But I expect he'll have to produce a good result this time," Richard said. "The pressure from the media and government will be back on very quickly, and they'll be skeptical about the next individual charged with the murders of Vachon and his bodyguard, so Fortin better get it right."

That made sense to Burke.

"Maybe Fortin will consult you on the Vachon case, too," Richard said.

"What do you mean?" Burke asked.

"A variety of sources, including a TV program two days ago, have suggested you produced some information that led to the arrest of that bike mechanic."

"Just coincidence," Burke said.

"Yes, well, my sense is you don't miss much, Monsieur Burke," Richard said. "I'll be in touch if you're needed for Claude's court appearance. In the meantime, good luck with trying to tell Hélène she shouldn't visit her uncle when he's away."

"I think I'll need it," Burke said.

"I guarantee you'll need it," Richard said and then left.

CHAPTER 43

AFTER THE MEETING, BURKE needed to digest what he had heard from Claude and Olivier Richard. Not wishing to return home, he drove near the Promenade des Anglais, parked and found a bench overlooking the turquoise water and the rocky beach below. He sat, letting the gentle sea breeze caress him. He closed his eyes.

So, Claude had misled him—and Hélène—about the depth of his anti-FP Developments activities. He had been foolish, even reckless, but Claude believed in a cause and had tried to help people.

And now Hélène was facing a different future, one that involved him in a fairly serious way.

He smiled at that idea.

But who was responsible for the hit-and-run against Vachon and his bodyguard? Fortin was a smart guy, but Burke felt he might need some luck, too. So far, the police hadn't discovered the culprit despite most of their resources being committed to the case.

He sensed that Olivier Richard's comments about the police getting closer reflected wishful thinking by the flics.

As for the large black car, there were thousands of them in the region. Obviously, no videocam showed the vehicle's license plate or the features of the driver or any passenger. If it had, there'd have been an arrest, which would have been trumpeted to the media.

His mind drifted to Léon Petit. Something was niggling at Burke. Something that made him wonder about Petit murdering both McManus and Den Weent.

He put aside those thoughts and watched the ferry from Corsica coming into port. It was a massive vessel, but it moved with ease and speed.

Once it was out of sight, he decided to go and have a word with André Rousseau. He expected his friend would have some comments about Léon Petit.

And he did.

"I thought I'd hear from you about our friend Léon," Andre said as soon as Burke walked into his shop.

Burke looked around. No customers.

"Were you surprised?" Burke asked.

"After all you said before, I was only a little surprised," Rousseau said. "This is all a whirlwind adventure you've involved me in, Paul."

"It's definitely been strange," Burke agreed.

"And now I need another mechanic," Rousseau said. "It will be tough to get one as skilled as Petit. Hopefully, though, the next one won't be a murderer."

"Too bad about his mother," Burke said.

Rousseau didn't know that part, and so Burke explained. At the end, Rousseau shook his head.

"They're very close," he said.

"It seems that way," Burke agreed.

They talked a few more minutes, and then Burke turned to leave.

As he got to the door, André had a final thought: "I can see Léon killing McManus, but I'm surprised he murdered Den Weent, especially in that way. I guess you just never know."

Suddenly, Burke realized what it was that was bugging him.

Instead of heading home, Burke went to Nice police headquarters. He wanted to talk with Fortin.

After parking, he was going up the stairs to the station when Fortin and Côté came out.

"I was coming to talk to you," Burke said, stopping in front of the two detectives.

"Ah, Monsieur Burke once again," Fortin said.

Burke figured he wouldn't waste time. "Did you ever find the knife Léon Petit used to kill Mark Den Weent?"

Fortin seemed surprised by the question. "Since you aided us somewhat in our investigation, I will tell you that Léon told us he threw the knife into a garbage bin a few blocks away. The knife wasn't found because it was taken to the garbage site and impossible to find. Besides, it was no longer necessary since he had confessed."

"Second question, did you confirm the whereabouts of Karin Petit when Mark Den Weent was being killed?" Burke asked.

"What are you getting at, Burke?" Fortin said, dropping the formality.

"Was she in the area?"

Fortin's pause told Burke the detectives hadn't gone in that direction. Or at least not very far.

"Do you know something we should know?" Côté asked.

Burke shrugged. "No, I'm just wondering about some things."

Fortin and Côté exchanged a glance.

"We have to be somewhere now, but we need to talk again—and soon," Fortin said.

Burke agreed, then watched the two detectives stride away.

It was time to head home.

After parking his car, he was strolling to his apartment when Jean called his name and motioned him to come over to his shop.

"You know how we've been talking about Madame Marois having some, you know, mental troubles?" Jean said.

Burke nodded.

"Well, this morning, she drove her car into that stone wall over there," Jean said.

"Is she all right?" Burke asked, noticing a pile of stones knocked out of the wall.

"Yes, she's fine. Just shaken up," Jean said. "I think she got distracted."

"Was she going too fast?"

"I saw her, and she was going very slow, just enough to crumple her front right side. She must have been thinking about something else."

"Where is she now?"

"I helped her make a report to the police and then took her home. She's resting now."

"It was lucky she was going slow," Burke said. "Is Plato OK?"

"I expect so," Jean said. "He wasn't with her."

Plato missing a car ride? Burke was surprised.

"Did she say where she was going?" Burke asked.

"Shopping in Nice," Jean said. "I think she's reached a time when she shouldn't be driving."

Burke agreed.

"Too bad she's alone," Jean said. "Madame needs help."

Burke nodded. Madame Marois was struggling. Yet he couldn't stop thinking there was something about the old woman that he was missing.

CHAPTER 44

A FEW MINUTES LATER, Burke knocked on the old woman's front door. He wanted to check how she was doing. He half expected she'd shut the door in his face or accuse him of meddling, but he was curious.

He could see the peephole being filled. She was looking to see who was visiting her.

The door opened.

"Monsieur?" she asked in a wispy voice.

Her hands quivered slightly as she held the door handle.

He said he wanted to check if she was all right.

"I see my incident has become village news," she said, waving a finger at him.

"Not at all," Burke replied. "Jean told me because he saw it happen. He's the only one."

The old woman shook her head. "He's a nosy man. He did help me, but he should keep what happened to himself."

Burke looked down. Plato was by his mistress's feet, tail wagging, ears perked up. Burke bent and scratched the dog's head. Plato seemed to grin with appreciation.

"Jean is only concerned, Madame," Burke said, standing back up.

Madame shook her head once again, still agitated. "Well, he doesn't need to be. I had the sun in my eyes, and that's all."

"I'm glad you're doing well, Madame," Burke said.

"Quite well, monsieur," she said. "Thank you for your concern, but you can rest assured that I can manage."

And then with a nod, she nudged Plato back into the house and closed the door, leaving Burke standing there like a rebuffed door-to-door salesman.

Burke wasn't bothered, though. He returned home and called Antoine in Antibes.

The paper's tech wizard was busy wrapping up some postings for the paper's internet site, but would be available in a few minutes. Burke arranged to call back.

While he waited, Burke went online to read the latest reports about Vachon and the investigation. The media were spending a lot of effort analyzing the new FP Developments CEO and how the stock markets were reacting, not just in France, but elsewhere on the continent and even overseas. It seemed Vachon's successor was highly regarded, but the markets were reflecting some unease.

When Antoine called, Burke wasted no time.

"I'd like you to check into some video for me," he said.

"Video?"

"Yes. Are you available to meet in person for a few minutes? It would be easier," Burke said. "It's important, too, and might help you and your newspaper. I don't want to say anything more right now."

There was a pause. Antoine was obviously piqued by Burke's secrecy. He asked when Burke wanted to get together.

Burke said sooner was better, and to his surprise, Antoine agreed. They'd decided to meet at a café in Antibes in a half hour.

Antoine was nursing a cassis when Burke showed up precisely on time. They shook hands.

"So, what's this cloak-and-dagger routine about?" Antoine asked.

Burke looked around. There was no one near who could hear them.

"I'm wondering if you'd like to try doing a hack?" Burke said.

"A hack? Into what? What are you talking about?"

"The city of Nice has video cameras posted in several spots," Burke said. "I expect the city's tech department keeps those video records somewhere. That's what I'm interested in."

Antoine leaned forward. "For what reason?"

"I want to look at the video where Vachon was hit and killed," Burke said.

"The police have probably studied that tape many times," Antoine said. "If there's anything on that tape that's valuable, they'd have it."

"I know, but I want to check something. I want to check the tape from not just that day, but two or three days before."

"It's a worthless exercise," Antoine said, finishing his cassis and motioning to the server for another.

"Probably, but, hypothetically, could you do it?" Burke said.

Antoine thought about the question. Finally, he nodded. "I think I could. The city of Nice's security measures are second-rate. They've been hacked a few times and still haven't done much to improve their security."

Burke said, "Good."

"But it's serious business to hack into a city's database, Paul. I mean, if we get caught, we could be heavily fined or, worse, go to jail."

"Are you good enough to avoid getting caught?"

Antoine grinned. "Between us, I'm very good. I doubt they'd catch me. But why take such a risk?"

"Because of the payoff," said Burke. "We might get some information that would solve the Vachon case. That would be big news."

Antoine looked skeptical but then nodded. "That would make François very happy. He'd be even more full of himself."

"And maybe he'd give you a raise."

Antoine shrugged. "You're baiting me, but that's OK. I like the idea, and if it gets me a raise, all the better. Besides, I'd like to know what happened to Vachon, too. If we could find out who did it, I'd send that person some flowers."

They agreed to meet later at Antoine's place because it would be safer and because Antoine had a powerful computer at home.

After leaving, Burke went to Claude's café. Hélène was there, working with the staff to get the tables prepared for the dinner crowd. She was her usual pleasant, friendly self, but Burke picked up on a little more decisiveness in her suggestions to the other servers and even to the chef. She was asserting herself as the new owner, and the staff seemed happy to respond.

Sometimes, it seemed Claude had been too busy visiting to ensure the café ran smoothly.

They chatted for a couple of minutes and then decided they'd get together the following day, since Hélène would be closing the café that night and Paul would be working with Antoine for what could be an extended period of time.

After a small salade Niçoise at home, Paul headed out to Antoine's. It took a while to find the address since it was tucked up a hill, in a cul-de-sac overlooking Antibes. The exterior of the small house was prettily painted in sea blue and pastel yellow. Flowerpots rich with color stood on the terrace. Burke wasn't sure what he had expected, but this handsome, manicured house was definitely a surprise.

Burke rang the doorbell, and a foghorn inside sounded. This was getting stranger by the second.

The door opened, and there was Antoine, dressed in blue linen pants and an orange, long-sleeved linen shirt. The big man filled the doorway.

"Enter and let the games begin," Antoine said, stepping back and motioning for Burke to step forward.

The living room featured a black leather couch, a huge glass coffee table with a stone sculpture of a black elephant in the middle, and two black chairs that looked like they'd only be sturdy enough for a child, let alone a mountain of a man like Antoine. On the walls were two small Impressionist paintings.

"My tastes are eclectic," Antoine said, noting how Burke gawked at the room.

Antoine led Burke down a short hallway and into a partially darkened room. It felt as though he'd stepped into some futuristic vision of an office. There were two computers on two different, plexiglass desks, which stood on black tile floor that contrasted dramatically with the white walls. The monitors were enormous, and the definition on the screen savers—featuring more elephants—was astonishing; Burke had never seen such detail. On one wall was an enormous plasma TV screen. An oversized metal chair on rollers was in the middle of the room, almost as if awaiting the captain of a starship. Two tiny gunmetal lamps on extended rods stood in opposite corners and were dimmed to produce a minimum amount of light.

Burke noticed there was not a single sheet of paper in the room, nor a pen or pencil.

"This is my hideaway from the world—and my way to connect with the rest of the world at the same time," Antoine said.

"It's incredible," Burke said.

"I'll get you a chair," Antoine said.

He returned with a small black chair that he placed beside the large chair. Then he sat and rolled toward the nearest computer, his fingers attacking the keyboard with a speed that once again stunned Burke.

"I've already done some work," Antoine said. "I've been into the city system and found the path to the video security site. It was remarkably easy, even with their new security measures. Their technicians, or whoever designed it, should be embarrassed. It was like it was designed by children. Nevertheless, I've taken extra precautions to ensure there will be no footprint leading back to me." He paused. "I mean, to us."

He spent a few minutes doing tasks that left Burke totally perplexed, and then suddenly, a dimly lit street showed up on the screen.

"This is from the night that Vachon and his bodyguard died, and this is the street where it happened," Antoine said, pointing to the paused scene. "The image is dark because the street isn't lit well and because the city's videocams are of questionable quality. The one showing this view is at least four hundred meters away."

Most of the vehicles were dark, and it was impossible to read a license plate. The brightest lights came from two nearby cafés, but they weren't enough to provide clarity to the two individuals about to walk onto the street.

"Here's the scene from a camera up the street a bit," Antoine said.

The scene switched angles, but the view didn't improve. In fact, it was darker and blurrier.

"No wonder the police have had trouble figuring out what happened," Antoine said. "I can enlarge the view, but watch what happens."

He toggled back to the first street scene and enlarged the section with the two men. Burke thought one of them could have been Vachon, but it could also have been someone's Uncle Jacques.

"So, are you saying this is Vachon and his bodyguard?" Burke asked.

"Watch."

The scene switched back to full view, and Antoine let the video run. Just as the two men got a third of the way onto the street, a black sedan tore around a corner and drove right into the two, sending one man flying forward and the other backward.

"Keep watching," Antoine said, excitement in his voice.

Then a second vehicle—another dark sedan—roared onto the scene, almost colliding with the first vehicle. The driver, obviously surprised, swerved to avoid contact.

The second car hopped up, then down.

Burke gasped.

The second vehicle had rolled over the man who had fallen forward, crushing him in the midriff. It was brutal.

The first vehicle sped away. The second car slowed for a moment, and then the motorist floored it, and it, too, disappeared.

Left behind on the street were two bodies.

Vachon and his minder.

CHAPTER 45

BURKE POINTED AT THE screen and asked if it was possible to identify the two license plates.

By way of answering, Antoine went back, captured the first car just before it struck the leading walker and then enlarged the rear of the vehicle. The license plate appeared like it had been blacked out. There was no possible way to see the numbering.

Antoine ran the video ahead a bit and did the same to the second car. The numbering hadn't been blacked out, but the plate was clearly dirty, and Burke saw there was no way to distinguish anything more than a single figure.

"Even if the numbers weren't covered in muck, it would be difficult to read the plate from this distance," Antoine said. "There is software that can work on scenes that lack appropriate pixels, building the image from what is likely, but not in this case. So, no plate numbers."

Antoine sat back and pointed at the screen.

"If I was to bet, I'd say the first vehicle had its numbers blacked out on purpose, but the second car's plate numbers were dirty by accident," he said.

Burke agreed with Antoine. He had thought the same.

Antoine leaned back in his captain's chair.

"So maybe the first driver did what he wanted to do, while the second one got caught in a bad circumstance, then got frightened and drove off after running over Vachon or his minder," Antoine said.

"It seems likely," Burke said. "Let's look at it again in slow motion."

They spent ten minutes watching the cars move toward and then strike the two pedestrians. Nothing new showed up.

Burke asked if there was any way to see where the first black car had come from. Antoine reversed the video slightly and enlarged the bottom left corner where the first vehicle initially appeared. The front half of the car showed up, but from what direction was still unclear.

"Can we see if there's a street view on Google for that area?" Burke asked.

"It will only show the view taken during some day well before the accident," Antoine protested.

"I understand, but let's try anyway."

Antoine went to the other computer and pulled up a street scene of the corner where the first sedan had appeared.

"That's a fairly sharp turn," Burke said.

Antoine nodded.

"You'd have to know how to handle a vehicle to carry some speed through the turn," Burke said.

"I expect so."

Burke asked Antoine to focus on the buildings on the left side of the curving road.

"Stop it there," said Burke, pointing at the screen. He leaned forward. "Can you twist the angle to our right?" he asked.

Antoine managed that in a couple of seconds.

Burke moved even closer. Then he pointed.

"Look through the gap between those two buildings. You can see the café where Vachon had supper on the night he was killed," Burke said.

Antoine studied the scene. "Were you expecting to see that?"

"I had an idea," Burke said. "If we accept that the license plates of the first sedan were blacked out on purpose, then that individual had something in mind. It's possible the driver was waiting for Vachon, but then how would the driver know when Vachon was coming out? That view there tells us the driver could park in that area of the street and watch the front door of the café."

"But how would the driver know Vachon was eating there?" Antoine asked.

"Vachon was widely known to be a creature of habit. Same cafés, same times, same days."

Antoine scratched his neck. "But the flics aren't stupid," he said. "I expect they'd have done the same thing we're doing."

Burke thought about that for a moment. "True," he said. "But knowing it and getting the driver's identity are two different things."

"Wouldn't the flics probably have talked to residents in the neighborhood about a parked sedan?"

Burke acknowledged that was likely.

"Let's go back and look at the surveillance video from the night before Vachon and his bodyguard were killed," he said.

"Why?" Antoine asked.

"It's possible the driver didn't have this one night picked out to drive into Vachon and his minder. The conditions had to be right—very little moonlight, virtually no traffic, no one parked in the viewing area up that street, no other people walking nearby. Maybe the driver was there the night before and we can get a better view."

"When you put it that way, that's a lot of things that had to go right for the driver to kill them, and get away," Antoine said.

"It is indeed," Burke said. "But I think the driver was someone with a lot of patience."

"Or a lot of hate—or maybe it was someone who was hired to kill Vachon if he was the real target," Antoine suggested. "After all, it sounds like Vachon made a lot of enemies over the years."

Burke mentally ticked off Claude and Lemaire as two, but he said nothing about that.

"Go into the kitchen in the back and make some coffee," Antoine said. "The coffee machine and the coffee are by the sink. I'll start checking the video from the day before."

Burke nodded and went to the kitchen. Once again, he was surprised. Unlike the modern living room and the space-age office, the kitchen was circa 1850 with superb, chestnut woodwork and cooking utensils hanging from the ceiling over a wood table that featured a huge cutting board. The entire kitchen was immaculate.

Back in the office with two steaming cups of coffee, Burke found Antoine leaning forward, examining the screen with a frown.

"Anything?" Burke said.

"I think this is the same vehicle that initially struck Vachon and his bodyguard," Antoine said, pointing at a black car. "I can't be sure, but it's the same size and shape, and the license plates are impossible to see."

Burke leaned over and checked the screen. Antoine was right.

They watched the car glide around the corner and merge into heavy traffic.

Burke pointed at the top part of the monitor. "Look. There are several people coming out of the café."

Antoine stopped the video. They both moved closer to the screen.

"Those two men look familiar," Antoine said.

"They do, indeed."

"If it's them, there are too many others around and too much traffic," Antoine said. "The conditions weren't right."

"The conditions weren't perfect," corrected Burke. "Let's go back to the same general time from the day before."

It took a half hour before Burke and Antoine spotted a familiar-looking vehicle coming around the corner. Once more, there was a group of people leaving the café, and once again, it seemed like the leading two figures could have been Vachon and his minder.

"I wonder if we're seeing things that aren't there, though," Antoine said, leaning back and sipping a new cup of coffee.

Burke had been thinking the same thing, but he didn't mention it.

"Let's go back one more day, and then we'll quit," he told Antoine.

Working on the theory that Vachon would be leaving the café around ten, they needed just fifteen minutes before they stopped the video and studied the scene.

"That's our sedan, isn't it?" Antoine said.

"It could be."

"And, look, there are Vachon and his minder—maybe—leaving the café," Antoine said.

Burke agreed.

"But they're alone, so if it's really our driver, why doesn't he take them out now?"

Burke was wondering that, too. The traffic was virtually nil. The area was dark. No pedestrians around. Perfect timing.

"What's that white blotch in the car?" Antoine said, almost touching the screen.

Burke had seen it, too. It was near the windshield. Not big, just a small white spot. It clearly had nothing to do with the camera or the monitor. It was something in the vehicle.

"I don't know," Burke said. "Run it forward slowly."

They watched as the vehicle slowed and the two men crossed the road without a glance at the approaching car. When they were across, the sedan drove off without any urgency.

"I lied about this being our last day. Let's go back one more day," Burke said.

Antoine didn't complain and started working on the video from the previous day. Again, he used 10 p.m. as a reference point.

He stopped it when he thought he spotted Vachon and the minder exiting the café. They were alone, and the street was quiet.

They crossed the street. No vehicle approached them.

"Keep it running," Burke said.

Vachon and his minder got into a car and drove off. Then, a few seconds later, a black sedan slipped around the corner and followed.

"Did you see it?" Burke said.

"See what?" Antoine asked.

"The white blotch in the front of the car," Burke said. "That's twice."

Antoine rewound the video and then stopped it. "What the hell is it?" he said.

Burke was writing down dates in a notebook.

"What are you doing?" Antoine asked.

"Years ago, I had a directeur sportif who always used to tell us, 'The devil is in the details.' I think he might have been right," Burke said, snapping his notepad shut. He stood and stretched. "That's good, Antoine."

The big man pushed himself out of his chair. He looked tired. He also seemed perplexed.

"Did we learn something tonight?" he said. "I mean, beyond getting a sense that Vachon might have been stalked."

"I don't know yet," Burke said. "I have a couple of matters to explore."

He thanked Antoine and promised to keep him in the loop about what he did or learned in the next couple of days.

"But keep all this just between us, Antoine," Burke said as he walked into the balmy night air.

Antoine snorted. "I wouldn't tell anyone about this little game you and I are playing," he said. "It's more than a little dangerous."

He shut the door.

Burke took a deep breath. Antoine was wrong. They weren't playing any game. They were investigating murder.

CHAPTER 46

THE ALARM WENT OFF at 7 a.m. Burke groaned. He hadn't been able to fall asleep until almost three, his brain overloaded by the images he and Antoine had spent the evening researching. The late-night coffee didn't help either.

Burke struggled into the kitchen and turned on his coffee machine. He'd need caffeine to keep awake. He turned on the TV to watch the morning current affairs program. A few minutes into the program, he found himself studying an interview with the new head of FP Developments—a husky, moon-faced man around forty-five who was loaded with heartfelt comments about the late, much-missed Yves Vachon. Maintaining a serious demeanor but adding a few smiles, he launched into the corporation's plans for the future and overwhelmed the interviewer with polished charm. After the interview, a business analyst told the program host how the new CEO was performing so well that share prices were rising.

After two cups of coffee, Burke walked down to Jean's newsagent's shop to pick up a couple of papers and maybe have a chat. When he got there, Jean was in conversation with a neighbor of Madame Marois—a retired government bureaucrat who was always eager to share his views.

"Bonjour, Jean. Bonjour, Monsieur Picard," Burke said, adding a smile.

He shook hands with the two men.

Jean explained they'd been talking about the new developments west of the village.

"Monsieur Picard believes no amount of protest will stop the new resorts from being built," Jean said. "He said it's a *fait accompli*."

When Burke turned to look at Monsieur Picard, Jean eased away, leaving Burke to handle the listening duties while he attended to other chores.

Picard didn't need coaxing and immediately launched into a monologue about the onslaught of resort developments not just in their area but around the country. He wasn't entirely opposed though, managing to say the new developments would increase the tax base for communities, which, in turn, would allow for more government projects.

It took a few minutes before Burke was able to gently turn the direction of the conversation.

"With all this new development, I expect noise pollution will become a greater issue," Burke said.

"It already is becoming a problem," Picard replied.

Before the older man could get going, Burke said, "We're lucky to live in this quiet little village. Hardly any noise."

"True," Picard said, nodding, "but we are getting noisier. Those machines paving the new bike path can disturb a man's lunch. And then there are neighbors who can no longer control their dogs."

Picard had arrived at Burke's goal.

"What do you mean?" Burke asked, hoping he wouldn't sound too eager.

"My neighbor, Madame Marois, has a little dog who is normally very quiet, day or night, but he was howling one night this past week. It's annoying when you're getting ready for bed."

"Did you talk to Madame Marois?"

"I did, but she was quite difficult," Picard said, frowning. "She said her dog doesn't howl, but when I told her that he had and when, she said she couldn't believe it. She said she'd left home for a few minutes to run an errand and Plato would have slept while she was away. Then she turned and walked away. I felt quite foolish."

"Did any other neighbors hear the dog?"

"Yes, Madame Lecocq told me yesterday she'd heard the dog howling on the same day," Picard said. "She lives a little farther from Madame Marois, but she had her windows open and was reading when Plato howled so she heard it clearly enough."

"Did she complain to Madame Marois?"

"She said she asked Madame Marois about the dog, hoping he wasn't hurt or ill. Madame Marois said her dog was in perfect health and that there was no need for people to worry about him. Then Madame Marois left. Madame Lecocq said she seemed annoyed."

Puzzled by Madame Marois's behavior, Burke figured it was time to wind up the conversation. Five minutes later, he escaped with his newspapers and a sympathetic nod to Jean, who was being approached by Monsieur Picard, likely with more views to share.

As Burke walked back to his apartment, his phone rang. It was Jean-Pierre Fortin. The detective said he was nearby and wanted to talk with Burke. It was an order and not a request.

"I'll be over in ten minutes," Fortin said and then rang off.

The detective was again true to his word, showing up at Burke's door—with Côté beside him—in precisely ten minutes.

"Your comments yesterday about the murder weapon used to kill Den Weent were a little strange," Fortin said, standing in the living room. "We were in a rush, but now I want to pursue the matter a little more. What did you mean?"

Burke shrugged. "I was just thinking out loud," he said.

"No, you weren't," Fortin said. "You were fishing."

"What do you mean?"

"Tell us what you know or think. No more games."

Burke looked from Fortin to Côté and back. They were both leaning toward him.

"Did you find out where Karin Petit was when Den Weent was killed?" Burke asked.

"She wasn't at work," Fortin said.

"Where was she?"

Fortin's aggressive posture eased. Then he smiled, almost coyly.

"You have an idea," Fortin said. "You tell us."

Burke glanced at Côté; she resembled a pit bull ready to be unleashed.

"I don't know, but I'd be curious to learn if she was in the area where Den Weent was when he died," Burke said.

Fortin nodded. "When you talked with Karin Petit, I think you saw something in her, something that made you wonder if she had somehow been involved."

"Her hand," Burke said.

"Please explain what you mean," Fortin said.

Burke described Karin Petit's bandaged wound in the palm of her right hand, as well as the couple of nicks he'd noticed—one at the base of the index finger and the other on the thumb. Since she was an experienced gardener, it seemed odd that she would hurt herself doing a job she'd done thousands of times before.

"I think she hurt her hand doing something other than her job," Burke said.

"How do you think she got hurt?" Fortin asked.

"Using a knife, but in a different way from what she does at work."

"Explain your thinking," Fortin said.

It would sound foolish, but Burke went ahead, mentioning the TV detective show in which one of the investigators mentioned how a knife-wielding killer often nicks their own hand when stabbing someone.

"Yes, the power of television," Fortin said. "I understand those CSI shows are very popular in North America. I've seen some dubbed episodes on our TV, and they make some fundamental errors from time to time, but that investigator was correct about knife wounds on the person doing the stabbing."

Burke nodded and kept quiet. Fortin seemed to have a plan for their conversation.

"After our little talk yesterday, we went and did some further checking and learned that Karin was indeed in Carpentras on the day Den Weent was killed," Fortin said.

Burke wondered how Fortin found that information, and he was puzzled why Fortin was telling him, an ex-pro cyclist who did a blog for a small newspaper operation.

"I can see you are wondering why we're talking to you about this," Fortin said. "You could say I'm repaying a debt. Some of your questions prompted us to go beyond what we were looking at, to the point where we got a result."

"So did Karin kill Den Weent?" Burke asked.

"Patience, Monsieur Burke," Fortin said. "I will get there. You deserve to know the latest information before it's released, and as a blogger, you may want to use it ahead of your competition."

Fortin looked at his watch.

"However," he said, "you'll have only one hour to post something since we'll be having a news conference in one hour to announce the latest development in the Den Weent case."

"Which is that Karin Petit killed Den Weent," Burke said.

"No, you're wrong," Fortin said.

"Karin Petit did not kill Mark Den Weent," interjected Côté.

"So who did?" Burke asked.

"Léon Petit did," Fortin said.

Burke felt lost. Fortin was telling him there was a new development in Den Weent's case, and yet the flic was saying Léon had murdered Den Weent, just as the bike mechanic had confessed he had. What the hell was new?

"It's a little difficult to follow," Fortin said. He checked his watch once more. "Less than one hour before the news conference—fifty-five minutes to be precise."

Burke didn't care about the soon-to-be-breaking news. He just wanted to understand what had happened with Den Weent.

"We're keeping the charges of double murder against Léon Petit," Fortin said, and then he paused for dramatic effect. "And we're adding an attempted murder charge against Karin Petit, plus a couple of other charges."

Then Burke saw what had happened.

"Do you have it?" Fortin asked.

"Karin Petit tried to kill Den Weent for some reason…" Burke began.

"Because Léon told her that Den Weent had noticed some unusual drugs in a corner of his tool chest and had started to develop suspicions about Léon's involvement with Pierre McManus's death," Fortin added. "He told his mother the drugs were what he'd used to stop McManus's heart so suddenly and what would link him to a murder charge."

"And since Karin Petit was very protective of her son, she believed she had to do something to get Den Weent off the track," Burke said.

"Correct," Fortin said. "She went to Carpentras and met with Den Weent."

"How did she get him into the alley?" Burke asked.

"Karin Petit told us that she—"

"She confessed?" Burke blurted.

Fortin checked his watch once more. Burke felt ready to explode.

"Interruptions will delay you in getting your blog out," Fortin said. "Karin Petit did confess for reasons I'll explain later, if you'll allow me to continue."

"OK, just tell me," Burke said, almost pleading.

"Karin Petit told us she phoned Den Weent from one of the few public phones still in Carpentras and asked to meet him outside the hotel, away from anyone. For some reason, he went along with it. In the alley, she told him her son was innocent and if Den Weent persisted with his little investigation, Léon could lose his job. Den Weent said he still had questions. They argued. When he was about to leave, she pulled out a knife—one she used for her job—and stabbed him."

"But she didn't kill him," Burke said, the scene playing out in his mind.

"No, she didn't," Fortin said, this time not admonishing Burke for the interruption. "She didn't know how difficult it can be to kill someone with a knife. It takes a good degree of strength, which Karin Petit clearly has from her job, but it also requires good aim. You need to hit the right spots. She hurt Den Weent badly, but he was in excellent shape and started to fight her off. That's when Léon showed up."

"Where had he been?" Burke asked.

"Léon was staying in the same hotel with the team and was desperately looking for a chance to get Den Weent alone to talk to him. When he saw Den Weent go out late that evening, he followed. He saw Den Weent meet a woman in the darkened alley, heard the voice and recognized it was his mother. When she stabbed Den Weent, he ran toward them. He got there just as Den Weent was starting to get the upper hand, even though he was badly hurt."

"And Léon took over, finishing off Den Weent," Burke said.

"That's right," Fortin said. "Léon had the element of surprise and that little extra strength to kill Den Weent."

Burke thought about the nicks he'd seen on Léon's hands. He had been puzzled to see the hands of a gifted mechanic damaged in such a way. Now he knew why. And why Karin Petit had similar injuries.

"But why did you go looking into Karin's whereabouts?" Burke asked.

"Because of your question to us yesterday, Monsieur Burke," Fortin said. "I have learned that you sometimes have something useful to say."

Burke was surprised to hear that.

"Once we considered her as someone involved in the case, we tracked her banking and credit card activity for the period and discovered she had taken out money in Carpentras just a few hours after Den Weent was murdered," Fortin said.

"Then we traced her purchases to a nearby women's clothing store," Côté said. "Basic police work."

"She had come just for the day, driving up on her own, and she expected she'd be going home the same day," Fortin said. "She hadn't planned to end up covered in blood and needing a new top."

"But she had brought a knife," Burke said. "Doesn't that mean she thought about using it? So, if she was thinking about killing Den Weent, why wouldn't she bring different clothes to change into, at least to avoid anyone noticing her?"

Fortin shook his head. "She had only thought through the part about protecting her son. Karin Petit is not a criminal, probably not even that bright. She just brought a knife in case. That's it."

"After they killed Den Weent, Karin and Léon figured it was safer for her to use her credit card than for him," Côté said. "It might have been, but it didn't matter. We interviewed her, did some DNA testing and discovered Mark Den Weent's blood on her body. She thought she had washed off everything, but she hadn't. It's a tough task to eliminate all DNA residue."

Fortin took over. "When we had that, she confessed, saying she had killed Den Weent all by herself and that Léon had taken the opportunity to save her."

Burke was puzzled once more. "But you had Léon for the McManus murder," he said. "Why would she confess to the Den Weent murder?"

"She wanted to protect him from a double murder conviction, which she thought would guarantee him an even worse situation in prison," Fortin said. "But when Léon heard his mother had confessed to murdering Den Weent, he told us what really happened—to save her from a murder conviction."

"A mother's love and a son's love," Burke said, feeling some sadness for the plight of the two Petits. Then he thought about his friend Mark Den Weent and brushed aside any sympathy for Léon and Karin Petit. "And thanks to them, there are two dead people, one of them a good man."

"Indeed," Fortin said. "Now you have the story, although the news conference will convey most of that information in"—he glanced at his watch—"forty minutes."

Fortin stood and headed toward the door, Côté on his heels.

"Better get to writing your blog," Fortin said. "And by the way, this will only ever happen once."

Then they were gone.

CHAPTER 47

BURKE SAT THERE, TRYING to digest what he had heard. Fortin and Côté had confirmed some of his suspicions and filled in some gaps.

He shook his head at the tragedy of what had occurred and then picked up his cell phone. He called François Lemaire. It took just one ring before the newsman answered.

"I've got an update on the murders of Pierre McManus and Mark Den Weent," Burke said.

"What do you mean?" Lemaire asked.

Burke told him about the visit from Fortin and Côté, and added there would be a news conference about the charges now facing Karin Petit. There was a pause at the other end of Burke's phone. Lemaire was obviously sorting out what to do.

"OK, you'll give me all the basic facts that the flics and the prosecutor or investigating judge will provide at the news conference," Lemaire said. "After that, I'll write something quickly and post it on our website, with your byline."

"It's not necessary to add my name," Burke said.

"It is. You're the contact, and you're the one who deserves the credit," Lemaire said. "Next, I want you to do a background blog on this within the next hour. Three hundred words. Tell people what you did, what you think about it all. Then do a video version within a half hour of that."

"But..." began Burke, about to say he wasn't sure he could handle such efforts—or even wanted to.

"You can do it," Lemaire snapped. "Now, give me the basics."

Burke expanded on his initial comments to Lemaire. He could hear the editor punching a keyboard as he related how new DNA testing and other police work had brought Karin Petit into the picture.

More than once, Lemaire exclaimed, "Shit!"

"Good work, Paul," Lemaire said when Burke had finished. "I can polish this and get it online in ten minutes. I'll also use social media to let the world know what to expect."

Burke said nothing.

"OK, quit sitting around and get to work on those blogs," Lemaire said. "I want them fast. Don't worry about the news conference; I'll get someone to cover it." Then he added in a more subdued tone, "I expect we'll have to increase your payment for your blogs after this. I shouldn't have any issue with senior management. You're about to boost our visibility."

Lemaire rang off.

Burke went to his computer. He'd have to work fast, but he didn't know if he could. His stomach flip-flopped. He wasn't any kind of journalist, and he didn't want to be one, especially when they had to write under such deadline pressure.

But to his astonishment, the words came out quickly, although he had no clue if they were any good. He recycled his "a mother's love and a son's love" and tied it to how such devotion can lead people to perform terrible deeds. He doubted he was saying anything original, but it felt right to focus on how Léon and Karin Petit had been very regular people until a few comments triggered a series of deadly actions. He figured Lemaire would clean up any legal issues in the copy.

Burke was done within forty-five minutes. After sending it to Lemaire, he got to work on the video version. He had a rudimentary script—he doubted he'd be able to do anything better with the time restriction—and then grabbed his camera, figuring that shooting the video blog in the village green would work well as long as there weren't many people around making noise.

And there weren't—just two maintenance workers pruning bushes.

It took ten minutes to get an acceptable video blog done.

As he started to head back home to upload the video, he felt something by his feet.

It was Plato sniffing where he had walked. Holding the dog on his leash was Madame Marois, dressed, as usual, in black.

"He is definitely fond of you," Madame told Burke as he bent and scratched the dog's head.

"I like him, too. How's he doing? I heard he was upset the other night and was howling."

Madame frowned and snapped, "Nonsense. He didn't howl. He's as quiet as a mouse. That was just the active imagination of some of my silly neighbors." She paused then said in a calmer voice, "So, you were doing another one of your—what do you call them? Video blogs?"

"I was," Burke said. "Now I have to get it to my boss as quickly as possible."

"You have an unusual job, young man," the old woman said.

That made Burke pause for a moment. "I guess I do," he said. "Excuse me, but I do need to rush this off to my employer."

"I expect you don't have much time to go cycling," Madame said.

"Well, I think I can manage a ride right after I get this video to my boss," he said. "It's a perfect day to go out on the bike."

"Good for you, young man," Madame Marois said.

Burke excused himself, jogging up the stone stairs of the pathway and around the corner to his apartment. Fifteen minutes later, he was relaxing on the couch, his video blog now with Lemaire. It had been a hectic two hours, and he was tired. Maybe a bike ride wasn't a good idea.

He was just starting to nod off when his cell phone rang. It was Helénè, wondering if they could get together for a glass of wine in midafternoon before she started work at the café.

Burke readily agreed. He hadn't seen as much of her the last couple of days as he would have liked.

They decided she'd come to his place around three.

"But I won't have time for anything more than a little wine," Helénè said.

Burke laughed. He would like to get her into bed, but he was happy just to spend a little time with her. Maybe when they both had settled on routines, they could manage more time together.

The phone call had energized Burke, and he decided he'd go for a bike ride after all. It would be good to work on his fitness, and some hard exercise would clear his mind of the morning's developments.

He was munching on a pre-ride sandwich when his cell phone rang once more. It was Lemaire.

"One of these days, I'll get Antoine to show you how to do a better job of lighting, but overall, you did well," Lemaire said. "It's online already, if you want to check it out."

Burke didn't, but he didn't say that to the newsman.

"Anyway, it would be wise to do another blog for tomorrow," Lemaire said. "I expect there'll be a lot of noise in the media after Karin Petit's arrest."

Burke agreed to Lemaire's suggestion, and they rang off. He'd do the blog either before Hélène showed up or early the next morning.

He definitely needed a ride to freshen his mind. For a moment, Burke thought about going to the news conference, but he figured he wouldn't learn anything new, and besides, Lemaire had a staffer to cover it.

Ten minutes later, he was walking his bike down the pathway. The sky was cloudless, and the temperature was at least thirty degrees Celsius. As he strolled past the lovely stone buildings with their outdoor flowerpots crammed with vivid colors, Burke could hear songbirds, plus some voices from a couple of nearby cafés, including Hélène's. He smiled, his desire to stay in the old village of Villeneuve-Loubet never a doubt.

When Burke jumped onto his bike, he opted to do some climbing, and so he turned right and started on the long hill that would ultimately lead him to Grasse. It would be fun. And a perfect escape.

CHAPTER 48

AFTER THE INTENSE INTERVIEW with Fortin and Côté, and the time-pressured blogs for Lemaire, Burke was surprised he had, in cycling parlance, "good legs" as he hammered the pedals for the first couple of kilometers. The sense of strength could quickly disappear, but until then, he made the most of it and kept the power on.

He passed a handful of other riders, a couple of whom praised him for his efforts as he shot by. The compliments felt good. Bit by bit, Burke knew he was getting fitter. Maybe he'd go into some veterans races if circumstances allowed.

When he saw a side road that would lead him away from Grasse and into the hilltop villages farther north, Burke took it on a whim. The first village was at least another ten kilometers, but he expected his legs could handle the challenge.

And they did. Feeling strong, he rode past the first village and then past the second, pushing higher as the scenery grew more rugged with craggy hills that climbed and climbed. Behind him, the communities along the coast got smaller and smaller.

After forty kilometers of nonstop climbing, Burke stopped by the roadside, gasping for breath and sweating profusely but happy with his efforts. There might be prettier views in France, but Burke struggled to believe it. It seemed he could see all of the Côte d'Azur stretched out far below him. This was one reason he wanted to stay in the area, regardless of what happened to taxes. Hélène, though, was rapidly becoming the real attraction to remaining.

To the north were steeper hills. Stone farmhouses were scattered along the distant slopes. The people who carved out a living up this high were tough indeed. Much tougher than a pro cyclist and definitely sturdier than a blogger.

Burke relished that his mind had largely cleared away all thoughts of the Petits, Fortin, Côté, Lemaire and everyone else who had burrowed into his brain in recent days. All he had thought about on the way up was working on a good cadence and enjoying the spectacular scenery. Cycling could do that—take you away from your worries and into a different place.

Burke decided to do one more hill. He didn't have to worry about time since the descent would be fast—maybe forty-five minutes at most, and that would leave plenty of time to clean up before Hélène arrived. And after all the wild traffic along the coast, it was a pleasure to ride along a road that had virtually no traffic; he hadn't seen a vehicle in twenty minutes.

He did the next hill in five minutes and then turned his bike around. He thought about detouring into one of the villages, but the thrill of the upcoming descent appealed far more.

With a gentle breeze behind him, Burke let his machine go, and soon, he was flying down the hill at sixty-five kilometers per hour. Always a good, fearless descender, he leaned into the twists and bends of the road with just the slightest touch on his brakes. He knew any car behind him would struggle to keep pace.

On one stretch, he hit eighty on his odometer. His heart pounded with excitement.

As he took another curve at maximum speed, Burke heard the engine of a car behind him. It must have come out of a country lane.

As usual, he let his ears tell him what was happening behind. He had long ago learned that if he listened well, he could judge the exact position of an approaching vehicle by sound, as well as the distance between them. He didn't need a mirror.

The road straightened, and Burke shot a glance over his shoulder as he heard the driver accelerate.

It was a black car, and it was coming quickly.

The road turned gently to the right, and Burke kept a tight line near the side of the road. He was doing eighty-five kilometers per hour.

The driver was getting closer, taking greater risks than even he was. It was time to let them pass. If another vehicle approached them at that moment, they'd all be in trouble, especially Burke.

He feathered the brakes, instantly dropping to sixty.

The vehicle was right behind him.

"What the…" Burke glanced once more over his shoulder.

He had only enough time to register that the car wasn't lined up to go around him. Instead, it was only a few meters directly behind him and getting even closer. The driver seemed intent on hitting him or driving him right off the road.

Burke yanked his handlebars to the right. It was his only chance.

His bike jerked off the road surface, and for a second, he was airborne, flying over grass and rocks and right toward a clutch of trees. When his bike touched the ground again, he had no control. The front wheel struck a large rock and crumpled on impact, stopping the machine and dislodging Burke like a human payload.

As he flew through the air, Burke knew he was going to die. This was his last millisecond on the planet.

He crashed into the widest part of a tree trunk, his left shoulder, hip and leg taking all the impact. Blinding-white pain shot through his body as he rolled along the gnarled surface of the small forest.

He came to a stop. Then he tried to move.

The world went dark and silent.

CHAPTER 49

BURKE HEARD A VOICE in the distance. It was a woman's, but he couldn't understand the words.

He opened his eyes with some effort, but he could only see shapes and bright lights. He couldn't focus. When he tried to lift his head, little stars exploded in his vision.

Burke retreated into unconsciousness.

When he heard another voice, he wondered how long it had been since he'd heard the first voice.

This voice was a man's, but again, he couldn't make out what was being said.

He tried opening his eyes again. Everything was still fuzzy and bright. He remembered to avoid lifting his head.

He tried to say something, but his mouth didn't work. He couldn't produce a sound. His lips were gummy, and his tongue was limp. He shut his eyes and told himself to get control. He needed to know where he was and what had happened.

Then he remembered flying through the air and hitting something hard. He recalled feeling pain that overwhelmed him and took him far away.

"Monsieur Burke," came a soft voice.

Burke opened his eyes. A man's fuzzy face leaned toward him. The face had a moustache, dark eyebrows.

Burke tried to answer, but still, he couldn't make a sound.

"Do not try to speak, monsieur," the man said with a voice that was deep and warm and somehow reassuring to Burke.

Burke shut his eyes. The simple effort of trying to communicate with this person had exhausted him.

"You're in a hospital, Monsieur Burke," the voice said. "I'm Dr. Rossignol. You've had a terrible accident, but you're alive, and you'll get better."

Burke managed a single nod.

"Good, you understand me," Rossignol said. "Right now, you're in a recovery room. We had to operate on you. I know you're very tired, so don't fight it. Go to sleep. I will see you again later."

Burke nodded again. An operation?

Then he drifted off.

When he awoke, he felt like he was floating, but he was able to focus better. He was in a different room. Not so many shapes or bright lights. He managed to turn his head slightly and saw a wall. By the wall was some machine that made odd humming and beeping sounds. He couldn't distinguish what it was.

He closed his eyes to focus his mind.

He remembered the doctor in the large room telling him he was in a hospital and had been operated on.

The doctor had told him he would live.

There were voices, this time farther away. Maybe from a nearby hallway. He couldn't understand the words. Too distant.

He dug into his brain. What had happened? He had been riding his bike. Hills, lots of hills. People telling him he was fast and strong. Distant villages, stone farmhouses.

A speeding car behind him.

A car that meant to hit him.

To kill him.

Then the tree, the crash, the pain, the darkness.

Burke could remember. He felt fortunate. Next, he wanted to see if he could talk.

His tongue was still thick, but Burke, with a steely effort, managed to mutter, "Bonjour," although he sensed he was alone in the room. It was enough to know he could speak. His brain, while still groggy, seemed to be working.

Next, it was time to take inventory of his body.

He lifted his head a centimeter or two and instantly felt a jab of pain in his torso. He slumped back again. He rolled his head slightly and saw his left shoulder and arm were wrapped up and stabilized in some kind of contraption.

He wondered about his legs. He told himself to wiggle his toes. He felt them move. *Bloody good*, he thought. Not paralyzed.

But something was wrong. There was some kind of packing against his left leg, right up to the hip. There was also some kind of contraption at the end of the bed. His eyesight was still blurry, and he couldn't identify much beyond a meter or two.

Exhausted from this brief self-assessment, Burke closed his eyes again. He was thankful to be alive. He remembered the moment just before he collided with the tree. He had expected to die.

"Monsieur Burke, I see you're awake," came a new voice.

Burke fought off sleep and looked up to see the face of a pretty young woman bending over him. He gave her a weak smile.

"That's good, that's very good, Monsieur Burke," she said. "I'm Nurse Peplinski, and I'll be looking after you tonight. I'm going to put a small control panel in your right hand. If you need me, you just push this button."

She showed him a small remote connected to a cable, identified the button and then placed it into his right hand.

"You have some very bad injuries, and you need to stay still," she said, gently rubbing his right forearm. "Your surgery went well. You just have to rest and get your strength back. If you feel too much pain, just push that remote. I will be in and out to check your vitals. Now, get some sleep."

Before she was out of the room, Burke was asleep—and dreaming about birds and gardens and the sea.

CHAPTER 50

WHEN BURKE AWOKE AGAIN, he felt slightly more alert. His eyes took less time to focus, and his brain didn't struggle as much to establish his whereabouts.

"I'm here, *chéri*," said a soothing voice at his side.

There was a welcome familiarity to it. He rolled his head toward the sound.

Hélène. Yes, it was Hélène.

Even though she was smiling, tears slipped down her cheeks.

"I'm here, *chéri*, I'm here," she whispered into his ear. "You're safe, and you will get better."

Burke smiled at Hélène and teared up as well. She was the person he most wanted to see. The world wasn't so bad. She could rescue him.

"I love you," she said.

"I love you," Burke mumbled.

"OK, that's enough," said another voice.

It, too, was familiar. A figure stepped closer—a man. André Rousseau. Burke's friend wore a strained smile, and he wondered just how bad he must look.

"You scared the shit out of all of us with this accident," Rousseau said.

Burke smiled back and then closed his eyes to concentrate. Had it been an accident? Had he screwed up on a ride? Then, in a rapid-fire series of flashbacks, he remembered the black car and having to ride off the road to avoid being run down. Then the crash into the tree. And then the waves of pain. Crushing, unbearable pain.

"No accident," he said, opening his eyes and looking at Rousseau.

Rousseau's eyebrows shot up. Hélène looked equally surprised.

"No accident," Burke repeated, feeling more tired by the second. His reserves were low, and this minor interaction was depleting them. "A car tried to run me over."

"Really? We all thought it was an accident," Rousseau said. "Are you sure? I mean, you've been badly hurt."

Burke nodded. "It's true. I don't remember much after, but that driver tried to kill me."

"Maybe the driver wasn't paying attention," Rousseau said.

Burke's mind filled with the last moments before he hit the tree.

"No accident," he repeated.

"Did you see who was driving?" Rousseau asked, sounding like he was beginning to believe Burke.

Once more, Burke replayed the incident.

"No, I couldn't see the face," he said.

Hélène held up a hand to Rousseau. "Paul's exhausted, André," she said. "He'll tell us later what he remembers."

"But the police..." Rousseau said.

"Later," Hélène said.

André nodded. He smiled at Burke and then said, "While you've been away—so to speak—hardly anything has happened, except Léon Petit and his mother are in jail and supposedly have pled guilty, him to murder and manslaughter and her to attempted murder. Lots of stuff about it on the TV and in the papers."

Burke recalled talking to Fortin and Côté the same day of his accident. And doing blogs for François Lemaire. And then he'd finished his work and gone for a ride.

"How long have I been unconscious?" he asked.

"The accident was Wednesday, and this is Saturday," Hélène said. "The doctor and nurses said you were awake for a couple of minutes the other day, before the surgery. Do you remember that?"

Burke shut his eyes and shook his head.

"*Chéri*, we've tired you out," Hélène said. "You need to sleep now."

With his eyes closed, Burke nodded. Just before he gave himself over to the overwhelming need to drift away, he heard Rousseau tell Hélène, "We have to talk to the police about what happened."

Then Burke returned to his dark world.

CHAPTER 51

WHEN BURKE OPENED HIS eyes, he looked about his room. He was alone. Had Hélène and André really been there? Had it all been a dream? He recalled their faces and what they had talked about. And he remembered how Hélène had cried and said she loved him. And how he had said he loved her.

But how long ago was that? The room seemed darker. Maybe it was night. Maybe it was a totally different day.

He tried to move, but a bolt of pain shot up his left side, and he froze. It took a half minute before he was relaxed again.

He lay there, his eyes taking in the machines beside him, the two chairs at the end of the bed, the TV to the side and the half-closed curtain.

Burke figured he was going to be in the hospital for a long time.

"I see you're awake, Monsieur Burke," came a voice from the door.

Burke focused and found a face that seemed slightly familiar. He thought he should know her name, but he couldn't find it. He shook his head. He knew the drugs were helping him handle the pain, but they were also preventing him from grasping a full thought.

"I'm Nurse Peplinski," she said with a smile. "We met last night, but I think you probably don't remember."

"Sorry," Burke said.

She took his pulse and blood pressure, and then examined the plastic bags hooked up to the machines. As she did, she told him about the remote control he could use to summon her.

"Is it night?" he asked.

"Yes, it's almost nine o'clock," she said.

"What day?"

"Sunday," she told him.

"How badly am I hurt?" Burke asked.

Nurse Peplinski looked around. Behind her appeared a man—tall, thin, a stethoscope around his checkered shirt. She introduced him as one of Burke's doctors, providing his name, though Burke instantly forgot it.

With Nurse Peplinski at his side, the doctor checked the information on a chart. Then he pulled up a chair.

"You're more alert than last time," he said.

Burke couldn't recall meeting this man "last time."

"First, I want to assure you that your surgery went well, and we expect you to make a good recovery," the doctor said. "But your injuries are extensive and serious, and it will take time to recuperate. I expect you will be with us for a while."

Burke prepared himself.

The doctor listed the injuries almost like reading a grocery list: a broken collarbone, a separated shoulder, two broken ribs, a badly bruised sternum, a broken hip and a broken femur.

"Damn," Burke said.

"Indeed, it's a long list," the doctor said. "The worst were the hip and femur. We had to put in some rods to keep the leg in place. The shoulder is back in place, and the sternum should heal quite quickly. As for the other broken bones, they were not as severely damaged as the hip and femur. Unfortunately, given that your entire left side has been essentially incapacitated, you will not be moving much at all for several weeks."

Burke couldn't believe how badly injured he was. He had suffered broken bones during his racing career, but nothing like this. Still, he was alive, and that's what counted. It could have been much worse.

"An average person would not have survived such damage, but you have," the doctor said. "I think your past as a professional cyclist gave you the strength and determination to get through. You'll need it in the future, but I expect you're a strong individual and will manage."

He explained how the medical staff would use drugs to ease the pain but wanted to keep the dosages away from becoming addictive. There would be discomfort, but he expected Burke could handle it. "Mild therapy" would begin in a day or two. Later, once Burke's bones were relatively healed, more extensive therapy would take place.

Then there was a knock on the door. The doctor added that he or another doctor would be back in a few hours to see how Burke was coping. Then he stood and left, nodding at the two people by the door.

Fortin and Côté.

CHAPTER 52

AFTER A QUICK WORD with Nurse Peplinski, Fortin and Côté approached Burke's bed. Burke noticed how they scanned his injuries, exchanged raised eyebrows and then turned their focus on him.

"You're a mess, Monsieur Burke," Fortin said. "It seems you've broken most of your body, but we understand you will recover, given time."

Burke managed a small smile.

"However, we're not here for a social call," Fortin said. "It has come to our attention you are claiming someone deliberately ran you off the road."

Burke nodded, thinking Rousseau had likely contacted the police.

"Normally, this matter would go to someone else, but since we've been dealing with you on a couple of other matters and heard you were the cyclist who smashed into a tree, we thought we should talk to you," Fortin said.

Burke wished Fortin would get to his questions; following long explanations was tiring.

"I understand you did not recognize the driver," Fortin said.

So, Rousseau had passed on the gist of Burke's few comments about the accident.

"No time to see a face," Burke said.

"And the license plate?" Côté said.

Burke shook his head.

"Tell us everything you can remember," Fortin said, sitting down in one of the chairs. As usual, Côté remained standing, her notebook in hand.

In halting sentences, Burke gave them a rundown of his route, how he had seen virtually no traffic until he heard a car come out of a country lane on the descent, and how he had sped downhill but found the car accelerating until, finally, he had to ride off the road to avoid getting run down.

"Is it possible the driver misjudged a turn and accidently got too close?" Fortin asked.

Burke replayed the last few seconds before the crash. The memory was surprisingly fresh, right up to his crash into the tree.

"The driver was in control of the car," he told the two detectives. "I have no doubts about that."

"And you didn't spot the vehicle before?" Côté asked.

Burke shook his head.

Nurse Peplinski came over and studied Burke's face.

"Are you getting too tired, Monsieur Burke?" she said.

Burke liked her. He had heard complaints from some people that the new generation of French nurses tended to be cold and distracted. Nurse Peplinski was the opposite.

"I'm fine," he said.

"We won't take too much more time," Fortin told her.

Then he switched his attention back to Burke and asked him about the last few seconds before the crash. How fast had Burke been going? Had Burke hit any gravel or other debris on the edge of the road? Had the driver honked his horn? Had there been any oncoming traffic? Which direction was the sun shining from?

Burke sensed the two detectives believed his claim. They just had to ask all the appropriate questions. He managed to provide the answers.

Burke had a question of his own.

"Who found me?"

"A truck driver noticed the sun reflecting off something metal by the roadside and then spotted a damaged bike leaning against a large rock not far from the road," Fortin said. "He stopped and found you a few meters away. He checked to see if you were still alive, and then he called it in. I understand that if you had lain there much longer, you could have been in real trouble. You're lucky that driver spotted your bicycle and that he stopped."

Burke didn't remember anything involving the driver or the ambulance or even the next two days, but he felt fortunate to be still around. If the sun hadn't reflected off his bike at that moment, he might not have been found for hours or even days—and that would have been the end of his story.

"I owe him a beer," Burke said.

"I would say you owe him several beers, monsieur," Fortin said.

With a quick nod to Nurse Peplinski that suggested he was almost done, Fortin asked if Burke had recognized the car.

"No, I didn't get much chance to look at it," Burke said. "It was black or maybe a dark blue. A sedan. Dirty in the front."

"Dirty?" Côté said.

"It had mud on the grill," he replied.

"And on the license plate?" Côte said. "Is that why you didn't notice any numbers?"

Burke closed his eyes and dug once more into his memory. It took a couple of moments before he returned to that near-fateful scene and the split second when he had glanced down at the front of the advancing car.

"Yes, a license plate where the numbers weren't visible, like they'd been blacked out," he said, surprised he had noticed it, but sure about what he had seen.

Just like the license plate of the car that he and Antoine had seen run over Yves Vachon and his minder.

A dark sedan. Maybe black or deep blue.

"Damn!" he muttered.

CHAPTER 53

FOR ALL HIS EXHAUSTION, Burke was alert.

"Monsieur Burke, do you remember something?" Fortin asked, leaning closer.

Clearly, Fortin had caught him recalling something important, and he knew the detective well enough to know he wouldn't be put off.

"Maybe," Burke said, stalling while trying to consider what to say next. He didn't want to admit to hacking into the city's network, and he definitely didn't want to repay Antoine's assistance by landing him in jail.

"The faster we act, the better our chance of identifying the person who was driving that car," Fortin said. "It's already getting late in the case."

Burke nodded but said nothing.

"Monsieur, I believe you're stalling," Fortin said. "I don't know why, but you need to answer the question."

Nurse Peplinski jumped in, saying, "Please, Monsieur Burke is very tired. We must be careful."

"I understand, Nurse, but this is crucial," Fortin said. He looked back at Burke with a frown. "What do you remember?"

Burke took a big breath, winced in pain and began.

"I remember the way the license plate was covered up, the style of the car and the car's color, and I believe I've seen that vehicle before."

"Where did you see it before?" Fortin said.

"I think maybe you've seen the same car, too, Inspector," Burke said, half expecting to surprise Fortin.

But Fortin's gaze never wavered, and Burke wondered if the flic was somehow ahead of him.

"Where would I have seen it?" Fortin asked quietly.

"I think it might have been the car that ran over Yves Vachon and his minder," Burke said.

"How do you know about that car?"

"I heard a general description in the news," said Burke, hoping that would satisfy the detective.

"Your description is more detailed than what was provided to the media," Fortin said. "So, how do you know about the covered-up license plate and style of car?"

Checkmate. He had nowhere to go—except to the truth, or his version of it anyway.

"I have my sources," Burke said.

"Not true," Fortin said. "I think you've seen the video of that hit-and-run that killed Vachon and his bodyguard. In fact, I think you know more than you've told me."

Burke was trapped. He also felt ready to slip into sleep. If he did, he could at least escape for a little while.

Nurse Peplinski started to walk over, but Fortin stopped her with a hand held out.

"Tell me," Fortin told Burke.

"You're right. I have seen the video," Burke said. "I won't tell you how. Call it protecting my source."

Fortin said nothing. For her part, Côté moved silently to Burke's bedside.

"When you looked at the footage, did you check the video from the same place on previous nights at about the same time?" Burke asked, his voice sounding weaker by the second.

Fortin nodded.

"Did you notice a small white blotch inside the car on a couple of evenings?"

"We did. Do you know what it was?" Fortin asked.

"I think I do," Burke said, almost ready to pass out.

"Monsieur..." came Nurse Peplinski's insistent voice.

"Tell me," Fortin said.

Eyes shut, Burke nodded once.

"I think it was a dog," he said.

And then he passed out.

CHAPTER 54

WHEN BURKE AWOKE, NURSE Peplinski was gone. So was Côté.

But Fortin was still there, slumped in one of the chairs and dozing. With his suit rumpled, he looked like he'd been there for a while.

Burke wondered how long he'd slept. He twisted his head to look at the clock on the far wall. It was almost seven. Since the room wasn't very dark, he figured it was morning. He thought it might be Monday.

As he readjusted slightly on the pillow, jolts of pain shot through his shoulder, hip and leg.

He fumbled for the remote and pushed the button. He hoped Nurse Peplinski or whoever might show up quickly. He didn't feel great.

"You're finally awake," Fortin said, rubbing his eyes.

Burke managed a nod.

"Do you remember what we were talking about before you fell asleep last night?"

Burke tried to assemble his memories of their previous conversation. It took a moment, and then he recalled where he'd left off.

He nodded.

"Why did you suggest it was a dog?" Fortin asked.

"Because I think I know the driver, and I know how her dog, who is small and white, usually stands against the dashboard when she's driving," Burke said.

The door opened, and Nurse Peplinski came in. She smiled wearily when she saw Burke awake. She asked what he needed.

Burke told her about the pain, and she made a couple of adjustments to one of the bags hooked up to his wrist.

"That should help you," she said. "If it gets worse, you know what to do. It'll be another nurse coming, though, since I'm done in a few minutes." She glanced at Fortin and then back to Burke. "Don't try to do too much," she warned him.

Burke nodded, thanked her and watched her leave.

"So who was the driver?" Fortin asked.

"One of my neighbors, Madame Marois," Burke said.

He knew he'd have to explain his reasons, and slowly, he began. As he spoke, Fortin took an occasional note.

"It's because of the dog, Plato, that I know about the car and Madame Marois," Burke said.

He thought that might confuse Fortin, but the detective's face showed nothing.

"I'm a dog person," Burke said. "I love dogs, grew up with them. If I hadn't been a pro cyclist and hadn't been forced to travel so much for work, I'd have had one."

"I have a dog," Fortin interjected.

Burke was surprised. Fortin didn't seem a dog person. He seemed more an anti-pet guy.

"The first few times I met Madame Marois, Plato greeted me with affection," Burke said. "He's an excellent dog—very smart, nice manners. He doesn't want to hump your leg or piss on your shoes. I think Madame Marois saw how much I liked him."

"And Madame is devoted to this Plato?" Fortin said.

"Totally. She told me once that he knew her moods better than anyone. If she was upset, he'd be upset. I never gave that any more thought because that's the way with a lot of dogs and their owners. Then, in recent days, Madame became agitated. She lost her keys, forgot other things and generally was in a very emotional state. I thought it was a case of an old woman starting to show her age. I felt sorry for her. And then just a short time ago, I remembered one thing—Plato had remained calm throughout all those occasions. That struck me as odd."

"That is interesting," Fortin said. "Like that Sherlock Holmes story about being aware of the dog that didn't bark."

Burke didn't have a clue about Sherlock Holmes and a dog.

"That told me," Burke carried on, "that if she was telling the truth about Plato reflecting her real moods, then she was acting on those occasions when she seemed upset, because Plato remained calm. And if that was the case, I asked myself why she would fake her emotions or mental state."

"If you're correct in your assumption, why do you think she did that, Monsieur Burke?" Fortin asked.

"Because I think she was planning to do something that, if caught, she could claim she was suffering from dementia and wasn't in total control of her mind," Burke said.

Fortin sat back, obviously digesting Burke's theory.

"That wouldn't be the first time someone has used a mental disorder as an excuse to kill someone," he said.

"Before the hit-and-run, she started to act scattered, and I think that's because she had this planned," Burke said. "After Vachon and his minder were killed, she kept it up, maybe even increased how often she seemed out of her mind."

"So she's very methodical, according to you," Fortin said.

"I believe Madame is a very calculating individual with a very long memory," Burke said.

"You're talking motive now," Fortin said.

"I think if you check into her past and Vachon's past, you'll see there is a crossover. They knew each other years ago from business, and it did not end well at all for Madame and her husband. I don't know the exact details, but I believe she blamed Vachon for a number of things. I think she held a grudge."

"I'll accept that for the moment. You talk about this Madame Marois as if she is elderly."

"She's in her eighties, I think," Burke said. The increase in pain medication was helping, but he felt a stab in his ribs once again. "But I think she has as much dementia as you or I have. I think it's all an act. That brings me to the howling Plato."

"The what?"

His mouth dry from all the talking, Burke gestured toward a cup of water with a straw in it. Fortin grabbed it and gently put the straw into Burke's mouth. A few sips later, Burke felt ready to continue.

"On the morning of my accident, I talked to one of Madame's neighbors, and he told me Plato had been howling one evening."

"And when exactly did Plato howl?" asked Fortin.

"I believe it was on the same evening when a certain black sedan struck and killed Yves Vachon and his bodyguard," Burke said.

Fortin nodded. "But what about the white blotch in the city's videos from the days before the hit-and-run?" he asked.

"She knew Vachon was a creature of habit because she knew him in the past. Plus, the newspapers always talked about how he was a person who liked order and discipline. She wanted to know where he ate and when. So, she followed him. She took Plato with her, and, as usual, he propped himself up against the dashboard. I've seen him do that. Once she established Vachon's routine, she left Plato back home and went out alone with the intention of running him over and killing him."

"But why leave Plato behind?"

"She didn't want him to get hurt if something went wrong," Burke said, hearing his words start to slur as the increased pain medication began to get a firm hold of him. "That dog is her life."

Fortin scribbled something in his notepad.

"And then there was Madame's accident the other day," Burke said.

"Accident?"

"She turned a corner in the village and crashed into a stone wall," Burke said. "She damaged the front right of the hood of her car."

"The same part of the car that would have struck Vachon and his man," Fortin said. "We naturally checked the body shops after the accident, but no car matching the description showed up anywhere."

"After Vachon's death, I think she put her car in the garage to hide the damage," Burke said. "I don't think anyone saw her drive during that period. Then she took it out and crashed it into a stone wall to disguise the real damage."

"And her car is a dark sedan," Fortin said.

"Four doors, black with the same grill as the car that drove me off the road," Burke said, feeling a powerful urge to sleep.

"Stay with me just a little longer, monsieur," Fortin urged. "So maybe it was the same car that tried to run you over on your ride in the hills. But why do you think she tried to run you over?"

"Before my accident, I mentioned to Madame Marois that a neighbor told me he'd heard Plato howling. I asked if Plato was OK. She said he hadn't howled and the neighbor was just being stupid. She was agitated and quickly switched the subject. A minute later, she left, but she still seemed bothered."

"By what?"

"Madame told me Plato didn't howl, but it was clear I didn't believe her and that made me a threat although I didn't recognize that at the time. She was worried I'd keep poking around and find out what she'd been up to on the night Plato howled. The person behind the deaths of Vachon and his minder wasn't Claude Brière or one of his friends. It was her."

Fortin rubbed his chin. He wrote a few words in his notebook and then shut it.

Burke had nothing left. He was mentally and physically exhausted. He closed his eyes.

"What did you mean about Sherlock Holmes and the dog that didn't bark?" he whispered, his eyes still shut, seconds from finding peace.

"It was in a Sherlock Holmes story," Fortin said. "Holmes was investigating a case and heard about a dog that didn't bark when it should have and that..."

Burke heard no more.

CHAPTER 55

FORTIN WAS GONE WHEN Burke awoke.

But Hélène was there, sitting at his bedside and smiling at him. She looked almost as tired as Burke felt. He sensed she was less worried than the last time he'd seen her.

She leaned over and kissed him gently on the lips. Then she told him it was early afternoon. She said the nurses had been in several times to check his vitals and had been pleased at the results.

"They say you're doing well," she said. "Or as well as could be expected."

Burke couldn't recall nurses poking and prodding him. His last memory was his conversation with Fortin.

He wondered what the flic was doing now.

Hélène had visited Claude that morning and mentioned he'd been in good spirits even though he would be spending the next half year in prison. Somehow, she said, his calm state of mind had been a relief. He would be facing tough times ahead, but he was ready for whatever came his way.

She also updated him on the Petits. The news was overflowing with the latest details, and some outlets, especially a couple of newspapers, had turned the story into something lurid and nasty. Still, people seemed fascinated by what they were hearing and reading.

Burke enjoyed hearing her voice. His energy was returning, bit by bit, but he felt no urge to do anything other than listen to Hélène chat about her uncle, the Petits and how her café was doing.

"Bonjour, Paul," came a familiar voice from the doorway.

It was Jean. Burke was surprised to see him, and even more surprised to see him holding a small vase containing yellow flowers.

"You're not looking so good, my friend," Jean said, putting the vase on Burke's small table and then standing by Hélène. "Maybe these flowers will brighten you up."

Burke thanked him for coming and waved him to sit down. The newsagent was happy to comply, all the time talking about how people in the village had heard about Burke's accident and were concerned for his well-being.

"Thank you," said Burke, who had thought the longtime villagers still considered him an outsider.

"And there has been some other activity in our village," Jean said.

Burke wondered if a cat had gone missing or someone's husband had been arrested for public drunkenness.

"The police were over at Madame Marois's house for a few hours today," Jean said. "There were police in uniform and two detectives—at least I think they were detectives."

"A tall, middle-aged man and a chunky woman who looks like she'd like to bite you?" asked Burke, fully alert now after Jean's news.

"That's them," Jean said, looking surprised at Burke's accurate description. "I watched for a little while. I think they were searching for something. Madame wasn't there, and so they talked to a couple of neighbors."

"About what?" Burke asked, figuring Jean would have chatted up the neighbors as soon as the police were gone.

"As strange as it sounds, they asked about Plato."

"Where was Madame?"

"No idea," Jean said. He studied Burke. "You don't seem too surprised by this news I have, Paul. What is it you know? You must tell me. After all, we often share information."

Usually their information was gossip, but Burke took Jean's point. Still, he didn't want to say what he knew or anticipated.

"Do you know if the police looked at Madame's car?" Burke asked.

Jean's eyes narrowed. "They did—for a long time," he said. "In fact, they brought a tow truck and took it away."

"The police?"

"Yes, the police," Jean said. "Why do you ask?"

"Madame might be in serious trouble, Jean," Burke said, glancing at Hélène, who was glued to the exchange.

"How?"

"I can only say what I have said," Burke said.

Jean snorted, clearly disappointed. He sold news, and he embraced news, and Burke wasn't giving him much about what was happening with one of the village's best-known residents. Burke wondered if Jean might leave and take the flowers back with him.

But then Jean smiled, surrendering to his usual bonhomie.

"I don't understand, but I accept it, Paul," Jean said. "But one day, you'll have to tell me what all this intrigue is about and how you're involved."

Burke had a feeling that Jean—and everyone else—might learn sooner than later, thanks to the media, but he didn't say that. Instead, he agreed to tell Jean a little story when the time was right.

Then a thought tickled his brain.

"You've lived in Villeneuve-Loubet most of your life, Jean," Burke said.

"That's right."

"You've known Madame Marois for many years then," Burke said.

"I know her, but I wouldn't say I know her well at all. In fact, I don't think anyone in the village knows her well."

"Have you seen her drive often?" Burke asked, knowing the question would probably seem odd to the newsagent.

Jean's frown indicated he was indeed surprised by the question. He shrugged. "I've seen her drive into and out of the village many, many times," he said. "On occasion, I've seen her driving in Nice and Antibes."

"Is she a good driver?" Burke asked. "And forget about that small accident she had the other day with the stone wall."

Jean still looked puzzled but went along. "I'd say she is a competent driver, as long as the traffic is not heavy. But I wouldn't like to be a passenger when she drives on a highway. I think she's a little nervous, a little unsteady."

"Has she been that way just recently or for a long time?"

"For the last decade or so," Jean said.

Burke's brain was functioning better each day, but he still didn't have the physical stamina to think too hard for too long. Whatever reserves he had, he needed them to heal his injuries and fight the pain that threatened to explode at any time. He had to think fast before his will diminished.

They chatted for a few more minutes about other matters, and then Jean, likely noticing Burke starting to fade, left.

"What was all that about, *chéri*?" Hélène asked when they were alone.

"I've relived the accident in my dreams the last day or so and something just occurred to me," Burke said.

"What?"

"That Madame Marois isn't as good a driver as I thought she was."

That made little sense to Hélène, he knew, but he didn't have the strength to elaborate.

As Hélène told him about her chef's new recipe that she was going to feature that night at her café, Burke's mind drifted to Madame Marois and her car.

Was he wrong about everything he had told Fortin and Côté? Had it been someone else studying Yves Vachon and then running him and his bodyguard down on that fateful night? Was Plato's howling just a dog being unhappy? Had the driver who'd almost killed him up in the hills been some stranger?

Yet the more he thought about it, the more he felt Madame was in the middle of everything. He just wasn't so sure she'd been behind the wheel for all of those trips.

And if she hadn't been driving, who had been?

CHAPTER 56

THE NEXT MORNING, A physical therapist helped Burke into a wheelchair and took him to another floor, where he would begin his therapy.

"We'll start slowly, monsieur," said the physical therapist, a rangy young man. "Nothing strenuous at this point. We just want to get your body to function a little."

He was there for an hour. The therapist moved him gently, getting Burke to do some slight twisting of his torso and stretching of his legs. For a healthy person, the session would have been energy-sapping; for Burke, the hour left him exhausted.

"You did well, monsieur," the physio said. "It's important to get the blood flowing to your extremities. We'll do some more tomorrow. In a week to ten days, we might try walking a little."

Burke could only nod. On the way back to his room, he started to doze.

When he got back to his room, he had two visitors.

Fortin and Côté.

Two nurses helped Burke onto his bed. He was barely stretched out when Fortin, sitting close to him, began.

"We have examined Madame Marois's car and discovered some interesting things," he said.

Burke waited, still trying to recover from the therapy session.

"For example, Madame's car appears to have been in two accidents, not just one," Fortin said. "The original damage was in almost the exact spot that was damaged when Madame drove into that stone wall you mentioned."

Burke nodded. He wasn't surprised.

"We also discovered some blood below the bumper," Fortin said. "The car was otherwise extremely clean, but a couple of drops were missed."

The flic left those words hanging in the air.

The blood wasn't Burke's. He'd veered off the road before the car could touch him.

"Do you know whose blood it is?" Burke asked.

"Yes, we do," Fortin said.

"Yves Vachon's?"

"Close enough," Fortin said. "It belonged to his minder."

That was it. Madame Marois had been the hit-and-run driver, and she'd gone after him for asking questions and maybe getting too close to the truth. She was totally ruthless.

Fortin said they also discovered something else that was interesting.

"Madame's car is nine years old and has almost 300,000 kilometers on it," Côté said. "And in case you are wondering, she has been the only owner."

The numbers seemed strange to Burke.

"That's more than thirty thousand kilometers a year," he said. "That's a lot of driving."

"More than thirty-three thousand a year," Fortin said, "and you're right—it is a lot of driving. Not just for an elderly woman, but for anyone."

Burke wondered what Madame had been doing to rack up all those kilometers.

"And forgetting the damage to the hood from her crashes, Madame's car is not in very good shape," Fortin said. "In fact, our experts believe she'll soon need to put in a lot of money to keep the vehicle roadworthy."

That surprised Burke. Her personal attire was immaculate, if a little out of style. Her home had the same austere elegance. And yet her car was in rough shape.

"I see you find that intriguing as well, Monsieur Burke," Fortin said. "Maybe she didn't want anyone to know how much she was driving, so she kept the car away from the attention of a regular mechanic."

That made sense to Burke.

"Now, I have a question for you," Fortin said. "Have you ever seen her drive with anyone else in her car?"

"No, just Plato," Burke said.

"Yes, Plato, the dog who knows his mistress's moods," Fortin said.

Burke studied Fortin's face to see if the detective was being sarcastic. He didn't think so. Fortin's tone and his face actually seemed to suggest he believed Plato had some powerful connection to Madame Marois. As a dog owner himself, maybe Fortin could understand the bond between dog and owner.

Burke had his own question. "Have you arrested Madame Marois?"

"We're in the process of conducting an interview with her," Fortin said. "Her lawyer is anxious that our interviewing process be shortened, but that remains to be seen."

Once again, Burke wondered why he was getting all this behind-the-scenes information from Fortin. He kept that thought to himself, though.

Fortin leaned over the edge of Burke's bed.

"I know you're tired, but I need you to do something," Fortin said.

Stretched out in a hospital bed with virtually no mobility, Burke figured he was useless, but he nodded anyway.

"I need you to go back in your mind to the day of your accident, to just before you went off the road," Fortin said.

"OK."

"I need you to recreate the scene in your mind," Fortin said. "I've asked you to do this before, but I need you to go deeper this time."

"Why?"

"Never mind. Just close your eyes and think back to what happened," Fortin said. "Go second by second, meter by meter. And I want you to focus on the front windshield. Nothing else."

"The windshield?" Burke asked.

"Go back to the split second when you first looked over your shoulder and saw the car speeding toward you," Fortin said. "Relax and try to look at the windshield. Meter by meter…"

Burke felt like he was about to be hypnotized and went along with the request, closing his eyes, trying to remember…

"Do you see two body shapes in the front seat—not one, but two?" Fortin asked.

Burke focused on clearing his mind. Then he was back at the accident scene, when he first glanced back and saw the car speeding toward him.

"Just the windshield, nothing else," Fortin said.

Burke cleared away all the distractions in the scene: the road, the hills, the sky. He saw only the windshield.

He had originally seen only one shape—the driver—but now, he wasn't so sure. Maybe he was thinking more clearly now, or maybe it was because Fortin was putting an idea into his mind, but Burke had a strange sense that maybe there were two shapes.

A large one and a small one.

The large one was behind the wheel.

Burke wondered if he was just imagining it. He recalled the second time he looked back at the car, right before he decided he needed to ride off the road.

Fortin started to speak again, but Burke, with his eyes still closed, shut him up with a wave of his non-pinioned hand.

The car was ten meters back, maybe even closer. The sun was overhead. No shadows.

Yes, it seemed there were two figures. He couldn't see faces or clothing, just body outlines—one large and one small. Burke was now convinced there had been two people in the front of the vehicle. Why had he thought he had seen only one? Because he'd believed Madame Marois had been behind the wheel. It had fit into his theory.

Opening his eyes, he told Fortin what he thought. The policeman seemed satisfied, almost like he had always suspected there'd been two persons in the automobile.

"Good, Monsieur Burke, very good," Fortin said.

"But can you use what I just said in a courtroom?" Burke asked. "I'm still a little vague."

Fortin waved away the objection. "I have other plans for what you just told me," he said.

Then he excused himself and, with Côté behind him, marched out of the room.

CHAPTER 57

THE NEXT THREE DAYS passed slowly and painfully for Burke. He slept fitfully, with the pain meds sending him to sleep and bizarre dreams awakening him. He was starting to eat better, but he was a long way from finishing a plate of hospital food. He tried to make the hours go by faster by watching some television, but he couldn't maintain his focus on the tiny screen by his bedside.

The physiotherapist was working him a little harder each time, once commenting that Burke was progressing so well that they might try walking a couple of days ahead of schedule. Burke almost laughed at that suggestion. He felt as ready for walking as a newborn baby.

The two doctors who visited him twice daily also seemed pleased with his progress. They agreed Burke was getting stronger by the day, although the healing process would be lengthy and might involve some minor follow-up surgery.

He had visitors, most notably Hélène, who came at least once every day and chatted to him about the café, the weather and how much better Burke was looking. Her spirits seemed much improved, but she still looked tired.

When he was alone, he thought mostly about Madame Marois. And Fortin and Côté. And what could be happening outside the hospital.

He waited for any news at all.

Then one morning, Jean bounced into the room, holding a few newspapers. He sat by Burke's bedside.

"Have you been watching the news or read a paper today?"

"No," Burke said.

Jean held out the front page of a local newspaper. The headline across the top said:

"MOTHER AND SON CHARGED IN VACHON DEATH"

There was a photo of Madame Marois with a tall, husky, middle-aged man beside her. They were being escorted up the stairs of a building and both looked miserable. Police surrounded them.

"Damn!" Burke's jaw dropped.

"Absolutely!" Jean said. "The story is everywhere. But Madame Marois?"

Burke could only shake his head.

Jean studied Burke. "Did you know this was going to happen?"

"The police asked me some questions on a couple of occasions, but that was it. I didn't know what would happen."

Burke, shocked by the involvement of Madame Marois's son, asked Jean to give him the gist of the story, and his friend was more than happy to comply.

It seemed Madame and her son Gabriel had worked together for the last few months to target Vachon. The old woman had made several trips out of country to connect with her son, who, in recent weeks, had traveled back to the Côte d'Azur and was living quietly in a studio in Antibes. As for the motive, the police said it involved a family matter "going back years." Burke was left with plenty of unanswered questions.

"You know more than you're saying, Paul," Jean said. "I can see it in your eyes."

Burke managed the mildest of shrugs.

"I didn't anticipate anything involving the son," Burke admitted. "I thought Madame wasn't close to him."

"I did as well," Jean said. "I've never seen him in all the years Madame has lived in the village."

"Maybe she and her son mended fences years ago but chose to let everyone think they were still estranged," Burke said.

"Why do that?"

"Because she and her son shared one overwhelming desire—to get revenge against Vachon for something he had done to their family. I bet their estrangement was just a ruse to keep people from linking them while they plotted away. Do the news reports get specific at all about their motive?"

Jean told him the information was a little thin due to the case going to court. Burke asked for the charges. Jean checked one newspaper and said they were both charged with murder, attempted murder and conspiracy to commit murder.

"You said attempted murder—of whom?" Burke asked.

Jean fingered a column of the news story. "It isn't specific. It just says it involves an attempt to run someone off the road," he said.

Burke watched the light bulb go off.

"You're the one they tried to run off the road!" Jean said, pointing at Burke. "They tried to kill you. You're in here because of them."

"I suspect you're right, Jean," Burke said, convinced Gabriel had been behind the wheel when the car had forced him off the road and into the trees. The driver had been aggressive and skilled, able to handle the road's challenges with ease while dealing with Burke on his bicycle. Burke guessed the son had also been driving when the car struck Vachon and his minder. To handle the sharp curve in the road at speed and then drive away quickly after striking the two men had required talent, more than Madame Marois had displayed in recent years.

Burke could see Jean was reviewing recent conversations they'd had. Then Jean nodded to himself. He was connecting the dots.

"But what had Vachon done years ago that was so bad that they wanted him dead? And why did they try to kill you?" Jean asked.

"They tried to eliminate me because I was asking questions that needed to stay unasked," Burke said. "As for why they killed Vachon, I expect we'll have to wait to find out."

"Our little village will never be the same," Jean said.

There was a knock on the door.

Fortin and Côté stood there.

"We need to talk to you privately, Monsieur Burke," Fortin said.

Jean looked at Fortin and Côté, then back to Burke. Understanding crossed his face, and he got out of his chair.

"I'll talk to you later," Jean said.

Burke knew his curiosity would drive him to return soon—probably later that day—to find out what the two flics wanted.

Once Jean was gone, Côté closed the door, and Fortin took up his customary seat by Burke's bedside.

"You heard what's happened?" Fortin said.

Burke nodded.

"There's a chance you'll have to testify after all," Fortin said.

Burke nodded again, although he wasn't sure what he could contribute to the case against Madame Marois and her son.

"If you do, it will likely be about Madame Marois's strength of mind and what you have observed, not about your accident in the hills," Fortin said. He must have noticed Burke's puzzled expression, because he added, "The old lady's lawyer is already arguing diminished capacity on her part."

"That she's senile and didn't really know what she was doing?"

"That's it. The lawyer has listed a number of recent events that indicate her diminished capacity. He might be able to persuade the presiding judge to consider other options besides serious charges."

"Other options? What does that mean?" Burke asked.

"Hospitalization on a long-term basis," Fortin said.

Burke shook his head. A weak mind? Madame Marois was as sharp as a tack. The more he thought about it, the more sure he was that Madame Marois had plotted well in advance to look like she was suffering from dementia in case she was arrested for what happened to Vachon.

"I believe she's extremely clever, but it will be difficult to prove she had all this worked out weeks, or maybe even months, before Vachon's death," Fortin said. "As for your observations that her dog is able to identify Madame's true moods, that will never stand up in court. Not a chance. So her lawyer's got a good case."

"But aren't there tests to determine if she has dementia?"

"There is some diagnostic testing that can help, but there is also some vagueness with the results, at least as far as legal responsibility is concerned. A psychiatrist attached to the police told us about the causes for memory loss. It can be a result of dementia, but it can also be because of stress, depression, vitamin deficiencies or a brain tumor. So we're looking deeper into our case against her."

Burke had a sudden thought.

"What happened to Madame's dog Plato?" he asked.

"As soon as we took Madame into custody—she's been placed in a hospital for further testing—her dog was put into an animal shelter," Fortin said.

"If she never returns to her home, will they put Plato down or give him up for adoption?"

"I don't know," Fortin said.

"Did Madame Marois ask about him once she was in custody?" Burke asked.

Fortin nodded. "About every fourth sentence, she asked. I think she's petrified he'll be euthanized."

So the old woman was clear-thinking enough to be worried about her best companion.

Burke asked about Madame's son.

"That is a very interesting story," Fortin said.

Burke settled in to hear it.

"But I can't tell it to you until later," Fortin continued. "For now, let's just say it's about a mother and son seeking revenge."

Burke had an instant sense of déjà vu.

"The Petits and now Madame Marois and her son," Burke said. "Same story."

"Indeed," Fortin said.

CHAPTER 58

AS BURKE EXPECTED, JEAN was back that afternoon, asking about Fortin and Côté. Burke told him they'd stopped by to ask him some questions involving the case against Madame Marois and her son.

"I can see you aren't telling me everything, my friend," Jean said, waving an admonishing finger.

"For the moment, I can't tell you everything," Burke said. "Now, I have a question for you."

Jean sat back and waited.

"Would you and your wife be willing to take in a dog?" Burke asked.

"Ah, you mean our little friend Plato?"

Burke nodded.

"As it happens, we've already spoken at home, and I'll be picking him up tomorrow morning," Jean said. "We had to clear it with Madame's lawyer. Like you, we were concerned Plato might get the chop."

Burke was relieved. Plato was a fine animal.

They talked a few more minutes, and then Burke got a new visitor—François Lemaire, with big Antoine in tow, who was carrying an oversized camera bag. Satisfied he wouldn't get any more new information, Jean excused himself and left.

"We came once before, but you were sleeping like a baby," Lemaire said.

"You're not such a good-looking baby, though," Antoine added.

The two newcomers made idle chat with Burke about his injuries, but he sensed they were there for other reasons.

"I'm glad you're feeling better," Lemaire said. Then he motioned to Antoine.

The big man hauled out a video camera from the bag, turned it on and approached Burke.

"When we were here the other day, we took a couple of photos of you and some video, too," Antoine said. "We were probably not supposed to do that, but no one was around, so we did."

"Why?" Burke asked.

Lemaire jumped in, saying the newspaper had to explain what had happened to their top blogger, adding that photos and video would help emphasize the seriousness of the situation.

"We ran the photo on the website," Lemaire said, showing Burke his smartphone, which had the website pulled up for viewing. There Burke lay, stretched out sleeping. He was not a pretty sight, and with all the machines hooked up to him, he looked like his next breath could be his last. "We put up a little video, too. If the hospital authorities ever see it, we might hear from them, but I'll worry about that later."

Burke was too tired to care one way or the other about what Lemaire had done.

"We had a lot of response, a lot of hits," Lemaire said. "So here we are hoping you can give us a few comments, which we'll post as a video blog."

Burke smiled to himself. Lemaire was always thinking news and seeking an angle. Burke relented and said he'd cooperate.

Lemaire suggested Burke discuss how the accident happened, as well as if anyone had been charged in connection with the incident. Burke took a minute to think and then said he'd describe what happened but couldn't get into specifics about the criminal case.

"Fair enough, I guess," Lemaire said.

Burke took a few moments to compose his thoughts, and then, with Antoine filming him from a meter away, he recounted what he remembered.

After he was done, Lemaire suggested a second take, urging Burke to put more volume into his voice and more drama into his words. The editor could be a pain, but Burke agreed and did a second take, which seemed to please the newsman.

"That's much better. Now, we'll need to follow this up soon," Lemaire said after watching Antoine double-check the quality of the video. "Maybe tomorrow, Antoine can come back and do a follow-up video. You could talk about how you're coming along."

"I'm coming along OK, according to the doctors," Burke said.

"OK, but you can be a little more dramatic than that," Lemaire said.

"I'll think about it."

That was the most Lemaire would get out of Burke on the matter.

"Any chance you can type on a computer?" Lemaire asked, frowning at Burke's extensive injuries.

"Only with one or two fingers on my right hand," Burke said. "So I'm going to say no."

"That's a shame," Lemaire said. "It would be nice to have you do some written blogs. No matter. That's not a big deal. We can work around that. Right now, the video blogs will be fine. You're a hot commodity, Paul."

Burke didn't feel so hot. For the first time, he wondered about his new TV gig. He doubted the station would wait for him to recuperate. Television worked with the here and now. In a few months, he'd be just a distant name in someone's memory.

Lemaire and Antoine excused themselves and left. Moments later, though, the big man was back in the room.

"I told François I forgot to tell you something about working on your next blog," Antoine said. "I didn't want him around when I ask you if I have anything to worry about from the flics."

"What?"

"Do they know about our hack into the city video system?" Antoine asked with a worried expression.

"They know I was somehow involved in a hack, but they don't really care who got into the system," Burke said. "They wanted my information. The person who did the hacking is a small fish to them, so you don't need to worry."

"Really?"

"Really."

Antoine nodded. Then he smiled.

"That's good," he said. "Maybe we can work together again on something similar."

"You mean another murder or hack?"

"I vote for both," Antoine said, grinning.

Then he left.

A few minutes later, Hélène showed up. She was unusually bubbly, talking about new adventures at the café. After discussing a new menu she was working on with the chef, she leaned close to Burke's bedside.

"I have a suggestion," she said, smiling gently.

"For what?"

"You're going to be in here for a while, and someone needs to look after your apartment," Hélène said. "And then there's what happens when you're released and can go home. You'll need someone to help you. I think that person should be me."

Burke hadn't thought at all about his apartment or what he would need when he was released. His mind had been tied up with his injuries and then with the Madame Marois situation.

She was right. He would need help, and there would be no one better than Hélène. But he didn't want her to be a housekeeper or a nurse, and he told her that.

"I wouldn't be there as either," Hélène said. She blushed a little. "I'd be there as your partner."

There it was. She wanted to move in with him, and this seemed the perfect time.

Burke's heart beat faster. He had never lived with a woman before. He'd dated and had had a few extended female guests, but a full-time, live-in companion was an entirely new matter. He liked the idea.

"I accept your proposal," he said with a smile.

"Excellent!" Hélène said, and they kissed.

Burke told her he would likely be in the hospital at least two more weeks.

"With your key, I'll move in over the next two days," Hélène said. "I'll tell your landlady so she doesn't think I'm squatting."

Burke asked about her own apartment back in Nice.

"The lease is almost up, so this is perfect timing," she said.

He wondered if she was actually just looking for a cheaper place to live, then dismissed the idea. Burke believed in their relationship. Now he just had to accept this new direction.

"I'll pay my share of the rent, of course," Hélène said, almost as if she had read his mind.

They kissed again.

"This will be perfect," she said, beaming. "I'll be close to the café, and I'll be nearby to help you. And then when you're better, you can pay me back."

"Pay you back? How?"

"In a variety of ways," Hélène said, "but I guarantee you will enjoy every one of them."

CHAPTER 59

THE NEXT TWO WEEKS drifted by in a routine of waking up, eating, doing physio, being updated on his progress by the doctor, getting visits from a handful of people—mostly Hélène, André Rousseau, Jean and Antoine—and trying to catch up on what was happening in the outside world.

Whenever she visited, Hélène had a load of stories about how well her move into his place was going, how much better it made her life and how she was looking forward to when they would share the apartment. She also disclosed she had changed his ragged bedroom curtains for something lavender-colored and willowy.

One day, he received a new visitor—a producer from the Nice TV station that had wanted to use him on the sports program. Burke expected he was going to lose the gig and paycheck.

But the producer surprised him, saying the job offer remained.

"A lot of people have been watching what's been happening to you," the producer said. "We've kept them up to date on your progress and have been promoting your participation on our panel."

Burke was relieved. The TV gig would never make him rich, but it would pay a bill or two.

Another day, Fortin and Côté showed up.

"You won't likely be called to testify in a courtroom," Fortin said, forgoing any small talk. "It seems the lawyers for Madame and Gabriel Marois are ready to work something out."

"But how could they do that? I mean, they plotted to kill Vachon—and then they killed him. That's murder."

"I'm aware of that," Fortin said.

"And they tried to kill me," Burke said, getting angrier by the second at the idea of some kind of plea bargain.

"There are other matters involved, and I can't disclose them to you," Fortin said.

Burke couldn't change anything, and so he tried to calm down.

"Have you found out who drove the second car that hit either Vachon or his minder?" Burke asked.

Fortin shrugged. "Not yet, although we know it was the minder who got run over by that second vehicle," he said. "We're confident it was a genuine accident for that driver, though he or she should definitely not have driven off. If we find out who that person is, there will be charges, but we aren't pushing hard to find out the driver's identity. Right now, it's just a case of someone being in the wrong place at the wrong time."

Fortin told him he wouldn't be making any more visits. He had all the information he needed for the Marois and Petit cases.

"You've been a pain from time to time these last two months, Monsieur Burke, but you've helped us in subtle ways that allowed us to resolve the cases."

Burke recognized he was being thanked.

"And because of our successes in making good arrests, we are no longer being hammered by the media and the politicians and everyone else," Fortin said. "In fact, we're receiving praise from some quarters."

Burke wondered if Fortin had been promoted.

"So, thank you, monsieur," Fortin said, standing.

"You're welcome," Burke replied.

"And I say this with all respect, I hope I never see you standing in my office or in my police station again," Fortin added and then left.

Burke watched him disappear.

He had the very same wishes as Fortin.

EPILOGUE

FOUR WEEKS LATER, BURKE was released from the hospital. Hélène and André Rousseau collected him and took him home.

Using a cane with his good arm, he struggled up the stairs to his apartment, but he didn't complain. He felt fortunate. The medical staff at the hospital had done a superb job mending his injuries without further surgery, and he was improving by the day. Still, the routine at the institution had been stultifying. He had ached for fresh air and freedom.

When Hélène opened the door to his—their—apartment and Burke shuffled in, he was met with a cry of "Surprise!" from Jean, his wife, several villagers, Lemaire and Antoine. Instantly, a lump formed in his throat.

And so he visited and partied with his friends until he ran out of energy and sought the comfort of his bed in the bedroom, which looked surprisingly good with the new lavender curtains. He didn't mind at all that the celebrations kept going on despite his absence.

A month later, the two Petits were sentenced after pleading guilty to different charges.

Léon Petit got life imprisonment for the assassination, or premeditated murder, of Pierre McManus. His guilt in the killing of Mark Den Weent guaranteed he would never be released. During the sentencing, he said nothing and barely moved. In one story, a reporter described Petit as being "sphinx-like" as he heard his future.

Karin Petit received six years for attempted murder, her lawyer arguing with some success that her mental capacity had been eroded by overwhelming concern for her son's well-being.

A week after being incarcerated, Karin Petit suffered a fatal heart attack.

After Léon Petit heard about his mother's death, he waited a week, then committed suicide in his cell.

When Burke learned about their deaths, he felt strangely depressed and even sought out André Rousseau for a beer so they could bid some kind of adieu to the Petits—two lost souls soon to be forgotten except in the annals of the Tour de France.

Two months after that, Gabriel Marois pled guilty to assassination. He got the same sentence as Léon Petit.

Before sentencing, Gabriel Marois's lawyer argued his client had been driven by uncontrollable revenge to kill Vachon. He explained the head of FP Developments had once been business partners in both real estate and various developments with Gabriel Marois's father, and had victimized him through some insider trading that had never come to light and couldn't be proven in court at the time. Vachon had profited hugely, while Gabriel Marois's father had lost almost all the family fortune and suffered such shame that he'd died a broken man, a weakened heart finally claiming him.

Moreover, it turned out Gabriel had largely turned his back on political activism years before for a career in small business, using financial support from his mother. Madame Marois hadn't rejected him. She'd kept loving him, and they had reconnected after his prison term and after the death of Gabriel's father. They made a pact that, one day, if the opportunity came, they would kill Yves Vachon, and until then, they would keep up a semblance of antipathy toward each other to avoid being linked to Vachon's death whenever they had the opportunity to dispose of him. In the meantime, they found ways to see each other, driving thousands of kilometers each year to prearranged places for short visits.

The opportunity to deal with Vachon had come when he started to spend more and more time on his Riviera super development, not knowing that Madame Marois lived a short distance away. When protests erupted around the development, Madame had contacted Gabriel, and they agreed they could masquerade Vachon's murder as the work of a crazed protestor.

Madame Marois's age was a mitigating factor in her sentencing. It was also discovered she was suffering from the early stages of vascular dementia. Doctors suggested she sustained microscopic bleeding of the brain as a result of being in her car when it slammed into two people and later into a stone wall. In turn, those two incidents prompted some minor strokes. Considering her age and her deteriorating mental condition, the judge sentenced her to five years for conspiracy to commit murder, but not in a prison. Instead, she was sentenced to a mental health institution after doctors testified she wasn't likely to live more than another two or three years, given her rapidly failing health.

One day, on a whim, Burke went to visit the old woman in the hospital.

They sat opposite each other in a large, sterile room among other visitors and patients. Hospital staff were tucked in corners to ensure nothing went amiss during any of the conversations.

Madame Marois stared at Burke like he was a dot on a wall.

"Do you remember me, Madame?" he asked.

She stared and said nothing. He studied her eyes. Was she playacting like she had been all those times at Claude's café, her vision fixed on the opposite wall? Her eyes remained glazed, and he thought she was truly someplace else.

"I live—lived—near you in Villeneuve-Loubet," Burke said. "I'm a cyclist. You were in the car that ran me off the road. I was badly hurt, but I'm much better now."

Madame continued looking ahead.

"How are you feeling?" Burke asked, knowing it was a dumb question since she was in a mental hospital and, physically, looked even frailer than before.

Nothing from Madame.

"I know the story about your husband and Yves Vachon," Burke said. "Vachon was not a good man."

No reaction.

He looked around. The place was totally depressing.

"I see your dog Plato all the time," he said. "He's doing very well. Jean and his wife are treating him to all kinds of walks."

Not to mention all kinds of treats. Plato was at least two kilos heavier than he'd been a few months earlier. On a small Jack Russell frame, Plato was looking a little chunky.

"I miss him," Madame said, breaking out of her trance. "Who did you say has Plato?"

"Jean, the newsagent in our village," Burke said.

He could see Madame trying in vain to put a face to the name.

"Would you ask him to visit me, please?" Madame said.

Jean, as bid, paid Madame Marois a visit the next day. Afterward, he came knocking on Burke's door, with Plato on a leash at his side.

"I met with the old lady this morning," Jean said. "She's in rough shape, but she knows one thing: She wants you to have little Plato here. She says you understand him, and he understands you."

"But you've been looking after him," Burke protested.

"Yes, we have, and he's a fine dog. But Plato is Madame's dog, and we have to go with her wishes. I know you'll treat him well, Paul."

Jean handed Burke the leash and a bag that contained food, toys and a dog bed. The newsagent had a sad smile on his face.

As Plato strained at the leash to investigate his new apartment, Burke wondered about adding Plato to his life. He realized he was fine with the idea, even after Madame Marois had plotted to kill him. Plato was a grand dog.

"Who is this?" came Hélène's voice. "Ah, it's Plato."

The dog rushed to greet her. It was clear they felt mutual admiration.

Burke explained Madame's request, and Hélène looked at Jean with sympathy.

Burke had an idea.

"You know, Jean, they say it takes a village to raise a child," he said. "I think it also takes a village to raise a dog. We'd love to have Plato with us, but only if we can share him with you and Bianca. How about if Plato lives with us but spends part of his days with you folks while we work at whatever we do? That way, he gets the best of both worlds: a home with us, plus exercise and a chance to say hello to everyone when he's at your shop. After all, he's a very social dog."

Jean smiled at the idea and looked at the small dog. "He is very friendly," Jean said. "I think that's an excellent idea. Agreed."

They all shook hands, then looked at Plato, whose tail was wagging madly.

Standing there, Burke thought back a few months to what his life had been like.

It was definitely different now.

AUTHOR'S NOTE

THE STORY AND CHARACTERS in *The Bastard is Dead* are fictional.

However, the issue of too much development along the French Riviera has its basis in fact. Many people are trying to figure out how to maintain the culture, beauty and accessibility of this special area of France. It will not be an easy task, given the limited space and the increasing day-to-day costs of living. The same challenge applies to Provence in general.

As for the Tour de France, which began in 1903 and has run annually except for breaks during the First and Second World Wars, it continues to attract twenty million spectators a year, all eager to view cycling's preeminent race in one of the most beautiful countries in the world. The race has faced scandals in recent years, but organizers have corrected many of the problems, and today, it can be argued that professional cycling is tougher on itself in terms of doping than many other sports. As an event, its spectacle, beauty, difficulty and history are unparalleled. Whether you are a cycling fan or not, if you ever see a single stage in person, you will never forget it. The Tour de France is indeed special.

LOOK FOR THE NEW PAUL BURKE MYSTERY: A VINTAGE END

THE LEADER OF THE vintage bicycle race followed the Mediterranean coastal road around the bend and studied the next stretch ahead. It wasn't going to be fun. The road ramped up at a 10 percent elevation gain—a steep climb for anyone riding a new, lots-of-gears carbon fiber bike, but a nasty challenge for someone using an old-time steel machine with half the gears.

But that was fine, since he had trained for the race and was well ahead of everyone, feeling exceptionally strong on his 1970 Peugeot bike and cycling in flawless spring conditions—sunny, mild, no wind. Plus, the finish line back in the French working-class resort of Saint-Raphaël was not much more than thirty kilometers away.

Ahead were two people sitting in lawn chairs under a beach umbrella by the roadside. There had been plenty of spectators along the out-and-back 110-kilometer-long route that had started in Saint-Raphaël, gone to Antibes and then backtracked along the winding, scenic coastal road. But for this patch, there was virtually no one around—except for this couple.

When he was seventy-five meters away, he saw they looked a little odd, as if they were frozen in motion. They were also wearing bulky clothes and strange-looking headgear.

When he was fifty meters away, he noticed the headgear resembled German helmets worn by soldiers during the Second World War.

At twenty-five meters, he could have no doubts about what he was looking at.

The two people weren't people—not anymore.

They were skeletons.

ABOUT THE AUTHOR

AFTER FORTY YEARS AS a journalist and journalism instructor, D'Arcy decided it was time to put his writing skills to work in a fictional way. And so he's created a mystery series featuring Paul Burke, an ex-pro cyclist from Montréal, Canada who lives on the French Riviera and is killing time while figuring out what to do next. Trouble, however, is never far away from Burke wherever he is in Europe. To ensure the authenticity of the areas (and the food, wine and beer) he writes about, D'Arcy and his wife Lynda spend six weeks each year in Europe cycling the areas featured in his next novel and discussing plot strategies. (Suggestion: Never discuss murdering someone while you're in a public place.) When he's not pounding on his keyboard, D'Arcy is a Celtic musician. He lives in Lethbridge, Alberta, Canada.